Cryptic Spaces

Book Two:
Eight Queens

Deen Ferrell

Curio Creative

American Fork, UT USA

Cryptic Spaces
Book Two: Eight Queens
by Deen Ferrell

First Printing – December 2014
ISBN: 978-1-60047-477-4
Library of Congress Control Number: 2014954762

Printed in the U.S.A.

0   1   2   3   4   5   6

An old Chinese proverb says, "One generation plants the trees, another gets the shade." In my life, there have been many planters, and I have been blessed with much shade. I owe so much to so many, it is hard to single out only a few. Parents, teachers, friends, and fellow authors, past and present, challenge and inspire me. I wish to offer special thanks to a few who have made a considerable contribution to "Eight Queens." First, I wish to thank my editor and friend, Sherry Wilson. She has been my advocate for many years and I appreciate her attention to detail and her subtle suggestions. My agent, Whitney Lee, of The Fielding Agency, made early suggestions that impacted the direction of the book. My immediate family has long been a part of my work. Melanie's insights and literary instincts are invaluable. Ashley is a valued set of secondary eyes. TJ has advised me on technical and computer related issues. Austin is a sounding-board and advocate with his teenage friends. Benjamin is a continual source of wonder and heart to all my imaginary worlds. There are also many in my extended family who have taken time out of their busy schedules to support and champion my work, and I have received valued and insightful feedback from a small circle of volunteer readers, some of whom are accomplished writers and editors in their own right. I offer each my sincerest gratitude.

OTHER BOOKS BY DEEN FERRELL

Cryptic Spaces: *Foresight*, 2013
Winner, "The Book Pick" 2013, BookBundlz.com
Winner, "Best Sci/Fi, Time Travel" 2013, The Dante Rossetti Young Adult Fiction Awards
Honorable Mention, Young Adult Science Fiction category, Reader's Choice Awards, 2014

CONFIDENTIAL MEMORANDUM
TO: Aito Senoya
FROM: Hathaway Simon
SUBJECT:James Arthur Washington
DATE: Early April

Relative to our discussion of how this entity learned of us and when they began tracking our team, I recalled a comment from the day James Arthur was recruited.

I had taken him to our observation post in Egypt. I'd told him that we were actually observing the retooling of the Sphinx, supervised by the royal architects of Pharaoh Djedefre, 2522 BC. I know he recognized the crouching body of the Sphinx, and he could see a good portion of the original lion head that rested on that body. He watched intently as the stone masons chipped away at the head, reshaping the snout of the lion into the features of an Egyptian face. I explained that the snout of the great beast would soon become the likeness of Pharaoh Khufu, Djedefre's father. He considered for a moment and then turned to me.

"Are there others?"

"Others?"

"Yes. Are there other travelers—like you?"

"We have not come across any."

"Is there a girl—or maybe a young woman—with injured eyes in your group?"

"Injured eyes?"

"Yeah, black—like they were burned?"

I shook my head. He turned back and watched the work on the Sphinx. I studied him carefully. He was aware of my gaze and gave a sheepish grin. "I guess we all have mysterious women in our pasts."

At the time, I attributed the Doctor's quick acceptance of time-travel technology to his keen insights. Perhaps he had sensed the subtle interactions between the brain and the temporal world before. He had written a brilliant thesis on *time-mapping*—the process of reading biological signs hidden in the brain and body to chart a successful life course through temporal time. Perhaps he even had a degree of ancient *foresight*. His talent was not mathematical in nature, but a sense of time paths seemed to be there. Since our recent encounter, I have begun to question my original assessment.

James Arthur, of course, was fully vetted by our security team before we approached him, but I took the liberty of reviewing his full file in more detail. You will find the full digital profile of James Arthur Washington on the attached disk.

Under Profile Exhibit 4A, in a folder labeled "Papers and Essays," you'll find a rather odd note, originally scrawled on yellow tablet paper and tucked inside the front cover of a 1994 version of Ray Bradbury's *The October Country*. I have transposed the hand-written message and provide it for your scrutiny.

The security team labeled the note "Beginnings of Healing Abilities." While our interest in James Arthur was specifically in his healing powers, I am beginning to think we may have missed something. Could "sucked backward" refer to the pull of a time hole? Was this ghost-girl real and if so, is she in league with those that seem to stalk us? Could he be the weak link?

(Transcribed from handwritten note)

6.8.2011: It actually happened, but I know no one will believe me. They'll lock me up if I even mention this. So, I'm just writing the experience down so it is recorded.

I know there are ghosts because I saw one. It happened on our trip to New Orleans. At first, it sounded and looked like a girl. I was walking along a back street, alone, when I was suddenly sucked backward and felt like I was falling. It felt strange and scary, and then I was on the street again. Only, the street seemed different. It was covered in mud, and the lights were all oil lamps and torches.

I heard crying, and walked into an old Victorian mansion. On the second floor, I found the girl. I couldn't see her face at first. She was crying and begging for somebody to help her. I tried to talk to her. She looked up. Her face horribly burned across the ridge of her nose and around the eyes. The girl screamed that someone was coming and I should get out of there. Then, her eyes opened wider, and suddenly they were GLOWING COALS! That's the only way to describe it—glowing coals.

The girl screamed and light exploded from her face, blinding me. I staggered back, then, this girl's shape passed right through me. Now, I have strange dreams about her. Since this experience, there have been other odd developments. I seem to have an ability to heal myself. Last month, when I came down with a bad cold, I lay in my bed and something told me to just concentrate on getting well. I focused my thoughts on my throat, which was very raw. As I focused, I felt a sense of—of power. I can't explain it. It seemed like my whole throat and nasal cavity buzzed slightly. When I woke the next morning, the cold was gone and my throat was completely healed.

Oh, I forgot to say, after the ghost, there was that same feeling of being sucked backward and falling—the same one I had just before I saw the mansion. I found myself flat on a barren wood floor, and when I got up, everything seemed normal. The mansion was old and boarded up. I wondered if I had stumbled into this old fire trap, tripped, and somehow hit my head, hallucinating the whole thing. I ran. From the outside, it seemed like nobody lived in the old mansion. Except maybe that ghost lived there. I didn't want to wait around to see.

End of Transcript
End of Message – H. S.

1

New Orleans

James Arthur steeled himself, determined to focus. All around him was heat—a gritty, bitter, dry heat. He could taste it. He could smell it. He wanted to spit, but his mouth was too dry. His lips were cracked. He tried to think. *Where was he?* Disjointed scenes flashed through his mind. He was on a ship, hands tied. He was trying to escape from someone. He jumped into a closet and pulled the door closed behind him. The strange metal door locked and its doorknob glowed. Then, he was jerked forward and was falling. There was an odd, disjointed memory of some kind of underground catacombs where he was hit from behind. When he came to, he was laid out, mostly naked, in a dark, rock tomb. He knew something terrible had happened. Something had gone very wrong. He had been… *Where had he been?*

He couldn't think clearly. His head hurt too much. Everything in his mind felt tangled and fuzzy. He tried to open his eyes to get his bearings. He immediately closed them. He couldn't move his arms or legs. It was too bright—everything was heat and confusion. *Better to focus, to concentrate, to heal,* he thought. How had he become so broken? *Heal,* his mind commanded. The thought came from somewhere deep inside him. It was the hidden voice, the soothing balm that sprung from somewhere deep in his soul. Immediately, he began to relax.

Where had it come from—this power for healing? He wasn't sure. But, he knew when it had started. He knew the first time he had recognized the power, the energy inside him that could be focused and harnessed.

Heal…

He turned the word over and over in his mind. He had done this before. He felt the mechanics of his battered body. He located the centers of pain. *Breathe in*, he told himself, feeling his veins pulse with oxygen-rich blood, then, *breathe out*. He followed the blood with his mind as it passed through the body. He was an eye inside the body—a careful, critical eye, flowing in the river of fresh blood, observing the long journey through the neck, the heart, across the organs, to the tips of his fingers and the toes of his feet. He touched each point of pain, stopping with his mind to fully visualize the damage that had caused it. He infused the points with power—*heal!*

He was a doctor. He remembered this as he strained to retain focus. It was how he knew the body so well. It was how he could visualize so effectively. He knew how the damage would look from the inside, and how to reconstruct the tissues, the inner linings of each organ, the muscles…

He oversaw the removal of wastes from repair sites. The thought of *wastes* gave him a sudden urge to relieve himself, but his mind would not yet let him fully wake or move. Healing was the important thing. He refused any sense of embarrassment as a warm trickle ran down his leg.

"*Heal!*" he commanded his body.

With the mechanics of this healing process set in motion, his mind began to drift. *When had this started? Where had he learned to heal?* He followed his mind back, gaining speed, as if running toward an answer. He felt legs below him, moving now, touching pavement. He was somewhere, deep in his mind, deep in his past. A black, tangled fog around him began to clear. He looked down. He was no longer in his late twenties, but a much younger boy. He felt another surge of heat, but a different heat—a more humid, thicker heat. He felt like he was swaying in invisible syrup. The air swirled, clinging to him like an uncomfortable skin.

Step, step, step—*he'd been going somewhere—fast— but where?* A street materialized around him. It was dusk. The sun had sunk below the horizon, but the city before him was far from dark. Despite the absence of direct sunlight, he could see and feel shimmers of heat radiating up from the asphalt, mixing with a rainbow of neon colors from dozens of signs of various shapes and sizes. Small shops, bars, and cafes lined the street on either side. Some had already closed, but most were still open and crammed with people. Lively music spilled out of a dozen doorways—inviting music.

James Arthur paused. The night, the place, the stifling heat, it all seemed familiar. *He had been here before.* He wiped at his forehead and then pushed on, letting his tennis shoes slap down on the uneven black-top with a dull *thwack*. Strains of piano, fiddle, and guitar joined and parted around him as he moved, charting an ever-changing ocean of sound that ebbed and flowed. The thick air crackled with an inner vibrancy, carrying the unmistakable lightness of jazz and Dixieland. A voice piped up over the music. It came from the side, just slightly behind him.

"Sho' is hot," the rambling voice exclaimed with a thick southern accent.

James Arthur turned toward the voice, its identity immediately recognizable to him. It was his brother, Stephen Alexander. He studied the form beside him. Stephen was young. He had the sleek nimbleness of a gangly youth. Sweat poured down his face. That was not unusual for Stephen. He was always dripping with sweat, usually spouting tales of conquest and athletic glory, a sour smelling t-shirt flung over his shoulder like a drape of laurels. Tonight, though, the sweat was filled only with agitation. "Man, if it tried to rain here, the droplets would melt before they hit the pavement!"

"Show is something you see in a theater," James Arthur wanted to say, "and water can't melt. Ice can melt, but water would evaporate." Of course, he didn't say anything. His brother would have no interest in the technical correctness of his speech. He was trying to get a point across and he had. Everything else was just nit-picking. James Arthur had learned that his brother, who was several years his senior, did not take kindly to being corrected. "Yes, it's hot," James Arthur finally agreed. He looked up again at his brother.

Stephen was tall for his age. He stood at least two feet taller than James Arthur and sported a wiry, athletic frame. His eyes were fierce, full of determination. James Arthur had always admired that about his brother. The eyes distinguished him. They set him apart.

In contrast, James was remembering what it was like to feel gangly and awkward in his young boy skin. He looked down at his well-worn sneakers beneath his skinny, scratched calves and knobby knees. So, maybe he didn't look athletic, but he did share one of Stephen's traits—he was tenacious. Stephen pointed to a sign to the side of the road and slightly ahead of them. The sign was made from scrawled letters on what looked like the back of a pizza box. It read, "Westside Rugby Krewe."

"Get a load of that."

Another voice piped up from directly behind James. "Yeah. Crazy swamp rats don't even know how to spell." James Arthur looked back to find his middle brother, David Christian. David was stockier, but shorter than Stephen, and the word *Christian* was not a word James Arthur thought of in relationship to this brother. He had no problems correcting David.

"First, New Orleans is inhabited by people, not *swamp rats*, and second, the words on that sign are spelled correctly," he said. "They just chose to use the Old English spelling." His voice sounded unusually squeaky.

"Oh, sorry—I forgot! It's been a whole two minutes since we heard from you, *Professor!* When I want your opinion, I'll ask for it! How would you even know Old English from Swahili? It's not like you've been there, although you were born *old*. You're like, what? Thirteen? You're not even in high school."

Stephen glanced across at his younger brothers trying to contain a laugh. "He's got a point there, James Arthur."

James Arthur stubbed the toe of his tennis shoe on the pavement. "The word 'k-r-e-w-e' is Old English for the word c-r-e-w."

"And you know that because…?"

"…because I have a brain, because I like to read, because I wrote an essay on Old English root words for extra credit last year."

"Really," Stephen grunted, still smiling; "in the sixth grade? I think you're bluffing."

James Arthur eyed him severely. "I don't bluff. I only educate."

"Well, why don't you go *educate* somewheres else," David Christian started, but James Arthur cut in.

"Why?" He was about to point out that a person who uses the non-word *somewheres* has obvious deficits in education, but instead, he just added. "We were discussing the sign. Stephen brought attention to it, and I just told you what ya'll should know."

He purposely used the contraction "ya'll," which was not appropriate English, but less high-brow, to help diffuse the situation. He really wasn't trying to start a fight.

Stephen spoke up. "I thought it was funny that they even got rugby in New Orleans. Rugby is English, right? I thought New Orleans was French."

"It was named after Phillip II, the Duke of Orleans, who was very definitely French," James Arthur stated with conviction. "The French play rugby too. They completed a Grand Slam last year in the Six Nations Championship."

His middle brother, David, snorted. "Holy cow, does this guy just plug himself into a wall socket at night? You sure he's our brother and wasn't switched at birth? Why don't we just find a computer terminal and he'll be happy for the night while we go have some fun."

James Arthur frowned. David Christian was always trying to ditch him. He felt the pang of hurt inside that he had always felt, a pang that worsened as he noted Stephen actually appeared to consider the suggestion. Stephen had always been his hero. He looked down as Steven addressed David.

"No. Ma said stick together."

"Did Ma know we'd be lectured all night on the history of Old English?"

"New Orleans," James Arthur corrected.

"What?"

James looked back at David. "I spoke to you about the history of New Orleans. I only identified the Old English on that sign."

"Well," David said, "how about you identify yourself a rock and crawl under it!"

Stephen laughed.

Again, James Arthur looked down. He knew he did not have the seemingly effortless physical abilities his brothers exhibited. He had to work hard to even be average at most sports. But he did have brains. Why did they begrudge him that? They didn't know what it was like to be picked last on every team at recess and to be taunted and teased because he preferred a good book to an afternoon in stinky gym shorts. Oh, it wasn't that he didn't try. He made constant efforts to get better at sports and was determined to master the intellectual side of every sport well enough to beat any of them with strategy, and not just physical prowess, but it *was* lonely to be smart in an urban, middle-class neighborhood. His teacher had called him "highly gifted," while David Christian had dubbed him "highly embarrassing." He glared back at David.

David Christian was not studious in any way, shape, or form. He loved to show off his flexed chest and rippling biceps, and lived to watch and play football. He was two years younger than Stephen, and couldn't quite beat him in a fight, but could certainly flatten James Arthur with a single punch. If it weren't for the constant protection of Stephen, James was sure that David Christian would have maimed him long ago.

"Hey, I got an idea," David said, chuckling. "Let's let James Arthur stay right here and talk to his old rugby chums. They could all talk Old English, and the swamp rats would be happy, and he would be happy, and then you and me could just pick him up on the way back to the hotel."

Stephen shook his head vigorously. "I said no. You heard me."

"But how we supposed to enjoy ourselves with Mr. Professor analyzing the trees? He thinks he's God's gift to intelligence."

"I'm not analyzing trees—you see trees around here?" James Arthur contested hotly. He rounded on David Christian. "What good would it do even if there were? You don't even know the difference between a Poplar and a Giant Redwood. You probably don't even know the difference between rock and wood, except your skull is as thick as wood and you have the same IQ as a rock!"

David laughed, turning to Stephen. "See? There you go—now we're hearing about rocks and trees. How long did it take you to figure out the IQ of the rock, James Arthur?"

Stephen let go a laugh, looking over at James Arthur. "You walked right into that one."

That was it. It was one thing having David Christian chiding and bullying him. David always did that. But now Stephen was chiming in. He was seventeen, and a senior, and the high school quarterback and track star. He was the one who usually stood up for James Arthur, forcing David to back off. It hurt to see him laughing. This whole vacation had been a nightmare from the beginning, and James was tired of it. He turned away and ran, dodging Stephen's attempt to grab his arm. "Fine," he called back.

"I'll go back. Who wants to hang out with a couple of marauding losers?"

"Meradi loser? *Take that back!* What's a meradi loser?" David Christian was already trying to run after James, one fist raised, but Stephen held him back.

"Cool it!" Stephen said, but David shouted over him.

"I'll educate *you* when I get a hold of you, James Arthur! I'll educate you how it feels to get a fist in the face!" He shook his fist hard, and then swung it down, showing what he planned to do.

James Arthur had already reached the corner. He paused, looking one last time at his brothers. Stephen was still trying to hold David Christian back. James caught the boy's narrowing eyes. David mouthed the words, "You're toast!" Without another thought, James Arthur spun, turned down a side alley, and poured on the speed. He could barely make out the street signs in the dimming light. Street lamps clicked on. He noted that he was turning off of Royal and onto a narrow street called St. Phillip. "You won't find *me*," he huffed, straining to increase speed. It would take Stephen time to get David Christian to calm down. That gave him time to lose himself in the maze of streets and back alleys. He heard Stephen yell his name, but it seemed far away now. He didn't stop. They might be better athletes, but he could outsmart them. He could lose them anytime he wanted.

Panting, he zigzagged onto Decatur Street, and almost immediately ducked down a narrow alley. The alley came out on street called *Ursulines*. He stopped, bending over for a moment to catch his breath. No sooner had he bent than he had a strange sensation of being jerked back and upward. He opened his mouth to scream, the world spinning around, and then he was falling. Bile rose to his mouth as he fell to his knees. He swayed, dizzy, falling hard onto his hands and began to wretch.

When he was done, he looked up. *What just happened?* Had he pushed himself too hard and blacked out? He stared around him. The street seemed to be all mud now. Why hadn't he noticed that? He stared up at the street sign for a long moment. There was something about the sign—about the way the name was written on it—that gave him the shivers. The air around him felt strangely cold. Hair prickled at the back of his neck. He slowly rose to his feet and began to walk. Something told him to lie down, that he must be hallucinating, but he couldn't stop himself from walking. He was intrigued. He was mesmerized. The street seemed to have a hold of him, to control him, as if he were walking in a dream. The air felt heavy, as though a thunderstorm was building. Narrow buildings lined the sidewalk. The street lights were dark, but a segment of street was lit by torches.

"Flambeaux," James Arthur mumbled. He had heard about the torches. They had been used in the old days in New Orleans to light the Mardi Gras parades. But there was no parade here. There were no people. The noisy, reveling city had become quiet. All James Arthur could hear was a whimpering. He cocked an ear.

The sound came again.

It was a soft sound, like a girl crying.

The sound came from a two-story, Victorian-style house. The house had a high, wrought-iron balcony where two, gabled passages opened out from French doors. Long, shuttered windows stood to either side of the doors, each with a decorative, half-moon window above it. The doors themselves were shuttered tight, but he could see glints of yellow light bleeding out from between the uneven slats of the shutters.

The sobbing grew louder.

It came from behind one of the shuttered doors.

James Arthur could barely breathe. He was captivated by the sound. His eyes followed the contour of the house to where a screen banged open. The carved door behind it had been left ajar, leaking strains of faint humming onto the porch. James Arthur started toward the door, cautiously. He followed creaky steps up onto the porch and then entered the dark house. A sliver of light from somewhere upstairs illuminated a sweeping staircase. He approached and started up.

The sobbing came again. This time, it was punctuated by a voice—a young, and pitiful voice. She seemed to be pleading with someone. He felt a strange urge to run to her, to comfort her, but he resisted.

Slowly, he crept up the stairs. Near the top of the staircase, he could make out dim light from farther along a mostly barren corridor. He moved slowly, steadily toward the flickering light.

As he opened the door, he saw a girl. Her face was covered by her hands and she sobbed as if her heart was broken. He stepped into the light. It took a moment for his eyes to adjust. He guessed she was a bit older than he was, maybe fourteen. Her frame was delicate and petite. Her skin was rosy and slightly scented. She smelled of cinnamon and jasmine. Her hair flowed half-way down her back in thick, black curls. Her frilly, white dress was made from some sort of French lace and fashioned after the ball gowns of the 17th century. Of course, this was Mardi Gras, so that, in and of itself, was not unusual. She wore a pair of white, lace gloves that went almost to her elbows.

James Arthur waited, watching quietly, afraid that if he moved, he might scare her away. He was still unable to see her face clearly. She kept it completely covered with her hands. It almost looked like she was praying, quivering on her knees in the center of the room. Bright wall-sconces glowed with the flickering light of oil lamps. He allowed himself a moment to take in the room. It was full of antiques, Queen Ann chairs and couches, decorative floor lamps, ornate end tables and all manner of bric-a-brac, all in pristine condition. If he did not know better, he would guess he had been pulled backward in time. He looked back to the girl. She had begun to sob so violently that her shoulders shook. He took a step into the room, moving slowly, cautiously toward her. He wanted to see her face. He wanted to stop whatever suffering she felt. A deep sympathy welled up inside him for this girl. He reached out to touch her.

"Hey," he said.

She spun, looking up at him. James Arthur gasped, stepping back. Her face had suddenly become visible. He had expected to see a delicate, beautiful face, like the rest of her, but this was not what he saw. Her eyes were badly scarred. Dead, blackened skin ran across the bridge of her nose and spread out almost to her ears.

"Did you come to gloat—to laugh?" she barked, seeing his shock. "Are you going to run away like all the others?" The skin looked as if it had been scorched by some intense bolt of fire. *Had someone tried to put her eyes out?* Even more disconcerting, the pupils of the eyes were bright amber and appeared to glow like molten glass. James Arthur felt his own eyes begin to water. What could have done this? It was as if lightening had slashed the girl's face, scarring her skin and melting her eyes.

The girl dropped her gaze again, her face falling back into her hands. Sobs racked her even harder. James Arthur moved forward. This time he bent slowly down and lifted her chin. She stared up at him a long moment, then reached and grabbed his arm.

"Monsiuer," she cried, "*help me!*"

James Arthur's felt a pulse of electricity run through him. The woman gasped. "Can you, can you be the one, the healer? I sense the art inside you—*there!*"

James Arthur felt a stab of pain behind his eyes. He staggered for a moment, falling back, and then the pain was gone. He felt a momentary elation. His heart beat wildly. His senses were suddenly heightened and aware.

"What did you do?" he asked.

Her eyes bore into him. "I can only stimulate what is already there. But the power—it is too great! *I cannot control it!*"

James Arthur could make little sense of the words. The girl looked away quickly, the cadence of her voice changing. She was speaking quickly now, breathlessly, like a crazy woman. "No! Foolish! *Foolish!* You mustn't be here when they come! It is not safe when they come! Tell me, boy, *do you want to look like this?*" She gestured frantically at her face, tearing at it with her fingers. "You cannot help me! No mere boy can help me*! He, he would make me obliterate you!*" She fell into sobs.

"Who?"

James Arthur tried to make sense of everything that was happening.

"Who is coming?"

Before his question was even finished, the girl screamed wildly, dropping to all fours. She scooted away from him, sobbing and pleading.

"*Go away!* You must go away, boy! *Now!* Go!"

Her eyes glowed brighter. They were hot coals, turning her cheeks deep orange. A crack sounded, high-pitched and deafening as a blinding bolt of white light erupted from the girl's face, connecting her molten eyes and crackling across the room in a dozen spidery bolts. She screamed. The skin around her eyes and across the bridge of her nose sizzled and popped, and there was a sour tang of burning, yet the white fire continued. With a final scream, the girl slapped her gloved hands over the eyes. The motion sent her careening forward in a spasm of convulsions, her body seeming to stretch and grow as he watched.

Finally, choking and gasping, the body straightened and stilled. An odd calm fell over her form. The young woman, a good foot taller, her clothes now ill-fitting, stood and pulled her hands away from her eyes. She looked up at James Arthur. She seemed years older—possibly in her mid-twenties.

"Dry your tears, good doctor," her voice echoed through the room. James Arthur realized that her lips were not moving, yet he heard the voice all the same. "I am come," she said. Her eyes pulsed with glowing light and smoked. Her lips turned up in a wild smile as she flung out her arms, echoes of laughter pealing through the room.

James Arthur tried to take it all in. What had happened to the girl? Who was the "*good doctor*" the woman spoke of? He scoured the room. There was no-one else there.

A crack sounded behind him, as if the air had been ripped apart, and the girl swooped forward, coming right at him. He screamed, feeling the woman's fiery face tear through him. Then, with a bone-shattering crack, he was yanked backward, and up again.

Everything went black.

He felt the spinning, the falling.

Then, he was on his knees, retching again, this time into thick dust on a warped, wooden floor.

James Arthur listened to his own breathing as he wiped at his mouth. He'd pushed back away from where he'd been sick and huddled against the barren wall. He was staring out at a decaying, barren room. The French doors were long gone and the hole was boarded up with rough planking.

"What," he breathed, "what just happened?"

There was no answer. *Had it been lightning?* But it had come from *within* the room, out of the girl's face! There was no sound—no sound in the room at all. James Arthur peered around frantically. The girl, the glowing eyes, the furniture—everything was gone! As he slowly adjusted to the darkness, he saw streaks of dim light speckled around the dark corners of the room. The air was muggy again, and the empty room smelled musty and fetid. He moved slowly, cautiously to the planks covering the opening where the French doors had been. He leaned his face forward to peer through a crack. The light outside was not the flickering glow of a torch, but the steady, even glow of electric lights. James Arthur backed out of the room.

"Hello?" he cried out. "Who are you?"

He heard his name being called, but it wasn't the sobbing girl or the wild-faced woman. It was the voice of his brother, Stephen. They must have reached this street, looking for him. He no longer felt anger at his brothers. He only felt a desperate desire to leave this place. He spun on his heels, thundered down the rickety stairs, and ran, out through the cobwebbed door frame, and across the uneven and rotted porch. *What had happened?* Had he hallucinated the whole thing? Had he just had an encounter with a—a what? A ghost? A witch?

Spooked, he shot out of the house at a run. The street, free of mud, was a ribbon of black asphalt, covered with tire tracks and dust. He glanced back at the house behind him. It was nothing but a vacant derelict. He sped toward the end of the street, practically running into Stephen. He was breathing heavy, trying to get hold of himself.

"Sorry," he finally spit out as David Christian quickly caught up with them. "I, I thought I had lost you."

David yelled at him and cuffed him on the back of the head, but Stephen stopped him. "Can't you see he's shaken up?" he said. He looked down. "That was stupid and *dangerous*, James Arthur! I don't care how smart you think you are. New Orleans is no place for little boys to be lost and alone after dark."

James Arthur nodded, still fighting to catch his breath.

Stephan finally turned and led them away.

David Christian came up behind him, and gave him another whack on the head, making sure to make it quick so Stephen didn't see.

"That's for calling me a meradi loser!" he shouted.

James Arthur said nothing. He just kept walking, ignoring David.

A couple of blocks away, when David Christian and Stephen had fallen into a conversation about the music drifting through the streets, James Arthur slowly held his hand up to examine it. It was still shaking. It tingled, as if with a low charge. *Strange...* He tried to remember what the girl's voice had said. She called him *Doctor*. Earlier, she asked if he was *the healer*. Suddenly, without equivocation, he knew what he would do with his life. He was a healer, and someday, he would find this girl again and repay her for helping him know.

"*Heal...*" his mind commanded again. The street, his brothers, New Orleans, slipped away, into the dark. He was again focused on healing his adult body. He again felt the dry heat, beating down on him. The pain had lessened, but he still could not move his arms or legs. He tried again to open his eyes. The sun was still too bright. It must be mid-day. *Where was he?* He tried to lick his lips. He tried to move his arms. All he could manage was to flex his hands. He turned his head sideways. He forced one eye open a slit. Sand was all he could see, burning sand that seemed to go on forever. His arm was tied to some sort of pole.

Not again, he thought.

He shut the eye tight. His limb felt leaden, as if welded in place. He concentrated and could tell his other arm and his legs were also tied in place. He felt a residual, dull ache at the back of his head and in his groin. His lips ached too. They were so dry—cracked and bleeding. He needed water. A hot wind blew across him and sand stung his face. He thought of the scarred girl in New Orleans. It had been so long since he thought of her. For a brief moment, he heard her pleading voice in his head. It cried out from the heart of the desert, over the winds and sighing sand.

"*Help me, Monsieur!*"

2

Lucky-7 Emporium

Willoughby watched the golden-fire disc of the sun trace its silent arc across a canvas of powdery Bermuda sky. The scene had all the makings of a Monet painting—the ocean before him heavy with impressions. There wasn't a cloud in sight. Only a few white sails dotted the mirror-blue sea, and while the sun was bright, a steady breeze kept it from feeling hot. Willoughby sat next to the most beautiful girl he had ever met and he wasn't nervous. In fact, he felt almost *comfortable* as she leaned in close and let her shiny hair fall across his shoulder. The moment was more than a Monet impression. *It was real.*

"So, my dear Mr. Von Brahmer," Sydney sighed, "we've taken a lot longer here than we meant to." Her voice took on a serious tone. "I know we've faced some horrible things." She tried to catch his eyes. "I also know that we've got to find a way to go on. We've got to put it behind us and find our friends. We've got to try to return to—to some flavor of normal."

They had stopped a few dozen feet from the lip of the bowl-shaped cove, sitting together on an old sea wall. Willoughby took in the expanse of the Atlantic Ocean beyond the edges of the cove. Behind him, the pastel-and-white houses of Bermuda rose above low, rock cliffs. The girl, Sydney Senoya—a sixteen-year-old, world famous concert violinist and fellow member of the secretive organization, *Observations, Inc.*—had claimed she needed to put her sandals back on. So, they had jumped up onto the sea wall, where they had sat for almost two hours. Willoughby brushed a little more sand from his still damp jeans and put his own socks and shoes back on. They were well within sight of the path that led back up to the Villa where Willoughby had been recuperating. He had been shot and poisoned.

He shuddered. "*Flavor of normal?* Can there be such a thing for us?"

"There has to be," Sydney said, her dark eyes brimming with intensity. "We've got to find it. We've got to get to where we can see fun and joy in the day again." She looked away, narrowing her gaze as if contemplating before turning back. "Maybe it's one of those *hidden things* H.S. likes to talk about. Maybe we've just got to look hard enough and we'll find it." She smiled at him.

Willoughby's shoulder was still numb and bandaged. He felt physically spent, but somehow, this visit with Sydney had left him feeling emotionally, well, energized. The two of them had lived through a bloody hijacking and they had survived. Many others hadn't. Sydney was right—he needed to keep his thoughts positive. He needed to concentrate on those they might still save, on their friends who were missing.

He had come to the cove because he wanted to see Sydney, to speak with her about the frightening events that had made him seem distant and insensitive, which was not at all how he wanted to be with her. Now, the explaining was done. She knew all about the stranger—the time-traveler who created zombie minions and claimed to be his grandfather. He told her about their first meeting in his friend Antonio's barber shop. About his second, more terrifying visit earlier that morning. It was time to move on now. With a thin smile, he met her gaze. He didn't say anything. He knew that they had sat here for so long because neither of them really wanted to return to the villa, to the mission, to the confusing and dangerous life that had suddenly engulfed them. He turned away and looked once again over the gently breaking waves.

What would it be like to be here with her as a boyfriend? He couldn't help wondering how different it would feel to hold her hand while having no more pressing concerns than where to go to grab lunch, or the test in trigonometry next week. He inwardly chuckled at himself. Trigonometry would *not* be a concern for him. He was a brilliant young mathematician who had already solved the Riemann Hypothesis, one of the longest unsolved mathematical puzzles of the past two centuries.

"If wishes were fishes… " He said quietly.

"Yeah," Sydney echoed after a slight pause.

Willoughby squinted up. "How long do you calculate it will take the sun to reach its zenith?"

"Me, *calculate?* That's your specialty." She leaned back. "But we better start back soon. Not that I wouldn't like to stay and pretend that we had this cove, this island, to ourselves for a day. But you know H.S… He'll have the hounds out searching by noon."

Willoughby chuckled aloud. H.S., the director of their team, was punctual and demanding. He was also becoming a friend and a strange sort of mentor in this world of the unknown. The secret organization he had become a part of, *Observations, Inc.*, traveled in time.

Time, Willoughby thought as he scoured the small, abandoned bay with his steel-gray eyes. Time with Sydney was something he wished he had more of. This was not the first time the two of them had been alone together, but it was the best time. Something had happened between them. They had faced death together. An unspoken bond had developed. He didn't fully understand it, but he liked it. They had shouted out their frustrations at the horror of the past week, berating the gently breaking waves. It had felt good to let go—to empty the pent-up tension. Now, their moment together was all but over, yet neither wanted to be the first to admit it.

The time-traveler, who called himself Beelzebub, Prince of Demons, surfaced in his mind. When he had told Sydney about the veiled threats the being had thrown out, about his brute zombie thug, and his claim to be related by blood, she had been quick to change the subject. He appreciated that. She had told him about a concert she once did on a small island just north of Japan called Miyako Island. "The sands there were a little pinkish too," she said. "I remember taking a little vial and collecting some of the sand because I didn't know if I would ever see pink sand like that again. Funny how we do that sometimes isn't it—how we hold on to things as if that can somehow stop the clock?"

How could he hold on to this moment? He felt an urge to take Sydney's hand and never let go. Instead, he rambled on to her about his school, Worthington Hills Academy. She said she would like to go there. He assured her that she would find the place stuffy and boring, though some of the architecture was nice. He gave her a sly grin.

"You know the kids at Worthington Hills wouldn't have a clue what to make of you," he teased. "You're, like, culture and fame rolled into raining lava."

She smacked him lightly on the arm. He feigned great pain, making her think for a moment she had hit his bandaged shoulder. Then he laughed, assuring her that his injury was on the other shoulder and he barely felt the swat. When she let her head rest on his good shoulder, however, he did feel a slight twinge of pain. He shifted slightly, causing her to pull away.

"I'm sorry. Is that hurting you?"

Willoughby, suddenly embarrassed, winced. "Yeah, a little... I guess I still have some healing to do." He looked down at the wound on his opposite shoulder. The bandaging was light—it had not been as bad a wound as it could have been. The bullet must have been deflected by the leather strapping on the trunk where he and Sydney had been hiding. A thought of her body pushed up against him in the tight space made his face flush. Perhaps she had thought of that too, because she straightened, looking slightly embarrassed. Stray bits of her silken hair danced on the sea breeze and her bracelets jangled softly.

"It's peaceful here," she finally said. "We'll have to come back some day."

"Yeah, I'd like that." Willoughby threw a shy glance at the girl. He liked the fact that she had used the word *we'll*. He broke into a grin. "But let's leave out the requiem."

Willoughby could still see the image in his mind of Sydney, waist-deep in the waters of the cove, passionately playing her violin to an audience of seagulls and the percussion of waves crashing softly on rock outcrops.

"Hey, I'm a musician. When I feel something strongly, I put it into my music."

"Yeah, but a requiem is for dead people. I hope you don't go plan a funeral every time you feel blue or someone upsets you."

"No. But, I am good at planning big events for myself. You know, Academy Awards, Musical Fellowships, the Nobel Prize for music… "

"There's a Nobel Prize for music? Really?"

Sydney nodded.

Willoughby whistled. "Well, I think you have a lot of years before you need to start submitting requiems." Truth was that he didn't doubt that she could be up for a Nobel Prize. Sydney didn't do anything halfway. She was shrewd, smart, and talented. If she really wanted something, well, let's just say you wouldn't want to be standing in her way.

Sydney kicked her feet, tapping against the wall slightly. She sucked in a deep breath and seemed to come to a decision. "Okay, truth time," she blurted out. "I've got millions of fans out there—you know this. They seem to love me, to accept me, even to revere me. But it's from a distance, you know?" She squinted, looking out over the gently capping waves. "It's like nobody wants to get up close, to really get to know me." She tucked a strand of silken, black hair behind her ear, looking down at her bare feet. "So… What's wrong with me?"

"Is this a multiple choice?"

She looked up, fighting a smile. "I'm serious!"

Willoughby studied her a moment. "Okay… It's buck-teeth."

Sydney swirled on him, horrified. "I don't have buck-teeth!"

Willoughby grinned. "Of course not, but other people do. Other people have pimples, and weight problems, and hair that won't cooperate. But you—you're, well, you're practically perfect. You're beautiful, you're intelligent, you're talented, you're famous, you're, you're…"

"Yeah?" she said, wide-eyed.

He fought down a smile. "You're just so incredibly humble."

Sydney snorted loudly. "Yeah, right!" she said, shaking her head. "Humility is certainly one of my strong suits, and thanks for pointing that out so clearly."

"I live to serve."

Willoughby caught the smile in Sydney's dark eyes, but didn't let his gaze linger. He had to be careful with Sydney. If he looked too long in those dark eyes, he knew he would betray himself. Those eyes were dangerous. They pulled at him, like strong riptides, threatening to swallow him whole, threatening to drown him in hidden depths.

"So," Sydney said, with a more relaxed sigh, leaning back again. "You think I need to be more humble?"

"Well, yeah—a little bit," Willoughby offered.

Sydney's eyebrow rose.

"Okay, well, a lot." He couldn't help smiling back at this girl. Despite all they had been through, Sydney had a way of bringing a smile to his face. He thought of how he had been drawn into and survived the jerk of a real time-hole, how he had met and survived a time zombie, how he had seen the very air rip apart as number strings poured from the breach and Beelzebub appeared—a being seemingly able to waltz through time without technology. He had even witnessed a live battle between a pack of Plesiosaurs and a prehistoric eel fish with fangs the height of his body, yet, none of these terrors had power over him when he was sitting next to, and staring into the eyes of Ms. Sydney Senoya. She leaned forward, her eyes widening. He felt his own face caught in her gravity.

"Uh, excuse please, Master Willoughby, sir?"

The voice startled them. It came from behind, breaking the moment. Willoughby had actually jumped a little, causing a jolt of pain to shoot through his stitches. He breathed in sharply, pausing a moment before he turned. He had been so intent on his conversation with Sydney, on the moment, that he hadn't heard the dark-skinned boy, no older than thirteen or fourteen, walk up. The boy stood near the curved edge of the path, sinking his toes into the sand. He was dressed in the casual porter uniform of the villa staff. His voice had a definite South African flair to it. He offered a toothy grin and a slight bow.

"You be Master Willoughby I presume?"

"Yes?" Willoughby smiled. The *I presume* part of the boy's questions tempted him to claim that he was none other than Dr. Livingston, but he resisted.

The porter seemed to suddenly remember his duty. He stood erect, presenting a practiced poise, despite his bare feet. He had stopped about a dozen yards away from them in the sand. "You see how I am much sorrowed by this intrusion, Master Wil—"

"Just Willoughby will do." Willoughby continued to smile.

The boy coughed, a little taken back. "Ah, yes, Sir Willoughby—"

"No, not Master, or Mister, or Sir, or anything—just Willoughby."

The boy seemed flustered now. Sydney bit back a snicker. Willoughby prompted the boy to continue.

"Yes, then, *just* Willoughby... uh, the Master, Lord H.S., has had to leave for the ship. A car is waiting for you, *just* Willoughby—back at the villa."

Sydney chimed in. "Ah, *just* Willoughby," she said in crisp Oxford accent, "It appears the *master*, Lord H.S., wants to pull you away from me as quickly as possible. How right he is to be concerned about your formidable influence on such an impressionable and dainty wildflower such as myself."

The porter remained rigid, almost as if at attention, but his eyebrows furrowed at the barrage of words. Sydney's face spread into a devious smile. "Of course, who could blame him? Was it not rather wicked of you to follow me to the cove—just to get me alone—and then refuse to kiss me? You're such a despicable boy!"

She ducked in, giving Willoughby a quick peck on the cheek. "There. That's an appetizer to tide you over. For the full-course meal, you'll have to do considerably better than two hours alone on a sea wall." She hopped from the wall, swooped to pick up her violin case, and turned to leave.

"Now, young sir, I say Adieu, to you, and you, and you..." she bowed several time. As she spun away she passed within inches of the porter, sweeping a hand lightly over his cheek. She wheeled from the path, danced to the top of a low dune, and turned back, putting a hand on a bit of wind-swept rock. "I've got shops to accost and many, many suitcases to fill." She once again donned her Oxford accent, waving an arm toward the villa; "Go my brave soldiers! March up those sands, my own *just* Willoughby! Go with your good lieutenant! I must flit away, off to the nether-lands of commerce where I shall lavish myself as the mermaid princess I secretly am!"

She whirled her arms, allowing her drooping sleeves to create a swath of color on the air and then stepped behind the rock, out of sight.

"Hey!" Willoughby called after her. "The villa is the other way." He started to point, but realized it was useless.

Her Oxford voice, brimming with mischief, floated back to them on the breeze. "*To the mysteries, young soldier—to adventures that lie hidden, and lands of tomorrow, and the wide, curious expanse of those yester years.*" Her words had a musical quality, as if she were chanting to some unheard melody, each word executed in perfect harmony to the restless sea and the stirrings of ocean breeze.

Willoughby waited a moment longer to make sure Sydney was really gone. When she didn't reappear, he stood, with a sigh, taking care to safeguard his shoulder. He turned back to the porter, whose eyes trailed after Sydney, his mouth ajar. Only the boy's eyes moved, scanning the folds of the wind-swept rock.

"I believe, sir, that I would have kissed her," he stammered. "Does she really think herself to be a mermaid, or princess?"

"Most likely both," Willoughby admitted, cocking his head, "I'd steer clear of that one if I were you. She would skewer you on a spit and roast you for lunch." He stepped toward the boy, throwing a fleeting glance back toward the place where Sydney had made her dramatic exit. "Still, when you consider that you're dealing with a *Type-A* personality who has *Type-B* through *Z* aspirations, a mermaid is as good a choice as any. I can't actually say I've seen anything that screams *mermaid* to me, but I can say that her eyes are dangerous and mesmerizing. They'll pull you in if you let them and devour you whole. That's quite a neat trick for one with the bearing of a princess." He let his focus turn back to the boy, who had raised both eyebrows, his mouth still open.

"*Devour you whole?*" the boy mumbled.

Willoughby grinned. He was enjoying himself. "Uh huh—she told me she was a mermaid once before. I researched it, of course. I couldn't find a single visible scale on her arms, back, stomach, or legs. Then there's the obvious issue—she has no fins and no tail, at least, none that I could see. Of course, I didn't see everything…" He paused, as if in deep thought. The boy didn't respond. "There was one night that I saw her playing alone on her Stradivarius, though. You know she's a world famous violinist, right? She has millions of adoring fans. Her concerts are things of legend, you see, but on that night, she was playing alone, in front of a foaming, green sea. A pale moon was shining down on her silken hair. I could have sworn voices answered her from the waves and the mist. They called out, '*Sister…*'"

The porter's eyes stretched wider as though he didn't know if Willoughby was teasing or not. Willoughby grinned as he passed the boy, reaching out a hand to close the boy's mouth. He patted him once on the cheek, the same one Sydney had stroked, and then continued on up the path toward the villa. He was almost halfway up the hill when the boy caught up with him.

"Still," the boy said, "I would have kissed her, *just* Willoughby. It would have been an interesting thing to do."

Willoughby smiled to himself the rest of the way to the villa.

As they crested the hill and left the rows of quaint condos behind them, the porter pointed to the extended drive that circled around in front of the huge villa door.

"That car—it is for you. I believe that is your driver loading your luggage."

Willoughby knew he didn't have any luggage. Everything that he had brought with him on this trip had been sunk deep in the waters of the Atlantic Ocean. He was lucky to have the clothes on his back. They had been cleaned and laundered after his experience, but as soon as he could replace them, he planned to. He didn't want anything to remind him of the horror of the hijacking of their proud ship, the *Aperio Absconditus.*

The young messenger didn't know this, though, so he thanked the boy. He reached into his pocket to provide a tip and realized that he had no money with him. He panicked a moment until he recognized the figure at the car. He broke into a run.

"Sam!" he shouted. The man turned and waved. Willoughby glanced back at to the porter. "Sam is my chauffer from back in the States. He'll have a nice tip for you."

"It is not necessary, *just* Willoughby. I work for Observations, Inc. too."

Willoughby appraised the boy with new eyes. With his khaki shorts and a colorful blue shirt, the boy could easily pass as one of the island youths. There did not seem to be anything extraordinary about him. Then again, that was what Observations, Inc. was all about—hiding things in plain view.

"What's your specialty?" Willoughby asked.

"Fish," the boy said with a toothy grin.

"Fish?"

"Yes," the boy continued. "I am very good at catching and selecting the best fish. I work for your head of island cook." Willoughby looked perplexed, so the boy continued. "You know the big boss. I believe you call him 'H.S.' He is quite particular about his fish."

Willoughby barked a short laugh. "I didn't know he was the island cook."

"Yes! He is the best cook on all the island," the boy said, beaming, "and I select his fish."

"Very good," Willoughby said. "It was a pleasure to meet you."

"And you," the boy said. He started to turn, then hesitated; "Also, the princess, who may or may not be a mermaid…"

Willoughby jogged the rest of the way to the car. While he took a moment to catch his breath, he noted that Sam really was loading a trunk into the back of the sparkling black automobile. The tall man finished the task and turned to Willoughby, offering a firm handshake and a warm smile.

"Good to see you, young Willoughby. H.S. took the liberty of asking me to pick up a few things, since you lost your belongings in the, uh—the unfortunate incident with the *Absconditus*. I put them in a trunk for you. Sydney helped me pick out the clothes. I hope they're to your liking."

For the first time since leaving the beach, Willoughby frowned. "You didn't let her get me anything with smiley faces or hot wheels cars on it, did you?" He was thinking of a pair of pajamas Sydney had put on him after his surgery.

Sam grinned. "She tried, but I reined her in."

"Thanks," Willoughby said with relief. Sam opened the back passenger door and he climbed in. As Sam closed the door and walked around the front of the car, Willoughby stared back toward the beach. For a few moments, he had felt a peace of sorts. He had almost felt that he could put the horror of the past behind him. Seeing the villa, however, forced him to remember the unfortunate *incident* Sam referred to. He couldn't pretend anymore that it hadn't happened. The ship *had* been hijacked. Its crew *had* been brutally and systematically murdered. He, Sydney, and Dr. O'Grady *had* escaped through a time door. Some of their scientific team— Antonio, James Arthur (or Dr. J as he liked to be called), the pretty, blue-eyed cabin girl, T.K., and the strange Hindu girl who had helped them escape (the one named *Hauttie*, with an *au*)—were still unaccounted for. Their handler, H.S., believed that they each found the hidden time door and escaped. *But to where?* If the door had been compromised, or had been improperly controlled, his friends could be anywhere—lost across unknown corridors of time.

"Are we ready?" Sam said, abruptly interrupting his thoughts. He looked over.

"Uh, yeah, I am. Thanks, Sam. Let's get out of here." He had no interest in spending one second more than he had to at this villa.

Sam nodded and started the car. Willoughby's mind churned. *How had he become part of all this madness?* Observations, Inc. had studied and then recruited him, partly for his mathematical brilliance, and partly, as it turned out, because of his birth father, Gustav, who they had an interest in. They tricked him into stepping into one of their time-holes, and then dazzled him with a level of technology that he still had a hard time believing could really exist. He had stepped back in time to observe a

Jurassic Era sea in a prehistoric world. After that, anything academia could offer had seemed drab and predictable. *Why hadn't he understood the full danger?*

As predictable as his old life had been, and as boring as his old school had seemed, he would take them back in a moment if he could undo what had occurred on the *Absconditus*. Seeing Sam, his chauffer for almost two years at Worthington Hills Academy, brought thoughts of his family. What would his mom and stepdad, Klaas say if they knew he was traveling in time and had almost lost his life? They would come unglued. What if he never saw his half-sisters, Densi and Cali again? He missed them terribly. But things had begun to unravel around him, and the past could not be changed. He was part of something now— something that had begun long before he joined *Observations, Inc.* Even H.S. with all of his technology, had not foreseen the danger Willoughby brought to the organization. One question burned inside him. *Why?* Until he had some semblance of an answer, until he knew how to safeguard his family and friends, going home was not an option.

He sighed, staring out the window as Sam rolled slowly to the end of the villa drive. His parents believed he was on a three-week educational cruise, a prize he had won by writing a brilliant essay on historic mathematics. Best that they keep believing that for now.

Sam had pulled out onto the main road. He looked up into the rearview mirror. Willoughby would welcome any comment right now—a "You're quiet today," or a "What do you think of the island?" Anything. But Sam was the quiet type. It wasn't his way to make small talk.

At least he was here, though. As Willoughby turned back toward the window, he thought of his birth father,

Gustav. Somehow, his father—a man who had walked out of his life when he was barely two—was mixed up in all of this. Gustav had left for no discernible reason. There had been no goodbye. He had just left for work one day and never came home. For years, Willoughby had heard his mother crying quietly at night. Then, she had met Klaas, an immigrant from Sweden. Klaas was a superb architect, and a good man.

"Don't worry about the clothes," Sam said, causing Willoughby to look up. Sam had been watching him in the rearview mirror. "H.S. had all your measurements and I did have some input. After two years of driving you to school, I do have some idea of your tastes. I added toiletries, the latest *Artemis Fowl* installment, a Nintendo DSI gaming device, an iPod mini, various electronic gear you may need or appreciate, and snacks and such." He drove cautiously and lazily. "Given the circumstances, H.S. thought it best you not go back to your room."

Willoughby nodded. "Thanks," he mumbled. He couldn't disagree with H.S.'s assumption. He had been visited early that morning by Beelzebub and his zombie henchman. The white-eyed zombie had been called *Gates* when he walked among the living. H.S. had sunk the *Absconditus* as soon as he learned of the massacre. It was his way of keeping sensitive technology out of the wrong hands. Somehow, the being Beelzebub had snatched the drowning Gates seconds before the finality of death. He kept the brute in a half-alive stasis as a zombie slave. The bouncer-thug had tried to serve Willoughby breakfast, among other things. Willoughby shuddered at the thought. He intensified his gaze out the window, trying to clear the image from his mind.

The rustic green of the island passed slowly. He rolled the window down slightly to smell the fresh breeze and hear the crash of the surf. The sands of Bermuda really did look pinkish from a distance. He caught glimpses of bits of beach, and his mind drifted back to thoughts of Sydney. They were much more agreeable and less frightening.

At that moment, Sam broke in on his thoughts. "So, what do you think of the ride?"

Willoughby glanced about him, noting the car for the first time. He grinned. "Not your usual junk." Sam was driving him in a snub-nosed Rolls Royce with a pristine interior. The chauffer gave him a grin in the rear-view mirror.

"We could have taken a taxi."

"Are you kidding?" Willoughby gave a quick wave to a boy on a bicycle. "And pass up the chance to feel like Prince Charles?" He forced a smile.

Sam stared into the mirror for a long moment, his sunglasses masking all emotion. Finally, he said quietly. "You okay?"

Willoughby shrugged. He glanced over his shoulder. "The further we get away from that place, the better I'm feeling."

Sam nodded, as if he understood. "You want to go straight to the yacht, or do you want me to take you somewhere else?"

Willoughby thought for a moment. Sydney would be out shopping for hours, which meant he would be hanging out at the yacht with Sam. He really liked Sam, but the idea of just sitting on a small boat docked at the pier all afternoon did not really hold much appeal. He remembered his promise to his half-sisters to bring them back a souvenir. Would he have a better chance than this to pick something up for them?

"Are there any shops near the pier?"

"They're mostly tourist and curio shops."

"Good. That's exactly what I'm looking for. I need to pick up some souvenirs for the family and I think killing some time in a public place with a lot of other people around would be helpful."

"Would you like me to go with you?"

"No, I'll be fine. I'll walk on over to the yacht as soon as I'm done." Willoughby thought for a moment. "Oh, but I'll need some money. Is that a problem?"

Sam let go a rare laugh. He glided through a round-a-bout, then reached into his shirt pocket and pulled out three $100 bills. "Compliments of Observations, Inc." he said, handing the bills over. The two did not speak again until Sam pulled over to the curb about ten minutes later. "These shops should do nicely. You are less than a mile from the pier. When you're ready, just follow the road to the bottom of the hill, and then turn right. You'll see the wooden pier and the Rolls parked at the end by H.S.'s yacht, The Pesci Picolli. You can't miss it. Stay in public areas with lots of people around. If you run into any trouble, use this to call." He handed Willoughby a cell phone. "I'm speed-dial one."

"Thanks Sam," Willoughby said, sticking the phone into his shirt pocket. He opened the door. "How long do you get to keep the Rolls for?"

"As long as necessary," Sam grinned.

"Cool." Willoughby stepped to the curb. He started to shut the door, but then opened it again. "What?" he asked. He thought he had heard Sam mutter something just before the door shut. It had sounded like, "*Since I own it.*"

"Nothing," Sam said. "I'm just reminding myself to phone H.S."

"Why?"

"I need to let him know where you are."

Willoughby shrugged. "Oh. Okay. See you in a bit." He closed the door hard this time and turned toward the area of shops. Sam pulled slowly away and disappeared over the crest of a small hill. As soon as the Rolls was completely gone from view, Willoughby ducked into the first store. He found little there, but continued to comb through the small shops one by one. He found a plush Scottie dog complete with hat and cape for his half-sister, Cali. He thought of getting Densi, his older half-sister, a plush cat as a joke (cats were currently the bane of her existence) but he thought better of it. Instead, he found her a genuine paper parasol with a delicate print of exotic island flowers and fauna. He picked out an Edinburgh Crystal candy dish for Mom, and got Klaas an old, working sexton from an antique shop.

Just as he decided to call it a day and head back to the ship, an odd roofline caught his attention. It was from a low roof down a narrow, zigzagging alley between two older buildings. The buildings were nothing out of the ordinary, but the roof tiles didn't seem to match up when viewed from one corner of the alley opening. Willoughby could swear there was a small gap. Most people wouldn't even have noticed, but then, Willoughby wasn't most people. He stepped into the alley to investigate.

About fifteen yards into the alley, as he drew close to the supposed gap, he discovered that the roof was actually split, opening to an even narrower alley that shot off at almost a 40% angle from the main one. The roof on the left side of the opening was stretched out to cover the roof line, effectively hiding the narrower alley from all but the most particular observer. Turning into the narrower alley, Willoughby was forced to turn sideways as the opening was barely two feet wide. He walked about ten yards and found himself in a square courtyard, maybe fifteen feet by fifteen feet. Three sides of the courtyard were solid brick wall up to the roof. The fourth side held a door, with a rocking wooden sign hanging over it, and a window, divided into thirty-six rectangular panes of glass in six rows of six panes. Each pane formed a Golden Rectangle—a rectangle based on the Golden Ratio. Observations, Inc. used the ratio heavily in their time-travel technology, much as the ancient Greeks had relied on it in much of their architecture. *Was this a hidden base or time-hole of some kind? Why wouldn't H.S. have told him about it?*

Willoughby peered at the rocking wooden sign. What was making the sign rock on its rusted chains? This hidden alcove was pretty protected from the sea breeze. He caught a glimpse of a light blue glow at the top, right corner. He could feel his heart pounding harder in his chest. Fancy, hand-painted lettering on the sign read *Lucky-7 Emporium*, though the words were barely legible due to the faded and peeling state of the paint. The sign itself was cracked and weathered, as if it were at least a hundred years old.

The light blue glow came again and the sign rocked as if to some hidden rhythm. Willoughby narrowed his eyes. A pale blue string of numbers curled around the top, left corner of the wood sign. The string was made up entirely of the number seven repeated over and over. It flickered, disappeared, and then flared back. Willoughby stood alone on the cobblestone courtyard, trying to determine if these were numbers he alone could see, or if some sort of holographic trick of the eye was creating the odd display. The numbers winked out again. This time, they did not return.

Willoughby looked at the door and the cobwebbed window. The shop, at first glance, seemed abandoned. A clutter of contents strewn across ancient-looking shelves, though, attested to the fact that it was not. He thought of the marina, and Sam, and H.S. He could see in his mind the neat row of boats docked at the pier with Sam's Rolls Royce parked near one of the larger yachts. *Should he go to the yacht first and ask about the shop?* It had to be an Observations, Inc. facility. Who else would hide a little shop front like this in a back alley? He searched the brick over the door and around the window, looking for the tell-tale symbol the company always hid near a time-hole or an Observations, Inc. facility. The symbol was a spiral of right triangles with the numbers 313 underneath, the last 3 backwards. He could not find any hint of the symbol anywhere. The more he searched the more certain he became that there was no symbol hidden in the walls of the courtyard or in the door and window of the storefront. But if this wasn't an Observations, Inc. facility, what was it? It felt different from anything he had experienced before. He felt a slight shiver run down his spine.

Sam had warned him to stay near other people. He had already ignored that advice. Now, he had the strongest impression that he should enter this dark building, completely alone, completely away from anyone who could help him. He stopped himself, screaming in his mind, *"Are you mad? Think of what you've just been through! Turn and run!"*

As if hearing his thoughts, the circle of sevens appeared again, this time rotating three turns around the shop's doorknob. The numbers faded. Willoughby couldn't help himself. He moved slowly forward as if pulled by an invisible string.

The door to the Emporium creaked slowly open.

3

Open Wounds

The beast, with its great fanged mouth, was rearing to strike T.K. a final blow. It was mad with fury. One of T.K.'s knife slashes had wounded its left eye. As it sprang, Antonio instinctively shot up, ignoring the searing pain in his leg. He grabbed the nearest jagged rock and flung it at the thing's enormous, black head. *He had to do something!* By some miracle, the rock hit the monstrous head in mid strike, cutting a deep gash in the corner of the beast's one good eye. It twisted in mid air, its strike going awry as it howled in anger and pain, jerking toward the new threat, toward Antonio. It tried to attack, but blood was filling the good eye, and it could not seem to find him. Antonio held his breath, pushing himself tight against the cave wall. Howling, the beast jerked back, its long neck coiling protectively around the wounded eyes and then plunged below the dark waters of the cave. Antonio sat for a moment, panting, grabbing at another rock, sure that, at any moment, the black head would burst up again, ready to strike.

He was right. The beast thundered up in a rush of water, throwing its huge flippers against the rock shelf in an effort to pull itself out of the water. Its fangs plummeted toward him. He threw his rock, but it only hit the beast's chin, barely slowing it. There was no time to pick up another rock. There was no time to do anything but bravely die. Antonio steeled himself, roaring back at the beast with all his strength, and waiting for the fowl mouth to close down on him. The noise filling the cave shook his whole body. The head of the beast descended, teeth closing...

Bolting upright, Antonio screamed. His eyes had snapped open and he tried to focus. He held a hand up, protecting his face, ready to fend off the beast's teeth. But there was no beast. The cave was dark and silent. The only sound was his heavy breathing. *How was he here?* The beast's fangs had been only yards away. *What happened?*

He tried to think back, but his mind was muddled and confused. If he was already dead, how could he have heard himself screaming? If he wasn't dead, how had he survived? He fought a sense of growing panic inside him as he desperately scanned the darkness.

Where was T.K.? He tried to move but the pain from his leg was intense. Jolting upright had already made him nauseous, and moving his head only made things worse. He felt suddenly weak and dropped back onto the cold rock. He faded for a moment, coming back to consciousness just in time to hear himself gasp. He turned his head slowly this time. He could not hear or see the beast. Neither could he see or hear T.K. He squinted into the dimness.

The cave appeared empty. The darkness was only broken by a pale glow from below the surface of the dark waters that covered much of it. Calming his breathing, he tried again to gather his thoughts. His hands trembled. His forehead was wet with fever and the cold rock he lay on was hard and rough. He groped at his body, assessing the damage. He was bare-chested, but everything above his waist seemed in workable condition—only bruised and scratched. He couldn't reach down past the waist, but he could see in the dim light that his jeans were in tatters and one of his legs was badly swollen. The air smelled of sulfur. Agonizingly slow, he remembered how he'd come here. Not just to be lying here, alive, but how he had come to the cave of beasts at all.

He was in a small shop—The Corner Barber. He had been recruited earlier by an ultra-secret organization with a grasp of inter-spatial dimensions and time travel. He had been asked to evaluate a boy. Willoughby turned into a regular customer and then a friend. He had been worried about recruiting the boy—he was too young. But he was also brilliant in mathematics and there was something unusual about him…

Their first mission together had gone terribly wrong. Willoughby, and most of the rest of team, were missing and very possibly could be dead. Antonio closed his eyes, trying to hold back the frustration, the anger. *Was it his fault? Was it the team leader, H.S.'s fault?* Their ship had been hijacked by brutal thugs who had killed most of the crew. He and one other team member had been freed by one of the crew—a feisty, petite blonde who went by the name of T.K. She had led them to H.S.'s quarters. His other team member, James Arthur, had gotten separated from them. While trying to find him, they had stumbled onto a time-door and had been sucked in, thrown back to this dim cave to fight an angry, giant plesiosaurus. Now, all of the cool technology and his excitement at being able to use his advanced architectural skills to build across dimensions meant nothing. He didn't know where his friends were or if he would ever see them or his home timeline again.

He closed his eyes tight, his head throbbing. There was so much to think about, so much to sift through, and he knew there were details he wasn't remembering. *What had been the purpose of their mission?* It had something to do with the seer Nostradamus and a crystal pendant. He did vaguely recall the shape of a tattoo the hijackers had on their thick necks. It was an eye over a pyramid dissected by a line, with a number three in front of and then a backward 3 behind the bottom of the line.

His thoughts turned back to the girl who had helped him escape. She had been a cabin-girl on the ship, a beautifully crafted Windjammer called the *Aperio Absconditus.* T.K. had the bluest eyes he had ever seen. *How had she escaped the hijackers?* She had been close with the Captain of the ship, even referring to him as a second father. As Antonio mulled the question over, he remembered that he had talked to the Captain about turning back when he noticed irregularities with the crew. Had the Captain, in turn, spoken with T.K.?

He thought of James Arthur. Had Dr. J, as he liked to be called, also been sucked into the time-hole? If so, why hadn't he also fallen into this cave? T.K. didn't think so. She seemed to know the cave. *How?* One of the attackers had called her *Princess.* Why?

There were many questions and few answers. He looked down at his swollen leg. The beast had attacked even before they could swim to the bit of rock ledge in the cave. It had bitten his leg and would have pulled him under had not T.K. pulled a knife and slashed its eye. He gritted his teeth as his whole body shook with a fever-induced chill. The wound throbbed. *Where was T.K.?*

In time, he was able to force himself up onto his elbows. "T.K.?" he called out. There was no answer. Surely, if the beast hadn't fled, he wouldn't be here, alive. Did T.K. do something at the last minute—something foolish? A sense of panic welled up in his chest. "*T.K.,*" he grunted again. He was desperate now. He searched his mind again, playing over his last few seconds before his blackout.

He saw again in his mind the terrible beast bursting from the water, its gaping mouth and sharp teeth striking down at him. This time, however, there was a whir of movement out of the corner of his eye. T.K. had moved with such speed, grace, and skill, brandishing her long knife like a warrior, that she had been undetected. She had slashed at the beast's throat, and then everything went black.

"T.K.?" he croaked, only a little louder.

The only answer was a slow, dripping sound. He strained his neck. *What was that sound?* It was maddeningly slow, echoing in the silence of the cave. Finally, he located its source. A few yards behind and to the side of him, he saw a bedraggled shirt, draped over a ridge of rock—*his* shirt. He looked down, noticing again that he was bare-chested. He also saw that someone had moved him under a ledge of the rock wall, well away from the dark waters. A few feet above him, the thick overhang of rock offered some level of protection. The beast wouldn't be able to get to him here. *Who had dragged him into this shallow alcove?* It had to have been T.K., so she must be *alive!* But where was she?

He tried to scoot out to the edge of the overhang, to look down into the water, but every muscle in his body hurt, and his leg burned like fire. He could not inspect the leg, but he was sure it had become infected. It was badly swollen and it smelled. He remembered the sharp rip as the beast had sunk its teeth into his flesh. *Why hadn't he listened to T.K.? Why hadn't he swam faster?* His brain had frozen. He had never seen anything like the beast—at least, not living, not outside of the pages of a book. He remembered pictures he had seen as a boy of what artists imagined a plesiosaur to look like. *They were wrong!* It was much, *much* bigger, and uglier, and meaner…

His head throbbed in time with his leg. He focused his eyes outside of the overhang. How long had he been in and out of consciousness? The water was darker than he remembered, but it still glowed—brighter in some spots, dimmer in others. *What made it glow?* He suddenly noticed that the walls of the cave glowed in spots as well. *Why?* Was there light filtering up from somewhere deep in the water? Were the cave walls and lake-bottom both covered with phosphorescent algae? Everything was silent. There was only the drip, drip, drip of water from his shirt. He tried to move again, but pain shot through his leg. He glanced down. He could see his leg a little clearer now. It was *not* a pretty sight. The viscous bite on his leg had started oozing a dark green puss.

From the water's edge, he heard a faint gasp. He turned to see T.K.'s head bobbing above the surface of the water. He sighed with relief. The sleek, fit shape of T.K. pulled up onto the rock shelf. She had the long knife again, holding it in her mouth. She had stripped down to her under garments. She looked over.

"It's about time." She motioned for him to turn away as she wrung the water from her short-cropped, blond hair and pulled her tattered ship uniform back on. "It was getting old—just watching you lay there." He looked back over just in time to see her pull a wad of pale weed up from the water. She dropped it onto the rock ledge a few feet away from the water's edge. After resting a moment, she bent down to clean her knife blade.

"I am glad you are safe, Senorita," Antonio managed to mumble. "But how is it I am alive?"

"Well, that's a very good question." T.K. took a deep breath. "You were an idiot to throw that rock, but thanks to you, I had time to find my knife. I carved a six-inch gash into the right side of its neck only seconds before it would have taken off your head. It was close."

She looked down for a moment and then over at him. "You do realize how stupid it is to attack a striking plesiosaurus, right? You don't throw rocks at a predator that outweighs an elephant. It only gets them mad. You were lucky hitting its one good eye. Lucky, *comprendes?* Try it again and you'll be dead."

Antonio stared up at the rock of the overhang. "So, you wish to say '*thank you?*'"

"Well, yes, sort of." She sighed. "Don't mind me. I'm a bit put out at the moment." Her face cracked into a wry smile. "But it was nice to hear the little beastie wail!" Her voice betrayed a sense of exhaustion. "Despite our slight victory, though, I don't think we blinded it for good and the gash was only a flesh wound. It will be back and it has plenty of brothers and sisters. If we're lucky, we bought ourselves a few days. That's probably it."

Everything seemed surreal to Antonio. *Was this a dream?* He tried to make sense of the black, snake-like thing that had attacked him. "Where," he began, staring weakly around; "Where are we? What is this place?"

T.K. sighed, grabbing the bundle of dripping weed and dragging it further from the water's edge. "You, my friend, are now a proud guest of Hotel Jurrasica."

"Hotel Jurrasica?"

"Yes. You check in, and then our friend's black, ugly face—or one of its buddies—constantly tries to check you out."

Antonio forced his thought to his surroundings. The cave was oblong and sloped at both ends. The damp rock beneath him fell away from its high point near the alcove to plunge steeply into the now still waters that stretched beyond his line of sight. T.K. dropped the weeds just outside the overhang.

"What do you remember? You've already asked questions, but you were fighting the poison, so it's possible you don't remember. Do you recall Belzarac's men banging on the outside of the closet door? You told me it had to be the time door because the knob glowed and the walls were metal. You said to just *trust* you. Then you flung us into an eternal free-fall, and we splashed down here—running from one bloody nightmare directly into another. If the beast hadn't made an appearance, I probably would have killed you myself... *Trust you?*" She gave a sarcastic laugh.

Antonio tried to focus through the growing pain. He ignored her snide tone. "*You seem to know this place?*" he managed, between ragged breaths.

T.K. dropped to the cave floor and pushed up against a smooth bit of rock-wall near the edge of the overhang. She stared straight ahead, not letting her eyes drift from the sight of the foul waters.

"Yeah. I know this place. I shouldn't have trusted anyone who plays with time."

Antonio started to respond, pushing up slightly, but as he opened his mouth, he inadvertently moved his leg and pain wracked his body. All he managed was a low moan and belabored breathing. He fell back to the cool rock. T.K. watched, and then looked away with a loud sigh. "Sorry. This is not your fault. I should have known whatever *gateway* H.S. built would lead here."

Antonio tried to use his good leg to push the injured one over, but a blinding pain stopped him. His muscles clenched and he screamed. T.K. moved quickly to bind him down, pinning his shoulders to the cave floor. He saw the barely-contained fury in her eyes. He had seen that fury unleashed as she had stabbed at the monster when it attacked. There had been a cold, calculated fierceness in her every move—the feel of predator facing predator, not predator facing prey. She had stabbed her knife instinctively, knowing just where to penetrate the beast's slick hide, and just how to disable the mindless eating machine. As the huge, black neck had first jerked up from the water, the beast had exposed a sleek, seal-like underbelly and huge flippers. But she hadn't gone for those. She had waited until she could swipe at the eye.

Antonio turned away, shaking slightly. His muscles finally released. When he looked back over, T.K.'s eyes had softened. She bit her lip. "I've got to take a look at that wound." She scooted over and inspected the swelling.

"The—beast—was it a Plesiosaurus?" Antonio groaned, gritting his teeth against another throb of pain.

"Yeah. I already told you that. You don't remember?"

Antonio shook his head. "It seemed big—bigger than I would expect."

"I take it you're no paleontologist," T.K. said as she peeled back Antonio's tattered jeans. "A few scattered bones don't tell the whole story of an entire species. I doubt he's the biggest of his kind, but he's a good size. I've seen bigger."

Antonio forced a smile. "You are sure it is a he?"

T.K. gave a low snort. "The males are larger and more aggressive than the females. I am fairly certain it is a *he*."

"I've known my—my share of vicious *she's*," Antonio mumbled. "How do the walls and the water—glow?"

"You probably think I'm vicious," T.K. mumbled. She looked over toward a patch of glow. "I think it's a form of phosphorescent algae under the water's edge. The walls are lined with some sort of lichen that glows as well. I can't tell you more than that. I'm no botanist."

She turned and moved closer. Carefully, but without warning, she lifted Antonio's leg. He screamed from pain. She quickly slid a flat rock under the calf, effectively elevating it. Antonio's whole body convulsed for a long moment, forcing her to hold him down again.

"Sorry," T.K. said, trying to steady him. "You're burning up with fever. I have no choice. I have to lance that bite and suck out the poison or it will rot your leg away."

Antonio balled his fists, fighting to regain control of the pain. "You said before that I was fighting poison. That, that thing had—had poison?"

"It's in their saliva, sort of like a Komodo Dragon. I had one graze me once. I went through much of the same thing you're going through. I still have the scars on my arm. The procedure won't be pretty, but it will help your leg heal." She placed a wad of salty, rubbery weeds into his mouth. "Bite down."

Antonio wanted to ask how she knew this—how she knew of this place, these plants, these beasts, how she got injured before—but he couldn't talk. The taste of the weed in his mouth was bitter and slimy. He was debating in his mind whether to chew the wretched stuff or spit it out when T.K.'s knife punctured the wound. A searing jolt racked him, and he bit down hard, fighting an urge to shove T.K. away. A thick, bitter juice squirted out from the weed and seeped down the back of his throat. He felt a tingling and a numbing sensation. It helped him manage the pain.

T.K. cut in quick strokes, dropping her head after each cut to suck and spit. She repeated the operation over and over, until the ordeal was through and then washed the wound with salt water. The smell was almost unbearable. During the course of the procedure, Antonio had felt the weed in his mouth dull his mind, not only to the pain, but to everything else. He watched with detachment as T.K. carefully rinsed out her mouth with dark cave water. She brought handfuls of the water again and again to wash and rewash the cuts in his leg. The salt prickled, but did not openly burn.

Finally, she moved back to the dark lake, wretched, washed her hands and mouth again a little further away, and then washed her knife blade. She moved even further down the rock ledge and rinsed her mouth a third time. When she returned to the overhang, she grabbed a stalk of the pale weed and bit off a mouthful. At the same time, she picked up one of the weed stalks, dipped it in the water, and tried to sweep the area clean.

After she had chewed the weed into a sticky pulp, she spat it onto the largest of Antonio's cuts. She chewed and spat again and again, until all the cuts were covered.

Finished, she pushed back against a stretch of smooth wall, breathing heavily, and collapsed. The cave grew quiet.

Antonio felt the pulp on his cuts go to work. A tingly numbness seeped into his wounds, further dulling the pain. At last, he turned his head and rid his mouth of the remaining weed pulp. T.K. used a bit of fresh weed to pick up the spent wad and throw it toward the dark water. Antonio slowly wiped a hand across his parched and battered lips.

"I remember… They were beating on the door. I thought they would break through or destroy the mechanism. We found the gateway. That was our only option. I thought it would take us to an observation window, to a, a safe place," he said softly, his voice trailing off.

"Wrong, wrong, *wrong*," T.K. murmured, her tone defeated and bitter.

"I think," Antonio began, haltingly. He was fighting to keep his eyes open. "I think that you are not what you seem to be, *senorita*… "

"In that, you are right," the girl said softly, staring out over the dark waters.

Antonio managed to glance sideways at the girl for a moment and then mumbled softly. "That man who chased us—I think you called him Belzar—or Belzarac, or something like that—he called you *Princess*. Why? How do you know this place?"

"That man is a fool and a liar. He used to be an assistant of the man you call H.S."

Antonio's eyes widened. "One of the—hijackers used to assist H.S.? Why would… "

T.K. interrupted him, looking over at him with a withering glance. "Just suffice it to say there's a lot you don't know about H.S." She turned away. After a long, tense silence, she said more softly. "This place brings back memories I've fought with all my strength to forget, Antonio. Yes, I've been here before. Like I told you, I was wounded much like you.

"What I haven't told you is that my older brother was with me. He wasn't as lucky as you. I wasn't old enough to help him. I had to watch, helpless and screaming, as he fought a beast even bigger than that demon. I was only a child. In the face of such brutality, I—I froze. I saw the beast finally defeat my brother and drag him under. He'd fought bravely. At one point, it even backed off and dove away, deep into the dark water. I thought it had gone. I thought my brother had won. He started swimming back toward me. He yelled at me to get to the rock shelf. He said he would be right behind me. *I believed him!* When I pulled up onto the shelf, I looked back. He had barely moved. For the first time, I saw that he was wounded. I dove back into the water to go to him, but then the hideous black head of the beast shot up from the water and struck. Its fangs sunk into my brother's waist, and it pulled him under, its neck coiling..." T.K. stopped, the words caught in her throat. Her lower lip quivered. Finally, she managed a whisper. "I never saw him alive again. I never found his body—only bits of his bone. No, Antonio. I am far, far from what I seem."

Antonio sat quietly, stunned. "I am—sorry," he finally managed.

"Save it," she said bitterly. "If we don't find a way out of here soon, you may be sorry for yourself. We have to get out of here." She glanced down for only the briefest of moments, but it was enough for Antonio to see the glistening tracks of half-dried tears. "I thought I had buried this part of my life. I thought I was finally free of it. Now, you bring me back to it."

Antonio heard a slow drip and thought of his shirt. He wasn't sure what to say. After a long silence, he finally said, "The weed helped. Thank you."

T.K. roused herself, grateful for a chance to change the topic of conversation. She wiped an arm across her face. "I came upon it by accident. It grows on the rock face, just below the waterline. I tried it for food. It left my throat numb for an hour."

The cave was fading in and out around Antonio. He roused himself, fighting to focus his eyes. "You spoke of— finding a way out." His eyes fluttered closed, but he forced them open. He could tell that his mind was slipping away even as he fought to remain conscious. "Can you get us out of here?"

"Maybe," T.K. said, almost to herself, "but I warn you, getting out—getting out alive, that is—is considerably more difficult than getting in."

4

How Loa

Willoughby crept carefully forward, stopping to peer inside the dimly lit shop. Piles of wrapped goods sat on dusty, wooden shelves surrounded by shiny trinkets, painted parasols, and mounds of other imported goods and curios. His eyes flicked across the shelves. Beneath a fine layer of dust and a patchwork of delightfully decorative cobwebs, they sported cat clocks with eyes and tails twitching and jade carvings of fat Buddha's. A row of bamboo planters and bonsai trees further into the shop also seemed laced with cobwebs and dust, but they *were* green and alive, which meant that *someone* had to be tending them. The shop might not be visited that often, but it was by no means abandoned.

In the rectangular well of the window itself, an array of Chinese dolls in bright, traditional costumes towered over slender jade figurines and a selection of orange and green jade vases, some fat and rounded, and others tall and oval. Paper-thin wood carvings were tucked in and out of the top-most shelves depicting palace scenes or beautiful landscapes.

Willoughby again noted that the thirty-six panes in the window were small and rectangular, roughly following the dimensions of a *golden* rectangle—a rectangle based on the Greek ratio called the *golden mean*. He had already learned that this ratio was integrally connected with the time-travel technology used by Observations Inc. The organization had first attracted his attention with golden triangles, carved into a slab of stone above Antonio's shop, *The Corner Barber*. As he looked closer, he guessed that the entire storefront may be in the dimensions of a golden rectangle. He wondered again if this could be the work of Observations, Inc., and if so, why H.S. had not told him about it. Then again, there hadn't been a lot of time for chit-chat since he had arrived in Bermuda, and H.S. certainly had other things on his mind. Willoughby also realized that H.S. had not known that he would want to go souvenir shopping before boarding the yacht.

He glanced one last time at the wooden sign as he stepped under it. He could no longer see the circling numbers. After a long moment, he turned back to the shop. Could the dimensions of this shop hide a time door? Slowly, cautiously, he stepped in. The door creaked to a close.

"Ah, so you come!" a wispy voice whined from behind him. "I wonder if you just counting bricks in wall, or if you right customer. You right customer, yes? This good shop for right customer. You come, you see. Much to like! You buy."

Willoughby had jumped at the voice. It had seemed to just materialize out of thin air behind him. As he turned to see who it belonged to, he found himself looking up at a tall, bony man. The man had long, white hair and an ornate silk robe. He sat perched atop a tall stool in a cobwebbed corner. The small pipe in his hand exuded a sweet, herbal smell. He smiled as he placed it to his lips.

His mouth was framed by a long, white, Fu-Manchu moustache that drooped several inches below a bony chin. The crown of his head was covered by an embroidered silk cap that somehow clung to the wild tangles of his hair. Willoughby let out his breath.

"Do you always sneak up on customers like that?"

"Like what?" The man spoke with an obvious oriental accent. "You right customer, I think. We much like right customer." The man's smile widened, showing a row of thin, yellowed teeth as he puffed once on his pipe. He hopped down from the stool to give Willoughby a shallow bow. "I only open door for right customer. You lucky man! Today, you lucky day. That mean we do much good business. Come. Come. Lucky-7 bring you much fine, lucky days."

Willoughby had to smile. "Okay," he sighed. "I could use *much fine lucky days* right now." He paused for a moment as the man brushed by him with a rush of excitement. "By the way," he called after the man, "what do you mean you only open the door for *right customers?* How do you know a customer is *right?*"

The man turned with eyes wide. "You make joke, Mr. Willoughby? How Loa know? That not good question. I tell you good question: *What Loa's first name?* How! *What How's second name?* Loa! How Loa, can you go? No. How Loa want to stay. Always know right customer for right time. Always right time for right customer at Lucky-7. You listen, okay? You listen, you learn, you no see with confusion, okay? How Loa make you plenty good bargain." He motioned Willoughby forward with a sort of gliding shuffle. Once Willoughby caught up to him, he turned abruptly and held both arms out wide. "How Loa so happy, he give right store happy bow." He gave the store a slight bow and dozens of tinkling alarms went off, chiming from all around the shop. "Shop say: 'Welcome, welcome—you right friend of Loa.' Wow! Now How make right friend of Loa good bargain. Yes, yes. Holy cow! Quick, yes—hurry, How."

Willoughby shook his head at the sing-song lilt of the man's speech as his smile widened. He started to reach out to shake the man's hand, but How Loa didn't notice. He had already spun away and was hurrying down one of the narrow aisles. Willoughby followed wordlessly for awhile, but spoke when he stopped to pick up a long bamboo stick with something that looked like a real bumble bee attached to the end of it by way of a small, sparkling cloud.

"What's this?"

How turned, shrieked, and grabbed the stick from Willoughby. "How know this not right gift right now," he said, taking the stick from Willoughby and carefully placing it back onto the shelf. "Come! Quick! Loa have many good things. Loa keep best shop on island—Lucky Seven."

Willoughby tried to think through the maze of words. He saw other strange gadgets and trinkets. He remembered the ring of numbers he had seen circling the sign. His eyes narrowed as he tried to make sense of everything. This Chinese man seemed a ball of energy—almost larger than life. He padded forward, taking small steps and motioning with a frantic hand for Willoughby to follow.

"How Loa own all this." He motioned with a sweeping arm. "Now How very lucky. You see? Okay." He gave a low chuckle. "That mean How make you only best, only right deal."

An image jogged Willoughby's mind. He and his mother were watching TV together when the late show came on. It was an odd movie called *The 7 Faces of Dr. Loa.* This man had many of the zany characteristics of the *Loa* character, played by Tony Randal. He studied the man.

"Are you Loa as in Dr. Loa from the movie?"

"Only one face, twelve hands, plenty-good fingers. Ha! You funny man, Mr. Willoughby. Lucky-7 Loa pretty more handsome, you think? Yes, okay?" He gestured to the shelves around him. "Look, you customer now."

Willoughby decided to let it go. The man, the shop, they seemed harmless if a bit odd. If the man tried to be a character from an old movie in order to charm customers and make bigger sales, hey, who was he to knock it? The number string still bugged him, though, as did the man's comment about only opening the door for "right" customers. He stepped a little quicker, trying to catch up. "I was wondering, how long—"

"No, How *Loa*," the man barked, not pausing to look back. "How Long is other man. Next question?"

"I mean, has it been a while since you last had a customer?"

"Yes. Too long... Next question?"

"How long is *too long?*"

"No, Too Long is also different person—much shorter than How Long. Next question?"

Willoughby sighed. "Wow. Okay, let's just say you are the undisputed champ of the *Long* conversation."

The man turned with a sad smile. "Ah, yes... Very Long have to leave Lucky-7 soon." The man looked down for a moment, pursing his lips, and then jerked his head with a quick smile, speaking rapidly. "How Long too sad, so bad—you think so? Okay. We go."

Part of what he said seemed completely nonsensical, but Willoughby sensed a truth beneath the word play. The man spun and continued down the aisle. Willoughby followed. A jade figurine caught his eye. It was a fat, smiling Chinese man, sitting with his legs crossed. He had thought he saw the jade eyes glow for a moment. He slowed and picked the figurine up. The eyes did, indeed, glow. They pulsed a bright blue. Before he could say anything, the lively Chinese man snatched it from his hand.

"No, no, not for you. No good deal. That How's happy god and you no happy boy." He put the figurine down. "You make jolly fat man lose too much jolly fat, I think. How Loa now find you more better deal!" The man pulled his arm and Willoughby tore his eyes from the figurine. He couldn't argue with the man's pronouncement that he wasn't a happy boy. *Did it show that much?* He thought of the glowing eyes and the strange man. *What was this place?* How led him around the end of the aisles and up another even more haphazard one that eventually led back to the front window. How stopped abruptly in front of a group of wooden boxes and rummaged around, making a big show of pulling brass tools out then throwing them back into the box. Willoughby moved closer.

"What are you looking for?"

The Chinese man raised no eyebrows. "How know when How find."

Willoughby turned away. He saw a stack of decorative Samurai swords and walked over to them. "Look," he finally said, not turning back to face the man, "I saw a circle of seven's at the top corner of your sign, glowing with the same bright blue that your happy god's eyes pulsed with." He turned. "The circle of numbers was floating in the air. How?"

"Yes?" the strange man interrupted, looking up.

Willoughby plunged on, trying not to be annoyed. "Your window panes are shaped after golden rectangles. Is this a front for a time door? Is this owned by Observations, Inc.?"

"We right store for right customer! How no good question for How—too confusing."

Willoughby didn't understand. "Who are you, really?"

"Who no good question."

"Okay," Willoughby said, trying to play along, "*Why?* Why am I the *right* customer? And if you're not a part of Observations, Inc., how do you know my name?"

The man looked into Willoughby's eyes. His own eyes flashed mischievously. "Ah, yes, How know your name, and *why? That* very good question." He turned and continued rummaging in the box, talking over his shoulder. "*Why* is reason How knows your name."

Willoughby didn't move. "What is it you want from me?"

The Chinese man kept rummaging. "Don't know. How not find yet." He went silent for a moment, and then, with a grand flourish, he pulled a brass tube from the box. "Yes!" he cried. "How find *why!* How find *why!*" His excitement was infectious. He held out the tube. Willoughby studied it for a moment. It had an eye-piece at one end, extension bevels, and a rounded glass at the other. He lowered the bags that held souvenirs he had bought from other stores to the wooden floor. He then reached out and took the brass tube. "It looks like a spyglass."

"No. This much, much more." the man said.

Willoughby studied the piece closer. It was surprisingly heavy. The brass was worn and blackened in places and had a line of Chinese characters etched onto the barrel.

"It best for you—very special!" How said, smiling broadly. "Used by Grand Master Foo Ton. He fold out to bed, you know. He give spyglass to How Loa for right customer. You right customer. You like? Okay, yes, very much, you buy."

Willoughby extended the brass tube and put the spyglass to his eye. How hummed happily, as if he knew Willoughby wouldn't be able to resist the trinket, as if the question of what to sell Willoughby had been indisputably settled. Willoughby blinked and then gasped. *How was right.*

Pointing the spyglass out the window, he knew immediately that his was no ordinary glass. He saw the same numbers out the window that he had seen before, but instead of one small circle of numbers, he saw hundred, even thousands of them. They were everywhere, flowing around the room and through the outside air as if following invisible currents. The rivers of numbers winked in and out as if charting invisible eddies. They bobbed in tight circles around objects on the shelves, and especially along all edges of glass. A shadow caught his attention. A man ducked out of the narrow alley that opened to reveal How's store. He moved through the number flows as if swimming, bobbing this way and that way. As he peered at the storefront window, Willoughby noted that his clothes were odd. It looked like he had just stepped out of the 1930's or 40's. The man stepped toward the window, as if seeking a closer view. The face was unmistakable. It was a face he would recognize in any time period. His lips fought to form the words; "*Dad!*"

The Chinese man waited excitedly, his hands clasped behind his back. "You like?" he said.

Willoughby lowered the spy glass. The number streams vanished. So did the image of his father—his birth father—Gustav. He went to raise the spyglass again, but the Chinese man stopped him, pulling the spyglass away.

"You like, you buy. I have special deal for you. Lucky Seven make this you lucky day." He tapped the brass of the spyglass with his manicured fingernails, bouncing on the balls of his feet for a moment, then suddenly turned and rushed away, around the end of the aisle. Willoughby hurried to catch up. How led him to a dark, seemingly empty area of shelf. He reached a hand far back into the shadows. After a long moment, he pulled out a beautiful jade box. It had a tiny gold lock. He made a show of trying to open the box, but it was locked tight. He looked up, holding the box out to Willoughby with a frown.

"You take! How Loa no like. Look, you see in glass very customer that bring box to me!" The man pointed toward the spyglass and then toward the window. "He want How Loa to make trade. It bad trade, I think. He leave box, but no key. Box unhappy. Box want key. Key want boy. Happy god want jolly fat. Sad face make eyes flash, numbers glow. Box make dark on shelf, make shop unhappy. But, two sad face make one happy. This you lucky day! You take box—you be happy boy. How Loa give you spyglass in trade if you take box. You like?"

How again handed him the spyglass, gesturing for him to raise it to his eye. Willoughby slowly did. He pointed the brass instrument at the jade box first. Through the eyepiece, he saw glowing numbers—bright and crisp, gushing from the box. They sparked in brilliant, blinding flashes. Willoughby swung the spyglass again toward the window. He could see that the numbers were flowing out from the shop. The further from the box they got, the dimmer the numbers became. It was as if whatever was in the box illuminated, if not actually created the numbers. He searched the window again for Gustav. After a long moment, a man's outline again began to materialize from the glowing numbers. He walked slowly, purposefully toward the window. He was taller and thinner than Gustav, and wore a familiar gray trench coat… Willoughby felt his pulse quicken. The man outside the window this time was not his father. It was *Beelzebub*, the man who traveled time, who had orchestrated the massacre on the *Absconditus*.

Willoughby lowered the spyglass. There were no numbers, no shape in the window. They could only be seen with the spyglass.

"What is this—instrument?" he said softly. "Was it left by my father? You indicate that he left you the box. Why? What's inside it? How can it make me happy? *What are you're trying to tell me?*"

How's voice was softer this time, though his excitement never faded. "I tell you look. I tell you see. All things connected. I make you good deal—right deal. I only open door for right customer. Today you lucky day. You right customer—okay, you buy."

Willoughby barely heard How. He was still staring at the window. His heart was a drumming hammer in his chest. He raised the glass one last time to his eye. The man in the trench coat was still there. His eyes burned like blue flame around black coal. They stared at Willoughby— *through* Willoughby—as the figure loomed large in the frame of the window. Drops of cold sweat formed on Willoughby's forehead. He expected the man to stop, to cup his face against the window and peer in, but the image of the man passed right through the glass and wall. His lips were turned up in a twisted smile. He tensed, bending his elbows as if preparing to lunge.

Willoughby ripped the spyglass away from his eye. He felt a scream start in his throat. *No—it was an illusion*, he forced himself to realize, panting for breath. There was no man at the window. In fact, there seemed to be no-one in the shop at all now. The image of Beelzebub—or whatever he called himself today—was gone, trench coat and all. He looked around for How. The store suddenly smelled different. It sounded and felt different. The spyglass had only been pushed to his eye for a few seconds, but in that short span, the store had changed. He stared around in the dim light. The window was now crusted over with a soft sheen of grime. It let a ghostly, diffused light through. In the dim light, Willoughby could see that the store was now *empty*.

"How?" Willoughby called. He somehow knew there would be no answer. "Mr. Loa?"

Circling slowly around the empty shelves, now covered with nothing but layers of dust and cobwebs, he thought of what How had said; "*I only open door for right customer!*" He twisted his head to one side. By *door*, had the shopkeeper been referring to a *time door?* Who was this strange man? He had come across as an actor, a cartoon caricature, but the technology he provided was real and strangely powerful, and this shop had transformed in the blink of an eye. If he walked away from it, if he went down to H.S.'s yacht and tried to come back, would it even be here? Could he have been pulled into a, a—what had the tall man in the trench-coat called it—a time *junction?*

Willoughby turned to find the door. His foot hit upon something in front of him on the floor. He bent down and picked it up. It was a small, box shaped package, wrapped in old, brown paper. *It was the jade box!* Next to his other foot were the bags of souvenirs he had purchased from the other stores. He picked the wrapped package up and placed it and the brass spyglass carefully into one of the bags.

"Thank you, How Loa," he mumbled, picking up the bags. "I think."

He knew that the mysterious gifts might be able to help him find his friends and father, but it could just as easily get him into worse trouble. Something made him want to trust the strange shopkeeper, though. As he located the door and made his way out, he thought he heard an echo of Mr. Loa's voice. "*This you lucky day!*"

Once he had shut the battered and weathered wooden door behind him, he looked up at the old worn wooden sign. You could barely read the name *Lucky Seven Emporium.* No numbers floated around its corner now. He made his way back along the narrow alley until it rejoined the wider one. *Was Mr. Loa to be trusted?* Could he be someone H.S. did not know about? Willoughby was beginning to believe he had stumbled into some sort of underground war—one played out against the backdrop of time itself. Where had the spyglass Mr. Loa gave him come from?

He was soon back on the sidewalk, milling around the shops with the other tourists. He gave a low sigh. His fists unclenched. He hadn't even realized how tense his body had become. He stopped at a small, wrought-iron bench that looked out over the harbor. On a whim, he took out the spyglass and fingered it. After staring out at sea for a long moment, he placed the eyepiece to his eye.

At first, he saw only the capping waves out to sea. He worked the glass slowly around toward the pier. He found H.S.'s yacht. A Rolls Royce was parked on the pier beside it. Faintly, but unmistakably, he could see glowing number strings swirling lazily around the prow and stern of the boat. The spyglass *was* unique. What was the jade box? How could he find the key to unlock its mysteries?

Carefully, he put the glass back into his bag. He stood and sucked in a deep breath of the fresh sea air, then made his way down toward the pier. The small, trim yacht, the parked Rolls Royce, and the faces of his friends—some new, some old—suddenly meant safety to him.

And safety gave the feel of *home*.

5

The Barking Camel

It was some time before James Arthur had mastered and conquered the pain in his body. He breathed steadily now. The air had cooled a little. He opened his eyes. A swirl of sand came over the dune. Within it, he thought he saw a slash of black and a glow of bright amber, flashing out at him from charred, smoking sockets. He tried to push up. "*Monsieur!*" called a faint voice on the wind. Then, the swirl of sand parted and a figure stepped through. The figure became more distinct as it got closer. It was not the girl he had seen so long ago. It was a full-grown woman in a flowing desert robe.

The woman walked past, not paying him any notice, even as he tried to call out with a weak, raspy voice. He watched her turn away to the south and disappear behind a low rise. The rise was formed from red rock, scrub brush, and sand—lots and lots of sand. He pivoted his head. The surroundings were much the same on every side. He mumbled to himself.

Okay, first important question: Who am I? He smiled. *Why, I'm the good doctor, of course. Now,* he hesitated; *where am I?*

He squinted, taking another look at his surroundings. He realized this time that his left eye was the only one that could open all the way. His right eye was still swollen partially shut. He also felt the tenderness in his groin each time he shifted, though it was not as sharp as before. He tried to twist to see what was under him. *What was he lying on?* He wasn't on the ground. At least, his head wasn't. It was a good three feet above the sand. His feet, however, were close enough to feel the sand's radiating heat. His arms and feet were strapped fast to something. As he squirmed and craned, he surmised that he was on some sort of makeshift cot. It was tilted up in an incline of about thirty degrees. He heard footsteps behind him. They stopped a short distance away. He heard a deep voice boom out in a language he didn't understand. Though deep and resounding, the voice had an odd feminine quality. There was a rustle, as if the person were fumbling with something, then a goatskin bag of some kind was held over his head.

He tried to force a grin as warm water trickled out of the bag onto his cheek. He tried to catch as much of the trickle as he could in his mouth, feeling the water stream down behind the nape of his neck and down his back. He felt a sudden surge of thirst as he gulped at the warm liquid greedily.

The water tasted nasty, but he didn't much care. When the bag disappeared, his thirst was far from abated. "Hey," he mumbled in a harsh croak. He forced his eyes open again, squinting at the still harsh glare of the sun. A huge face dipped into view, looming over him with a broad, crooked grin. Despite his weakened state, he flinched.

"Uh, hello big, *very big* person," he mumbled. "You are a, a giant-ess?"

The big head nodded. "You spreak Englisa?" it said, its grin opening into a smile.

With a sickening feeling, James Arthur realized this giant head belonged to a woman. He couldn't help but wonder how enormous the rest of her was. Then, he had a fleeting memory of the huge woman. She had rolled him into a carpet and thrown him over her shoulder. He cringed.

"Uh, hello," he choked out, grunting as loud as he could muster. "More water?"

He couldn't help wondering if he had stumbled into some kind of desert circus troupe. Or perhaps he had discovered a previously unknown Neanderthal race.

The woman finally moved around to the front of the cot so he could see her clearly. She was undoubtedly the largest woman he had ever seen. He gulped, pushing back on the cot. The woman had to be at least nine feet tall and a good three feet broad. She was not fat. On the contrary, her arms and legs rippled with thick cords of muscle. If a ripped body-builder had six-pack abs, this woman's were easily a forty-eight pack or more. Everything about her was large. She had large eyes, large hands, large feet, large— well, James Arthur turned a little crimson—large *everything!*

She carefully held up the goatskin and poured more warm water into his mouth. "You," she said a word that was not in English, and sounded like "fluidish." Her silver-dollar sized eyes watched him. She motioned to the water she held and grunted the word again, "Fluidish!" She made a gulping gesture and he understood she was asking if he was finished. He shook his head vehemently, opening his mouth again. As water soothed his parched throat, he didn't care that it was warm. He couldn't gulp fast enough. Once the giantess was done pouring, she stepped back and he noticed for the first time a rolled carpet behind her on the sand. This time, more than just a fleeting glimpse came back. This time, he remembered everything.

Closing his eyes to stem the flood of memory, he tried to pick out moments that may be important to him now. He worked with a unique organization that had the ability to travel in time. He was a part of a team. His friends on the team called him Dr. J, a nickname he liked because it put more emphasis on his athletic ability. The rest of the team included a Spanish-American architect, a boy-wonder mathematician, a feisty yet beautiful teen violinist with fans all over the world, and an Irish astronomer. Everyone on the team had a unique skill set. His was an ability to heal. He thought of when he first became aware of his skill—of the odd experience he had in New Orleans as a boy. He had never told anyone about it. *Why did it seem suddenly important to him now?* Was it because he was fighting to heal himself?

He returned his thoughts to his team. They had been assigned a mission, to go to sixteenth century France to discover more about the seer Nostradamus. They had boarded a fully rigged clipper ship called the *Aperio Absconditus*, and that's when the fun really began. From the moment their voyage had begun, things had gone terribly wrong. H.S. brought them up to speed on concerns about some sort of brotherhood that had been caught stalking them. Two days later, the ship was hijacked, most of the crew brutally murdered, and had it not been for the antics of the ship cabin-girl, a striking blonde who went by the initials T.K., he and his older teammate, Antonio, would likely have been casualties as well.

Then, there had been falling through the time-door, waking up in a cave, being walled into a tomb, and finally, finding himself here, wherever *here* was, tied to this cot.

The hot sun poured down as the warm water churned in his stomach. The giantess had slung the water skin back over her shoulders and picked up the rectangular square of carpet. She shook it out and carefully began to re-roll it. When it was tightly rolled, she strapped the rug to the side of a heavily burdened camel. He watched for a moment, trying to make sense of what came next in his memory.

The cave he had first found himself in had seemed a cross between a catacomb and an underground temple of some sort. After being assaulted with a blow to the head, he had actually been stripped naked and walled up in one of the tombs. In an attempt to escape, he had crawled over scorpions, dodged cobras, and finally dug his way out through a crack in the rock. Once freed from the cave, he had run into the giantess. She had wrapped him in the very carpet that lay on the sands and had flung him over her shoulder like a sack of flour.

How long ago had that been? Had it been days or only hours?

The giantess was free with her jovial laugh. He had heard it more than once bobbing helplessly over her shoulder. She was still smiling to herself now, and smiling at him whenever she looked over. She seemed aware of his stare. Her long, dark hair was braided down her back and each braid was tied around a small piece of something (*was it bone?*) that dangled and clanked as she walked. A shudder ran down Dr. J's back. *Was there such a thing as a tribe of desert-dwelling cannibals?* He racked his mind, trying to remember more, but that was as much as he knew. He had no idea how he came to be tied to this cot.

The giantess turned and walked away, pulling the burdened camel after her. A short distance away, another two-hump camel came over a ridge as she called with a shrill yelp. The other camel trotted over to her and she tied the two together. In a single, swift movement, she mounted the larger camel, resting between its two humps, and spurred it on. In a different place and time, James Arthur may have laughed, imagining how the camel's eyes must have bulged, straining with the huge woman's weight.

He didn't feel like laughing today, however. His mind drifted back to his team. He had actually met the girl violinist once before. Though a bit loud-spoken for his tastes, she was amazingly attractive and as good a musician and performer as her reputation suggested. She had actually put on a concert for them on the ship, but he had also heard her perform at a sold out concert at Carnegie Hall. Young fans had filled the hall, chanting her name over and over—*Sydney! Sydney! Sydney!*

The brilliant mathematician was a good-natured kid named Willoughby. They had been bunk mates, and Dr. J had taken a bit of a shine to the boy. He was sort of like the little brother James Arthur never had. *Had his team made it out okay?* Had Antonio and the cabin-girl—who, curiously, went by the initials T.K., much like their infamous leader, H.S.—escaped? They had been only a few minutes behind him, T.K. helping Antonio, who had been beaten badly.

His thoughts were interrupted as the giantess prodded her camel forward, yelling again in words he did not understand. A slender man approached from a distant rise.

He seemed absolutely terrified by the huge woman. Dr. J let his head drop back heavily against the coarse fabric that made up his cot. He felt another throb of pain from his head and stiffened, closing his eyes for a long moment. When he opened them again, he looked down the length of his body. He was no longer naked. He eyed the strange tunic he was dressed in. Where had it come from—the giantess?

He tried to turn his head to see where the huge woman was going. She was still yelling at the thin man. He finally nodded, turned resignedly, and headed in his direction.

James Arthur tried to get a better look at the cot he was on. It was made of course fabric, sewn around tall, thin poles that angled up from the ground where they were tied to—to what? He tried to turn his head to look, but just at that second, the top of the cot shifted moving a few feet forward. Whatever it was tied to, it was living, and not stationary. He heard a gurgle of gastric upheaval directly behind him, and followed the sound to a sandy-brown hide and a spindly leg with large splayed toes. The gasses gurgled again. He leaned away from what he knew to be coming. He was tied to a camel, one that was about to blow. The back end of the camel erupted in a disgustingly loud fart that blew just over the top of his head. The camel grunted, as if relieved. Dr. J wrinkled his nose as the putrid smell brought water to his eyes. He gasped. The thin man, who was fast approaching, had heard the fireworks and seen James Arthur's reaction. He laughed heartily. James Arthur wanted to punch him. He stared at the man's slightly cleaner robe and thick sash. A curved sword hung at the man's side. Forcing his mind beyond the smelly camel, he tried to place the sword. *What desert cultures had used curved swords—Persia? Arabia?* Was he somewhere in the Middle East?

Dr. J leaned forward, pulling against the cords that held him tight. They were made from strips of leather and held fast, unwilling to budge. In fact, it seemed as if, the harder he pulled, the tighter they got. The thin man had come to within a few feet and laughed even harder.

"Oh, you think that's funny, do ya?" James Arthur began as the Camel again perfumed the air. The thin man was literally holding his sides, rocking with laughter. He smacked the camel on the rump and the beast started moving forward, bellowing in complaint and leaving a nauseous trail of fumes on the air behind.

James Arthur shut his eyes, gasping from the stench. He held them closed for a long while and must have nodded off. He vaguely remembered waking up to gag from the smell now and again, but he wasn't sure how many times it had been, or for how long he had been on this cot. In a daze, he squinted down at the uneven cot tracks stretching off into the sand for as far as he could see. The terrain slowly began to change. They had entered some sort of rock and sand ravine. There was no wind except the foul gusts from the camel. He twisted his head to the side, hoping to catch a glimpse of the thin man who had started the camel moving. He could see nothing but more rock faces and tan-colored sand. *Had the scrawny guy with the sword been with the giantess when she first wrapped him in the carpet?* He tried to remember. He certainly recalled the giantess' booming laugh. She hadn't even flinched when she'd hefted him onto her shoulder like a sack of wheat.

He looked around him, trying to find some landmark he might recognize. He still had no idea where they were.

Someone approached from behind him. It was not the thin man, but a shorter, barrel-chested man with a thick, black beard. When he reached the cot, he made expansive hand gestures to indicate the horrid smell. He spoke in a strange language and laughed a booming, good-natured laugh. He patted Dr. J on the shoulder.

James Arthur forced a smile.

"So, where's the other goofball sidekick? Too bad you don't speak English. I'd love to give you a good-old American rant, you pathetic oaf!"

The bearded man laughed again, showing rows of crooked, rotting teeth. "No, no—I be Mahadin!"

"You speak English?" Dr. J asked.

"Yes, fine. He is happy," the man said. "Happy to like you."

"Happy to like me?"

"Yes, many more crumpets, please!" the man smiled, bobbing his head excitedly. "Much Englas in Yankee Doodle Dandy, all right?"

"Much something," James Arthur mumbled, "but I wouldn't call you a Yankee, although you do remind me of something a cow would *doodle*."

The man kept jabbering brightly. "Yes, yes, with two lumps, not three. I speak news, old chap, chop, chop." His head bobbed as he spoke. "You do me plenty cricket, okay?"

Dr. J tried to ignore the man. Taking a deep breath, as the air had now cleared slightly, he whispered to himself. "Please, somebody, tell me this couldn't get worse…"

The camel offered a foul-smelling commentary of its own.

6

Eyes of Fire

As Willoughby approached the yacht, he took a moment to study the name painted on the side. In white lettering it read, the *Pesci Piccoli*. Sam clambered onto deck from the lower hold. He carried a box filled with—cleaning supplies? He gave Willoughby a weak grin.

"Back safe I see. I trust you found items to your liking?" He proceeded to a bin near the back of the craft and stowed the box. After straightening, he smiled. "Don't just stand there. Come aboard."

Willoughby complied, lumbering up the gang plank. "Has Sydney gotten here yet?"

Sam glanced quickly toward the end of the pier. "Willoughby, when Ms. Senoya arrives I am confident that the entire marina will know."

"Just the marina?"

Sam's grin widened. "Well, I would wager on the entire island if someone had not kept her busy all morning. She's had little time to prepare for too grand of an entrance."

Willoughby glanced around the deck. "Is Dr. O'Grady here? I haven't seen much of him since we got here to Bermuda."

"Yes," Sam pursed his lips. "He's been on board for a while now—stays locked in his cabin. He's not a very talkative sort."

Willoughby thought of the skittish professor from Ireland and nodded. He opened his mouth to say something, but Sam cut him off.

"Ah!" he said, glancing up the pier. "I believe Ms. Senoya is arriving now."

Willoughby turned. Seven taxis were headed their way. When the first pulled up beside the yacht, Sydney jumped out, flashing a perfunctory smile. She walked around to the driver and directed him to a stack of boxes and a suitcase on the back seat. Each driver in the entourage jumped out and also shuffled to either the trunk or the back seat of their cars, each retrieving a mountainous stack consisting of boxes, suitcases, and shopping bags. Sydney walked to the end of yacht's short gang-plank and began to direct the heavily-laden group onto the ship and across the deck to the cabin. Willoughby's eyes widened as he counted. "Boy, she wasn't kidding about accosting the stores and the number of suitcases..." he mumbled. As the final driver stepped onto the ship, Sydney followed.

"Hi, *just* Willoughby!" she said with a grin.

Willoughby rolled his eyes. "Did you leave anything for the good people of Bermuda?"

Sydney's smile tightened. "Oh, you are funny. I am a girl, in case you haven't noticed, and girls need their—things." A driver stumbled on the gang-plank, dropping the top box in his stack. Sydney grabbed for it, just catching the small box before it plunged beyond her reach over the edge of the *Pesci Picolli*. She handed the box back to the driver with a sigh and helped him across the gang-plank. "Do be careful," she said, fuming. "The bracelet you almost lost is a Carolyn Pollack original!" She looked back and shrugged at Willoughby apologetically. The taxi driver seemed less than impressed. He hurried forward, as nonplused as ever. Sam stood stiffly at attention.

"Will you need your bed at some point, Ms Senoya, or do you plan to just sleep on your... boxes?"

Sydney didn't respond at first, but just before ducking into the passage to the cabins, she turned to eye him. "Well, someone—*misplaced* my original trunks. I had to do something."

Sam held a somber face. "We weep for your pain, Madame."

Willoughby and Sam watched Sydney disappear down toward the cabins. "It could be worse," Willoughby ventured. "She could have charged all that to Observations, Inc."

Sam sighed. "Oh, I'm sure she did." He turned back toward the gang-plank. "Your trunk is in your cabin berth, Willoughby—down the stairs and to your right. As it appears the show is over, at least for the moment, I will beg you to excuse me. I've duties to attend. We cast off within the hour."

In a blink, Sam was gone and Willoughby found he was alone on deck. He stepped to the rail, taking a moment to breath in the fresh sea air. He stared for a long moment out at the rolling horizon of sea. Then, he turned back and looked toward shore. The green of the island was punctuated with white and blue, red and yellow, and dozens of other color combinations that made up the residential and shopping areas of this side of Bermuda. He narrowed his eyes, trying to pick out the alley where How Loa's shop had been hidden. On a whim, he bent down and pulled the spyglass from one of his bags. He pointed it at the row of shops along the top of the first low hill. It did not take long to pinpoint the faint, blue numbers, floating above a section of one of the larger shops. *It has to be a time hole or a junction of some kind*, he thought. He turned the spyglass one hundred and eighty degrees to view the deck of the *Pesci Picolli*. A churning haze, composed of hundreds of tiny glowing lines, escaped from the decks below. Intrigued, Willoughby pulled the spyglass from his eye, picked up his bags, and started toward the narrow cabin steps.

As he reached the bottom of the steps, he found himself in a richly furnished lounge with a low ceiling and bright sconce lighting along the walls. Two large, underwater seascapes by Robert Wyland hung on the back wall to either side of a small, rounded nook. A cushioned bench followed the contour of the nook. Other smaller seascapes adorned the room, all lit by barely perceptible light bars along the bottom of their stretched frames. The room was fairly spacious, extending about eighteen feet from the back wall to the stair itself, and then another six or eight feet behind the stairs. It was tastefully furnished with a smattering of cushioned chairs and couches. Following the right-side curve of the yacht and beginning just behind the staircase, a narrow hallway led to the crew quarters and a couple of guest cabins. Willoughby had to dodge the crowd of taxi drivers who had deposited their loads of goods and were now heading back to their taxis. He moved quietly to the first guest cabin. The door was still partially opened. He smiled as he heard Sydney grunt and then moan with exasperation behind a wall of boxes and bags.

Beyond Sydney's cabin was his. The door to his cabin was also open. The trunk Sam had provided was at the end of a narrow bed. An open closet space, a row of drawers, a small desk, and two shelves surrounded a small porthole window, centered over the desk. To the left, a small sink was bordered by a thin door that led to a toilet and a cramped shower stall. All in all, the bunk room could not have been more than ten feet deep and possibly eight feet across.

He placed his souvenir bags in the small closet, put the strange box without a key under his bed, and took a quick peek at the room through his spyglass. No number strings were visible here. He heard another loud groan from the other side of the wall, followed by a thud, a bang, and a short scream.

"You okay over there?" he called out.

"Just appreciating the spacious accommodations," Sydney spit back, punctuating the words with another bang. A stream of energetic words in perfect provincial French greeted the sound of toppling boxes. Willoughby didn't catch all of it, but he knew enough French to understand that a certain stack of boxes was being accused of plotting with the devil. He tried to envision the volume of boxes and bags that had come out of the taxis and wondered how Sydney could even move in there. Stepping back into the hallway, he closed his bunk room door.

Four other doors in the hallway were marked as *Guest, Sam, Angel,* and *Racci.* The door to Sam's cabin was at the end of the hallway and suggested a cabin considerably larger than the rest, but then Sam *was* acting Captain of the *Pesci Piccoli.* Willoughby padded softly back to the larger lounge. He placed the spyglass back to his eye. The churning lines had become visible, faintly luminescent numbers. Their flowing strings tangled and wove in a thick rush. They seemed to be flowing from a second narrow hallway, this one following the left-side curve of the yacht. He proceeded down this hallway cautiously.

A closed cabin door which read "H.S." stood across from a small conference room, about twelve feet long and ten feet deep. The far side of the room was walled from knee height up to a low ceiling with angled glass windows. The glass slanted inward and appeared to be thick, but was spotless. A six foot table in the room was surrounded by six chairs.

The second door to the left opened to a ships galley. It was relatively narrow for a kitchen, but elegantly furnished with stoves, grills, a menagerie of shiny pans and utensils hanging over a center island, white carved cupboards, shelves, and a stainless steel double sink. At the far end of the galley, a glass door and screen opened onto a small porch.

Willoughby passed beyond the kitchen, wondering where the dining area was. *Did they dine on deck?* Were tables brought out to the expansive lounge at every meal? The hallway dead-ended into a wide door that opened into a dimly lit room. He again checked the spyglass. *The number strings were flowing from this larger room.* Keeping the glass raised to his eye this time, he cautiously entered. The room seemed like an office or library of some kind. To the left, bookshelves lined the walls with rows and rows of books from floor to ceiling. To the right was what looked like some sort of electronics hub. The wall directly in front of him, however, took his breath away.

The whole expanse of wall seemed to be made of dark obsidian. Inside the blackness, shapes flickered. A low step led to a triangular-shaped alcove near the center—just large enough for a single, narrow pedestal. Something rested atop the pedestal. It glowed and pulsed. As Willoughby stepped closer, he saw that it was some sort of triangular crystal. The pulses of the crystal rippled through the numeric lines and changing, three-dimension shapes that populated the obsidian wall. He studied the wall with his spyglass. The crystal was not only the source of the shapes that flickered in and out, but the hub of all glowing number strings. It gushed in fountains of pouring content, belching numbers into the air like some sort of mathematical smokestack. He did not see anyone in the room.

Pushing the glass tighter against his eye, he carefully focused on the crystal itself. He could see a deep blackness near its center. It was as if he were peering at a mini black hole—a point that was sucking all light from the space immediately around it. At the edges of the clear crystal, however, an almost blinding white barrier glowed, isolating the internal dark core. No matter how he tried, his eye couldn't remain fixed on the intense white barrier. It shifted, moving like some sort of liquid prison set up to contain the penetrating black. Willoughby felt something in the black. He sensed a presence—something moving, struggling to get out—something *alive.* The presence seemed to call to him, pulling him forward, drawing him close. Suddenly, two eyes within the blackness of the obsidian wall blinked awake. They glowed white-hot, a piercing fire that burned words into his mind. "I AWAKE!" He gasped, scrambling back, ready to scream or flee. A hand touched him.

"Willoughby?"

Willoughby spun, jerking the spyglass from his eye as he jumped slightly. Sweat beaded on his forehead. His breathing was shallow and his heart pounded. He forced himself to take a long, deep breath. H.S. stepped into view, still holding his elbow.

"What are you doing? This is a rather odd place for a spyglass. What did you hope to see?"

"You—you startled me," Willoughby managed. He glanced over at the crystal. With the spyglass removed from his eye, he could not see the darkness in the crystal. It appeared to glow with a soft, pulsing. H.S. reached down and took the glass from him.

"You were staring at the crystal computer through this." He passed a hand over the worn, brass tube.

"It's a computer?" Willoughby asked.

"Of course—a computer of sorts," H.S. answered. He put the spyglass up to his eye. After peering through the eye-piece for a long moment, he handed the glass back over to Willoughby. "What did you see?"

Willoughby countered with a question. "What did *you* see?"

"I saw the pulsing crystal. In the center, however, there was—there was an odd darkness. Where did you get this instrument from? It has a curious workmanship."

"An odd man in a hidden shop..."

Willoughby looked down at the spyglass in his hand. *What was this thing? Who was calling to him from the crystal?* When the spyglass was not at his eye, the triangular crystal looked like some sort of webbed sculpture. Tiny hairs of activity seemed to make its surface shimmer and dance to the beat of the shapes on the obsidian wall. He tore his eyes away from the artifact.

For the first time, he took in the entire expanse of the room. It was even larger than he had first suspected. The long, obsidian wall, split by the triangular alcove that housed the pedestal and the triangular crystal, was perhaps thirty feet in length. The wall to the left was filled with beautiful, polished-wood bookcases and harbored hundreds of leather-bound books. A dark, mahogany desk ran parallel to the bookshelf on the left. The wall to the right was made entirely of segmented glass panes. Behind the panes, a smaller room obviously housed the computer center of the ship. Racks of computer equipment seemed to extend almost the full length of the wall and ran at least three banks deep, each bank composed of at least six individual racks of various high-tech equipment.

Cables from the computers ran on silver rails that snaked above the equipment racks like some futuristic monorail, leading to various conduits built into the sides and ceiling of the room. Willoughby stared at the room. It was obviously *not* an ordinary control room for an ordinary ship. *Did this ship house another mobile time door—like the Absconditus?* He made out a small, electronic keypad to the far right of the glass wall. A digital display marked the temperature and no doubt managed access to the room. The keypad had a small round scanner or camera built into it. He wondered if a retina scan and fingerprint match were required to enter the computer center. They probably were. The room was lit by a soft, bluish glow, though Willoughby could see no light source. All in all, it appeared to be the cleanest, most sophisticated technology center he had ever seen outside of a sci-fi movie. He let his eyes return to H.S.

"What have we stumbled into, H.S.? I don't know what we're about anymore. As fantastic as it seemed, I got my head around Observations, Inc. Now, it's like the world changes every time I turn around."

H.S. cocked his head. "I find it hard to believe that this control room, or even my crystal computer, would solicit such an impassioned response. Something has happened. You started to tell me about an odd man from a hidden shop. Please, continue."

"Things...*change* when I look through that spyglass. They wink in and out." Willoughby looked down, hesitant to continue.

H.S. thought for a moment, and then gave him a soft pat on his good shoulder. "The world is a stranger place than you could ever imagine. It *can* change in the blink of an eye—and does, routinely. That's why we observe, why we're here to notice." He was quiet, stepping to stand closer to Willoughby and staring at the obsidian wall. "As you don't seem quite ready to jump in with your thoughts at the moment, I shall endeavor to answer your question. I don't really know what's going on. I do know you've awoken—something. Wheels are turning. There was a tremendous spike in the magnetic flow just before you walked into this room. It continued until I moved to touch you. It was the kind of spike that usually identifies a time event." His words fell silent.

Flickers of light drew Willoughby's attention to the mahogany desk. Holograms flickered into life, hovering inches above the smooth surface of the desk. One gave numeric read-outs in a cube-shaped form. The numbers winked in and out of equation strings. Another showed a fluctuating landscape wave with a bright, stationary point that Willoughby guessed was the *Pesci Picolli*. *It must be some sort of 3-D GPS*, he thought. A section of obsidian wall toward the corner winked into a montage of various video feeds from around the boat. For several seconds, Willoughby saw Sydney, Dr. O'Grady, cabin crew, and

Sam puttering about. He had to smile when he noted that Sydney was in her room, fighting with a mountain of boxes that collapsed on her more than once. Then the smile froze on his face—*would H.S. also be monitoring him in his cabin?*

H.S. looked at where his eyes were focused and smiled.

"She's determined to keep those boxes. I've already told her to just take out the contents and throw the silly boxes away, but Sydney is—Sydney." He clasped his hands behind him. "You needn't worry, dear boy—there is a large button above your door that glows green when the camera monitor is on. I always let you know if I'm monitoring, and I never peek." He led Willoughby toward the center of the room. "Welcome to my personal command station," he said softly. "Now, why don't you tell me what happened since I last saw you, walking toward the beach to find Sydney."

Willoughby sighed. "Okay, the spyglass... I got it at one of the shops at the top of the hill, a very unusual one. I asked Sam to drop me off so I could pick up some souvenirs for my family. When I came out of the first store, I caught a glimpse of numbers floating on the air in an alley—7,7,7. I was curious. I followed the string. It led to a hidden shop that I thought might be part of Observations, Inc... "

He looked to H.S. for confirmation, but the man only raised an eyebrow.

"An odd man who called himself *How Loa* said I was the 'right' customer and gave me this spyglass."

"He just gave it to you?"

Willoughby nodded.

"Tell me more about this hidden store. Why did this man ask you to take the spyglass?" He looked down, studying the markings on the brass more closely. "Lights up to half," he said softly. Light in the room brightened.

"I don't know," Willoughby said. "The whole conversation was odd. The man was oriental and the shop had typical import stuff. Like I said, it had numbers floating over it, so I thought it was a front for Observations, Inc. I went inside... "

Willoughby outlined the entire encounter for H.S., but while he spent considerable time describing the strange Mr. Loa, for some reason, he chose to leave out certain details, like the box with no key and seeing his father and Beelzebub through the spyglass.

H.S. listened patiently, and then pursed his lips. With a short wave at the air, he called out a numeric command. A low, cushioned bench appeared from the seemingly hard floor. He made himself comfortable on the bench and motioned for Willoughby to sit.

"Multiple time-events have occurred since your visit this morning with Beelzebub and his zombie thug. As I said, it is evident that something out there is stirring, but we haven't a lot to go on as yet. One thing seems absolutely clear—we are not alone in the time stream. What is more curious to me is that, after years of discovery and observation across the timeline, we've only become aware of this now, when we invite you to join our team."

"Are you saying this is my fault?" Willoughby tensed on the couch. H.S. was quick to backtrack.

"No, I'm not saying that at all. What I'm saying is that you seem *central* to these events. *We* are the ones that seem to have stumbled onto something by finding you."

Willoughby opened his mouth to speak, and then closed it again. He thought of the implications of what H.S. was saying.

H.S. continued. "Though this Mr. Loa does not sound dangerous, he obviously has technology that I do not recognize. Until we know what and who he is, and know more about your abilities and talents, we must proceed with caution. It is absolutely essential, however, that we do *proceed*, and with all haste. I don't think these people will let us run away and hide—at least not you. They seem to have your *address* so to speak." He was silent for a moment, studying the brass spyglass. He looked up with narrowed eyes. "I would like to keep this for a while if you don't mind."

Willoughby gave a shrug. "Why does it seem that I'm at the center of this? I never even knew time-travel was possible before I met you. What does it all mean?"

H.S. shook his head. "I can't tell you, Willoughby. I wish I could. I can tell you that something found you that day when you saw time stand still at *The Corner Barber*. Whether it was looking for you before, or whether we, inadvertently, helped it find you, I don't know, but we need to figure out what it wants—and soon."

Willoughby took a deep breath. He thought of How Loa and of his final words; "*This you lucky day!*" The day did not feel very lucky. The image of the weird fiery eyes, pulling at him from the darkness, flashed across his mind. It was not his imagination. Something was after him, even H.S. could see that. *Was anywhere safe?*

He looked back to H.S. with a sudden sense of urgency. "Through that spyglass, I saw number strings spewing out of the, that crystal computer. Did you? You saw the black thing at its heart. Did it speak to you? A few moments ago, I saw eyes open out of that blackness, H.S. They said, 'I awake!' They called to me, pulling at me. They were like fiery coals. *Could this spyglass be a way for it, or them, or whatever, to track me, to track us?*"

H.S. thought for a long moment, studying the tube. "I don't think so... My gut tells me that your finding that hidden store may be a counter against the visit from Beelzebub. Something tells me there may be forces working in opposition here. If that is the case, this tool may be very valuable."

H.S. looked up, his face stern. "I will send people to look for this hidden store, but my guess is that we will not find it. Forces of great dark often stir forces of greater light. Of course, we are shooting a bit in the dark here. As Issac Newton surmised, the more we come to understand, the more we come to realize how little we know." He forced a smile. "Whatever our role in what is happening, Willoughby, I believe we will need all the help we can get."

7

Aert Olaneas Tis

The shaking and the sweats had seemed worse for a time, then, mercifully, they began to ease. Antonio still thought his leg was on fire, though. He mumbled, sliding in and out of consciousness. Hazy dreams were filled with fanged monsters and tattooed men. At times, he was vaguely aware of T.K.'s hand, lifting him up to squeeze water into his mouth, or stuffing bits of partially chewed pulp down his throat, causing him to choke. The pulp left a taste in his mouth, a salty, sour taste, like over-cooked turnip greens.

At last, he opened his eyes and kept them open. The throbbing in his leg had not subsided, but the burning had eased. He could tell he was weak, but he was no longer sweating from the fever, or shaking with chills. He forced himself slowly to his elbows and searched the dimness. He could not see T.K. He touched a hand to his face. Ragged stubble covered his chin. He must have been out for days. He felt an intense hunger. *How long had he been teetering on the edge of oblivion?* Had the vicious black beast, the plesiosaurus, been back? As if from a dream, he remembered a terrifying moment when he was sure the thing had come back—crashing its great bulk against the rock edge, struggling to pull its slimy body up the overhang. He thought he had heard its loud trumpeting and felt blasts of foul breath while the dark silhouette of T.K. hovered in front of him, screaming back at it with knife drawn.

Crawling slowly to the side of the overhang, Antonio propped himself up against the stone. He stared out over the strange, luminescent waters. It was not long before T.K. bobbed up and slid onto the rock ledge. He marveled that he had not seen her surface before. She couldn't have held her breath for the full ten or so minutes he had been awake. Had she been in another area of the cave, one he could not see from here? She stood, wreaths of leafy, green seaweed draped around her neck and down over her torn shirt.

"You're up," she said in a sort of breathless whisper.

"Yes… Do we have—water?" Antonio croaked, his voice little more than a rasp.

"No. I already gave you all the fresh water I could find. We get enough to keep us alive from chewing the weed. Well, sort of. I'm glad you're up, though." She walked to where he sat near the overhang. "I was getting sick of chewing your food." She dropped half of her wet bundle beside him. "I'm afraid fresh water is hard to come by in this cave. I found a little that had collected in a shallow pool under one of the cracks in the ceiling, but I've checked back and there's nothing." She plopped down. "The drips from the ceiling come so slow that it may take months for any substantial amount to collect. All I can offer you is this," she cut a piece of the green weed from one of the stems in her wet pile and popped it in her mouth. "It may not be a taste sensation, but it'll keep you alive—at least until I can get a fire going and distill some fresh water." She handed Antonio the knife. He took it with shaky fingers.

Antonio picked up a piece of the seaweed, cut it with some effort, and stuffed it into his mouth. He, at once, recognized the taste.

T.K. continued to talk between chews. "I've been storing some of the giant kelp over there. I can only go for it after the plesiosaurus has visited and I'm sure it's gone. The bed is near the underwater entrance to the cave, and I don't want to meet one of those things down in their element."

"There are more than the one?" Antonio asked.

"Oh, yeah," T.K. said. "There's a whole herd of them—herd, or gaggle, or school, or swarm, I'm not sure what you call it, but there's at least seven or eight of them. They seem to be a bit afraid of the cave due to its luminescence. They only come in here by ones and twos. I think it's like a test of bravery or something. They swim around a few times, like they're really hot stuff, and then leave. Of course, now that they know we're here, I'm sure their visits are a bit more frequent. Anyway, I think I've dried almost enough of the giant kelp to manage a small fire. We can boil some salt water and collect the condensation. It won't quench our thirst, but it should help with that parched throat. We need to get you strong again."

"You have a plan?"

T.K. was quiet for a while. "While the luminescent may spook the plesiosaurus, the thing that terrifies them the most in this cave is what I call the ring of fire."

"Yes," Antonio said weakly. "I remember. You mentioned that."

"It's like that closet that brought us here, I think—a time door, or hole, or whatever you call it," T.K. continued. "This one, though, H.S. didn't create. I don't know if anyone created it. I found it a long time ago. It was before H.S. started recruiting, and building time-doors, and whatever else it is that he does with you guys. The ring glows about every five or six days. When you're strong enough, we need to swim into it—and hope that no plesiosaurus is bold enough to follow us. I don't know if all of them would face it, but one followed me through it. If it hadn't been for the cold and the murk of the lake, I would never have made it to shore."

"The lake?"

T.K. looked at him blankly. "Loch Ness," she said cooly.

Antonio's eyes widened. "Who are you?" he finally blurted out. "You say you've been here, but how did you get here? Where are you from?"

T.K. took a long time to answer. "My real name is Tankien Keilhar," She looked at him with a wry smile. "And yes, I was a princess—a princess of a long lost people that have been silenced and buried by the cold cruelty of time." She was not as emotional as the last time he spoke to her. She wasn't exactly cheerful, but she did seem resigned to their situation. "You probably remember my name and the princess part from the ship."

Antonio waited, but she only popped another bit of seaweed into her mouth. He decided to try another line of questioning. "What are your thoughts on James Arthur? Do you think he was brought here?"

T.K. shook her head. "No. I've thought about it, but the beast was hungry when we dropped in. James Arthur wasn't more than a few minutes ahead of us. There were no signs of struggle and whatever else you want to say about James Arthur, he *is* a fighter. I don't think he came to this cave at all."

Antonio pondered the answer and then picked at another small strand of the weed and put it into his mouth. "I much fear," he finally grumbled, "that I am at a great disadvantage, *senorita*. You obviously know more about time travel and about H.S. than you have let on. You say you were not a spy, but why did you masquerade as a cabin girl and pretend to know nothing of Observations, Inc. and of time doors? Once again, what is your relationship to H.S. and our organization?"

T.K. barked a short, vicious laugh. "I have *no* relationship with H.S. or his secretive organization. Had he the slightest clue I was on his ship, I assure you, he would never have let her sail."

"Where are you from then? You know things about H.S., about time holes and this cave, as if you have been following him for a long time. You seem to know much more about what really happened on the ship than the rest of us. How?"

"I told you—I'm not the only one who knows Belzarac. H.S. knows him even better than I do. He used to work for H.S. I told you that as well. Don't you remember?" She looked over at Antonio. "I thought the man was dead, Antonio. If I had known—if there had been the slightest clue that he was alive and that he and H.S. were now pitted against each other—I would have done everything in my power to see that my adopted father never signed on to Captain the *Absconditus*. I would have never wanted him to get in the middle of that kind of blood feud."

"The Captain was a good man," Antonio said quietly. He let the silence engulf them until T.K. sucked in a breath and plucked another strand of the weed. Antonio watched her a moment, then asked softly, "Do you think Willoughby is okay?"

T.K. looked over. "He means something to you, doesn't he? I saw you take him swimming. You hover over him. What's the connection?"

Antonio saw an opportunity to perhaps win the girl's trust. He chose his words carefully. "I, uh, I recruited him. He is—a good friend—almost an adopted son. We needed a brilliant mathematician, and he came with added benefits. He's different. He's not your typical, cocky—"

"Uh," T.K. said, "I saw a bit of *typical* cocky, along with a lot of naivety. He may be bright, and he *is* different in a good way, but he's still a kid, Antonio, yet you guys put him on that ship."

Antonio looked away. "You are right," he finally said. "I blame myself."

T.K.'s gaze had now turned intense. "Don't. Things happen in life. We can't always be looking back, blaming ourselves. Besides, while I wish Willoughby hadn't been on that ship, I think he's tougher than you imagine. He's not a porcelain doll, you know. He may come out of this okay—maybe even stronger." She became quiet. It was a long time before she spoke again, turning to face Antonio. "None of us want to live in this kind of danger. I mean, maybe there are some masochists out there, or kids who think danger is cool because it gives them a rush, but that's not you, and it's not me. I passionately wish my life could have been different. I didn't have a choice. It is what it is, and I have to live with that. Sometimes, because of what we've had to deal with, we think we can protect others. A lot of the time, I think we just make things worse. Maybe we should just concentrate on being somebody to talk to, someone who will listen, who will understand. I think, in the long run, that's more helpful than thinking we can step in and protect people."

Antonio gave a frown and then a shrug. "Maybe... Still, he should have been older."

"I was nine when I lost my brother," T.K. said, looking out again toward the dark water.

Antonio toyed with the weed in his hand. "Well, I am sorry for you, but I still hope Willoughby got out okay."

T.K. waited a moment, letting Antonio's words simmer. "I do to," she finally said. "I even hope Miss Superstar *I'm-so-hot-and-I-know-it* Senoya got out okay. No one deserves to be butchered like, like..." Her voice trailed off for a while, then came back with a sob. "I guess we can't blame ourselves, Antonio. None of us knew any of this was coming. H.S. is persuasive—I know. Besides," she looked over at him; "Sydney was heading straight for H.S.'s cabin. He often communicated with her privately. He even spent several hours with her before the rest of you arrived on ship. That's one girl who is all about control. I think she would have known about the door and she was all over Willoughby. He's probably the first boy that she's ever had a chance to get close to—H.S. seemed to keep her on a pretty tight leash from what I could see. Anyway, I think she would have made sure she got him out safe. Maybe she got the old dotty professor out too."

"Dr. O'Grady?"

T.K. nodded. Antonio weighed her words. He started to ask her what people she was princess of, but thought better of it and just chewed, thoughtfully, pulling off another strand of weed. T.K. appeared to be done talking for the moment.

Over the rest of that day and over the next two, life in the cave became routine. T.K. had an old, spring-powered wristwatch which they used to mark the passing of days and she regulated their time accordingly. In his waking hours, Antonio explored the closer surroundings. The rock lip where they were camped was roughly thirty yards deep and about seventy yards across. The cave itself extended perhaps a hundred feet beyond the ledge to either side before its ceiling sloped down to touch the strange, glowing waters. There were no visible entrances or exits to the domed cavern, at least, none he could see. T.K. told him that the right side of the cave hid an underwater opening to the subterranean world of a Jurassic era sea. It was about twenty feet below the cave's water level—a frightening and deadly place. The left end of the cave held only narrow footholds and smooth, lichen covered walls. The rock lip became narrow toward the area where T.K. said the *ring of fire* appeared, making it hard to really explore that area, but they did watch the waters patiently for any hint of the strange shimmer T.K. promised would play upon the surface when the time hole became active.

Most of the time, T.K. was a good companion. She was tireless and attentive. But Antonio had a hard time getting her to open up. He knew scarcely more about her now, after a half dozen conversations, than he had known when she first cut them loose on the ship. She occasionally brooded about losing her friend and adopted father, the Captain. Once or twice, she also mourned the loss of her brother—usually after a visit from one of the snake-headed beasts, but she rarely said much about herself.

The beasts visited them on a regular basis. Antonio counted half a dozen visits with at least two different creatures making an appearance in the cave. The one with the wounded eye, the largest and foulest tempered of the two, came more frequently than the other. It would surface, screeching and bellowing, then pound against the rock wall in frustration, unable to get at Antonio and T.K. when they wedged themselves beneath the overhang. Once, it had followed T.K. up from a dive to harvest more weed. She had jumped onto the rock shelf, screaming for Antonio to get to the overhang, and had spun to face the thing, teeth bared and knife in hand. The thing had shot up from the water angrily, but cowered back when it saw the knife. The eye T.K. had stabbed was puss-filled and a sickly gray in color. It hissed and screeched as she backed up toward the overhang. Once it saw that she was safe, it slammed its head against the rock shelf, shaking the cave and knocking a chunk of rock free. It pounded and screeched for almost an hour until finally slipping back down beneath the waters.

After they were sure the thing was gone, Antonio turned to Tankien.

"I need a weapon, *Senorita*. I will not run to safe shelter and leave you alone to face the beast again. Had it chosen to strike, I would have come at it with rocks again—or with bare fists."

T.K. smiled. "Thanks, Lancelot, but you would have gotten yourself eaten and that *will not* do. You allow yourself to get eaten and I'm warning you—I'll crawl right down that beast's throat and kill you a second time for leaving me alone here!" She sunk down against the rock wall and let out a sigh. "Sorry, I do appreciate the thought, but most of the weapons around this place are organic and unfriendly. I had to abandon most of the harvest. Tonight's meal, I'm afraid, will be a bit meager."

"I should be harvesting with you too," Antonio added. "I believe I am strong enough."

T.K. studied him. "Okay. If you're sure you're up to it, I'll take you tomorrow."

Antonio sat quietly as she cut up the few strands of weed she had been able to save and gave him half. "I need the truth, my friend," he finally said, watching her closely. "How did you and your brother find yourselves in a natural time hole? What could this have to do with H.S.? You say you don't work for him, you do not spy on him, yet you know him very well."

T.K. sighed. "You don't understand, Antonio. You've stumbled into something. It's a long tale, and one that's—well, it's complicated."

"I have much time to be listening," Antonio said calmly.

Tankien looked around the cave as if hoping someone else would speak. "All right, but remember, you asked. The story starts with a horrible murder—my father's. I follow a boy who dies chasing the truth—my brother. I was barely nine years old at the time. To this day, there are parts of the story I don't understand." Her voice grew tense. "I'm not who you think I am. Neither is the man you know as H.S., or the devil who hijacked the *Absconditus*. None of us belong to your time."

Antonio raised his eyebrows, but motioned for T.K. to continue.

"I am from a lost culture, Antonio—one that existed thousands of years ago. My culture designed the technology H.S. has reconstructed. I was part of a city, of a people that made an unforgivable mistake, one that cost thousands of lives, and altered the history of your world."

"*Thousands* of lives?"

"The tale is sketchy in my mind," T.K. continued, "almost like a dream, but I can tell you this. Your myth about the great flood—it isn't a myth."

Antonio sifted through the silence. "So, you are telling me you knew *Noah*?" he finally asked.

T.K. laughed. "No. Would have liked to, but I don't know anything about that part of the story. I only know that there *was* an actual flood. It covered many lands, mine included. It was caused by my people."

Antonio frowned. "What land? Who are your people, *senorita?*"

"I don't really know who they were initially. That's the funny thing. I heard stories about my people coming from the stars. Many cultures have myths of their beginnings, only my father swore that ours was not just a story, that it was true. We were once star travelers, hopping from world to world, but something happened when we arrived on this world. My father's direct ancestors were what I guess you might call interstellar archeologists. They were interested in this world because some of your religions and myths had interesting parallels to a myth on our own home world. This myth tells about a group of banished elders who create a rift in eternity and create *time*. While they were investigating earth, something happened. They lost contact with our home world and lost the ability to transfer off your planet. In short, they became stranded."

"Why, I am thinking, did your home world not come looking for you?"

T.K. was silent for a long moment and then she looked up at Antonio. "My father said our home world broke the contact. He was convinced, and the council agreed with him, that something horrible may have happened to the home world. Much of our technology was grounded there, so when the connection was severed, what was left here on Earth didn't work. My people tried to recreate the parts of the system that were lost. It was difficult, because your minerals and resources are different here, and we didn't have the right scientist to build the whole array. This was an archeology team. They only had a few technology engineers, and those were more for maintenance. That meant that rebuilding the technology was not easy or quick. My father said it had gone on for decades. By the time I was born, we had developed an ability to travel the back corridors of Earth time. Then the great calamity hit and my people were wiped out—drowned in the depths of the sea. That's the whole story. I wish I knew more."

"Your father is a time traveler?" Antonio asked.

"No," T.K. corrected. "My father *was* the head of the council—our chosen leader. His grandfather headed the council when our people were originally stranded on Earth. The Head of Council position was traditionally passed from parent to child in our culture. In fact, my brother was being groomed to take my father's place. The great secret that everything in my city revolved around was the attempt to rebuild the time-door that could also transport us from this world—that could help us reconnect with our home world and try to uncover what happened. The door was built over something they called a *prime hole*. My father was very proud of that achievement."

"A prime hole?" Antonio rubbed his chin with interest. "H.S. is seeking a prime hole."

"Yeah, I know," Tankien continued. "He's searching for the same one. They built it deep in the mountain. It was supposed to help us return home when it was finished—whatever star our *home* is. At least, that was the plan. To my father and others, though, Earth had always been their home and they were beginning to have reservations about leaving. Has H.S. told you any of this?"

"Not in the same context," Antonio answered. "Why was your father murdered?"

"As I said, he was the chosen head of the ruling council. Remember, I was only a small girl, so I can only tell you what I think was going on from the things I heard and have mulled over for years. There was trouble in our city. We had been discovered by outsiders. Even though we tried to hide our city on a remote land mass outside of the normal trade routes, Greek sailors found us. Word of the wonders of our city began to spread. The trickle of sailors grew. My father was concerned that this could affect the timeline of your world. We could not share our technology. We tried to pass it off as magic, as favors from the gods, and that seemed to work at first. Then people in my city began to join with select outsiders. My mother was actually one of the outsiders. Once my father married her, his words of caution carried little weight. But he told me he had to marry her. He could not bear life without her. They say she was the most beautiful woman my people had ever seen. My father loved her."

"But these outsiders, my friend—they caused trouble in your city?" Antonio studied T.K., her body language, her face. He was a good judge of character, and he saw nothing in her mannerisms to indicate dishonesty or deceit.

"Not directly. But some of the offspring of mixed marriages between my people and the outsiders started the trouble. Some called them *half-breeds*, and members of the council argued that they should not have the same rights as the full-blood descendants of my people. Specifically, they were not allowed to be involved in any way with our technology. I can remember my father having heated arguments that lasted well into the night about this, though I do not remember which side of the argument he was on.

"Something else was wrong too—something to do with the time door itself, or the safety of the time-door. My father said the earth was trying to realign itself magnetically. Terrible earthquakes and tidal waves rocked the city. Rain fell for months at a time, raising the waters of the sea. The council, at first, was able to protect us by using their technology to build walls and reinforce buildings, but the quakes and floods got worse and did not stop." T.K. turned to Antonio. "I think that's why he was murdered. I think it had to do with his stance on safeguarding our technology, though the general unrest in the city may have allowed the murderers easier access to him. I know that's what my brother thought. He also believed he knew who did it. Though it's little consolation now, in the end, I believe he was right."

T.K. became silent.

Antonio weighed her words. "I do not say I am believing, or disbelieving, *senorita*," he said slowly. "But it is a fanciful tale. You speak of a murdered father and a dead brother and a lost city as if you read from a script. I am wondering how such a story should lead to this cave?"

Tankien bit her lip, picked up a rock and threw it. Sound reverberated through the cavern as the rock hit the far cavern wall and splashed into the water. "My brother found a trail that he believed to be the trail of the murderer's escape. We were following that trail—rather, he was following and I was shadowing him—when a great storm came out of nowhere. Part of our city began to sink into the sea. I stumbled after my brother, all the way to the mountain and the time door. He touched the door and was gone. I touched the door too. I was jerked here just in time to see a beast surface. It only grazed my shoulder—I still have a scar. My brother distracted it. I've already told you the rest. I watched, helpless, as the beast pulled him under. I couldn't save him.

"The horrid man who attacked you with his metal cane is called Belzarac. He's also from my world, only when I knew him, he didn't need that cane. He and a man named Habbus Soccees were the two my brother suspected of murdering my father. They were who he was chasing, and I think he was right. I think H.S. and Belzarac came to the cave before us. I found bits of a man's shoe and pants washed up on the rock shelf after my brother was gone. They were monogrammed with the initials *H.S.* I figured one, if not both of them, had been eaten in the cave too.

"When I finally escaped the cave myself, I had to learn to live in a different culture, a different time. I came out of the lake closer to this time. Fortunately, I had been schooled in Greek as my role was to be an Ambassador for the council. Though it took a while for the people who found me to figure out the language I was speaking, they were, at length, able to find someone to translate. After I learned English, after I had left my first adopted family, I gravitated toward the study of time travel. I don't know why. Maybe it was because I missed my people—because I hoped beyond hope that some had escaped the destruction of our city like I had. I stumbled onto the lectures of a professor teaching time theories that seemed vaguely familiar. Then, I learned the name of this professor. He called himself H.S. It was too big of a coincidence. I knew that at least one of the murderers of my father had escaped. Seeing Belzarac on the ship was like staring into the face of a ghost. I guess the beast only got a piece of him. Ultimately, both murderers had escaped as I did."

"Why, my friend, would this man attack the *Absconditus?* If you say the two were partners in horrible crimes, why would they now be enemies?"

"Habbus was a scribe, an assistant to my father. I saw him hurry out of my father's private chamber just before, before... "

T.K. fell silent. She stared blankly across the light and dark patches of water.

"I told you," she said evenly, "H.S. has to be Haubus Soccees, and I don't know why Belzarac is after him. I only know that the two once worked together, and I'm certain that they were responsible for my father's death. Why else would they have fled through the time door?"

Antonio furrowed his brow. "I am to believe, *amiga*, that H.S. is a vicious murderer from the past? That is not the man I know."

"He's a master of deception," T.K. said. "My father thought him to be a bright and loyal scribe. What I don't understand is why they did it." She turned brimming eyes toward him. "There's no mistaking H.S.'s blue eyes—haven't you noticed? They're the same as mine, the same as Belzarac's. Haubus has cost me my entire family. First, he took the life of my father. My brother was killed chasing him, and now, through Belzarac's heinous hijacking, the life of my adopted father, the Captain, has been cut short. I *will* find him. I *will* get my answers."

T.K. sat as silent as a stone, though streaks of tears glided down her face.

"You say the myth of the *great flood* is no myth," Antonio continued, softly. "It was caused by the attempts of your people to create a time door to return home, yet we have just stepped through a time door, have we not? H.S. has built several, and they have not caused floods or natural disasters as far as I am aware."

"Yeah," T.K. mumbled. "That's one of the things I can't figure. Maybe it's because he's not found the prime-hole yet."

Antonio rubbed his chin, deep in thought. "H.S. has always claimed that time will not allow itself to be changed. Is it possible, Senorita, that the catastrophe to befall your city was not caused by the technology, but by the growing interaction between your people and the people of the time?"

T.K. considered this and shrugged. "It's possible. I don't know Antonio. I'm not a scientist."

"How long have you been following H.S.?"

"About twelve years. I stumbled across his lectures closer to eighteen years ago, but it took a while to track him down and convince myself that it was Haabus. He's a dangerous man, Antonio, but a hard one to find. Now that I know Belzarac is also alive and pitted against him, and that both of them are trying to find the prime hole, I'm even more convinced that Earth is in great danger."

Antonio narrowed his eyes. "You could not be more than eighteen or nineteen years of age, yet you want me to believe that you have been searching for this, this scribe of your father's for almost twenty years? Your math does not work, my friend. "

T.K. shrugged. "I don't age like the rest of you. It must have something to do with the time travel. I age more slowly—about a year for every ten or so of yours. I don't really understand it, but I've had to move on from foster family to foster family because of it." She moved back toward the overhang, cut a piece from a pile of wet weed and chewed. She cut a piece for Antonio. Grudgingly, he took it.

"H.S. is..."

"Haubus Socees," she said.

"The assassin on the *Absconditus* is..."

"Belzarac. His last name is *Treec*."

"And you, my friend—you are an old princess in the body of a cabin girl?"

T.K. pursed her lips. "That about sums it up."

Antonio nodded, mumbling to himself. "Princess of a fantastical city, created thousands of years ago, with unimaginable technology imported from other worlds. Yet somehow, all of this is lost to our illustrious history, destroyed by the angry winds of time, or perhaps, washed away by the *great flood*?" He turned to T.K. "You must give me something more substantial, *amiga*—something I can hold on to."

T.K. sighed, puffing out her cheeks. Her blue eyes twinkled in the dim light. "My city isn't completely lost to your history, Antonio. It's a part of your mythology. In my tongue, the name of our fair city was '*Aert Olaneas Tis*,' meaning simply 'blue world outpost.'" The words lingered in the air a moment before she continued. "The Greek sailors who first visited us simplified the name. They called it merely '*At-lan-tis*.'"

8

Clear as Crystal

Willoughby's first night aboard the *Pesci Piccoli* was fairly uneventful. H.S. seemed preoccupied with studying the brass spyglass. Sydney appeared around dinnertime, looking ravishing despite the slight discoloration around her knuckles where it appeared she had punched a wall. Sam fretted over dinner, which was singularly delicious. It was thick-sauced chowder made from local sea bass, with fresh baked bread and a side of buttered asparagus. Willoughby couldn't help but think of the toothy grin of the young porter who had escorted him back to the villa earlier that morning.

"I met your fish specialist," he told H.S. They were seated at a crystal table. The unusual table top had descended from the ceiling in the main room, turning the central alcove between the two Wyland paintings into a dining nook. H.S. shifted on the cushioned bench.

"Oh. You met Bastion?"

Willoughby swallowed a gulp of honey tea and wiped his mouth. "Well, I didn't know his name, but when I tried to get him to take a tip for fetching us from the beach, he said he worked for Observations, Inc. He explained that his specialty was fish."

"Yes." H.S. smiled. "He is a maestro. He can literally call the most succulent fish to him. They follow him to market, and then flop willingly into his basket," he said with a bit of a twinkle in his eye. "He is a legend on the island."

"So," Sydney said, "Observations, Inc. employs a *fish-whisperer?* Does the board know this?"

H.S. dabbed the corners of his mouth with a napkin. "Sydney, my dear," he said, cleaning his teeth with his tongue, "the board is very busy and hasn't time to scour every fish purchase, or for that matter, every credit card statement. Else they might question a number of rather curious purchases, such as an entire collection of Tiger-Eye beaded anklets, which, of course, exceeded the daily expense limits by almost eight hundred dollars as I recall. Shall I go on?"

Sydney raised an eyebrow, considered the comment, and then decided not to respond. She took another dainty bite of asparagus. Dr. O'Grady then shuffled in. He looked as disorganized and disheveled as usual, his hair sticking up in odd directions as if he had been napping for most of the afternoon. His spectacles hung down on his nose, slightly skewed. He mumbled an apology as he made his way to his spot on the cushioned bench.

H.S. picked up his saucer and teacup, seeming a bit annoyed at the interruption. Willoughby noted him carefully turn his teacup a quarter turn every time he set it down on the plate. It was a little thing—something H.S. had always done from the first day he met him—but Willoughby found it oddly fascinating. He remembered the first day he had met Dr. O'Grady. He, too, had twisted his teacup a quarter turn before spilling it. The thought caused him to casually watch O'Grady during the dinner. Sure enough, very discreetly, O'Grady turned his teacup a quarter turn each time he put his own cup down. *What was it about these two?* Were they long time friends? Had Dr. O'Grady picked this up from spending time with H.S.? Willoughby had been around O'Grady since the beginning of their cruise aboard the *Absconditus*, but he was the one team member who didn't feel like a part of the team. In fairness, Willoughby had been too interested in getting to know Sydney and T.K., and his new bunk-mate, James Arthur. He had been interested in spending time with his friend, Antonio, and learning what H.S. deemed as critical for him to learn for the mission. He hadn't paid a lot of attention to the older, somewhat skittish Doctor O'Grady.

Sam poked his head around the corner of the hallway. "Is the food to your liking?" he asked no-one in particular.

H.S. gave a cheery smile and a wave. "Delectable, as usual…"

The stone-faced man nodded and disappeared back toward the kitchen.

Sam refused to join them at the dining alcove. He said he felt more comfortable eating with the staff. Willoughby looked around. How many staff did the *Pesci Piccoli* have? He had only met two other people on the ship—Angel, a petite, pleasant woman with red-hair and a coy smile who acted as cabin maid and maître-d', and Racci, a slender Portuguese man who served as chef and deckhand. He wondered if there were other staff he was not aware of.

So far, it was the wily Portuguese man who had won his immediately admiration, falling to the ground at the sight of Sydney. Lying completely prostrate, he had cried out in accented English, "Your eminence—welcome to our humble ship. May I raise my unworthy self from the dust to behold your magnificence?"

Sydney had sighed, shaking her head and rolling her eyes as she stepped over him. When he jumped back to his feet, he grinned broadly, giving Willoughby a wink.

After dinner, Sydney excused herself, claiming she still had to finish *arranging her room.*

"Don't punch anymore walls," Willoughby teased.

She looked down at her bruised knuckles. "Oh, that," she said. "I fell." She looked up with a grin. "Thank you for the concern, though." She spun, whirling her short skirt out. "By the way," she added, "do you know Morse code?"

Willoughby nodded.

She gave him a mischievous wink. "Keep your ears peeled. Tonight the moon is supposed to be full. It could be a sleepless night."

Willoughby wasn't sure, but it was highly possibly that he blushed. It was hard to imagine that this was the same girl who, only days ago, had set on the edge of his recovery room bed and wept at the thought of the horror and carnage of the hijacking they had lived through. How was she able to put that behind her so quickly? Maybe it was just her way of coping.

The rest of the night was a bit of a blur. He had gone to his cabin and looked through the trunk of things Sam had bought him. Amazingly enough, all of the clothes fit. He spent a few minutes arranging them before feeling a wave of exhaustion sweep over him. He was asleep before his head even hit the pillow. The next thing he knew, a grayish light was bleeding through the small porthole. When he stumbled up onto deck, pulling a windbreaker around him, he found that they had already left port. He could barely make out the outline of the island far in the distance. The tang of the brusque air did not hold the same magic for him as it had when they left Boston harbor on the *Absconditus*. He felt apprehensive and unsettled this time.

Sydney appeared on deck, shaking her head as if she, too, was having a hard time waking up this morning. She made her way over to him.

"Wow," she said, brushing silky strands of hair from her face. "I can't remember sleeping that hard for a long time. You think they put something in the chowder?"

"Either that or the honey tea," said Willoughby. "I noticed that H.S. had coffee." He smiled. "Actually, I think we were both due for a good sleep."

Sydney gave a nod of agreement. Sam appeared, directing Racci and Angel who were carrying a small table. He led them to a covered area near the stern of the yacht. After Angel had thrown a light blue tablecloth over the table, Sam made his way over.

"Breakfast is served. H.S. will join you momentarily." He turned and disappeared back down the cabin stairs.

Willoughby looked at Sydney, shrugged, and motioned for her to follow him over to the table. Low pedestals rose up from the deck and Racci laid down cushions for them to sit on.

"You know, you still look good," Willoughby said. "I mean, overall—with just waking up and everything." He felt stupid as soon as the words left his mouth.

Sydney narrowed her eyes. "Was that meant to be a compliment?"

Before Willoughby could respond, the food arrived. Breakfast consisted of Belgian waffles with strawberries, steaming cocoa, and thick, maple-flavored bacon. H.S. joined them just as a tray of syrups, butter, and orange slices arrived. The three of them ate, making only small talk. Willoughby was determined to keep his mouth shut so he didn't make a bigger fool of himself than he already had. For some reason, he found it hard to formulate intelligent sentences these days as he watched Sydney— and since he came onto the yacht, he was finding it harder and harder not to watch her.

H.S. broke the silence. "Sydney, I want you to work for a while with Angel today. She will help you practice your fifteenth century French. I've also asked her to go over the geography you are to have passed through once again to refresh your memory."

"What fun—I can't wait to get started." The sarcasm in Sydney's voice was notable. She gave H.S. a pout. "And what does our brilliant mathematician get to do today?

H.S. gave her a smile. "Willoughby and I have— issues to discuss."

Sydney rose from the table with a sigh. She looked Willoughby's way and gave him a wink and a crooked smile. "Well, good luck with your *issues*." She made her way back toward the cabins.

Willoughby looked at H.S. "We're still going through with the mission?"

H.S. pursed his lips. "Let's retire to my office downstairs. There is something I need to show you."

As he led the way down the stairs and through the small hall, past the galley, to his office, H.S. did not speak.

He ushered Willoughby inside the office, shut the door, and walked to his desk, ordering the lights up full. Using a thumbprint-lock to open one of the drawers of his desk, he pulled out the brass spyglass. He held the tube over the center of the desk and let go. The spyglass dipped a quarter of an inch and then held, hovering in mid-air. H.S. looked up. "It's a magnetic field. It holds the object while dozens of sensors probe its outer skin and inner electronics. I have peeled this onion to its very roots. What you see on the walls is the technical read-out from its flash memory combined with infrared sensor images of bits of internal construction. Can you make any sense of it?"

Willoughby looked to the obsidian walls. They were covered with spider-web schematics, dissecting the tube and outlining electric circuitry. The circuitry revolved around a power source of some kind, though not like anything he had ever seen. The source seemed to be a space, or tube filled with various shapes that rippled, like waves on a slope of beach. Some of them seemed almost recognizable, like a small cross, a shape that looked like a button, a bit of chain, and a polished stone of some kind. An electric arc seemed to ripple along its length, firing between and around the shapes. A read-out of number streams scrolled through various locations of the schematic grid, first in a slow crawl, then in a much faster burst. The number streams repeated over and over. He could catch most of the number combinations, but could make no sense of the overall display. It seemed a display of pure chaos. He could find no patterns in the number streams. They seemed random. He slowly shook his head.

H.S. came to stand beside him at the wall. "I was afraid of that. This is definitely *not* our technology. It is beyond anything we know. Yet I do have some clues." He walked over to where the faster burst of numbers began. "You said you saw number strings with this device—strings that led you to this room." He looked at Willoughby, narrowing his eyes. "Did you see anything else, anything at all?"

Willoughby fidgeted under the tight gaze. Finally, he looked up and met H.S.'s eyes. "I saw my father for a brief moment out the window of the shop I told you about… I saw the man with the trench coat, Beelzebub, or whoever. He was coming right at me."

H.S. listened intently. He then walked back over to the desk and plucked the brass tube from the air. The walls immediately went black. "Yes. I thought you may have seen something. I believe the crawl of number streams is a natural combing of the time corridors. The burst of number stream represents, I believe, an event."

"An event?"

"Yes." H.S. looked down at the brass spyglass, leaning back against the desk. "You may recall recorded incidents of certain individuals receiving premonitions—dreams, or visions, warning them of things to come and what to avoid." He walked slowly over and handed the glass to Willoughby. "I believe this is what your brass tube really is. Some sort of mechanism for seeing clues in time that may be important to you as this wave of time unfolds."

Willoughby stared down at the spyglass. "Clues from the future?"

H.S. raised his eyebrows. "Possibly… I don't know. But if I'm right," he stepped forward, clasping his hands behind him, "it means that we have an ally for whatever is to come, a powerful one. That could prove very important." He stepped brusquely to the door and opened it slightly. Turning back, he smiled. "Wouldn't want the others to feel we're too deep in secrets, now would we?"

Willoughby gave a slight shake of his head. His mind was reeling. *Ally?* Was he in need of an ally? What did H.S. mean by *"whatever is to come?"*

"So, we continue with the mission?" He finally said, repeating his earlier question.

H.S. walked back to the desk and seated himself in its high-back, leather chair. He gave a flick of his wrist over a section of desk and a curved segment of floor rose up. The segment created a chair, with a seat portion, curved arm rests and a curved back. He motioned for Willoughby to take a seat. As soon as he did, surprised at how comfortable the make-shift chair was, H.S. began to speak.

"I have explained to you, Willoughby, that whatever we have stumbled into, it does not appear to be by accident, nor does it seem to be something we can run away from. Both favorable and unsavory creatures seem to have fairly free access to us with technologies beyond our own. I have given a great deal of thought to our situation and believe that our best course of action is to train you as quickly as possible to use the gifts you have displayed—at least as much as I can. So, we start today."

"Now?"

H.S. smiled. "Absolutely." He leaned back in the chair, tenting his fingers. "You have told me you see number strings. Sydney has explained how you equated the number strings you saw to time holes, or doorways. Do you have an idea what the number strings represent?"

Willoughby thought for a moment and then shook his head. "The numbers are moving too fast. I don't have time to study them or see if they follow a pattern."

H.S. leaned forward. "They are representations," he said softly, "flavors, if you like. They provide you a cross-section of time. You have the ability, young Willoughby, to see them." He sat silent for a long moment. Then he leaned back again and tapped a finger to his lips. "There are an infinite variety of flavors to time, but a finite number are visible to us along our own timelines. When I explained time holes to you, I gave you the analogy of an eddy, or whirlpool, sucking in and funneling down materials from the river at large. These materials carry a *flavor*, or signature if you will, that connects them, as if by a thin thread, to whatever original point in the timeline they came from. If you know the point you are seeking for, and you recognize it in one of these trapped threads, the thread, or flavor, will lead you to that point in the timeline."

"How do you know the exact point you're seeking? Is there a numeric sequence to every point in time?" Willoughby scooted forward, perching on the very edge of his circular seat.

"There is," H.S. said, squinting up at the ceiling lights, "but it is not a sequence you can write down and pursue like you would a map. You see, every person who looks into the crystal computer, or who exhibits the skill of sensing the numeric sequences with their mind, sees something that is unique." H.S. was angled forward again now, leaning heavily upon the desk. "The flavors, or strings, you see, are as unique as a perspective. The ripples of infinity that form the life-blood of time seem to somehow know every finite particle—every cloud, every tree, every blade of grass. But each of us perceives them in a slightly different way."

"Every hair on your head is counted…" Willoughby mumbled, remembering something from Sunday school.

H.S. shook his head. "Yes. So, to better explain, you have a numeric relevance to the infinite. The number strings you see, then, are equated outward from the point of *you*—you are central to the equation. Caught in the time-hole, threads or flavors of time, you see, are not static, because you are not static. Remember, time is motion. You are moving through time, and the points at the end of each thread are moving through time. This should help you understand why you see a running string—a thread, an ever evolving equation and not a static number."

Willoughby realized that his fists had been tightening, his knees had tensed, and he had almost stopped breathing while H.S. had been speaking. He forced himself to take a deep breath now and push back into the circular chair. *This made sense!* He felt the truth of H.S.'s words in his very being. He breathed in again. "But you said that you could follow a flavor, or a thread to find a person or place."

H.S. nodded. "You must think of every person, of every place, of every particle we know of as always existing on two planes simultaneously. One plane, an infinite, ever moving one—a fluid ribbon of continuance—and the other, a finite series of events wherein that particle occupies a precise space at a precise mark in the time continuum."

H.S. walked around the desk and perched on the left corner of it. "Our finite selves, you see, are really nothing more than millions of precise events, occurring in tandem to create a sense of time and motion due to the framing and relevance of their occurrence." He snapped his fingers, giving a quick, wavy signal over a segment of desk and a film clip from a silent Buster Keaton sketch hovered in the air over that spot. "It is much the same as a motion picture. A *living* story can be created from thousands of still images, strung together and projected in a relevant sequence in a defined frame. If you see reality in this way, then you can begin to make sense of the number sequences that stream by you. In time, you will learn to recognize various flavors—times and places—or you may even be able to pick out from a thread or stream specific patterns, or events in space and time that are known to you, that may have direct relevance to your immediate needs." H.S. pointed his chin toward the brass spyglass, still in Willoughby's hand. "I think your spyglass somehow augments this process, helping you visualize the patterns or shape events may take."

H.S. fell silent.

Willoughby stared at the spyglass, his hand trembling. "It's almost too much to take in," he said, softly. His mind was a whir. There were so many ramifications to the information H.S. was casually throwing to him, not only from a mathematical standpoint, but from a personal standpoint. He felt like his core was shifting. The world that had seemed somewhat baffling before, yet now, to consider it as a mass of particle events held in check by some framework unique to himself—it was simply too much to process. He pushed the whirl of ideas flying around in his head away and focused instead on a simpler question. "How—how do you recognize things with the crystal computer? How do you know the places, the things you want to find?"

H.S. gave a slight grin and shrugged. "I see a specific number sequence as slightly brighter than the streaming numbers around it. I think that may be the infinite part in me, recognizing a particle, an event that has relevance. That is why I planned to send you to France for this mission. Once you can read the crystal computer, and we can get you to sixteenth century France, you will be able to find threads that relate to your father, which means more chance of finding *Michael de Nostradame*. We have spent a small fortune to buy artifacts from France crafted during this time period. These will help you find the threads to the right time and place."

"But how do you keep from making a mistake? The numbers are moving so fast. What if I think I see a brighter sequence and I direct the team there and it's completely wrong?"

H.S. pushed back in his chair, clasping his hands and bringing both index fingers to his lips. "Then you're wrong." He straightened. "Willoughby, one of the first lessons you need to learn before any training will be effective is to *trust* yourself. At any moment in time, there is a part of you that knows where you should be and what you should be doing."

Willoughby's head reeled. His shoulders tensed. "I—I can't do this, H.S. It's—it's too much."

H.S. studied him. "You don't *know* what you can do yet, Willoughby. Frankly, I don't think you have a choice. I am trying to prepare you as best I can to use the gifts you have to maximum advantage. I have no control over the events that have begun to affect your life. Had you never found us, or chosen not to join us, it is unlikely that your talents would have gone unrecognized for long. Remember, when you first saw the numbers—when you first came in contact with that most distasteful being who calls himself Beelzebub—you did not even know we existed." He paused for a moment, pursing his lips. "The fact is, you already saved your team, or part of your team, once. I'm sorry to throw so much at you at once, but we don't know how much time we have. There are team members who need our help. They need *your* help. Shall we continue?"

The thought of James Arthur and Antonio and what may have befallen them sobered Willoughby. He sucked in a deep breath and gave a curt nod.

"Good," H.S.'s smile returned. "So, today we start small. We start by helping you understand what a miracle you, and basically all humankind, really are." He waved a hand over his desk, signing a shorthand message. A three-dimensional image appeared at one corner of the desk. It was an olive-skinned, stocky baseball player coming to bat. His shirt read "Detroit" and his number was 24.

"Miguel Cabrera earned baseball's coveted Triple Crown when he hit a home run in the fourth game of the 2012 World Series against the Giants. It drifted over the right-field wall. The Tigers were swept in four games, but watch. This is a beautiful hit." The man crouched with the bat at the ready. He swung. There was the crack of the ball being hit and the almost immediate roar of the crowd. H.S. continued. "Matt Cain was pitching for San Francisco. He pitches a fastball at ninety-four miles per hour. We know that an object traveling ninety miles per hour would travel 7920 feet, or 1.5 miles, in roughly sixty seconds. If we set up the equation, $7920/60 = 60.5/X$, we discover—"

"That it takes 0.458 seconds for the ball to cross home plate," Willoughby interrupted.

H.S. barked a short laugh. "Well done! That means Miguel has less than four tenths of a second for his eyes to register the release of the ball, transmit that information to the brain, which then must determine what kind of pitch it is, estimate how fast it is moving, send instructions to the appropriate muscles on how and when to swing the bat, and for those muscles to then implement these instructions. How does the body do it?"

The clip of Miguel walking to the plate, crouching, then swinging the bat and hitting his home run played over and over in a continuous loop. Willoughby slowly shook his head, having a hard time taking his eyes off the three-dimension image that seemed so real he could swear a miniature man was standing in the air above H.S.'s desk, stepping up to a hovering plate.

H.S. knitted his fingers together. "The answer is simple. The body cheats. There is not enough time for the chemical and electrical processes that need to happen to take place in real-time. So the body makes use of other, shall we say more primitive, resources. It primes and starts the muscles, uses a shadow sense that marks motion much faster than our optical sensors, though not as precise, then when the optical information arrives, the brain predicts where the ball is at that moment, placing it not where the optical information says it is, but where its trajectory predicts it should be, and adjusts the burst of energy from the muscles to push the bat accordingly. It is an absolutely fascinating feat, accomplished at the edge of biological time."

The image of Miguel disappeared. Willoughby looked up. "What does this have to do with learning how to use the crystal computer, or to make use of the numbers I see in my head?"

"Everything." H.S. grinned. "I'm going to show you how to use numbers to *cheat* the finite, or physical, world."

9

The Desert Witch

James Arthur rolled his head, fighting to escape the maddening buzz of a fly. He wanted to swat at it, but he couldn't move his arms. He cracked an eye open. His throat was parched and his body was one, long bruise. His uncomfortable cot hung from the filthy, foul-smelling rump of a loping, gas-endowed camel. He swayed in staccato jerks as the camel navigated a deep fissure between high, rock walls. The sand to either side of the camel was empty. The stout, barrel-chested man who called himself Mahadin was nowhere to be seen. Dr. J had fallen asleep to Mahadin's strange babble of broken British phrases he had picked up somewhere. It was obvious the man had no idea what he was saying. The only real information he had gleaned from the conversation was that Mahadin's grasp on world history had the Duke of Wellington defending Yankee Doodle's donkey. When was that song first sung? Was it late 1700's or early 1800's? At least, he felt like he was honing in on a date. He wiped his eyes and looked around again. He and the camel seemed truly alone.

"Hello?" he called weakly. There was no answer. He studied the sandy wash they were traveling down. It was coarse and bumpy and a particularly jarring bump rattled the cot. The camel, yet again, expelled a tremendous burst of gas. Dr. J jerked his head as far away as his constraints allowed. *Lovely*, he thought. *He was tied to the one beast who could single-handedly match the natural-gas output of the cypress swamps!* The fly that had been pestering him was caught by the gastric upheaval and fell away, dead. The rumbles from the belly of the beast made James Arthur cringe and the fumes from the subsequent blast made his eyes water. He felt a sudden urge to be sick. Another bump left James Arthur bracing for the worst, but when no additional thunder-works came, he let himself relax.

Ignoring the stiffness in just about every inch of his body, he closed his eyes and focused his energy. *Repair, heal*, he encouraged his body. He had been fighting to heal himself every moment he could since being strapped like an old rug on the back of the camel that followed the giantess. The problem was, he kept drifting off into unconsciousness. He could tell, though, that the pain was lessening. He slowly sucked in a deep breath and concentrated his gaze, for a moment, on the walls of the rock cleft through which they were traveling. Multicolored and beautiful, the rock walls extended for hundreds of feet straight up on either side. Dr. J turned his eyes to a scruff of bushes in the wash that seemed to follow what had once been a shallow stream bed. He struggled with the cloth rope that had him bound. It wrapped across his chest, waist, and legs. He looked up at the sky, guessing from the deeper shade of blue and the coolness of the air that it must be early morning. How long had he been unconscious this time? He could swear that when he last listened to the babble of Mahadin, it had been early to mid-afternoon.

Examining what little he could see of himself, he discovered that someone had at least attempted to wash away the thick chalk that covered him, and had placed a loose fitting, vile smelling garment on him. It covered him to his ankles like a coarsely woven nightshirt. He wondered if the garment had always smelled vile, or if the smell was a lingering result of earlier gastric upheavals from the camel.

His thoughts were interrupted by the sound of two old men, talking fast in an unfamiliar language. As the cot steadily approached them, and then slid past, they stared down at James Arthur with detached interest, pointedly joking as they swatted away flies with their rakes of thin reed. The men were tall and dark-skinned, one with a stubbly chin, the other with a thick, matted beard that hung down to his chest. Both men wore turbans. One slapped the camel's rump, causing it to fart again. They fell into peals of laughter. Obviously, this particular camel had been hand-picked.

"Okay," James Arthur managed to croak. "I'm just biding my time, and then I'm going to lock you two in a phone booth with this exploding tower of hoof-humps. Then it'll be my turn to laugh."

The men just laughed harder, happy to get a rise from him, despite the fact that his voice was so faint that they obviously had no idea what he said. They threatened to swat the camel again and Dr. J turned his head away. The animal expelled more gas, even though it hadn't been touched. The two doubled over. *Okay—a Volkswagen,* James Arthur thought; *I'm going to fit you two and this camel into a Volkswagen.* James Arthur blinked rapidly to keep his eyes from stinging.

He tried to place the language the men were speaking. Perhaps it was the same as the one spoken by the old woman who pushed him over the sand ridge. He thought of the giantess, snatching him up and of her friend with the shovel. *Where were they?* He turned his head nervously, dubious at the thought of the two. There was no sign of either. The heckling from the two tall men faded as they fell, unceremoniously, into step beside the cot. The camel blew another gasket, and Dr. J choked, watching the other men wave their reed fans and give the beast a wider birth. "Try smelling it from this angle," he grumbled. He heard another sound, growing from up ahead. It took him awhile to identify. *It was the sound of trickling water!*

James Arthur licked his lips and realized how thirsty he was. It was agony hearing the water up ahead, but having to move so slowly toward it. He searched for something to occupy his thoughts. The rock walls, towering up on either side of the gorge, seemed vaguely familiar. He couldn't shake the feeling that he had been here before. *Had he walked this narrow gorge?* The walls abruptly widened as the camel slowed and then stopped. He could hear other camels and men ahead of them in a state of happy excitement. He realized that the camels all around him were being watered and the men's water skins refilled. His throat burned as he waited for someone to give him a turn at the trickle of water.

"*Wa... W—water...*" he pleaded, trying to get his voice to carry. He was ignored. He felt like crying, but he was determined not to. He steeled his thoughts, his eye catching on a series of carving on one of the rock walls. He studied the intricate carvings. They were of camels and camel handlers. This place in the gorge almost seemed like a shrine of some sort. He heard a flurry of commotion immediately to his right, and then three barefoot boys circled around the back of the cot, one dragging a bucket of water and splashing the other two. The two tall men scolded them roughly and they immediately stopped, traipsing away quietly toward a sound of even more camels further ahead. A sole drop of water from their antics had hit Dr. J's lip. He licked at it greedily. His own camel, or, at least, the one who was dragging him, moved forward a few paces, and began to make a slurping sound as it drank from either a pool or a bucket. James Arthur tried again to call out, but he could not get his voice to work. All that came out was a hoarse whisper.

"Please, *please—water!*"

Other men crossed his line of sight, as well as other camels. A few lined up behind him, the men slowly inspecting their beasts, making sure the camel's harness and rigging were tight, and the sacks and boxes of goods strapped to its back were secure. Dr. J could barely make out five or six camel teams, tilting his head back as far as possible. He tried to speak again, this time managing a short cough, but the men all around continued to ignore him. In what seemed to James Arthur an incredibly short span of time, the camel was refreshed and the men had fallen back into their place. The slow trek through the rock crevice resumed. Dr. J was beside himself with thirst and with rage. He tried one last time with all his might to cry out, thirst biting at his parched throat, but the words simply wouldn't come. He watched in fury as the opening, with its intricate carvings, fell away behind them and the sound of the trickle faded. He struggled again against the thin ropes, but it was no use. Even though his body was beginning to heal, he was too weak to escape, too parched to cry out, and too dehydrated to muster real tears. The trickle of the water was soon no more than a ghost wind in the gorge, somewhere far, far behind. James Arthur lolled his head back against the stick and hide cot.

As the air warmed, the walls of the crevice grew narrower and the rock sides rose even higher, barely letting in a hint of the sun. Once again, Dr. J had the sense that he had seen this place. A half-hour later, it dawned on him where.

They had crossed under an arch at some point. He had been drifting in and out of consciousness, but he distinctly remembered it. It had reminded him of the *triumphal arch* that had once marked the entry to *The Sig*, a ceremonial entrance to the ancient city of *Petra*. Petra had been famous, or perhaps, infamous as a key link along the famed *Silk Road*. Its ruins now lay in the country of Jordan. Of course, he had not seen the *real* arch before. He had never traveled to the Middle East, or to Jordan, and the real arch had long ago crumbled to ruin. He had, however, seen artists' sketches of it, made by early explorers. The arch had disappeared somewhere between 1839 and 1870, not long after Swiss explorer Johann Ludwig Burckhardt rediscovered the city in 1812. James Arthur stared in amazement. Was he being pulled down *The Sig* somewhere before 1870? *When?* He thought of the only tool he had seen so far—the shovel that had struck him. It had looked fairly modern to him. Surely, it couldn't date much earlier than the mid-1800s. He shook his head, cracking a weak smile.

Petra. Of all the places he could have wound up, this is the one he would have chosen. Few people, even in his own family, knew of his passion for archeology. He had learned early that the history of ancient civilizations wasn't nearly as prized in his house as sports statistics. While he smuggled home books on the glories of Rome and the ancient Greeks, hiding them at the bottom of his backpack, his brothers spent every spare moment in pick-up games at the local park, dreaming of sinking that winning basket at the buzzer.

James Arthur's fascination with Petra began during his final years of college. He wasn't sure why he had become so taken with it. Maybe it was the pictures he saw of grand temples carved into solid walls of rock. Maybe it was the adventure that surrounded a time when ancient trade routes crisscrossed the Middle East. Petra had not only been one of the most famous stops for travelers of the *Silk Road*, but had also been the seat of a thriving desert civilization, prized enough to be seized, in 106 AD, and put under the rule of Rome. Mentioned as Rekem in the Dead Sea Scrolls, the site was also described as "a rose-red city half as old as time" in a famous sonnet by the English poet John William Burgon and, more recently, served as backdrop for one of Hollywood's *Indiana Jones* films. The ancient people of Petra, the *Nabataeans*, were fascinating as well. They did far more than just build a breathtakingly beautiful city in the middle of a desert. They were ingenious engineers, turning the whole basin at the foot of Mount Hor into a water-gathering array.

James Arthur pushed his mind back to the present, watching the high cliffs above the gorge creep in and out of view as the camel train continued on. The crevice had begun to widen a little. Suddenly, the camel stopped. The men beside him spun, falling to their knees with much crying and commotion. Dr. J heard a booming, female voice calling out from somewhere above them. It took a few minutes to locate the voice. It was a slim, dark-haired woman, standing on the edge of a carved alcove about half-way up the rock face. He had seen pictures of such alcoves, once used by the city as lookouts or guard posts when Petra was in its prime. He stared harder at the woman. He could see her form clearly, but her face seemed obscured by the shadows. She, for her part, seemed to be staring right at him. He heard her shouted words in the same language as the other men. But in his mind, he heard a high-pitched, whining voice, speaking in French-accented English.

"You have finally come. You have found me. Pity you are too late. When we last met, I was in pain... Now, *I am* pain."

James Arthur sifted the words, the voice. There was something familiar about it. "*Last time we met...*" The woman's eyes flared and he, at last, saw why the woman's face seemed to blend with the shadows. The skin around her eyes was charred black.

10

Six Degrees

The concept was fascinating. H.S. Explained to Willoughby that the numbers he saw floating in air were mathematical representations of the "stuff" escaping from the time-hole, much like air escapes from the hole of a punctured tire. "Molecules, stray neutrinos, even human or animal pheromones, all can be sucked into a hole that is on the ebb out."

"Ebb out?"

"Yes. As you know, gravity creates ebbs and pulls across space that impact the flow of time. Of course, most of these are very small—invisible to the naked eye. But just as pheromones, also invisible to the naked eye, can be sensed by our brain, affecting moods and mating habits, it appears that some minds have the ability to sense these minute changes in the time continuum. Some call it *Déjà Vu*—the sense of somehow knowing a place or thing without ever having experienced it before. You, with your mathematical mind, provide an extraordinary chance to study the phenomenon up close. The theory is that the mind struggles to understand what it sees, what it senses, so it attempts to translate the information into something it understands. For you, this would be mathematics. You see what I am trying to say, do you not? Sensed information beyond visual plane can be *given* a visual representation by the brain, much like a computer uses programming logic to create visual information on a computer screen."

H.S. had walked over to the obsidian wall where a stream of numbers had become visible, spilling from all sides of the crystal computer on its pedestal. "So, the floating numbers are not actually there, I'm just creating them in my mind?" Willoughby asked, walking over to study the crystal computer more carefully. H.S. raised an eyebrow. "I'm saying the information is there, and your mind is finding a way to present it to you. Computer logic, after all, is a form of mathematics."

"You're accusing me of being a computer?"

H.S. smiled. "We are all computers, Willoughby— biological computers with—something else."

"That bit of infinity inside us?"

"Yes. Quite so." H.S. walked over and snatched up the crystal computer. The patterns on the wall changed, reflecting the changing location of the computer. "Have you wondered why the numbers seem to spill from the computer wherever it is, instead of from the physical location of a nearby time-hole?"

Willoughby nodded. He hadn't, really, but he didn't want to interrupt the flow of H.S.'s words.

"The computer," H.S. continued, "hijacks the information from nearby time holes and focuses, or somewhat controls the flow, much like a faucet controls the flow of water in a pipe." He handed Willoughby the "computer." It looked like a flat, crystal stone with microscopic veins of flickering color. It was heavy, even though it was very thin—no more than half an inch at its center with tapered edges to the sides. A sort of connector at the bottom seated it onto the pedestal much like an iPod to its dock. At the other end was an indentation that looked like it may be another connector, but unlike any connector Willoughby had ever seen. It was teardrop shaped.

"What's this?" He pointed at the teardrop indentation.

H.S. had been closing down the wall projections with a series of hand signals. The walls were now black and lifeless. He looked where Willoughby was pointing. "The original crystal computer was considerably lighter than this copy. As you remember, I used to wear it around my neck before your father snatched at it and fell into the time-hole. The crystal design of this duplicate is as close as we could make to the original with materials on hand. There were two pieces to the original computer. The tear-shaped piece was lost long ago."

"What do you mean by 'materials on hand?'"

H.S. frowned. "I mean exactly what I said. The original computer was not created in this time period. In fact, we are not entirely certain of its origin. There is much to discuss about the original computer, but for now, it would only provide distraction. The time I have to teach you how to use your gift, Willoughby, is limited. You must see that. We are far from in the clear. The ones who hijacked our ship and visited your rooms while you were convalescing are not far behind us. So, I ask you to concentrate. Hear me out before you pass judgment on what I have to say."

Willoughby nodded.

H.S. waited a long moment, and then turned back to the pulsing crystal, his eyes sharp and penetrating. "The second piece to the computer was a sort of memory base. On the original computer, this connector fit a small, tear-shaped crystal with unimaginable memory capacity. I'm not sure if this duplicate can deal with the size and complexity of the information on that crystal should we ever find it, but the information is important enough that we would try." H.S. sighed. He looked sidelong at Willoughby, his eyes overtaken with a sudden sadness. "There is so much, my boy, so much I would like to tell you. One day, I will. One day, you need to know everything about our secretive organization, but not today. Right now, it will make little sense to you."

He paused as Willoughby tried to take this in. *What was H.S. holding back?* He watched the man bend his head and chew on his lip. Then, he straightened and forced another smile.

"One thing I can tell you though—the lost crystal would have a substantial bearing on our ability to control the *prime hole* should we ever locate a path to it. I, personally, believe we will. I believe our path to the hole is somewhere in the arctic—hidden deep under miles of ice."

H.S. had first told Willoughby about the *prime hole* while he was recovering from his ordeal aboard the *Absconditus*. He had explained that every planet has entwined into its gravitational core, the makings of a very powerful time hole—one that, if tapped into and controlled, could not only give them the power to reach eons further into the past, but could even link them forward to the future, or link them to other planets across vast distances of space. Willoughby's ears perked up.

"It is possible," H.S. continued, "that, if we are unable to find the original crystal computer, yet we find the tear crystal and the prime hole, that this duplicate computer could give us limited power. But I have no clue where the tear crystal could be. It disappeared many long centuries ago and despite meticulous searches over the ages, no trace of it has ever been found. So, we follow what avenues are available to us. We search for your father and the original computer."

"So, you're saying we're risking our lives for something that may not even matter?"

H.S. frowned. "Life is risk, Willoughby. The best we can do is to insure we are taking risks with desired consequences. Now," he said, pointing back down at the crystal computer. "Unless I'm very much mistaken, you don't need digital wall read-outs or wirelessly equipped glasses to peruse the output from our crystal."

Willoughby shrugged and looked down at the computer in his hand. He tried to clear his mind, but nothing seemed to happen. He studied the internal flashes of the tiny color veins. They mesmerized him. "Anything?" H.S. asked. He shook his head and pulled his eyes away from the crystal, looking up at H.S. At that very moment, he noted a faint flicker out of the corner of his eye. "Wait," he said. He looked down at the crystal, and then back up at H.S. He did this several times, paying close attention to what he could see out of the corner of his eye. "I see some number strings floating—very faint, out of the corner of my eye. I can't really see them clearly."

H.S. smiled. "Of course...You are not seeing things with your physical eye. There is a part of your brain that you have not learned to exercise and control yet, but the ability is there. Our first goal is to help you learn to access and control this gift. Then we will begin to discuss how to interpret the number strings, and use them to help you navigate time."

For the better part of the day, H.S. taught Willoughby to clear his mind and reach for the almost mystic sense of numbers in the air around him. It was like trying to make sense of those 3-D puzzles that appear to be just a jumble of lines and shapes until, suddenly, a full image looms out at you and you wonder why you couldn't see it there before. "You're familiar with the theory called The Six Degrees of Separation?"

Willoughby frowned. "That's a valid theory? I thought it was just an internet myth."

H.S. smiled. "Myth usually carries a kernel of truth. This particular one was first proposed in a short story by Frigyes Karinthy. Later popularized in a play by John Guare, it has its real roots in early network theory. As mathematicians, sociologists, and physicists brooded over the optimal design for cities after World War I, some began to imagine the consequences of a shrinking world where dense human networks bring everything and everyone within reach. The theory states that any two people are always only six steps or degrees apart. As you widen your network from direct friends, to friends of friends, and then to friends of friends of friends, and so forth on to six steps or degrees out, you can eventually touch every living soul. Numerous studies conducted over the past fifty years support the theory."

"What does this have to do with my gift—with my seeing numbers?"

H.S. had brought up one of the round, stool-like chairs from the floor and seated himself on it. "As it turns out, this sort of connectivity also exists in the natural world. All things are interconnected. If you can see the patterns around you, if you can trace the path of those patterns back through their gradual evolution, you can develop a connection with the whole of our physical world—with *all* time, with *all* space. You seem to be able to visually see these patterns and trace these connections via mathematics. The chemical pathways of your brain have learned to recognize what, to the rest of us, is invisible. You see flowing number strings that allow you to locate inter-connections via mathematical bridges."

"Okay," Willoughby started, "but, we've already established that, haven't we?"

"Yes," H.S. agreed, "but a path found, Willoughby, can become a path remembered—a path frequently accessed. Once you learn to decipher the patterns, to understand the connections, you have taken a step toward learning to control the path, to navigate, without the need of outside technology, the time grid."

Willoughby listened as H.S. discussed the areas of the brain, the parts of the body associated with the brain, and meditations that help open these areas, passing conscious thought, degree-by-degree, to areas of unconscious performance. They had lunch delivered in and continued talking, working, until after 4:30. By that time, Willoughby's mind felt like mush. He was mentally exhausted and still somewhat physically strained. H.S. stopped in the middle of a question, noting the glazed look in his eyes.

"You're tired," he said, matter-of-factly. "We should call it a day and give you time to get some sun and air before dinner."

"I'd like that," Willoughby agreed.

"We'll hit it again bright and early tomorrow. We only have three days."

Willoughby stopped half way to the door. "Three days until what?"

H.S. was heading back to his desk. He looked up. "Until we reach the rendezvous… You will, my dear boy, have a chance to see one of our premier secrets. I'm taking you down to our seafloor base. You will see the very core of this strange, Bermuda Triangle—the reason for its sinister reputation." He smiled, moved to the back of his desk, and sat.

Willoughby watched him for a long moment, then turned, and without any more questions, left the room. Coming quickly to the ship's galley, he glanced in. To his surprise, Sydney was there with a cooking apron on. He saw Racci, visibly distressed, near the back of the galley with a steaming saucepan. Sydney was bent over a mixing bowl.

"You cook?" Willoughby couldn't help grinning to himself.

Sydney looked up and smiled. "Of course I cook!" Racci shook his head vehemently, but she didn't seem to notice. "I've also learned how to sew and, uh, I vacuum. At least, I think it was a vacuum…" She was staring into a cupboard now, mumbling. "It sucked a whole sock up, so, what else could it be?" She grabbed half a dozen spices and then looked back to Willoughby. "Anyway, I'm making a special dessert for tonight. Racci has convinced me to try one of my own creations." Again, Racci was shaking his head vehemently. "It's a flambé," she said.

Racci proceeded to mime gagging, throwing up, and dying, in that order. Sydney turned to face the Portuguese chef. The wiry man miraculously changed his final throws of death, to a pleasant smile, and a bobbing agreement, his chin bouncing up and down like the head of a bobble-doll. "I am happy to be recommending your fine culinary sensations," he sang. "Oh, to think your grace has honored my kitchen!" A sob caught in his throat. "My lips water at the very thought of banana-chili flambé!"

Sydney looked at him dumbfounded. "It's banana-*cobbler* flambé."

"Ah," Racci said, pulling a spice bottle from her hand. "Then we have no need for the chili powder, do we?"

Sydney shrugged, letting go of the spice bottle. "Anyway, cooking got me out of the tedious language lessons with Angel. Try some of the flambé tonight. I think you'll like it." She had started stirring a lumpy mass of something in one of the mixing bowls.

Racci glanced over at Willoughby, again shaking his head emphatically. Willoughby's grin widened. "Sure. I'll be happy to." As he headed up the stairs, he heard Racci's voice, sounding a bit panicked.

"Are you sure, Ms. Senoya, that you wish to mix garlic powder with the delicate cream and banana sauce? It will be difficult for taste buds to recover from such a surprise assault."

Sydney muffled a low snort of laughter. "Uh, no...I meant to grab the cinnamon. Hey, what does this nutmeg stuff do? Will dill weed make an interesting crust sensation?"

"Well, interesting fits, but maybe not sensation."

Sydney cackled again. "Dill weed—sounds like some sort of bad romance novel..."

On deck, the sun was just nearing the water. Sam was in the wheelhouse, navigating the yacht. He waved. Willoughby waved back. Then he walked past the wheelhouse to the front bow of the ship. In his brief experience with sailing, he had learned that he liked the front of the ship. He liked watching the bow neatly cut the waves. The ship seemed alive when it was sailing. He enjoyed watching the spray rise and fall in glistening sheets as it bounced ever so slightly. He liked feeling the wind on his face and the smell of the open sea. The sea had a smell that somehow spoke to him. Born under the sign of water, there was something of the seafarer in him. The sea quieted his soul. It let him think.

Sam came up behind him. "Ah, Willoughby... Good to see you're up for some sunshine and air."

Willoughby turned. "Don't you need to be sailing the ship?"

Sam barked a short laugh. "No. The ship is automated. It pretty much sails itself." He leaned on the rail beside Willoughby, looking out over the ocean. "I come up here mainly because it's quiet and I like to feel the sun on my skin and the wind in my face."

"Yeah," Willoughby said. "I like that too." He paused a long moment and then turned to Sam. "Is life always so hard, Sam? So filled with trade-offs? I joined H.S. and got to meet Sydney, and got to sail. The things I'm learning are fascinating—I couldn't want for better teachers. Yet, there's a part of me that misses my home, my old life where the most stressful thing I had to face was a mid-term, or putting up with the bully-jerks at school." He turned back to look out over the water. "Now the bully-jerks are a lot bigger, and a lot meaner, and have roots that even seem to hold time under their thumbs. And I'm supposed to be some boy-wonder to face them." He swung his gaze back to Sam. "What if I don't want all this? What if I want to put all the spilled milk back in the bottle and forget any of this ever happened?"

Sam was silent a long moment. "Some people spend their whole lives, trying to escape what life throws at 'em.

They do it different ways—turn to drugs, flood their lives with noise and activity, even run off to become chauffeur for some fool, secretive organization... Running doesn't work in my experience. Life is too much like skin. It molds to the core of who you are and whether you dress it up, or try to keep busy so you don't have to think about it, it doesn't go away. So, we're left with a choice. You embrace it and make it beautiful, or you can keep trying to run from it like a rat in the tread-wheel. It's up to you."

Willoughby felt a lump grow in his throat. His eyes stung. "Yeah," he finally said in a shaky voice, "but facing it is, is *hard*. That's all."

Sam waited a moment. "You're right," he finally said, "but it's the kind of hard that matters." After a long silence at the rail, Willoughby looked over to the leeward side to see the sun, in all its resplendent glory, sinking into the shimmering water, spilling gold and crimson across the waves.

"Well," he said to Sam, "I guess dinner will be ready soon. Sydney's is making banana cobbler flambé."

Sam groaned. "Don't tell me Racci let her back in the kitchen?"

Willoughby grinned and nodded.

With a heavy sigh, Sam turned and started back toward the wheelhouse. "I better check in and see that the galley is still standing—and that Racci hasn't used one of those knives he's always sharpening... "

Willoughby stayed on deck, watching until the final hints of crimson on the water were gone. Then he slowly started for the stairs and for the life that awaited him below.

11

Twelve Roots

The day T.K. caught a large, odd-looking fish near the edge of the cave opening, was a day for celebration. She jabbed her long knife up through its chin and into its brain. It almost got away, but Antonio helped her wrestle it to the surface and slap it onto the rock ledge. He thought it looked like a medieval Tuna, but T.K. claimed to have looked up this type of fish after she saw one as a young girl. She said it was something called a *Leedsichthys*. After whooping and dancing a bit, the two settled on the task of cleaning the large fish. Its scales were thick and tough, but the meat inside was tender. Antonio stoked the small fire burning near the back overhang of the cave. He had been nursing the fire for days now, feeding dry, kelp-like stalks onto it in order to boil seawater and collect the condensation. The process had proved achingly slow, and while the weed T.K. found was enough to keep them alive, it did not help much in Antonio's battle to regain his strength. Having so large a fish venture near the cave was a real stroke of luck. T.K. strained some of its blood into a bowl-like piece of shell she had found. Antonio carefully cut away the meat, placing thin chunks onto a flat rock at the base of the fire.

As the cave filled with a haze of smoke and the meat sizzled slowly, T.K. joined him. She lifted the blood filled shell and took a drink, throwing a hand quickly to her mouth. She coughed a few times and bit off a chunk of seaweed, chewing anxiously. Finally, she spoke. "We haven't had time for significant amounts of water to distill, so…" She nodded toward the shell of blood. Antonio stared at her blankly.

"So?"

T.K. sighed, coughing again. "So, we need to make the most of what God grants. You need to drink that blood, Antonio. You need the fluid. We're both dehydrated. I warn you though—swallow fast and have plenty of weed on hand! The weed's bitter taste will help you hold the blood down."

Antonio slowly lifted the shell and looked at the thick, crimson liquid. He breathed in deeply, closed his eyes, and downed the remainder in one gulp. He threw weed into his mouth between gags, fighting to keep the liquid down. Breathing heavily, and coughing, it took several seconds before his neck muscles calmed down.

"I think, *amiga*," he croaked, "that it was not God who granted us *that!*" He threw another piece of weed into his mouth. After chewing in silence, he picked up the knife he used to gut the fish and divvied out slabs of meat. Despite the numbness from the weed, his mouth came alive to the sweet-tasting meat. He savored it, telling himself that it tasted so good because they were half starved, but still, it was a feast to remember. After the bulk of the meat was gone, T.K. moved up beside him.

"That was delicious," she said grinning over at him. "I'd forgotten how sweet the meat is."

"You've tasted it before?"

"Yes—although the last time I was here, I could only eat things raw. I didn't know how to make a fire with flint. That's not the sort of thing they teach a princess. I was just lucky to stumble upon the edible weed. It was enough to keep me alive."

"How did you catch the fish as a young girl, *Amiga?* It was all we could do to wrestle it out of the water with your long knife and the two of us."

"I didn't catch it, I scavenged bits of it when two plesiosaurs got in a fight over it and were distracted. I made away with enough to feed me for a couple of days, and the beasts never knew." She leaned back against the rock wall of the cave and let out a sigh. "We can rest a while, but we need to make use of this energy while we can. The weed is almost depleted and we need to find a better source of fresh water."

"Yes," Antonio agreed. "The water distilling is not going so well." He had barely collected enough since they had begun their fire to cover the bottom of a glass, much less enough for a long drink.

T.K. shrugged. "When I was here before, I didn't stay for that long. I noticed the water was brighter five or six days after I got here. Then, about a week and a half later, the water near the back got bright again. This time, I swam over. There was a sort of bright ring about ten feet below the surface, and it seemed to be pulling water in. I stayed away from it, but it came again six days later. I never fully explored the cave. The whole time I was here, I was hiding from the beasts and finding ways to collect water and weed—to stay alive. Then, the ring was back and a beast came to the cave and swam right into the bright ring and disappeared. I swam over to investigate, the ring flared bright, and I got sucked in." She paused long enough to pull a small pebble from between her toes. "We'll need to swim into the bright ring too. I know it can be done because I've done it. I thought I was going to die. The swim is grueling and freezing. I thought my lungs would burst, but I made it."

"Ah, yes," Antonio added, "to the lake, right? You say the bright ring took you to a lake—to Loch Ness. Who's to say that wasn't just a fluke, *senorita?* If that is what I think it may be—if it is an unstable hole—it could take us anywhere."

T.K. pursed her lips. "I don't think so. When I was swimming up from the bottom of the lake, I found an empty, silver tube—a tube labeled in the writing of Atlantis. It was one of the tubes the Elders used to keep delicate plans and research dry and safe. I filled the tube with rock and flung it back into the lake, as close as I could estimate to the location of the hole. My thought was to keep it from being found, but it seems it continues to serve me." She handed Antonio a small scrap of thin metal with strange writing on it. "I found it washed up on the rock ledge when I was looking for some flint. I think it's from the same tube. Look at these markings here. They're part of a date—the same date that was on the tube I threw back into the lake."

Antonio cocked his head, confused.

"What I'm saying is that I think this hole connects us to only one point—that freezing lake in Scotland called Loch Ness. How else could this bit of writing have gotten back here?"

Antonio studied the writing with interest. "So, Atlantis is not enough. We are also to become part of the riddle of Loch Ness?"

T.K. ignored him. "Do you think you're strong enough to go?"

"*If* your story is true, *amiga*," Antonio said, "it would mean you arrived at a strange lake in a strange time as a child who spoke in a strange language. How did you survive? Did the captain find you right away?"

"No," T.K. said. "I didn't find the captain until many years later. I camped out around the lake for weeks, stealing food from tourists and sleeping wherever I could find shelter. Finally, a kind woman shared her meal with me willingly. I came back to her the next day. She made inquiries and came to believe that I had been abandoned. I couldn't speak English, so I didn't say anything at all. She thought I was too traumatized to speak. She set a task for herself—to get me to speak again. Gradually, I learned. I lived with her for almost seven years before she noticed that I wasn't aging. That's when I had to move on."

"Is that when you found out about the professor—the man you now believe to be a murderer as well as our leader, H.S.?"

T.K. sighed. "It was about twenty years before I found H.S. I've told you this before, Antonio. Don't you remember? I was looking for anything I could find on time travel technology, hoping I could figure out a way back home." Her eyes became cold and hard. "Those were long years I'd rather not discuss," she said softly. "It's not easy to be an abandoned child in your time. Finally, I came across a scientific paper on the mathematics of inter-dimensional travel. There were phrases in the paper that sounded so similar to things I'd heard when my father spoke of time-travel theory, I was amazed. Then I saw that the paper was written by one H. Simon, or H.S. for short. He was a professor at Oxford at the time. I guessed that it was Haubus—that maybe he had escaped just like I did, and had created a name using his true initials. I tracked him down and when I saw him, I was certain it was Haubus. I had only seen him a few times, but he had the blue eyes so prevalent among my people. I spent the last thirteen years learning everything I could about the man. It's what led me to the captain."

"The captain?"

"Yes," T.K. said. "I followed him from an interview with H.S. At that time, Observations, Inc. needed some heavy freight delivered to South America. They wanted someone they could trust who would not ask questions about their evasion of port inspections and the like. The captain needed crew. I presented myself and begged for a job. I told him I was an orphan, which was true. He took me in, treated me like a daughter. He was the closest thing I had to a father since—well, since my own father was killed."

"You have lost two fathers then," Antonio said softly.

T.K.'s face flushed. "Yeah," she looked away. "It's not fun."

"What happened to your mother? You've told me little about her."

T.K. stared over the dim, still waters of the cave. "I never knew my mother. She died in childbirth. My father raised me himself. He refused to remarry. He loved my mother very much. I had servant women, but it's not the same as a mother." Her voice trailed off. "Old wounds," she whispered. Veins in her neck seemed to strain. She sniffed and absently tugged at a necklace that hung beneath the tattered remains of her shirt. Antonio had seen her fingering it before—a teardrop-shaped crystal that dangled from a silver chain. The crystal was between one and two inches long and possibly an inch wide. It had strange markings scratched into it. The delicate chain upon which it hung shimmered like no metal Antonio had ever seen. He was mesmerized.

T.K. finally looked up. She turned away, brushing a quick hand over her eyes, and then looked back with a forced smile. "I swore to myself when I lost my brother that I wouldn't let myself cry again. But sometimes, it just happens."

"Yes, *Senorita*—to mourn is not a thing to be ashamed of. Sometimes, we must set pain free," Antonio said gently. "It is the only way for us to go on."

"It's a waste of time—and water—here in the cave." T.K. locked arms around her knees, still watching the rippling, black waters, still blinking her eyes. "We don't have the water to waste. Neither my father nor the captain would have wanted that. They were both practical men. The tide comes in, and the tide goes out. God bless the tide." She wiped again at her cheek and turned back to him. Antonio poked at the dying coals for a moment.

"This is the last of the dry stalks, my friend," Antonio said. "I will go with you this time to try to find more. I can at least keep watch if we have to venture beyond the underwater opening of the cave. Could we have better chances of finding fresh water if we tried for the surface—for land?"

T.K. gave him a grim smile. "This is the Jurassic era. It would be a miracle if we ever made it to the surface, and even if we did, the beasts up there are worse. At least here we're somewhat protected, and I believe the bright ring will flare again. No matter what year we come out of the Loch in, it's bound be more civilized than here." The glowing embers reflected in T.K.'s eyes.

He pointed to the necklace she held. "It has significance? I notice how you touch it."

T.K. looked down, suddenly aware of the crystal. "My father gave it to me just before he was murdered. He told me that it was my mother's and that she had wanted me to have it when I was of age. He made me promise to always keep it around my neck. *'It is our family, our world,'* he told me." She held it up for Antonio to view. He marveled at its complexity. He had never seen such a stone. It seemed to carry a light all its own. The outside was smooth and cool to the touch, but below the surface, colors swirled and glowed, creating patterns that seemed to react to movement or touch. Antonio held it close, trying to make out the symbols scratched onto its surface. With alarm, he recognized one of them. It was a part of the symbol H.S. had showed in their mission briefing on the ship.

"What are these?" he asked.

T.K. leaned over and looked. "They are symbols of the twelve roots."

"The twelve roots?"

T.K. sucked in a deep breath. "There is—was a legend among the ancients of my father's people. It told of twelve roots that sprang from the mother tree, representing the twelve royal families of the first council. The council became very wise and very powerful, and three of the roots entwined, believing they could forge their own tree. They failed and were cut off—banished by the good earth to a place where there was no solid ground and no blue sky, where time had no effect on them. These are the three symbols. See, they are separated from the others by the thin box." She looked up, pushing a strand of hair behind her ear. "This myth had something to do with why the early travelers came to your world. At least, that's what my father believed. He believed your world was both a wonderful and a dangerous place in the universe."

Antonio noted that the two symbols he recognized were in the box she pointed out. He turned the crystal between his fingers. He saw that, even though it appeared solid from a distance, its interior was actually fractured into millions of tiny honeycombs. He noted a flat indentation on the back, with grooves, as if the teardrop was only part of a larger piece. His mind was spinning.

"I have no idea what he meant when he gave it to me," T.K. mumbled as she tucked the crystal back under her shirt. She forced a grin. "Maybe he just wanted me to remember the stories and the myths of the ancients. '*Our family, our world?*' What's that supposed to mean? It's just another piece of the hopeless mystery of my people." Her voice fell away into silence.

Antonio noted her melancholy mood and pushed his own thoughts away. "Nothing is ever hopeless, *amiga*," he said softly, touching her shoulder. The two of them became silent watching the fire burn. Then, they both rolled out onto the cold rock to sleep.

After a short rest, they woke. Antonio could feel every muscle throb, it seemed. His entire body was sore from wrestling the fish and then sleeping on the hard ground. As they pushed to their feet, he saw that the fire had gone almost out. T.K. prepared to go out to gather more of seaweed stalks. Despite the disgusting taste of the fish blood, the foul liquid and meat gave him strength— enough that he finally felt more confident about going with T.K. to collect the weed. After eating some more of the partially cooked, partially dried fish, they took a short swim through the dim waters to the far side of the cave, he dove after T.K. The strange world outside the mouth of their underwater cave was both fascinating and terrifying. He stared at it with both wonder and trepidation. T.K., on the other hand, focused on the task and seemed unwilling to spend a single second more in the water than necessary.

While the water naturally brightened near the cave opening, it was still dim enough to only give a few feet of visibility. After the dim glow of the cave, though, it was like walking from a dark room into the sunlight. When his eyes adjusted, he took in the bizarre eco-system visible to him. The cave entrance was about thirty feet below the surface, partially hidden below an arching shelf of white reef. The deep blue of the water was dotted with vibrant color as odd plant and animal life teemed across half a dozen shelves of coral reef. T.K. struck out immediately to a patch of seaweed about twenty feet below them. He was impressed with how strong a swimmer she was. Her lungs were strong too. He had to go back into the cave for a breath while she was cutting the weed. When he dove back down, he found he couldn't take his eyes off of the girl's lithe form as she swam amid the color. He had already developed a soft spot for this strange girl who had the body of a teen, the mind of a mature woman, and the courage of a warrior. He also noted how tense his body had become. While the colors of this underwater reef were indeed beautiful, the strange animal life and hidden depths below the cave worried him. He twice glimpsed massive forms gliding by, lurking just beyond the shelves of vibrant color. He watched, ready to intervene if any of the beasts veered in toward T.K. and the coral shelf.

At last, T.K. had her arms filled and they headed back. When they had pulled themselves back onto the rock shelf of the cave, dragged the weed to the back overhang, and carefully laid out the stalks, Antonio sank down against the rock wall, breathing heavily. He had picked up other bits and pieces of T.K.'s story as they set the stalks out and she seemed to want to resume the conversation. She dropped down beside him, also breathing heavily. "Pretty wild out there, huh? You should see yourself. Every time we go, your eyes are bugging out." She made a face, gesturing at her eyes and gave a short laugh. Antonio found himself staring at her, smiling. The girl, or woman, or mystery, looked absently away, fingering a strand of briny weed. Antonio finally found his voice.

"You swim like a fish."

T.K. shrugged. "My people lived on an island. I've always been around the sea."

"When we get out of this cave, I will help you find your island and people. Nothing is hopeless."

"Tell me that after you've lost everything you've ever loved, Antonio…" The two breathed in silence for a while and then T.K. sighed. "When we've had some rest, we'll polish off the rest of the fish meat in one more grand meal. Then, we'll eat as much of the weed we harvested as we can. The bright ring should shimmer to life soon. When it does, we've got to be ready. By my count, we've been here over two weeks now."

"I think I can be ready," Antonio said.

The water still dripped from their clothes and, without the fire, the cave felt cold. T.K. instinctively squeezed closer to Antonio. Huddled this close, Antonio could not help but feel an urge to put an arm around her, to pull her close.

She turned toward him. "You've spent a lot of time asking about me and very little time talking about yourself.

Why are you involved with H.S.? I heard Willoughby say you own a barber shop, and you opened your own little shop on the *Absconditus*. Cutting hair seems a strange occupation for a respected architect."

Antonio considered the questions. "My father put me through college cutting hair. He taught me. This was a skill that was passed down through the generations in my family. My grandfather was also a respected barber. Even while in college, I would often help him on the weekends. My shop in DC is an extension of that relationship. The shop may have been created as a part of the Observations, Inc. network, but to me, it was a nod to my heritage. My father, younger brother, and older sister have all worked for me at various times. I had an older brother once." Antonio absently made a quick sign of the cross. "He was killed in a rough neighborhood in East LA. He owned his own small shop. It was robbed. I had tried to get him to move out of that neighborhood, but he loved the sense of community he felt there. He wanted to make a difference.

"You ask me, *Amiga,* why do I work with H.S.? I guess I am like my brother. I want to make a difference— only, I do not want to be shot in my shop. H.S. is a man who took a chance on me. This man that you say is a murderer and a thief gave me what many a struggling architect can only dream of. I do not dispute that he is secretive and I do not believe he has been completely honest with me about his aims and motives, but a murderer? I find that very difficult to believe, Amiga."

T.K. had been watching him. Her question caught him by surprise. "Do you have someone back home?"

Antonio raised an eyebrow. "You mean a girl? Yes, and no. I have many friends. One or two I thought may be special, but it didn't work out. My hours are long. I have not had much time for a private life. I have spent what time I have, working with the community, and taking care of my parents. All of my family have moved to safer neighborhoods, but they, like me, still contribute."

T.K. gave the faintest hint of a smile and turned slowly away. Antonio fought the urge to touch her. "I have a question for you as well. It is of a more personal nature. How old might you be, *Senorita*?"

T.K. laughed. "I don't know." She was quiet for a while, as if thinking, and then rolled onto her back. "In your years, I think I would be sixty-something."

Antonio gave a low whistle. "You keep a nice figure for sixty-something."

T.K. turned her face away from him. He didn't want to make an issue of looking, but he thought he saw, from the corner of his eye, her face break into a nervous smile.

12

Imprints

The scene was in sepia tones—somehow old, and yet fluid. Willoughby listened as his half-sisters, Densi and Cali, loudly planned their summer break. He turned toward them. They were in the kitchen of his home. This was perfectly normal, right? His Mom was cooking, and his step-dad, Klaas, was goading the girls. His sisters pleaded with Klaas. They wanted to take a road trip. Two years ago, the family spent ten days meandering along the gulf coast. He spoke up.

"Okay, okay! I have always wanted to spend some time in Charleston."

The girls cheered.

Willoughby felt a surge of excitement as well. He had seen pictures of Charleston's Georgian and Queen Anne architecture and it fascinated him.

He blinked.

When his eyes opened, he was sitting in a car with the family. They had just arrived at a beach along the South Carolina coast. He had no sense of lost continuity. Everything up to this point seemed normal, natural. He stepped out of the car. Why did the sand have this pinkish hue? For the first time, he felt that something was wrong.

This beach was wrong.

The sky was wrong.

It had become suddenly overcast, and the waves grew huge and violent. He turned, noticing his family had become silent. One by one, they winked out of existence. Clouds of glowing numbers rose up from the sands and swallowed them. Then, the numbers spilled away, back into the sand, and there was nothing. The sand was empty. His family, the car, they were all gone! He was all alone on the beach.

A scream tore through the air. He spun. He saw Sydney, running toward him in a one-piece swimsuit, trying to escape a monstrous wave. The beach was empty but for the two of them. What was he to do? An ancient pier in the distance groaned as the huge wave broke over its timbers, threatening to break it to bits.

"What's happening?" he screamed at Sydney.

She yelled back, but he couldn't hear her above the roar of the approaching wave. The wall of water rose up, towering over them. It took shape—the shape of a man, a dark, muscled man with bleached white eyes. Seaweed clung to his tattered clothes and barnacles were stuck to his pocked and crusted skin. The man moved in jerks of motion, as if he were barely alive, some sort of animated jelly. A huge, black hand grabbed for Sydney. Willoughby jumped to grab her, trying to scream her name, but no sound came out. He lunged again, grabbing...

He sat upright in his bunk, his fists out before him, clutched tight. Sweat beaded across his forehead. He sucked in shallow breaths, trying to calm his pounding heart. It took him a few minutes to get his bearings, to realize he was still in his cabin aboard H.S.'s yacht—that it had all been a dream. He glanced around the dark room apprehensively. No one was in the room.

"*A dream...*" He mumbled to himself. "It was just a stupid dream."

He closed his eyes, calming his panic before reaching to the side of the bed to click on a small desk lamp. The dim pool of white light took the edge off the terror that still lingered in his mind. He forced himself to let out a long, slow sigh.

What had brought that dream on?

It had actually been a rather pleasant evening. Sydney's banana-cobbler flambé was actually edible. After everyone had finished eating, he had spent time on the deck with Sam and Sydney. Sydney had rambled on about a lot of nothing, but it had been pleasant to watch her, radiant under the full blanket of stars and the sliver moon. He stared toward the door for a moment. Something wasn't quite right. Then, the hackles on the back of his neck rose. *The door was cracked!* He had not only closed it when he'd gone to bed, he had locked it per Sam's strict security precautions, and the lock had no key. How could it be opened unless from the inside?

Willoughby cautiously climbed out of his bunk, opened his trunk, and rummaged inside. He pulled out a metal flashlight and closed the lid. Flipping on the flashlight, he pointed the beam of light toward the cabin door and took a deep breath. He took a few steps toward the door, then stopped, turned back, and went to the desk. He opened the middle drawer and pulled out his brass spyglass. At the door, he grabbed his jacket off a hook and slipped it on. He crammed the spyglass deep into the jacket pocket and continued out into the dim hallway.

The ship was unusually silent. He did not hear the lap of waves, or the normal creaking he would expect, nor was the ship rolling at all. *No night at sea could be this calm.*

When he came up on deck, he knew immediately that time had frozen. There was no breeze. Puffs of cloud in the sky weren't moving in the moonlight. His form cast no shadow. He looked over the railing. The ocean waves had frozen. The surface of the water looked like dark glass—like some sort of massive, acrylic sculpture. The hair prickled at the back of his neck. Though the deck appeared empty, he knew it was not. He walked to the rail and clicked his light off. "Where are you?" he said. "Surely, you don't expect me to indulge you in hide and seek." He looked out across the unmoving expanse of water.

"No. I just knew how excited you would be to see me." The voice came from the shadows behind him, near the ship's bridge. Willoughby jumped slightly, even though he had expected to hear an answer of some kind. He turned slowly to face the being. It was strange how the spoken word carried in a frozen time bubble. It caressed the ear as if the speaker were directly beside you, even though this nemesis was at least forty feet away. Every word, every syllable, penetrated the silence with perfect clarity. The tall, gaunt figure who had spoken rose from his deck chair and strode casually from the shadows. His signature black trench coat hung limp past his knees. Willoughby had no trouble remembering what the creature, or man, or whatever he was, liked to be called; *Beelzebub*. The tall form clasped his bony hands behind his back.

"So, my dear *grandson* has come to join me."

It took Willoughby a moment to respond. "Why are you here? How did you get around our sensors? Is anyone with you?"

The figure meandered over to the ship's railing. "No one is with me yet. I'm concerned about you, Willoughby.

They pulled a bullet from your shoulder. How are you healing?"

"Am I supposed to be touched?"

The man ignored the cheek. "How did I get around your sensors?" he answered. "The simple answer is, what does it really matter? I go where I want to, when I want to, and right now, there is not a thing you can do about it." The creature looked out over the stilled waters. "But, if it amuses you, as you may recall, time is frozen inside a junction. I simply formed my bubble wide enough to encompass your ship. There is nothing for your ship's sensors to detect—only the briefest blip. Meanwhile, we have time to talk. The being eyed Willoughby with an amused grin. "Ever walk across the water, Willoughby? No. I suppose not. It would be too much show for you."

"Is that why you do the things you do?" Willoughby asked. "You're all about show?" He had experienced this type of frozen time before. Beelzebub had first introduced him to the term *time junction* mere days ago. He had explained that, by bridging two different time-planes, an intersect bubble was created, a point between time-lines. If one knew how, they could reside inside this bubble. They could walk and even talk inside this bubble. But Willoughby had actually created a junction months earlier. Beelzebub claimed this is how he found Willoughby. By accidentally creating a junction at Antonio's barber shop, Willoughby had caught the being's attention. He relived the moment in his mind. He had been sitting in Antonio's barber chair. Antonio was chatting away, and then he wasn't. Willoughby had looked up and found everything, including Antonio, suddenly frozen in mid-motion. He glanced again over the railing at the frozen dip and swell of the ocean. It was like a sort of dark crystal landscape.

"You have a sharp tongue," Beelzebub said, licking his lip. "But you missed the essence of what I said. The illusion of actually walking on gently rolling waves is not new to this world. There are few, however, who understand how to do it. Would you like to know how?"

Willoughby did not answer. The man waited a moment, a thin smile spreading across his face.

"It requires you to fluctuate between the live sea and a tightly formed junction. I need only to connect with the junction every other second to keep from sinking noticeably into the water. If I fluctuate between the two at quarter-second intervals, there is no hint of my sinking at all. It's the same principle as a movie projector. I appear to walk on water and it doesn't take magic or miracles—only physics."

Willoughby felt an anger bubbling up inside him. "What do you want from me?"

"To *illuminate* you," Beelzebub said. He walked over to a deck chair. "What need is there for faith when you can have fact? I am here because, in your heart of hearts, Willoughby, you want to know. You want to know it all." His eyes were dark, but glowed with an intensity that seemed to burn. Willoughby found himself edging back against the rail. He tried to think of a distraction. He needed information about this being—something to help him understand who or what it was. He needed some way to protect himself from these unwanted visits. He remembered the brass spyglass in his pocket. *Would it tell him anything?*

"You can create junctions that move with you?" he said aloud, stalling for time as he tried to think of how he could casually pull out the spyglass.

Beelzebub seemed to sense his discomfort and his smile broadened. "Of course I can. You have to be more exact and control the size, but it can certainly be done. As I have said, I can teach you. This is only the beginning of what you could learn from me."

"Did you bring your goon?" Willoughby asked, looking around. The *goon* he referred to was a huge man who had orchestrated the murder of most of the crew of the *Absconditus* crew before he, Sydney, and Dr. O'Grady had escaped. Beelzebub had somehow snatched the man moments before he drowned and held him in stasis, still underwater with the sunken ship, until he was needed. The gaunt man wrapped his trench coat tighter around his bony frame. Willoughby noted that the air seemed to be growing colder. "No," Beelzebub said. "I told you already, I came alone. Gates will not join us this time. He has roughly three minutes before all brain function ceases. You know the time calculation for beings out of their own timeline. That gives me only twenty-one minutes outside of a junction. True, we are inside a junction here, but there are precious seconds lost every time I call him. I can't afford to waste any more of his *usefulness* just to make a point. You are smart. I have no doubt you got my message."

Willoughby had learned that a being pulled outside of their own time aged at roughly one seventh the rate that they aged while in their appointed timeline. He pursed his lips. "You said no-one was with you 'yet.' What did that mean?"

Beelzebub was still looking out over the still sea. "Amazing isn't it? I am able to draw, here, upon one of the strongest holes on the planet. It allowed me to create a junction that extends for hundreds of feet on every side."

It was a fascinating sight, Willoughby had to admit that. The stilled sea lasted for as far as he could see. He thought of how no-one could see a junction unless invited or pulled in by its creator. It was like the tale of Brigadoon.

Beelzebub seemed able to read his thoughts. "Funny how science can be wrested from myth and legend, is it not? What other secrets await discovery, needing nothing more than a mind that can understand them?" The tall figure knitted long, bony fingers together. "You see what I'm offering you? I have asked so little. When I was called Baal, people cut off their arms for me. You see that I am fond of you, don't you Willoughby? I haven't asked you to cut off anything."

Willoughby backed away another step. "The thing I want to cut off is your access to me and my friends. I don't want to learn from you. I don't want to play your games. You think you can barge in on my life whenever you want. *I want you to leave!*"

"I...am not ready to do that, Willoughby. You interest me," the man's voice was barely more than a hiss. "I must watch you, manipulate you...I could send emissaries to visit—both to you and your friends—but I choose to be civil."

"I'm, I'm not afraid of you," Willoughby said, taking another step back.

The gaunt man raised an eyebrow. "Is that why you are still backing up?"

Willoughby forced himself to stop. He stuck out his chin and gritted his teeth, determined to hold his ground. "My door was open. Did you come into my cabin?"

"No."

"Then who did?"

"I do have an associate I wish to introduce you to, but she is not here now."

"Where is she?"

Beelzebub only smiled. Willoughby gripped his hand around the spyglass, ready to slip it from his pocket. "Who else did you visit on this ship?"

"If you mean the girl, I did not go into her room either—nor did my associate. We are here to see only you." The gaunt face turned into a tight grin again as Beelzebub watched every slight nuance of Willoughby's face.

Willoughby swallowed hard, trying not to shiver. "I'm warning you—keep him away from Sydney."

Beelzebub laughed. "Warning *me?* Oh, by all means, I shall take note. Oh, and I am certain Gates will be shaking in his boots. You remember the affinity he has for your girl. I could barely restrain him earlier. Do you plan to kill him too? Now I am interested. How do you plan to kill a man who is five times larger than you and technically already dead?" In the dead air, his voice came as the merest of whispers. "There is a way, of course, but I doubt that you know it. I could teach you to control him, to hold that meager sliver that is his existence in the balance, but you aren't interested. So, I'm left with no choice but to force your hand." He stepped closer. His voice became soft and soothing. "It doesn't have to be this way, Willoughby. You could control Gates, you could control H.S., and you could even control Sydney…Yes. You could have everything you want from her, everything. No guessing. No wondering if you said or did the *right* thing. You could have her at your beck and call."

The words hit home. Willoughby struggled against the pleasing thought of absolute control. He ground his teeth, forcing himself to breath. "Who did you send to my room?"

"Ah…I see. Hit a nerve, did we? I think you like the idea of control. I think you see yourself spiraling away and you desperately want order, you want everything to make sense." He was quite for a long moment and then looked away from Willoughby. "I sent an acquaintance of your friend James Arthur to your room. A female he met as a child. She used to have such silky black hair—much like your Sydney. She was a noted musician, again, like your Sydney. Interesting parallels, don't you think? Do you want to meet her? She is not what you might expect."

Willoughby's face darkened. "Why do you think I'd want to meet another of your zombies, male or female? I seriously doubt she knows James Arthur."

"Well, let's see," Beelzebub hummed. "You'll find this one is not like Gates at all. I wanted her to stay, shall we say, *unchanged*."

Willoughby tried to cover his fear by being assertive. "There has to be a limit to how long you can maintain this broad of a junction. With linear time pressuring the bubble from at least two planes, you can't hold it forever."

"Oh, but I can. You see, that's where you are wrong, Willoughby. You have no idea what it is like to hold real power. We are, in every sense of the word, standing in *forever*. Shall I call her now? Shall I call our friend? The people around the cave she inhabits call her the *Desert Witch*."

"I don't believe in witches. There are always explanations for things they can do." Willoughby stood stock still, determined not to move. Beelzebub, however, stepped ever closer, his hand tapping on the ship rail.

When he reached Willoughby, he stepped slowly around, his eyes studying every inch.

"You control your fear well, you analyze it," the silky voice crooned. "I like that. Analyze and the situation is not so frightening. It is what I would do if I still had to face fear."

Willoughby's voice came out in a wavering croak. "You, you no longer face fear? What do you think you are? God?"

The gaunt form seemed amused. "Yes…and yes. It all comes down to definition."

"My God," Willoughby said evenly, "wouldn't kill innocent people."

Beelzebub pursed his lips. "Oh, he only kills guilty people? One question; who determines who is guilty and who is innocent?"

Willoughby did not respond to the question. He took a slow breath and then met the being's dark eyes. "Are we done here?"

Beelzebub looked out over the still waters. "No. No, I do not think we are. You see, guilt and innocence are specialties of mine. I am afraid you have brought up an important point that needs to be clarified. I would argue that guilt and innocence are merely points of view. You are quick to judge me for no greater crime than having a different point of view."

Willoughby's head was beginning to ache. "Guilt or innocence is about what you do—what you make happen."

"Ah, but you make things happen too, Willoughby. You called me. How do you explain that?"

Willoughby was silent a long moment. Beelzebub had turned back to him. He forced himself to hold the being's gaze. "I, I just have a talent in math," he finally said.

Beelzebub cocked his head, and let out a loud laugh. He leaned against the back of a nearby deck chair. "Yes. It has everything to do with your talent in math." He smiled at Willoughby for a moment and then stepped over to the rail in a single, fluid stride, closing the distance between them. Willoughby gritted his teeth, once again refusing to move away. Beelzebub pushed close enough that he could smell the gaunt creature. The odor was that of old, worn leather, or ancient wood.

"You are conflicted, Willoughby. Your sense of right and wrong is misguided. It keeps you from claiming the things in life that could be yours. I want what any grandfather would want. I want you to be happy. I am here to ask you to reconsider."

"Reconsider what?" Willoughby whispered. "You kidnap people. You *murder!* You make people cut their arms off for you! I don't know what you are. I don't even know if you're human."

"Not human? Why? Because I travel in time? Because I'm hundreds of years old? What if I told you that you could cheat death too? Would that make you inhuman? What is *human?* Need I remind you that your team, the *friends* you think so much of, also travel in time and cheat the aging process? Are we that different?"

Again, Willoughby could not think what to say.

Beelzebub looked away. "Yes, Willoughby, I cause things to happen. I control people, armies, countries—sometimes, pretty close to the whole world. That is wrong because…?" He turned back. "I repeat, Willoughby, right and wrong are points of view. Time takes all life eventually—all life that allows itself to be taken. So, I occasionally help it along. What of it?"

"I believe life is something to…to cherish, to respect."

"Why?"

"Because it's rare, it's beautiful," Willoughby fought to find a way to express something he deeply felt. "I mean, it is to you, right? Why else would you work so hard to hold on to it?"

"Life is necessary, Willoughby. I need to move in time, to accumulate power. I find it neither rare nor beautiful. I find it merely, *necessary*…"

"I don't feel that way."

"Yes. That is part of your problem," Beelzebub said. "The first rule of real power is that you never cripple yourself with feelings. Either there is logic to be followed, a purpose to be gained, or there is not. I have no interest in rituals of human *feelings*."

The way the creature said the word "human" made Willoughby want to take a step back, but he refused the impulse. He looked up; "*Rituals of human feeling?*"

The being's gaunt face snapped back, like a snake recoiling. "I find the human emotional condition regrettable. I profit from your hot blood—your ability to hate, to love, to envy, to fully explore the vanities of greed. Your human emotions have spilled more innocent blood than I and all my kind ever could."

"And what is *your kind?*"

Beelzebub smiled. "Why, the immortals. You are cunning, Willoughby. You are persistent. As I already mentioned, you control your fear well—admirable traits." He stepped away from the rail. "I am what I choose to be. I choose to live in comfort, to live with power, to live forever. What is wrong with that?"

"How many of your *kind* are there?"

The gaunt shape bared his yellowed and pointy teeth. He said no more.

Willoughby turned from the rail. "One is plenty," he mumbled, starting toward the cabin stairs. The being called Beelzebub said nothing, but his thin lips remained frozen in a slight grin. Willoughby had taken barely a dozen steps when a girl stepped out from the shadows to block his path. Her frame was delicate and petite with skin that glowed white in the moonlight. She smelled of cinnamon and jasmine. Her hair flowed half-way down her back in thick, black curls. She wore a white dress made from some sort of lace. On her hands, she wore a pair of white lace gloves that went almost to her elbows. As she looked up, however, Willoughby gasped inwardly at her face. Her eyes were dark—not just the pupils, but the skin itself. A swath of burned, blackened skin was splashed across the bridge of her nose, both eyes, and extended almost to her delicate ears. Only the whites of her eyeballs glowed slightly, buzzing with a hint of blue electricity. As she stepped closer, holding out a bony fist, the electric eyes erupted in a zigzagging arc of pure, white, power.

Willoughby stopped in his tracks.

"Ah," the gaunt man offered, almost apologetic. "Where are my manners? I forgot to introduce you. Willoughby, this is Carolyn. Say hello, Carolyn," he commanded.

The young woman sent out a flash of spidery-sparks from her fingertips. She did not say a word.

"Now, now, Carolyn," Beelzebub crooned, "you will ruin your nice gloves. Besides, Willoughby, here, happens to be important to me. I expect a more civil welcome."

Willoughby stepped back as the girl took another step.

"Carolyn," the smooth voice continued, "has limited use of her skills here. My junctions are—essential to her. Outside their relative safety, she wreaks havoc. Her father, you see, was a traveler from one time, while her mother was a traveler from a different time. The child was actually *born* in a junction. Her parents were stupid enough to not realize what that would mean. They soon learned, though, that when the child was taken outside of the junction, things happened—bad things. So, they tried to create a world for her hidden within a series of cleverly connected junctions. The child never knew. But when she grew older and questioned all the rules and restrictions on her, she set her mind on getting outside of her boundaries. One day, she found a way out of the junction. One day, like many young people, she decided to run away. Do you know what happened?"

Beelzebub had walked quietly over to stand beside Willoughby, staring with glistening eyes at the girl, crackling before them. He gave his head a slight tilt.

"I'll tell you. She became time's executioner. She annihilated an entire town where she stepped out from the junction, including her parents. They came after her not understanding who she was—what she was capable of. She killed them. She killed them all—not out of anger or malice. She killed them out of ignorance. She had no idea of the power she controlled. The destruction broke her mind. She could not cope with what the power she had unleashed had done." Beelzebub paused. "Ignorance...few recognize what a powerful weapon it really is."

Beelzebub turned to face Willoughby. "A being from outside of time has a unique biological footprint. When it

169

enters time, it finds itself out of phase, a sort of negatively charged anti-time. Vast electrical charges build up within its biological form until it cannot hold them in. They erupt from the girl's very body as a sort of raw lightening.

"Her mind in chaos, she ran, tripping through time and wreaking havoc while desperately looking for someone to help her. That is how she encountered your friend, James Arthur. She sensed his healing gift, but with her mind in such a fractured state, she did not understand your friend was only a boy. He's lucky to be alive. I found her only hours after that." Beelzebub turned toward the scarred girl. "Now, I tell her what to do. If she's good, I help her keep her damage to a minimum." The gaunt man leaned forward, almost as if he would caress the girl, but he did not. Her eyes held a warning, a mix, Willoughby thought, somewhere between fear and hatred, like a trapped viper in a cage of glass. Beelzebub continued, turning away, he walked back toward his chair in the shadows.

"I keep her mostly in junctions, in a safe haven of my creation. Being born in a junction, she has an ability to grow in a junction even though it is a point devoid of time. I have helped her learn to control the power within for short periods. I keep her close to a time hole. She can only be outside a junction for an hour or two, so I have to watch her closely. I have to keep pulling her back. I have to keep corralling her in. Hers is a power that could unseat the world."

The creature called Carolyn crackled again, spidery threads of energy escaping her eyes, finding points of metal or water. Willoughby couldn't take his eyes off her.

Beelzebub chuckled. "You may not believe this, but she actually seems drawn to your friend, James Arthur.

Maybe that's why her power didn't kill him. Maybe she blocked it somehow, and funny thing—now he has found his way back to her. At this very moment, a group of desert misfits are bringing him to her. He may think he knows what is coming. But, he does not. What do you think will happen if he tries to touch her? Will he be able to heal her? Will he be able to heal himself after she is done with him? Interesting questions, don't you think?"

Willoughby stared at the girl's glinting, black eyes.

The tall man continued. "So, Willoughby, a test—a chance to prove the superiority of your own right and wrong. Should James Arthur try to save this poor, lost soul? Let us say that you control this reunion. I warn you though—she plans to kill your friend. He failed her. He must pay the price. Oh, and also remember that James Arthur is not the only one at risk here. Hundreds, even thousands of others could die if she loses what little control she has. What if you have no choice but to kill her? Are you prepared to do that? Perhaps I could take you back and introduce you to her before she left her safe haven. Perhaps you would develop *feelings* for her. Would that taint your decisions? You may have no choice—you may have to kill her or allow her to completely destroy your world? Not so easy to see a clear path when it is muddied by emotions." He gave Willoughby time to think, and then stepped closer. "You seem much less sure of yourself now."

Willoughby didn't move. He just glared at the man.

Beelzebub raised an eyebrow. "This is your show now. I do try to be ever learning. Perhaps you have something to teach me. I will not interfere. I will merely *watch*."

Willoughby finally spoke in a barely audible whisper. "Stay away from Sydney," he said, an unfamiliar menace in his voice.

"Or? Do you plan to kill me, Willoughby? This is the second time you have threatened me. I keep this unimaginable danger at bay, saving you from a painful death, and all you can do is threaten me? This is your idea of fair play?" His voice lowered to an icy tone. "I use what I need to accomplish what I must. It is clean. It is straightforward. It is uncomplicated. I *can* teach you. I have already taught you tonight. You have the skill to do more than just cling to a naïve concept of *right*. You could be a wielder of power, Willoughby."

"Like your *kind?*" Willoughby said, his voice clipped and icy.

The dark eyes of Beelzebub narrowed. "*Yes*, like my kind."

Willoughby turned once again toward the stairs. "But I'm not *like* your kind." He stepped forward as if prepared to brush past the softly crackling girl. She raised a hand instinctively, as if ready to throw a lightning bolt. He saw power charging in her eyes. Seconds before she released, her eyes glowed with a blinding intensity, and then, in a blink, she was gone. Willoughby's heart was racing.

"You will learn, Willoughby," the smooth voice behind him said, "that, in the end, power is the only thing that matters. Everything else goes away, but power—real power, stays. I think you are more like my kind than you know."

Willoughby had let the man speak, still edging toward the cabin steps. He had carefully maneuvered the spyglass from his pocket.

"Just so you know, you cannot run, Willoughby," Beelzebub added. "Time will always find you. You are awake now to possibilities. Your world has changed. You can never again be the boy you once were. Your life is not the easy, unchallenged life it once was. If you do not walk carefully, there will be more than one life laid at your feet." The man gave a grim smile. His eyes flicked up. "It is up to you."

Willoughby turned away from the voice and raised the spyglass. With a spin, he quickly pushed it to his eye. Beelzebub seemed amused. His mouth turned up in a hollow grin. "What—do you expect my skin up close to be painted rubber? Do you think a spyglass will help you see a monster lurking here beneath this suit?" He barked a laugh. "Perhaps you are looking for a heart? Trying to see through to my rotten core?"

Willoughby didn't say anything. He lowered the spyglass and had thought to stuff it back in his pocket, but did not. He felt the blood drain from his face. He felt a pull, a tug that seemed to grab at his insides. Beelzebub was working his fingers frantically, unbuttoning the length of the black trench-coat. "You want to get a clear picture of this inhuman thing that haunts you?" He jerked open the coat, spreading his arms wide. A bright rip burst out from the coat, hiding the being's torso." Look closely. *See what you can see!*" The words seemed to echo out, like a shockwave. The unseen force rocked Willoughby, forcing him to his knees. He nearly dropped the spyglass, but somehow managed hold on and raised it once again to his eye. "I am no villain," Beelzebub continued. "I am an artist, a master of the winds of time. I sculpt outcomes as others would sculpt clay. I re-align what is. I make *my* reality what others come to accept as real. *That* is true power."

For a moment, the intense brightness flared, like a great, white-hot oven. Willoughby felt himself sliding across the deck toward the radiating core of the man. Then the light was gone. Beelzebub was gone. Willoughby pitched forward, let go from the pull that had gripped him. He was panting, his arms and legs trembling slightly from the strain and shock of the experience. When he finally rose up again, he felt the cold night breeze on his face. The boat rocked and the waves rolled. The junction had been dissolved.

Willoughby stared at the place where the being had stood. Then, slowly, he put the spyglass away and pulled out his flashlight. He turned back toward the cabin stairs. His felt shaken and confused. He clenched his fists, trying to stop their slight trembling. What had he seen in the spyglass? There had been numbers streaming toward Beelzebub—hundreds, possibly thousands of complex number streams, melding and meshing into black cords before flowing into massive black clumps. The center of the clumps seemed to be ever compressing, sucking all light, all matter into a cavity of nothingness, of emptiness, high in the being's chest, *right where his heart should be.*

13

Hot Breakfast

Sydney was up bright and early the next morning. Willoughby put a pillow over his head in an attempt to block out the sound of her piercing violin. His sleep had been restless and uneasy. If what Beelzebub told him was true, James Arthur was in great danger. Not only that, but others could be in danger. How could he help his friend? Should he tell H.S.? Should he tell Sydney about the visit? She had seemed visibly able to put the horror of the past behind her. Wouldn't telling her about his concerns just bring all the horror of the hijacking back? He didn't even know how much to believe of what Beelzebub said. Was the being just messing with his head? Anyway, he had no clue where James Arthur was. How could he or anyone else help his friend unless they could figure out where he was? Beelzebub had said something about a desert. That really narrowed it down. Still, maybe there was something in this that H.S. could use.

The violin tune broke through his thoughts again. He groaned inwardly. When he had walked down the hall past Sydney's cabin door last night, he had stopped for a long moment. He had tried to analyze how he felt about her and ended up confused. On the one hand, he didn't want her out of his sight. He knew Beelzebub was dangerous and he might be the only one with a chance of keeping the fiend at bay. On the other hand, Beelzebub seemed to sense his concerns about her and had already threatened to use her as a pawn in whatever dangerous game he was playing. He didn't think he could ever live with himself if Sydney were ever hurt because of him.

The violin strains increased in volume. Doubts, questions, fears swirled and jumbled in his mind. Sydney was playing a cheerful, snappy tune. The upbeat tune pounded against his brain. He clamped the pillow tighter over his head, breathing out in frustration. Finally, the tune stopped. It was a good five minutes into silence before Willoughby was willing to take the pillow away. He sat up and took a book off the nightstand. It was a technical treatise based on Einstein's time theories. He had no real interest in reading it, but wanted to appear occupied as his mind fought in vain to visualize a course of action.

Despite the seeming silence from next door, Sydney was still very much on his mind. A knock sounded. Before he could even say "Come in," the door swung open to reveal a stunning Sydney. She was decked out in white shorts and furry boots, with a tight t-shirt that said something about New York Arts clinging to her form under a loose, off-white jacket. Half a dozen necklaces hung down from her neck and bangles adorned both wrists.

"Um, did you happen to note the time? It's after nine-o'clock. H.S. will expect your bright, shining face by no later than nine-thirty." She gave a conspiratorial grin. "I thought you might want to know."

Willoughby forced himself into a sitting position, wiping at his eyes. "Yeah, and speaking of notes..."

"Ah!" Sydney said, a smile creasing her face. "You heard my warm ups! It's how I greet the morning when I'm at home."

"Well," Willoughby noted, "you probably don't have someone on the other side of a paper-thin wall when you're at home."

"I'm sorry. Did I wake you up?" She looked anything but sorry. "In my defense, Vivaldi is a great choice to wake up to. That was a selection from *Recomposed by Max Richter, Vivaldi: The Four Seasons*. It's one of my favorite albums, especially the *Summer* piece. Does your sister play Vivaldi?"

Willoughby opened his mouth, intending to ask if her "warm-ups" could be put off to a little later in the morning, but then tried to remember when he had told her that his sister was taking violin lessons. "My sister barely plays *Twinkle, Twinkle, Little Star* so that it's intelligible," he mumbled. He put his book away, noting with a hint of embarrassment that he was bare-chested. He unconsciously pulled at the covers and looked up. "Well?"

"Well what?"

"Well, are you going to close the door so I can get up and get dressed?"

She cocked her head. "Why would you need me to shut the door so you could get up and get dressed? It's not something I haven't seen before—remember? I dressed you after your surgery." She smiled. "By the way, how's the shoulder doing?"

Willoughby looked over at the trim bandage that clung to him like a second skin. "I still feel it, but it's not bad," he said. "I'm still taking these." He held up a bottle of antibiotics. "They're vile." He used the distraction to cover his slight blush. Sydney had actually assisted the doctor who operated on him and dressed him afterward while he was still unconscious. He winced at the thought, rubbing a hand across his face. *She had seen him pretty much naked.* "I don't need a nurse at the moment, Sydney," he said quietly. "Now, if you'd just shut the door..."

"Okay," Sydney smiled again. "So, do you want me in or out?"

"*Out!*" Willoughby barked.

Sydney shrugged and started to comply, but he stopped her.

"Wait," he said, his stomach jumping flip-flops. He had no idea what he was going to say, exactly, but he had made up his mind to say something, and say it now before he lost his nerve. He steeled himself and took in a deep breath. "There's, uhm, there's something I've been meaning to tell you," he started. She had turned back to him and raised her eyebrows.

"Yes?"

He bit his lip. "I, uh, I have another girl," he blurted out. He wasn't sure why he said it and blushed slightly, knowing it a flagrant lie. *Would she see through him?* He just wanted some space, some time to work things out. He wanted to keep her away a little so that he could mask the fact that he cared for her. It was the only way he could think of to protect her.

Sydney narrowed her eyes, started to say something, and then stopped. She cocked her head. "Another girl," she said slowly, "you *have* another girl." She screwed up her face. "So, why are you telling me this?"

Of course she wasn't going to make this easy. "I, uh, well, I, I guess I need to be true."

"You need to be *true*," Sydney repeated.

Willoughby sighed. Every word the girl repeated made him sound more ridiculous.

Sydney raised an eyebrow. "And, why am I supposed to care about you *having* a girl and wanting to be *true?*"

"I don't know," Willoughby said. "I don't know why I said that. It's just; we've been together a lot, so—"

"So?"

"So, maybe it's not such a good idea—us spending time. Together."

Sydney stared at him, her mouth hanging ajar. "Together?"

"That's what I said."

"You're an idiot, Willoughby," Sydney concluded. "We're on a small yacht with four other people. How do you propose avoiding each other? Then, there's the issue that just two days ago, you were all, 'I enjoy all the time I spend with you,' and now it's, 'Stay away—I have to be *true!* So, what is it, Willoughby? Are you *tru*ly mental or just stupid?"

Willoughby narrowed his eyes. "Those are my only options?"

Sydney's eyes flashed fury. "You are *so* funny, but I have other boys, men, too—*hundreds*—"

"Probably thousands," Willoughby interjected.

"Yeah, well, they *want* to be around me."

"Sydney," Willoughby said, wiping his brow, "I *want* you to be around too. That's the problem."

"The *problem?*" Sydney spit out. He was sure she would spit fire if she could. "If my being around, being alive, is a *problem* for you, then I'll just have to stay out of your way. When I see you coming, I'll say, '*Danger! Danger! The untouchable is walking by. Contact is eminent!*'

That way, you can be *true* to your *other*, and I can maybe stop throwing up!"

"Does everything have to be an opera with you?"

"Yeah! I'm the musician, remember? Only, I wouldn't expect *Madame Butterfly*!"

"No, I was thinking more *Madame Barracuda*," Willoughby mumbled, at which point Sydney gritted her teeth, shook her fist, and slammed the door. Two seconds later, she slammed it back open. She burst forward, stopping at the foot of the bed to stab out her finger. "So, so, WHY—"

She stopped herself, biting her lip and smacking her fist against the cabin wall. Finally, she pointed the finger back at him. "Just you *stay out of my way!*" she barked, her nostrils flaring. She spun, and started back toward the door.

"Sydney," Willoughby started, but she cut him off.

"AND," she said, grabbing the door handle once again, "stay *away* from my violin!"

"Why would I touch your violin?" Willoughby was fighting to maintain his temper.

"I don't know," she said, spittle escaping her lips. "I just know that the bow has a pointy end!"

She stormed out, slamming the door. Willoughby sat up, snapping the covers back. "Hey—I, I'm just going to pretend I didn't hear that!"

Sydney groaned from behind the door. "Big surprise—you do a lot of pretending, don't you? By the way, I was *going* to ask if you wanted me to bring some breakfast. But I'm afraid I wouldn't be able to find you— I'll be too busy keeping my eyes on the floor. I have to make sure my head is always lower than that of your majesty!"

"*What?*"

"Of course, I guess I could still *throw* the breakfast from the end of the hall, couldn't I? Perhaps some of it would impale on the hook of your nose!"

"You're not making any sense, Sydney!"

Sydney grunted irritably, storming off down the hall.

Willoughby fell back onto the bed, barely breathing. He knew that if he lay there long enough, breakfast was liable to be flung at him through the open door. With a sigh, he got up and started getting dressed.

"That was brilliant," he mumbled to himself, "real brilliant!" All the smooth, carefully crafted conversations he had rehearsed in his mind as he lay awake had failed to materialize. It was her eyes, he thought to himself. Those eyes always got to him. Of course, she also had very shapely legs. Her shorts *purposely* accentuated that fact. And of course, there were her boots—something about her dainty boots got to him—and then there was the curve of... He closed his eyes trying to get the image of Sydney's figure out of his mind. She didn't fight fair. How could he think clearly when he was so, so distracted?

Sighing again, he grabbed at his jeans and shirt. When he finally opened the door to his cabin, a tray had been set out at the foot of the door. On it was a bowl of hastily slopped oatmeal with a half-peeled banana sticking up from its center, its peels draped over the edge of the bowl like an octopus' tentacles. Garlic bulbs were spread around the tray in an even circle, as if to ward off werewolves.

"Thanks Sydney," he called out. "This is nice. You've, you've really outdone yourself." He wasn't sure, but from inside her room, he thought he heard a soft grunt and imagined her violin bow make a quick jab at a nearby pillow.

14

Trap

Antonio flipped the giant sea-turtle onto its back with some effort. He inspected the slash across its throat. The throat had been severed cleanly—he could tell as he probed it with the tip of his blade. He was strangely quiet.

T.K. watched him. "What are you thinking?"

He looked up suddenly, sucking in a breath and moving back slightly. He wiped his arm across his forehead. The cave was getting hotter. "Did you ever read a short-story by Ray Bradbury called *"The Sound of Thunder?"*

"Ray who?"

"Bradbury," Antonio's voice was vaguely distracted. "The story is about a time-travel company that takes paying customers back to hunt prehistoric beasts. They kill the beasts moments before their research says that they would have died anyway. As the story unfolds, they are hunting a T-Rex. The customers come face-to-face with the reality of a beast far more deadly and ferocious than they ever imagined. One of their party panics. He steps from the path and tramples a butterfly that was not supposed to die. The domino effect of that one premature death changes history."

"So, what are you saying? You think we're changing history?"

"No." Antonio leaned forward, raised his sharp knife, and began cutting into the soft shell on the underside of the turtle. "H.S. taught me that time has a set course. Before it allows any event to change that course, it will find a way to stop the event and pull time back to its intended path. Thus, we can only affect small changes to time itself." He looked over at T.K. "I'm not so worried about history itself. I am wondering how long we can live off the bounties surrounding this cave before time takes an interest in us."

T.K. listened carefully, still watching him, but did not respond. He turned back to the turtle and continued cutting.

It was true that the sea had become bounteous to them. Lithe, strong swimmers, the two had developed a tag-team approach to diving that allowed them to steer clear of larger predators while adeptly preying upon the slow and the weak. They had also located a steady drip near the back of the cave that had grown into almost a trickle recently, possibly as a result of monsoon or seasonal heavy rains on the surface above. They collected the fresh water in a half dozen or so shells, each carefully washed, dried, and filed with rough rocks until their insides were smooth. The result was that, while even a week ago, they worried if they could survive, now, they felt they had a fighting chance.

As Antonio finished removing the soft under-shell, he cleaned and proportioned out strips of meat. T.K. stoked the dry weed fire. She still hadn't spoken. Her clothes having worn to mere rags, she had killed some sort of early whale. The creature had been young and had somehow become separated from its parent. She had washed and then dried the skin and was now scraping the inside of it with her knife to make the texture softer and more pliable. She finally looked up.

"We've been here almost three weeks now."

"Twenty days by my count," Antonio added.

T.K. went on. "We should see the ring of fire soon. I would have thought we would have seen it by now."

Antonio was actually glad it had been less regular as it seemed to be the thing that attracted the plesiosaurs. They had not seen them now for several days. "You have to remember that last time you were here may have been tens of hundreds of years earlier or later than now," he pointed out, laying some strips of the raw turtle meat over a specially placed flat rock on the fringe of the fire. "Its occurrences may be less predictable in this time."

"If we can't find the hole, what are we going to do?" T.K. looked over at him. She was more subdued than he had ever seen her, and despite the grime and the tatters she wore, he suddenly felt that she was beautiful. Not in a teenage crush sense, but truly, to the bone, beautiful as a person. If he had to be stuck in a prehistoric cave with someone, he was glad it was her. Just at that moment, T.K.'s head shot up. She jumped to her feet.

"*There!*" she shouted.

As if in response to their discussion, a faint glow had flared up deep in one of the corners of the cave. It was slowly brightening.

"How long does it last?" Antonio asked.

"When I was here before, I would say at least two to three hours."

Antonio turned back to the fire. "Let's give this meat a few minutes to cook, finish it up, and drink up the rest of the fresh water. Then, we'll swim into the hole."

T.K. nodded, moving swiftly and silently to collect the remainder of the fresh water. Antonio used a forked bit of dry bone to turn the meat. When she returned, they quickly drank the last of the water and Antonio hurriedly pulled the sizzling meat from the rock. They let it cool in the shell receptacles for a few minutes, and then wolfed the meat down. The glow in the corner of the cave grew ever brighter, illuminating the water for several yards out from the ring. Antonio was halfway through chewing the last bite of meat when he saw the first dark form dart across the illuminated expanse of water. He shot to his feet.

"*No!*" he whispered, the meat forming a sudden lump in his throat. T.K. became still.

"What is it?"

Antonio slowly pointed. There were obviously two shapes, one larger and the other noticeably smaller. "*Now!*" Antonio shouted as T.K. also pushed to her feet. There was no need to further explain. They had been through this drill at least a dozen times and were halfway to the rock overhang when the larger creature rocketed from the water, pushing itself high enough onto the rock shelf to cut them off from the overhang. They stopped abruptly and slowly back-pedaled toward the fire. The other beast threw itself onto the rock shelf behind them. *They were trapped!* T.K. had already pulled out her long-knife. She turned toward the smaller beast behind them and waived it menacingly, letting go a low, loud hiss. The smaller beast hesitated, glancing back toward the water.

Antonio also drew a knife he had fashioned out of a jagged bit of rock. The body of the monstrous plesiosaurus towered over him. He could see its milky eye and the scarred and calloused face they had given it. The beast threw back its head and roared at the smaller beast, urging it on. Antonio threw a glance toward T.K. He forced a grim smile. "Seems, *Senorita*, that the boys are back are back in town," he mumbled, preparing to take a stand.

T.K. shot a quick glance over at him. She pushed a strand of blonde hair back from her face, then, with a swift glide, closed the distance between them. She leaned over, looked up, and grabbed his shoulder. She pulled herself up quickly, pecking forward as their faces came level to catch him full on the lips. The lips collided with some force. Antonio jerked back, surprised. At first, he wasn't sure if she was trying to kiss him or take him out. The impact smarted and it fully busted his lower lip. He tasted blood as she jerked back down and slid away, breathing heavily. She wiped at her forehead and retook her crouching stance as if nothing had happened.

"Sorry," she finally said, glancing over. The beasts were making a show of it, waiving their long heads up and down as they trumpeted loudly and inched ever closer. The larger of the beasts, their old friend with the milky eye, seemed to be calling the shots. It had trapped them effectively, and now seemed to want to savor the victory, toying with them, taking its time. T.K. countered the movements of the smaller, more agile beast. She threw Antonio another glance. "I've wanted to do that for a long time," she said, again brushing hair from her face, "but, well, that didn't work quite like I imagined."

Antonio gave a quick nod, wiping the trickle of blood from his cheek. He circled, slowly, searching for the best moment and time to strike at the threatening beast. He had no idea what to say to this wild, unconventional girl.

His lip still burned. His jaw hurt. His heart was pounding. He was facing almost certain death, yet, he felt—*elated*.

A fire coursed through his mind, through his entire being. *Hope*. Unbelievably, inexplicably, he felt a surge of *hope*. It was like when Dr. J had helped him escape his pain on the *Absconditus*. He had been on the verge of giving up—hardly able to move and ready to give himself over to the hijackers, but then, James Arthur had touched him. In that very moment, everything had changed. Something deep within his own body, within his mind, suddenly surfaced. His thoughts became clearer, his breathing focused. He felt an inordinate sense of calm, a surge of well-being. Then, he could move again. He had somehow escaped from his own pain.

The calm, the strength, the sense of power over self was like that now, only he had no desire to escape. He wanted to *win*. His body bristled with a new awareness. His muscles flexed, and he felt a tingling as his reflexes readied themselves. His mind narrowed into one line of thought. He would dispatch this foe, and he would do it fast. He would dispatch this foe quickly and decisively, and then he would turn to help the girl—that crazy, wild girl who had so mangled her attempt at a kiss. It didn't matter the size or weight difference between himself and his foe. It didn't matter that the beast's teeth were as long as his forearm. He could and would beat his foe, he was certain of it. Victory *would* be his! It was natural. It was logical. He marveled at his sudden sense of power. What moment of magic had suddenly transformed him? *Was this really the result of one mangled kiss?*

He certainly would not admit it to anyone, but inside, he knew. He knew that no power could compare with the willingness to give all—to sacrifice whatever may be needed for the one you love. And he *did* love T.K. He knew it now, and he would face heaven or hell to protect her. Nothing—not man, nor demon, nor even beast— would take her from him.

15

Mirror, Mirror

Hathaway Simon prided himself on remaining calm in the face of crises. Perhaps it was the years he'd spent in England, or his regal status with his true people, but he was usually able to maintain a clear head no matter what ill winds blew. Now, however, he was rattled.

Sam—the same Sam, who had never had time for anyone and seemed perfectly happy to remain single and unattached and focused on the benefits and profitability of the corporation—had visited him last night. He had come with concerns about the boy, about Willoughby. He felt that, given the abilities Willoughby had, and the attention he had garnered during his scant exposure to time portals, that perhaps Observations, Inc. should not have recruited him. So, instead of sending the boy headlong into the time-stream again, teaching him to navigate and use his talents, Sam felt that the corporation should keep him from it, should *protect* him, or possibly hide him away.

H.S. had stared at the man incredulously. "Obviously, you have feelings for the boy. How do you propose to hide him from time?"

Sam had not answered.

Now, the record of portal activity on his very ship, right under his nose last night, confirmed it. They had no defenses against this being, whoever or whatever he was. Willoughby related everything he could remember about the visit right after breakfast. Whatever was happening, it was beyond the scope of his experience, and beyond the reach of their technology. There was no hiding or protecting Willoughby. Only if they could develop their talents and work together as a team could they face the challenge of a being like the one stalking Willoughby. *But was there enough time to do that?* Willoughby was a fast learner, but he had only a few scant days to train in, and then what?

He was still brooding when Willoughby came in. The boy looked tired and haggard.

"It was a disturbing night," he offered.

Willoughby shook his head. "It's not that," he said, falling into one of the overstuffed chairs with a sigh. "I'm finding that Sydney can be very dramatic."

"*Finding* that she can be dramatic? I would have thought that you, especially, would know how dramatic she can be by now. Most people figure that out within two minutes of meeting her."

Willoughby smirked. "Yeah, well, I tried to tell her we need to see less of each other. I don't want her too close until I figure all this Beelzebub stuff out. Was that—was that the wrong thing to do?"

H.S. took a quick breath. "Ah… Well, matters of love, Willoughby, are not my specialty, but, I venture to suggest that Sydney might want to make her own determination. Maybe you should tell her your concerns."

Willoughby shifted uncomfortably.

"But that means trying to talk to her again."

"Yes. It does."

"That didn't go so well last time."

"Well, you certainly are not the first to experience that sort of difficulty. In my time, I have determined that there is nothing for it but to try, try, and try again." He gave Willoughby a quick smile as he moved toward the pedestal that supported the crystal computer. "This brings me to the challenging day we have ahead for you." He picked up the crystal and handed it Willoughby.

After handling it for a time, H.S. put the crystal back in its pedestal at the edge of the stream. He had Willoughby put a hand on it, leaning his head against the back black wall panel. Willoughby had been surprised that the wall was not solid. He told H.S. that it felt almost like liquid. H.S. had encouraged him to stick his head in further and glimpse the inside of a raw time-stream. Willoughby had bobbed his head out, exclaiming that it was like trying to open your eyes underwater in a fast flowing, clear-blue river. He said he could see a jumbled chaos of numbers flowing around him, populating the flow. H.S. had been very clear. "Do not, under any circumstances, pick up the crystal."

Of course, that is precisely what Willoughby had done. *How could he have been so stupid!* Willoughby was a boy. Yes, a brilliant one, but still a boy. In no more than five minutes, that *boy* had suddenly pulled the computer off its pedestal and dove completely into the time stream. Had H.S. not been watching, who knows what could have happened. As it was, all the ship's instrumentation had to be repurposed to try to locate him. This was *not* a good time to have security systems down. Despite their mysterious breech of the night before, he at least had confidence that his system could block normal threats, and even *detect* abnormal ones, like the forming of the junction last night. He caught himself wringing his hands before forcing himself to sit at his desk.

"Any success ALVI?" he asked the ship's on-board interface. The soft answer was cold and clinical. The accent, of course, was British. "There is an eighty-two percent chance Willoughby has gone back less than five years. The trace stream initiated was unable to lock onto his signature. Estimated date range being probed currently is 2009 to 2014. I will notify of any events with historic significance"

"No idea on a location?" H.S. watched a projected hologram of the probability scores of various time dates. ALVI, short for Automated Language and Voice Interface, could speak in sixty-seven languages and dialects, and accessed the processing core at the speed of light. The answer came in less than five seconds. "Probability favors the European continent."

"Well," H.S. mumbled, "five years and one continent... That narrows it." He sighed. "Alright, keep probing the records—probe everything; newsfeeds, traffic cams, security cameras. I want to make sure we find him first."

***

Willoughby was not in America. He was on a snow-covered street, shivering, holding to the glowing crystal computer. Across the street was an ornate theater, displaying posters of Sydney. Cars were stopped, still in the street. He stumbled over to the theater, weaving between them. The posters appeared to be Russian. People were everywhere. A tall, burly doorman was standing guard at the theater door, staring straight at him. But no-one moved. There was no sound. The people, bundled in their heavy coats, were frozen in mid-stride.

It took Willoughby a moment, but it finally dawned on him that he had created a junction. It was something like his experience back in Antonio's Corner Barber. *So Beelzebub was right—he could create junctions!* He had no idea how he had created it, *but he did.* He had seen a string of numbers that had seemed familiar to him in the time-stream. As he had stared at them, they had begun to vibrate, and he heard music in his head. It was the very song Sydney had been playing that morning. What was the music from? Vivaldi? He had lifted the crystal off the pedestal and grabbed the vibrating string. There was the now familiar pull, and then he found himself here. *How long would the junction last?* He had no idea. He needed to act. He decided to slip past the frozen doorman and into the theatre while he had the chance. He stuffed the computer into his pocket and ran.

Only seconds later, the junction collapsed.

He ducked into a dark corner as sounds, and smells, and a flood of frantic movement enveloped him. The ushers were motioning everyone into the main hall. The language being spoken certainly sounded Russian, though he didn't speak the language, so he couldn't be sure. He followed the crowd toward one of the ornate entry doors into the great hall itself, smiling as people stared at his odd dress and appearance.

Sydney was playing as he entered. Her full form was hanging, suspended in the air halfway between the stage and the top curtains, dimly lit. As soon as he was in the theater, he slipped into a dim alcove along the back wall.

He watched as the crowd seated itself, thinking about his first experience in a raw time-stream.

At first, his surroundings had been incomprehensible. The stray numbers and number strings were so thick that he couldn't make sense of them. It was dizzying, like being in the middle of a kaleidoscope that was churning around you. In time, though, his senses calmed and his heart-rate slowed, a little. He grew accustomed to the pull of the stream, and began to discern patterns in the chaos of numbers around. That's when he had seen the rather large thread working its way toward him, as if drawn to him somehow. It wrapped around his arm and hand and he realized it was pulsing a familiar rhythm. That was when he had begun to hear the music in his mind, Sydney's music—the Vivaldi piece. His thought was that this was where the music was coming from and that he could just hop back and take another shot at his disastrous conversation with Sydney. He had taken the computer off its pedestal and stepped fully into the stream before he fully thought things through, and had reached out and touched the vibrating string.

It had been stupid—he had to admit that now. Of course he couldn't go back to a time that *he* was in. How had he been so certain it was Sydney playing the music? He could have been mistaken and ended up anywhere in time. But he wasn't mistaken. It was her playing all right, but was he any better off than if it hadn't been? He was somewhere in a foreign country where he didn't speak the language and he could only hope that the crystal computer could help him find his way back to H.S.'s yacht.

He sighed, sinking back into the shadows every time someone looked his way. The concert hall was packed. Lucky for him, Sydney's music was filling the hall with some sort of pre-show as everyone found their seats. He waited to see there was one empty seat at the very end of the back row and moved to it. The theatre was circular and massive. Balconies ringed the main floor, with private boxes extending up for a full four tiers on either side. Though the building was old, it was well kept, and grandly ornate.

As Willoughby sat, he couldn't help feeling that he had seen this theatre before. When was it? Had it been Christmas—or a TV special? Then he remembered, sitting on the couch watching with his Mom and his half-sister Densi. It had been the Nutcracker, performed by the Russian Ballet, he was sure of it. And what was the name of the ornate theatre? He racked his brain, trying to remember. It wasn't until more lights flooded the stage that he remembered—*the Miriinsky, in St. Petersburg.* Alarm bells sounded in his brain. *Hadn't St. Petersburg been where the first Observations, Inc. facility had been breached?* Why would the time-stream lead him here?

As Sydney stopped playing, Willoughby saw, now that the lights on the stage had come up, that the entire stage was adorned with dozens of full length mirrors. Each mirror held the same image. It was classic Sydney. She was dressed in antique clothes, looking like a woman from the nineteenth century. Her hair was pulled off her neck and piled into a bun. Her feet were laced with antique black leather boots. Her dress was fashionable but plain, and she wore a single silver locket around her neck. Her violin rested on her shoulder. She finished the lilting melody— the one that had brought Willoughby here. That was when he noticed that the figure of Sydney suspended in the air was not really Sydney, but her reflection in a hanging mirror. In fact, the same reflection of Sydney was visible in all the mirrors on the stage. He sat, studying each closely, trying to figure out where the real Sydney was. The lighting helped create an almost perfect illusion. Sydney's voice rang out. With his ear, Willoughby heard the language he had heard spoken outside the hall. In his mind, though, he *understood* the words.

"The great film director, Sergei Eisenstien, once stated that 'Perceiving is building. As we perceive our world...we rebuild it.' He started one of his famous student lectures much as I start this concert—with a wall of mirrors. Which is the real Sydney? Which is the illusion? We spend our lives looking in mirrors, trying to gage what we see. We look for reflections in words of a text, voices on a cell phone, comments in the mall, teasing in the locker room. All around us are mirrors, defining, displaying, trying to shape our perceptions, trying to construct our world."

The audience jumped as all mirrors across the stage shattered, then gasped as the stage was revealed as empty. The hall went silent. The lights burned down on the shattered glass. Slowly, from not more than a dozen yards away, a woman entered from back of the theater, her hair in a bun. She tucked a violin under her chin and played the same tune that the reflections had played earlier. This time, though, Willoughby detected sadness in the music. Sydney moved gracefully down the aisle, lost in the music. As she mounted the stage, walked to the center, and faced the audience, the tune was coming to a close. She smashed her antique boot down hard on a larger shard of mirror that had not broken. It smashed beneath her, marking a definitive note to end the sad tune. She looked up, her eyes flaring suddenly.

"I am not darkness. I am a beacon. I am not peace. I am the sword. I am not silence. I am the gathered storm. We start here, we start today! We build from within! We shatter the mirror-minions and scream, 'I am not acceptance. I am *revolution!*'"

The audience roared with approval as Sydney tore into the strains of another tune. She attacked it with a vigor and passion Willoughby had never seen before. Something was going on with her tonight. Something had set her ablaze and she was on the attack. Or could she really be that good? Could this all be just an act? Again he wondered, *why had the time-stream brought him here?*

He noticed that he had slunk down into the seat. That had been *too* close. What if Sydney had seen him? It could have changed something—could have affected time, messed up the little solid grounding he felt in this topsy-turvy world of time travel. He needed to slip out and slip out fast.

As Sydney moved to the opposite side of the stage, he ducked into the aisle and slipped past the usher. He made his way out of the theater. The doorman shouted something at him, but he ignored him. The cold was biting, and he had only a short-sleeve deck-shirt on. He huddled, rubbing his arms until the street was clear, and then ran, grabbing the crystal computer from his pocket and heading for the indentation in the snow bank where he had first tumbled out. He could see numbers as he neared the bank. The crack that spilled numbers was up a few feet from the top of the snowbank. He would have to jump. He needed more of a running start. He backed up just as a car roared past on the other side, honking. The doorman yelled at him again. A car was approaching from his side now—*fast!* He ran toward the snowbank. The car's horn sounded. He jumped not a moment too soon, feeling the wake of the swerving car as it skidded, trying to stop. The tug of the hole grabbed him, then the crystal computer seemed to take over. It followed rapidly a thin, elastic thread of numbers, pulling him back like a bungee cord. He held on for dear life, and then, with a jerk, found himself flung to the floor beside the computer's pedestal. A soft British voice was saying, "Computer beacon has been located in the time stream. Auto-return has engaged and is functioning. Boy's re-entry is eminent."

"Boy's re-entry has occurred," Willoughby corrected, rising to his feet and rubbing his shoulder.

16

Al-'Uzza

James Arthur recognized the woman's scarred face. The black around the eyes mingled with the French accented English left no doubt in his mind. *It was the girl,* the one he had met in New Orleans all those years ago. She had grown. Her frame was taller, though just as thin, and her face held the shape of a mature young woman and no longer a girl, but it *was* her, he was sure of it. She gave a slight twirl and her coal black cloak shimmered, like the skin of a cobra. *Was this why the time hole had flung him here? Was he somehow connected with her in time because of his experience as a boy?* Dr. J's attention was pulled away from the woman for a moment as he heard the sound of fast approaching horses. An entourage of four fine steeds burst around the flank of his camel. James Arthur gagged from the dust and grit thrown into the air, fighting to keep his eyes open while the horses whirled and reared, pulling up as the riders dismounted.

Three of the men were obviously guards to the fourth, a small, squat man with leathery skin and brilliant white pantaloons. The man's fine breaches were off-set with a silk embroidered coat and a deep maroon sash that completely covered his ample waist. An elaborately woven turban covered his head, seeming to rest on thick eyebrows. His horse was the finest of the white horses, and pranced proudly in its colorful finery. The three guards ran to the stout man, who waited impatiently on his fine horse. Two of the men formed a human stairway with their backs, while the third helped the stout man to step down from his horse gracefully. The guards were attired in older and coarser garments, including loose fitting pantaloons, threadbare sashes, stained shirts, and non-descript turbans. Two of them had wide swords, stuck through their sashes. The tallest had an antique looking pistol in his sash and a long knife. The small man had a thick, brown beard. He called a greeting to the woman and bowed. His guards fell to their knees behind him, shouting in unison; "Al-'Uzza! Al-'Uzza!"

The woman seemed unimpressed by the show of respect. She spoke harshly to the fat man, who looked up, fidgeting with the collection of large jewels that adorned his fingers. James Arthur had to pull against his constraints with all his might, straining his neck to see the little man. He finally gave up, letting his head fall back to the cot. The black-cloaked woman addressed the bejeweled man as *Hamoudi al-Jerusha*. She pointed at him, shouting for some time in the tongue of the people. The bearded man answered one or two questions, holding out his hands, as if to profess innocence. The woman shouted in a booming voice that echoed against the rock walls. It sent the fat man scrambling into a prostrate position, his face buried in sand. James Arthur could hear the camels growing restless, and felt his own camel jolt a little forward. The woman turned back to him.

"You," she spoke again in his mind; "You did not die, son of the future—I pity you. I once begged to die. I asked for your help. You did nothing. *Now, you will beg me!* When it is time to pay, you will beg. Always and forever, someone must pay. It is what binds those like you and me."

The woman pushed back into the shadows, seeming to fade into the rock itself. Shouts and murmurs rose from the men who lay on the ground. Evidently, there were some who had dared to look at the woman. James Arthur studied the alcove. To his utter astonishment, he found no visual trace of the cloak, a doorway, or the woman. It appeared that she had simply vanished. No smoke, no mirrors—only a slight distortion as the woman pushed back against the cave wall. Then, his eye caught movement in other clefts of the rock face. Nearly a dozen snakes hissed out from holes in the rock, including a large, black king cobra, which made its way to the edge of the high alcove. It coiled on the ledge and rose up, fanning out its hood. More screams broke out from the men as they jumped to their feet.

The fat man rose from the sand with only a hint of alarm. He carefully backed away from the ledge, shouting orders. Gruff voices echoed the orders down the line, cracking whips in an attempt to restore control and get the caravan moving again. James Arthur heard frenzied footsteps approaching. Two men lifted his cot and used it to goad the camel into starting again. As soon as they dropped it, and the camel lurched forward, he glimpsed a third man, approaching fast, snapping a small whip in the air. A large, bearded man with a head the size of a small boulder came into sight. He stepped brusquely toward the cot and raised a hooked knife.

James Arthur cringed, turning away from the knife. "Wait! T-tough meat on these bones..." He held up a bony leg. "See, too tough for good meat! That makes poor sacrifice!" He hoped he could make the big man understand, but there was no hint of comprehension. The man peered down, his face sweaty, his eyes somewhat crazed. The man's knife shot up high and then started down. James Arthur flinched, turning away. He was sure he was about to be sacrificed in some sort of ancient desert ritual. The swoosh of the knife came within inches of his torso, but with relief, Dr. J saw that the brute was merely cutting the cloth ropes that bound him. The man chuckled in a low growl.

"You show much tough leg?" He grinned, a row of rotted teeth lining his crooked grin. He stepped away, throwing the dregs of a water skin on James Arthur's lap. "Much pretty—you save for big one, yes?"

Dr. J was desperate to question the man's understanding of English, but thirst won out. He drained the water skin rapidly. The man yelled something at the two struggling with the camel and then moved on. James Arthur tried to call after him, but could not get his voice to be more than a soft croak. He had a good idea of who the "big one" was, but had no desire to show off his legs to her. He lay his head back against the cot and breathed in heavily. He drained the last dregs of the water. It felt soothing on his throat. Then, he pushed himself up to a sitting position, happy to be free of the cords. For the first time, he glimpsed the front of the caravan. It stretched on and on. Shading his eyes, he tried to determine its size and make up.

As far as he could tell, the caravan consisted of perhaps three dozen camels, at least eight or nine donkeys, and a handful of tall, ferocious-looking dogs. Men numbered maybe sixty in total, most of them dressed in dirt-stained robes. The camels stretched out in a long, jagged line. They were laden with sacks, wooden boxes, and clay jars. As James Arthur watched, he saw a number of burly men who looked much like the one who had cut him free. They were rough-looking men who seemed to be patrolling the caravan, keeping the camels and handlers in line. The bejeweled man—the one the vanishing woman had called *Hamoudi*—was leading his honor guard toward the front of the caravan. Not far behind, Dr. J saw the giant woman who had first snatched him from the floor of the ravine like a sack of wheat, and then given him water. How long had he been on that cot? *Had it been only a day, a week?* He watched as she caught up with Hamoudi and rode beside him.

James' cot hit a rut, knocking him sideways. He turned and lay back down. It was not long before the man with the boulder-like head appeared in view again, carrying a fresh skin of water. He threw it onto Dr. J's lap, picking up the emptied skin and throwing it over his shoulder. As he disappeared, heading toward the front of the caravan, he slapped the camel, making it lurch forward and expel another burst of gas. James Arthur had almost believed he was rid of the beast's foul explosions, but the way the man laughed told him this was an inside joke to the camel drivers. They had probably carefully chosen the loudest, most disgusting camel of the whole caravan to be his bearer. He thought of rolling off the cot, but he was too weak. So, forced to lay back and hunker down, James Arthur settled in for the rest of the trip. He looked up one last time toward the alcove where the woman had been. Most of the snakes had disappeared by now, slithering back into their respective holes. Only the king cobra was still visible, its head rose in a hiss, watching as the caravan moved away.

"Okay," James Arthur said to himself, trying to make sense of what had just happened. "Time has sent me to my old, dark-eyed friend, who also seems to scare the bee-jee-bees out of these desert folk. Her interest in me appears to have made them rethink my treatment—good! She disappears, like some kind of desert witch—bad. Her eyes didn't glow and explode this time—good. She seems to have some sort of control over snakes—bad." He heaved a sigh, wiping a hand across his forehead and closing his eyes. Beyond his throbbing head, his dizziness, and the pain in his joints and limbs, beyond the annoyance of the camel's smell and combustive constitution, he had a far more serious problem. *Where are they taking me—to her? Why does she want to kill me?*

Events were beginning to take on a surreal quality, as if he were living in a wild dream. The supposedly impregnable technology of H.S. had been undermined and the *Absconditus* lost. He had escaped into a time-hole only to find himself in a strange underground temple for a cult that seemed to worship snakes and was somehow tied to a mark tattooed on the people who had hijacked their ship and murdered the crew. He had been knocked out by a shovel, pushed over a cliff by a ghostly old woman, and picked up by a giantess. Now, he was being pulled down *The Sig,* entrance to the ancient city of Petra, by a gas-prone camel, and had come face to face with the ghost of his childhood—a girl whose eyes could explode with white fire. What if H.S. and his organization weren't the only ones who could travel in time? What if others had even more control of the time flows? Had he met the girl because somehow she knew they would meet again in the future, or had they met in the future because somehow their paths had crossed in the past?

He wasn't sure what the answers were, but he knew he would soon find out. He shook his head. It was a lot to try to make sense of. How did this Hamoudi, or whoever he was, fit into all this? How could he be sure that James Arthur wouldn't try to escape? Maybe that's what he wanted. Maybe James Arthur had become a liability he wanted to get rid of. He sighed, stretching his arms and glancing again toward the front of the caravan through the clopping feet of the camel. At least he was in Petra, a place he had always dreamed of seeing. That was worth something. The desert nomads he was the guest of now seemed inclined to be civil toward him, too. It certainly could be worse.

His mind drifted back to H.S. Why hadn't H.S., with all his brilliance and technology, been able to see this coming? He had told them about the men with the mark. Had he told them everything? Had he been completely honest with them?

Something was unfolding here that was far more significant than a mission to learn more about a supposed seer. Nostradamus was interesting, but he couldn't help feeling that the ancient seer was only the tip of the iceberg. There were too many frayed ends, too many coincidences. If H.S. knew others were traveling time, why hadn't there been more safeguards, more training? What had the team stumbled—or been pushed—into?

17

Deep Waters

Willoughby watched H.S. cross the room in no more than six strides. He grabbed the crystal computer from his hand, placed it on the pedestal, and then tightly gripped his shoulder.

"Are you mad?" the man shouted at him.

Willoughby waited for him to go on, but the man just stood there, as if expecting an answer. "I, uh, I guess that was stupid," he finally said. H.S. nodded, still unable to speak. It was a good minute and a half before the words did come from his mentor, and when they did, they were hot, and loud and fast. H.S. let him know, in no uncertain terms, what a fool he had been to attempt a trip into a raw time stream without the appropriate tether. "You could have been killed. You could have been lost. You could have gotten stuck in the stream. This is no game we are playing, Willoughby!"

Willoughby dropped his head. "I know." He looked back up. "But I wasn't. I made it there—to Russia, to St. Petersburg. Sydney's music drew me. It was her concert at the Minski…"

H.S.'s lips gave a curious twitch. "The Minski? What night were you there? Did you see me, near the front, center aisle?"

"No. You were there?" Willoughby asked.

H.S. nodded slowly. "I was there for two of the nights. The third night was the evening of the break-in at our St. Petersburg facility. I broke the news to Sydney myself just before her last performance. I had to do it by phone. She was devastated. She knew the people stationed at that facility. One was killed in the break-in."

Willoughby didn't mention Sydney's apparent anger at the concert. Maybe it was nothing. Maybe it had all been part of the act. He couldn't seem to get it out of his mind, though. There had to be a reason he had heard Sydney's music, why the time-stream had pulled him to that particular concert.

H.S. questioned him about his experience and as they talked it through, he slowly worked back into his instruction for the day. The lesson went on through lunch and well into dinner before his instructor finally let him go.

"Tomorrow, first thing, you will be transported with Sydney and Dr. O'Grady down to our Atlantic facility," he said as Willoughby left. "We will only have three or four more days to train before we project the timing will be right for your departure."

H.S. had already explained to Willoughby that the Observations, Inc. facility on the sea floor near the center of the infamous *Bermuda Traingle* was attached to one of the strongest time holes they had yet discovered. H.S. had not linked the facility to a counter-part facility in the past. He intended it to provide an un-tethered entry point to the time grid, one that could only be navigated with the crystal computer.

"Will you be coming with us tomorrow?" Willoughby asked.

"No. The three of you will go ahead while I wrap up some things here. I have a noon meeting with the board and a few other loose ends. I should join you by dinner."

Willoughby started to leave, but H.S. called out to him. "Wait. I would like, if you don't mind, to look at that spyglass of yours more closely today. I'm interested in the Chinese characters etched into the brass. Would that be all right? I'll bring it with me when I come."

Willoughby shrugged. "I'll drop it by." He turned and left the room.

Later that night, at dinner, Willougby sat next to Dr. O'Grady, who was making his first real appearance outside the walls of his cabin since they left Bermuda. When Willoughby mentioned this, the man apologized profusely, claiming that he had been "unaccountably busy." Willoughby carefully studied the man. Once again, he couldn't help wondering why O'Grady was on the team. He actually had asked H.S. about Dr. O'Grady earlier that day, but the big man had simply laughed, explaining that O'Grady liked his privacy. "He has been with Observations, Inc. for some time," H.S. added. "His ideas are singularly brilliant, even though his mannerisms may make it challenging to make him part of a team. This is really the first time we've sent him into the field. He usually prefers to provide background support."

Thinking over this conversation, Willoughby decided to try harder to get to know the man. He tapped O'Grady on the shoulder. The man's large eyes, magnified by his spectacles, swung up questioningly. "Uh," Willoughby started, "H.S. tells me that you can find time holes without the aid of technology, with only star charts and mathematical formulas. That's pretty cool." He didn't point out to O'Grady that he could find holes too, that he actually saw their mathematics representations floating on the air. Instead, he tried to bring up the paper the doctor had wanted him to read, *eternal sequence*.

O'Grady merely shrugged. "I'm working through some translation issues, lad. I just don't have the time," he said. Then, before Willoughby could ask any more questions, he turned back to his meal, his mind obviously somewhere else.

H.S. strode to the table like a five-star general and immediately began to lay out the details for their trip to the ocean-floor facility. The team would leave for the Atlantic facility almost as soon as the sun came up. It was roughly 19,800 feet below sea level. He was almost giddy as he spoke of the Triangle's reputation and how the time-hole was to blame. His voice dropped, however, and he frowned as he reported that they were having some challenges with the facility at the moment. The trouble began, he admitted, shortly after he had to scuttle the *Absconditus*. Its gateway had been connected to the hole at the time.

"The gateway on the ship," he further explained, "helped to stabilize the hole. Now that it is gone, the hole has become less predictable. It has had these periods before, but we take any issue with time-hole predictability very seriously. We want to be completely certain that we are sending you into prime conditions when you go. So, to make a long story short, the three of you may be down there for a while. Don't worry though. It is a pleasant enough facility, and some of the dark-sea sights are fascinating."

"Is there a staff already down there?" Willoughby asked.

H.S. smiled. "No. The facility is fully automated."

Great news…Not only would he have a slow descent in a cramped submersible, but possibly a long stay with just he, Dr. O'Grady—who liked to disappear—and Sydney. He realized now just how stupid his idea that they stay away from each other really was. Why had he thought having a "*talk*" with Sydney was the right thing to do? Why hadn't he just been honest with her? Now, she wasn't speaking to him and made it a point to be as far away from him as she could every time they had to pass each other. It was her way of pointing out to him, in her nice sort of way, how stupid he was. At dinner, she chose to sit at the very farthest chair from him, even taking out a measuring tape to make sure. When Racci asked what was going on, she told him; "We need to give Willoughby at least five feet, I think, so that his *other* knows that he is ever *true*." She smiled, the only time she looked over at him the entire night. In fact, it was her cue for everyone to look at him. *What was he supposed to say?*

After dinner, he went straight to his room feeling drained and depressed. He lay onto his bed with his clothes still on and must have drifted to sleep as the pulse of the alarm sent him jumping up in panic. As he realized it was just the clock, his heart rate slowed and he wiped his eyes. His light had been on all night long. Pushing lethargically through his shower, he put on the fresh, white coveralls that Sam gave him the night before and downed a quick breakfast. He saw Racci and Sam, but caught no sight of Sydney or Dr. O'Grady. As he finally walked up onto deck, he learned that he was late. Both Sydney and Dr. O'Grady were already inside the submersible, inspecting their gear. H.S. gave him a stern look.

"I suggest you square things with Sydney or you have a long trip ahead of you. I rather thought you would do that last night."

"I was thinking about it," Willoughby said, which was true—sort of.

The compact, light blue craft had been pulled out of the cargo hold sometime during the night. It had been moved into position, resting on a small platform at the aft of the ship. He felt his first rush of adrenaline as he walked slowly around it, staring at the bulbous windows, the mechanical arms, the large light canopies, and the gleaming oblong skin of the submersible. H.S. held their final briefing at the back of the craft near the entry hatch. It went quickly, full of fiery words, and a passionate farewell. Sam was there too, making both he and Sydney promise to stay safe, and wishing Dr. O'Grady *Godspeed*. Soon, all the gear was loaded and the three of them had clambered aboard. Sydney ran through a mechanical checklist of the various systems while Willoughby acquainted himself with the emergency controls. Dr. O'Grady checked and secured the packs and gear.

Finally, the hatchway began to lower. Sydney threw him a quick glance. She'd barely said two words to him all morning. There was just a hint of apprehension on her face.

"Keep your hands and feet in the ride at all times," Willoughby quipped quietly as the hatch sealed and then locked.

The faint glimmer of a smile flashed across Sydney's face.

"Hope there be no trouble from you with enclosed spaces," Dr. O'Grady said as he buckled himself in. His face was already a bit ashen.

Huge hydraulic arms lifted the craft from the deck, swung it slowly until it was positioned over the side of the yacht, and then lowered them into the water. As the arms let go, the craft began to sink below the water's surface. Willoughby tightened his grip on the armrests. The front windows reminded him of dragonfly eyes, reflecting the cold brilliance of the morning sun one moment, and then the light blue of the ocean world the next. Sydney sat to the left of him, straining in her buckle harness to complete the last items on a technical checklist. Dr. O'Grady was the only passenger in the second row, directly behind Willoughby. He had an empty seat to his left, piled high with an armload of books and notebooks. The flap of his backpack was open and he pulled a small bottle from inside to take a quick nip.

"Purely medicinal," he said with a nervous twitch. "Claustrophobia is never a friend, mind you."

Willoughby cocked an eyebrow, glancing toward Sydney, but didn't say anything. He checked behind him to make sure his and Sydney's packs were secure. Each pack was labeled with the team member's name and contained everything the member would need. In Willoughby's case, that included the carefully wrapped, crystal computer.

Trying to lean back in his seat and relax, he glanced at Sydney again and smiled. She had a way of looking good in anything, even plain white coveralls. She looked over, saw his smile, and raised an eyebrow.

"What?" she asked.

He wiped the smile from his face and gave a short shake of his head as H.S.'s voice boomed over the intercom. "Remember, the submersible has a remote guidance system. There's no need for you to pilot the craft, hence the absence of all but basic navigation controls."

Willoughby let his eyes wander over the interior of the small craft as H.S. droned on. The metallic ceiling and side walls were filled with banded air tanks. Brass tubing traversed the tanks like a small highway system, eventually leading to metal boxes, or disappearing behind bits of molding. Hanging tools and instrumentation covered most of the rest of the interior, except the areas where their gear-bags hung. The edges of their seats hugged the walls, leaving no aisle. In fact, you had to climb over the row of seats to get strapped in and there was little elevation to the seats in the front and a few inches more for the seats in back. O'Grady tried to get comfortable and found he had to turn slightly to stretch out his legs. Willoughby was barely able to stretch out himself. A few feet in front of him, a low dash ran the full width of the craft, divided into rows of gauges and a series of labeled control buttons.

H. S.'s voice grew softer. "If you need me, as I have already discussed, you need only press the red emergency button on the dash. Your descent will be slow to help you adjust to the pressurization. Breathe deep and slow."

The craft, which had bobbed lifeless about ten feet below the surface of the water since being released by the hydraulic arms, came suddenly to life. With a click, its internal and external lights flared. Streams of bubbles obscured the view for a moment as the craft's engines kicked into gear. Classical music faded in around them. Willoughby tapped Sydney's knee. "Hey, I hear this

Bermuda facility is a real dive." He grinned, knowing the joke was lame, but hoping it would break the ice.

Sydney barely glanced up. "Does that mean we're speaking now?" she said. "I would have thought you needed this time to meditate on your trueness to the *other*."

Dr. O'Grady had busied himself with his flask and a stack of bundled papers.

"Okay, let's get this over with. I made it up, Sydney."

"Which part—your ability to be true, or the existence of the other?"

"All of it."

"Why? You don't have enough drama in your life?"

Willoughby pursed his lips. "I have too much drama in my life. You should sell tickets, you know."

Sydney narrowed her eyes. "I do sell tickets—millions of them. What is your point?"

"That I'm not the one who turns everything into a drama"

"Drama is what I do, Willoughby. It's why people follow me."

"Is that what you want?" Willoughby looked over. "You want me to *follow* you?"

Dr. O'Grady looked up from his papers. He looked as if he were going to say something, and then took a swig from his flask instead. He wiped at his glasses with an old rag. Willoughby sighed. He wanted to *talk* with Sydney, not argue. As he glanced back at O'Grady, he saw that the doctor's hands were shaking. *Was the man really fit enough for this assignment?* He turned back to Sydney.

"What I mean to say is that I'm sorry." He spoke low so that Dr. O'Grady wouldn't overhear. Sydney had turned to watch out the window. "I don't want you to stay away. It's just… I don't know. Everything is confusing. There are things you don't know. I'm concerned. I—I need space to work things out."

Sydney glanced over. "You're confused. You're concerned. You need space to work things out. *What things?* Tell me what's going on, Willoughby. It feels like you've got a whole private life going that you don't want anyone else to be—"

"St. Petersburg," Willoughby blurted out. This was perhaps not the time or place, but the curiosity was eating him up inside. Why hadn't she told him that she had been there? Was this why she hadn't been drugged on the *Absconditus*? What did he really know about her? The questions were painful, but he had to ask them.

He leaned closer, speaking barely above the music. "I was there Sydney. I saw you play in St. Petersburg. It was the same night as the Observations, Inc. break-in. Why were you angry? Why didn't you tell me you were there?"

Sydney's eyes had narrowed and her mouth had gone slightly ajar. "How did you—did H.S. send you there?"

"No. It was nothing like that. He was teaching me how to read the time stream, how to use the crystal computer. I sensed your music—that song from Vivaldi. In the math, in the number strings, there were rhythms and harmonies. I could hear it in my head. I followed the string. It led me to St. Petersburg."

"You stayed for the whole thing?"

"No, I had to get back. I only stayed through the mirror smashing and part of the first number. I've never seen you so fierce."

Sydney looked back out the window for a long moment. "My Dad," she began. She turned and looked at him. "My Dad promised he would be there that night.

There was no call, no note. Someone left me black roses. Then, H.S. called. I didn't even have him there because my Dad had said he would be there. He didn't even call and I was alone—alone with everything, the black roses, the death at our facility. I didn't feel like performing, but..."

"But the show must go on," Willoughby said softly. Sydney nodded.

Sydney looked out the window again. "My father, Willoughby, is on the board of Observations, Inc. He helps fund H.S.'s ventures. That's why I'm involved. He's never around, that's nothing new. That's why H.S. found a place for me, I think. He learned I had a talent for languages and music and hounded my father into allowing me to develop them. H.S. is a good friend, but he isn't a Mom or Dad."

Willoughby studied her for a long moment. "A lot of people have absentee parents these days," he said. Sydney was biting her lip. Finally, she looked back at him.

"I think *father* and *mother* should be titles that are earned, not facts of genetic distinction. Your father may have left you, and taken the crystal computer, and who knows what else, but you and your mother are close, and you have a step-dad. I heard what he said to you that first day—when you stepped up onto the gang plank of the ship. He loves you, Willoughby. And you feel the same about him. You have *parents*. I don't."

Willoughby tried to think of something to say, but he couldn't. He followed her gaze, staring out into the darkening water. The mention of his step-father made him think of his family, and he felt a pang of regret. *Why had he ever gotten himself messed up in all this?* He could be home. He could be safe. But that didn't seem to be what his life was about. He turned back.

"My step-father and I are close, but when I go back to them, will I put them in danger?" His eyes flicked up and he leaned forward, speaking low. "That's what's bugging me. Am I being fair to the people I put in danger? The hijackers worked for Beelzebub. Beelzebub was after—still *is* after—me. What happened on the *Absconditus* could happen again. Don't you see that?"

"No," Sydney shook her head, also speaking low. "You don't know that. H.S. said they were after the artifact, the one he was sending us back to Medieval France to find. That *Hottie* girl told us that too."

Willoughby shook his head. "Like I said, there are things you don't know." He gave this a moment to sink and then looked over. "Why didn't you tell me about St. Petersburg and your father before?"

Sydney looked away. "That's, uh, that's the thing about being *practically perfect* and world-famous. You seem less willing to volunteer the information that you're a virtual orphan—that your mother and father don't really want you. My father wanted a son. He and my mother couldn't make it work, so they quit. If not for H.S., I'd be off in some private school in Europe."

"You all right, Ms. Senoya?" Dr. O'Grady had looked up from his papers and noticed that Sydney's eyes had become moist.

"Yeah," she said, giving him a smile. "Thanks for asking. I was just telling Willoughby some rather sad tales about my family."

O'Grady raised his eyebrows. "Ah. Well, I do know those kinds of tales, lass." He turned back to his papers, still mumbling to himself. "I do know those... "

Willoughby had still been thinking about what Sydney said. He looked up. "Did your father ever say why he wasn't there in St. Petersburg?"

"Oh, he was in St. Petersburg. He just wasn't at my concert. Or at the facility, or so H.S. said. He never gave me any explanation at all." Sydney went silent, staring out at the deepening blue outside the windows. It was obvious that she didn't want to talk about it further.

Dr. O'Grady looked up again. "How far down you think we are, lad?" He held a thin book in his hand and had started leafing through it. Willoughby strained his eyes upward, but could no longer make out the surface of the water. He looked over the gauges on the dashboard.

"It says one-eighty, but I don't know if that's feet or meters, or leagues." He noted that O'Grady's hands were still trembling. *Was he afraid?*

Dr. O'Grady drew in a deep breath. "Well, how 'bout some fascinating bits of trivia to pass the time?"

Sydney looked back and smiled. "I'm game."

Willoughby gave a nod and gestured for him to go on.

O'Grady opened his book and began to read an excerpt from his book.

The premise of the book, or at least the bits read to them aloud by O'Grady, seemed to be that a German scientist, based on strange magnetic readings in the Bermuda Triangle, in an area called the *Devil's Triangle* off the coast of Japan, and in a certain swath of Baltic Sea, were significant, and proved that there were areas around the globe that appeared to be linked somehow. The scientist argued that this was consistent with emerging theories of quantum physics and the idea of inter-dimensional travel. While O'Grady flipped to a chapter on unexplained disappearances with "And wait 'til ya hear this!" Sydney turned to Willoughby again.

"I always thought," she said softly, "that if I made good—if I did become famous or renowned, that it would make a difference, you know, with my parents. But it never did. So, I bury myself in my music, and in my persona, my drama."

"Ah! Here we go…" Dr. O'Grady broke in. "Over fifty ships, and twenty aircraft have disappeared here in the triangle alone. Over a thousand people have just vanished, without a trace. And it goes back a long while, mind you— listen: '*Christopher Columbus was the first to notice the strange qualities of the region. He wrote in his logbook about flaming balls of fire whizzing through the skies, and glowing streaks of white on the surface of the water—an observation that was echoed five centuries later, when US Astronauts orbiting the earth described mysterious patches of light and foam off the coast of Bermuda.*'"

Willoughby only half listened. His mind was still on Sydney's last comment. There was something about how she said, "*bury myself,*" that left him feeling agitated and panicked. He also couldn't get past the impression that there was more to the story in St. Petersburg. The time-stream led him there for a reason. He needed to learn more about her father.

He had become so intent on his thoughts that he hadn't noticed that Dr. O'Grady had stopped reading and was staring at him. He smiled, returning the gaze. "Uh, that's wild stuff," he commented, not sure what else to say. Sydney made no comment. She had turned back to the window. Dr. O'Grady shrugged, and buried himself in his book again, reading silently this time. Willoughby let his gaze return to the front of the craft. The water had become almost pitch black. With a start, he realized that he knew the music that was playing. He tapped Sydney's shoulder, glancing at her with a grin.

"Handel's *Water Music?* Did you choose this, or does H.S. have a perceptible, if odd, sense of humor?"

"I'm impressed," Sydney said. "Not many teenage boys would recognize Handel."

"And the composition—don't forget I got that right," Willoughby interjected.

Sydney smiled. "Yes, you did. Mention Handel and everyone thinks of the *Hallelujah Chorus*. His *Water Music* is not anywhere near as widely known. Do you follow classical music?"

Willoughby considered. "I wouldn't say *follow*. As I think I told you, I have a sister who takes violin lessons. I would define what she produces as more in the vein of classical noise, but my mom always makes it a point to have classical music on while we're doing homework. She claims that it helps us focus."

"Well, it probably does—at least, better than '*Deathcab for Cutie*'."

Willoughby smiled. "Mom had her own *death-thing* going on when it came to homework. So, you like alternative-rock?"

"I like all different kinds of music. Alternative-rock has some really good composers and songwriters—Elvis Costello, Beck, Tori Amos."

Willoughby looked over. "Elvis Costello? Wow. I didn't see that coming."

Sydney shrugged. "Why? His song, *Veronica*, is brilliant. Who do you listen to?" There was a sense of enthusiasm in her voice.

"Uh," Willoughby thought for a moment. "I like Taylor Swift."

Sydney let out a short guffaw. Her eyes bore into him. "Taylor Swift? Are you telling me you really like the music, or just her long legs and blonde hair?" She mimed flicking her hair back.

Willoughby opened his mouth to respond, but he paused. "Uh," he gave a short laugh, realizing that he better tread lightly here. "I don't know. It's sort of a package." Sydney rolled her eyes. He could see the enthusiasm draining out of her. Thinking fast, he added; "But I like a lot of different bands…How about Wilco?"

Sydney pursed her lips. "Better—they're good song writers. I like them."

"Hey, Taylor has written some good songs."

"*Taylor* is it? So, you two are on first-name basis?" Sydney smirked. "Wilco and who else?"

"Uh, I like the videos from the Piano Guys."

"Hmmm," Sydney tapped a finger at her lips. "Throwing in a bit of Classical…nice touch."

Willoughby gave a quick look over the gauges and read-outs. Everything looked okay. "So," he said, sticking with the subject of music. "You didn't mention any Country artists. You don't like Country?"

"I like older Country—what you would probably call folk music. I've listened to quite a bit of bluegrass. I also listen to some Opera, I even get into international Folk music, and of course, classical. My favorites on the classical scene include Barbara Woolf, Eric Lindsay, Kristin Kuster, Ciaran Farrell, Anna Rubin—the list goes on. I also have traditionalist favorites, like Mamoru Fajieda. Music is my life, Willoughby. You'd be hard pressed to stump me." She paused for a moment, her lips moving into a tight grin.

"Surprising what you find when you start peeling back the onion."

Dr. O'Grady, who had become engrossed in his reading, blurted out excitedly, "Flight nineteen, a whole squadron of bombers, twenty-seven crew, all just disappeared. Listen to the last communication from the lead pilot, 'Everything is wrong. We can't be sure of any direction. Even the ocean doesn't look as it should.' So, how many tons do you think that was? You really think H.S. can control such a thing? Even with all his fancy gadgetry, I seriously doubt it. What if we're passing through dimensions right now? What if we find ourselves suddenly in the path of spewing lava, or come face to face with some prehistoric monster?"

Willoughby pretended not to notice the panic creeping into the doctor's voice, nor the fact that he snuck another sip from the thin bottle. He thought of the observation window H.S. had shown him and of the feeding plesiosaurus he had seen. He looked back at O'Grady with a tight grin. "I think we're too far out, and too deep for carnivores," he said. "Maybe you should give the book a rest for awhile."

Dr. O'Grady looked up and for a brief moment, Willoughby thought he saw anger flash in the man's eye. Then, O'Grady broke into a smile and closed the book, mumbling to himself. He rummaged in his pack and pulled out a stack of old, Scientific American magazines.

Willoughby watched out the window for a long time, just listening to the music. Finally, he turned to Sydney. "So, H.S. said he didn't want you being sent on regular assignments. Does that mean your father—"

"Shhh," Sydney said, pressing a finger to her lips. She carefully undid her buckle restraints and turned to face

O'Grady. The man's head had started to bob slightly, and within moments, he sagged in his harness, his mouth open in a low snore. His magazine was still open on his lap, but had begun to slide. Sydney reached over and carefully slipped the thin flask from his hand and found the cap on the other seat. She closed the flask, leaving it where the cap had been, closed the magazine, and moved it off his lap. O'Grady did not stir. She turned and reset her own harness with a sigh.

"If you must know, Willoughby, H.S. was against me being involved with everything. He's always going on about how I should enjoy my youth—like that's going to happen. I indulge him because it's good to feel that somebody cares. I've known H.S. since I was eleven. In the years after things fell apart for good with my parents, I spent a good share of my time on his yacht. Mom was dancing and traveling and motherhood just wasn't her thing. My father has never been around, not since the hospital where they pronounced me a girl. So, H.S. took it on himself to be responsible for me. I'm the one who pushed for an assignment, especially when I heard they had recruited someone near my age. Even then, if I had left it up to H.S., I don't think I'd ever have been given an assignment."

"Why?"

Sydney shrugged. "I'm not sure. Maybe sometimes he wishes he had a daughter. My music career is also a great cover for Observations, Inc."

Willoughby frowned. "Cover?"

Sydney picked at the crisp white of her coveralls. "An eccentric public figure can get away with almost anything—from paying exorbitant sums for old relics, to wrecking hotel rooms."

"You wrecked hotel rooms?"

"No, I'm just saying people expect odd behavior from an eccentric artist. How do you think we were able to buy the Nostradamus staff and H.S.'s chain without causing suspicion? When I was in England performing at the Palladium last year, I took a day trip to Oban, Scotland and purchased them. You know about this, right? H.S., I believe, told you back at the villa, right after you recovered from the poisoning."

"Yeah… He spoke with me about it the night before we left Bermuda. I told you when we were talking in the cove."

"Right—back when you liked me."

"Well, I still like you."

Sydney smiled. "Anyway, H.S. said the stuff had something to do with the crystal computer. We still don't know if your father betrayed time, or masqueraded as anyone other than who he is. H.S. thought the stuff might give us clues."

"Well," Willoughby said. "There were numbers on the staff that I recognize as solutions to a puzzle my birth father, Gustav, was fond of. It was called the Eight Queens puzzle."

"There you go. That discovery was made a lot easier by the eccentric mystique H.S. and I have carefully constructed for my public persona."

Willoughby was still thinking about the staff and the chain. H.S. had told him the chain had held the original crystal computer, one much more powerful than his copy. He looked over at Sydney. "Why is H.S. so personally involved with the original crystal computer? He told me it contains information collected over thousands of years. How did he come to have it?"

Sydney scooted closer, speaking even more softly. "I don't know. There are a lot of things I don't know about H.S. I'm around him all the time, but he's always so, so secretive. One weird thing I can tell you—I've known H.S. for almost fifteen years now. Though I watched others around me age in that time, H.S. doesn't seem to age. He looks very much today like he did in my earliest memories, yet, he's not in the time stream that much—at least, not enough to warrant *no* passage of time. He's paranoid about letting anyone take his picture, too. I've asked him about it and he says it's due to his travels."

Willoughby watched something dart in and then back out of the light of the craft. H.S. had told him about time crawling to almost a stand-still while you are away in another time dimension. *Could frequent travel accumulate that affect?* His thoughts were interrupted as he became aware that he and Sydney's noses were almost touching. She had not moved away after speaking, but was staring at him intently. It made him nervous.

"Has there ever been an *other* in your life, Willoughby Von Brahmer?"

The question caught him off guard.

"I, I, I... "

She moved in and grabbed his lips with hers. Her eyes were closed, as if she were dreaming. She stayed there for a long moment. Willoughby could smell the faint hint of Jasmine from her hair, or her perfume. He could taste her. Something stirred inside his chest. He felt her eyes pulling at him again, even behind closed lids—pulling him as if she, herself, were some sort of time hole, and he was falling, falling... Sydney pulled abruptly back.

"Willoughby!" she said. "What are we doing?"

His cheeks turned crimson. "I, I, I, uh... "

Sydney sighed. "All right—I accept."

All Willoughby could do was stare at her.

"You wanted to apologize for lying to me," she continued, "so this is how I let you do it."

"Do what?"

"Apologize! You don't have an *other*. You don't need to be *true*."

"So, I'm forgiven?"

"I don't know. I think I need to evaluate the apology again." She smiled leaning forward again. "Besides, I barely felt that. I'll give you a chance to try harder this time."

"Wait, wait, wait," Willoughby said, shaking his head as if to clear it. "What are we doing here? What if O'Grady wakes up?"

"Let him."

"This isn't the time."

Sydney threw up her hands, exasperated. "Okay, Willoughby, this isn't the time. We're here pretty much alone, in the dark, side by side in a cramped space with nothing to distract us, but this *isn't* the time. Pray tell, when *is* the time? We aren't kindergarten kids." She flicked her hair impatiently.

"No, and I didn't kiss girls in kindergarten either. I just, you know, I mean," he looked at her as if praying for a lifeline; "I mean, *what are we doing?*"

Sydney barked a short laugh. "Well, it's obvious you didn't know what you were doing."

"Fine. Fine," Willoughby turned, quickly becoming perturbed. "You always have to push things, don't you? Everything has to happen to your timetable."

"*My* timetable? Listen, if I had to wait for *you* to make a first move, this *grand* first kiss wouldn't have occurred until the old-folks home. Sometimes a girl needs more than just standing alone in a field listening to the crickets chirp."

"What? *Crickets chirp?*"

Sydney spun on him. "Tell me, Willoughby—did you want to kiss me?"

"I, uh, well—"

Her groan cut him off. Willoughby watched her eyes flutter like a wounded bird and her fingers go taut. "If one kiss is *so* great an agony to you, Willoughby, then maybe you *should* just walk away."

"*Walk away?*" Willoughby gestured at the black waters outside the cramped cockpit. "That's a sound idea." He sighed. "Look, quit putting words in my mouth. Kissing you was not agony—you are agony to me, but in a good way."

Dr. O'Grady snorted awake just in time to hear Sydney say; "Just drop it, Willoughby."

"Hey, what happened here? I thought we were having a good talk. "

"For a genius, you sure—"

Willoughby jerked forward, pulling her into a sort of wobbly kiss. Stunned, she shoved him away. "I," she sputtered, recovering her breath. "I suppose you didn't want to kiss me then either?'" Her voice was sharp, but trembling.

Willoughby didn't answer. He just stared forward, blinking. Why *had* he done that? It was the most impulsive thing he had ever done his entire life, yet he felt strangely unrepentant. He turned, slumping slightly in his chair. She had been asking for it. She had been taunting him. Besides, *how else was he going to get her to shut up?*

O'Grady shook his head groggily, as though pretending not to notice anything. He wiped his eyes, found his magazine, and returned to his reading. Sydney sat in icy silence, rigid as an iceberg.

Willoughby looked out of the bulbous curve of his window. He leaned his head against the cool, smooth glass. "*Deep waters*," he whispered quietly to himself. "That's where you're headed—*deep waters...* "

18

Behind the Curtain

"How are we doing?" T.K. shouted, breathlessly.

Antonio looked over at her. She had blood running thick from a gash across her shoulder. He wiped blood from his own left eye. The bigger of the two beasts was slow, but powerful. His strikes rattled the ground, causing both of them to lose balance. The smaller one was quick and agile, but inexperienced. He had been watching both of them carefully and a plan had been formulating. He noted that the big one was throwing his strikes harder in an attempt to catch him before he could move. The younger, smaller one was darting rapidly in and out, its jaws snapping, trying to follow and adjust on the fly to where T.K. dodged.

"I have an idea," Antonio croaked. "Faint to your left, and then charge straight at me. At the last moment, dive and roll under me. I will dive just under the chin of the larger beast. If all goes well, we will cross them up and force them to attack each other."

"Okay." T.K. had barely spit the word out before she was forced to move. Antonio watched out of the corner of his eye as his own beast dove down hard. It seemed everything happened in slow motion. T.K. was screaming as she ducked back toward him. Then, she was rolling under his legs and he felt the small beast bearing down on him. He dove forward just as the larger beast's jaws snapped at him, spittle spraying across his neck. Then, there was crushing pain for a moment as the head slammed hard against him. The beast's head shot back up, trumping furiously, and striking at something above it. In seconds, the beast was completely off him. He pushed quickly to his feet. T.K. was unharmed a few feet away. Overhead, the larger and the smaller beasts were locked in combat. They hissed and lunged at each other. The smaller slammed right into the larger beast's milky bad eye, jaws agape. The larger beast, howling in pain, sunk its teeth deep into the smaller one's shoulder. The smaller one snarled back, writhing, and sinking its own teeth into the larger ones' flesh.

"Quick!" Antonio panted, motioning to T.K. He slid from under the battling plesiosaurus and scampered across the rock ledge, diving into the dark water. He heard T.K. splash in behind him. He doubted the beasts would stay distracted for long, and kicked off along the underside of the rock lip toward a dim back corner. The glowing ring was on the other side of the cave. There was far too much open water to risk swimming to it. Besides, even if they made it safely to the ring, they would be all but spent from the exhaustion of the fight and the fast swim. They needed time to rest and replenish their oxygen. But there was no time. Their one chance was to find a cubby or groove in the rock large enough for them to squeeze into. If they slipped out one at a time to replenish their air, and then dove back down to hide, maybe the beasts wouldn't find them. The larger beast was sure to be the victor of the fight above, and its nose and left eye were both badly damaged.

With the damage it inflicted on the smaller, it may not be in much better shape.

As Antonio searched the rock face frantically, he heard T.K. bob up to take a breath. He followed, his lungs burning. T.K. was ducking back down just as he surfaced, gasping. She pointed behind her and dove. Glancing over his shoulder, he saw the smaller plesiosaurus still on the rock.

The large one trumpeted, and then stumbled, falling heavy into the water. It was wounded and enraged, and on the hunt for them. Antonio knew that its speed and agility in the water gave them scant hope. He kicked down with everything he had. T.K. was floating, searching in the seams of the underwater rock face for somewhere to hide. Antonio saw a dark crease, as if the rock were folded over onto itself, about twenty yards away. He tapped T.K., pointed, and they made a mad beeline for it. As he approached, he slowed, motioning T.K. on. He could see the beast now, a dark shadow in the water, coming fast. T.K. shot past him and disappeared around the edge of the fold. Antonio followed, finding reserves of energy he did not know he had. Then, suddenly, he stopped. What was he doing? He was almost spent now. He would not be able to hide in the fold long enough for the beast to lose interest in them. Neither could T.K. He needed a better plan—he needed to swim *away* from the fold, put up at least a fair fight, and give T.K. a chance to get breath and stay hidden.

The beast was close enough now that he could see its undulating, eel-like glide. Its jaws opened, its one eye milky-white and its other bloody and blazing with anger. There was no time to swim away. There was no time for anything, except to become a dead man. He held his chin high, refusing to close his eyes.

The gaping mouth was feet away when a firm hand grabbed his hair from behind. It jerked, pulling him into an arm that angled around his neck. Then he was being pulled backward, faster than he could imagine, back toward the rock wall, and then into the dark of the crevice. There was a crash as the weight of the beast hit the wall somewhere to the side of them. The beast's scream of rage began even before it exited the water. Antonio felt it slam itself again against the rock wall. Then, everything was fading around him. He saw pin-pricks of light in his mind and his will was slipping. At least, he and T.K. would die together, he still clutched in her arms. Were they still moving? Where was she going? Was she pulling him deeper into the crevice? He didn't even know if she was pulling him up or down. His limbs felt heavy now—he could barely move—but the arms kept pulling him through the dark, dark water. He tried to fight the urge to breathe, the incessant demand from his body for him to open his mouth and inhale. He *had* to breathe. He had to open his mouth, to suck in. This was it. The fight was over. *Over...*

He parted his lips and prepared to suck in the foul tasting salt water. At that very moment, with a final tug, the arms jerked his head up, out of the water. He chocked, spitting and gasping, sucking in great lungs full of— what—*not water!* Not water at all. He was sucking in great lungs full of something far more wonderful—lungs full of cool, humid *air*.

19

Into the Hole

Willoughby turned from the window, tired of watching the dark waters. To his eyes, the world outside had become an uncomfortable black, a smothering black, one that left a sense of oppression, of bottled up tension. He felt changes in his body as it adjusted to the increased pressure. His ears kept plugging and he could hear the blood surging in his veins. Sweat broke out on his face. His lips tasted salty, and he felt with each breath that bindings stretched tighter across his chest. He glanced over. Sydney seemed uncomfortable as well. The craft rocked suddenly, as if hitting the wake of a passing object. Dr. O'Grady jerked awake, darting his eyes from side to side.

"What was it?" he asked.

Willoughby shrugged. "I don't know. I can't see anything."

Dr. O'Grady gulped from his flask, nervous and fidgety.

Tiny, glowing threads began to appear outside the craft, occasionally at first, then more and more frequently. Soon, it seemed like they had descended into an underwater snowstorm. "A glow-storm," Willoughby said, as a few of the flecks landed against the window.

"Zooplankton," Sydney said softly. She seemed anxious to put the kissing incident behind them. Maybe she, too, felt the intense loneliness of this alien world. "The rounder ones, I believe, are little jellyfish. Look—there's one up close." A tiny, undulating umbrella creature had brushed up against the glass. Then, as quickly as the storm had started, it was over. The flecks were gone, leaving only the emptiness and the darkness.

"A bit creepy down here, isn't it?" Willoughby said, smiling sheepishly.

As if to emphasize the point, the lights in the craft winked suddenly out. The engine sputtered and fell silent. The submersible was adrift. The blackness was so complete for a moment that you couldn't see the nose on your face. Then, emergency runner lights came up, bathing the cabin in a dim, blue glow.

Dr. O'Grady fumbled with words. "Wha-what's happening? Get the engine back on or we'll sink to the bottom of the bloody trench!" His voice rose in pitch with his panic; "If we sink too deep, lad, there'll be creatures— creatures you can't imagine! I, I—" He lunged forward, reaching toward the controls, snapping his belt harness taut. Tugging against the harness, his breathing became fast and shallow.

Willoughby turned to him. "Calm down! We're not going to sink, doctor," he said, sounding more in control than he actually felt. "We're not going to sink. The gauge is holding steady. We'll get this figured out. Just—we've got to stay calm." No sooner had the word left his mouth than something large hit them, causing the craft to jump and spin. A glowing, translucent tentacle wrapped across the glass, yanking them around and down, as if suddenly in tow.

"*Giant squid!*" Sydney gasped, pushing away from the glass as her eyes widened. Dr. O'Grady gave in to hysterics His shouts were high and shrill as he jerked and struggled, further jamming his belt harness.

Willoughby stared at the control panel, trying to think of something that might reboot the engine and help them shake free of the tentacle. The craft whipped about like a bumper car in a carnival. He managed to hit the glowing red emergency button; "H.S., *are you seeing this?*" he shouted, trying to be heard above Dr. O'Grady. The hysterical man was starting to hyperventilate.

Sydney undid her belt and turned in her seat to try and help the doctor. She twisted the loose belt around her arm for support. "I'm open to ideas," she yelled back at Willoughby, trying to push the still struggling man back into his seat. With a whimper and then a sigh, the man flopped backward, his head going limp. All Willoughby could hear from the intercom was static. Sydney was still bending over O'Grady. "I think he's losing consciousness."

Willoughby unbuckled his own belt and turned around. He saw the doctor's body jerk in a quick spasm. He looked back to the dash. "Which button lets down the oxygen masks? We need to get him oxygen—"

The glowing tentacle cut him short, yanking the spinning craft upside down. Sydney yelped, holding fast to the strap wrapped around her arm and using her feet to brace her from crashing into the roof of the craft. Willoughby wasn't so lucky. He tumbled down the side of the craft, barely able to cling to the arms of his seat. There was another jolt, spinning them sideways, and then all went quiet.

Willoughby and Sydney were both breathing hard. The doctor hung upside down, still strapped into his seat, his breathing barely audible. The squid, for its part, let go of the craft and moved away in front of them. It was an odd creature, unlike anything Willoughby had ever seen. Fully luminescent, its upper body was at least thirty feet long. Tentacles extended out from it like a hoop skirt, seeming rigid for ten to twelve feet, then going limp and hanging straight down. Its tentacles trailed behind like billows of a ghostly dress.

Lights clicked on and the craft suddenly righted itself, sending Willoughby tumbling onto his seat and Sydney tumbling on top of him. "Sorry," she mumbled, untangling herself from him. She was grinning despite the tense situation. Willoughby had a momentary flashback to an earlier conversation with Antonio about having girls fall into his lap. Care-free conversations with his friend Antonio seemed a lifetime ago. The thought forced Willoughby's mind back to the present. They needed to get Dr. O'Grady to a place with medical facilities, and they needed to find this underwater base so they could continue their search for Antonio, T.K. and Dr. J. He bit his lip, all but ignoring Sydney as he scanned the dark waters. The squid seemed to be gone.

Sydney didn't seem to notice his slight. She quickly recovered and focused her attention on Dr. O'Grady. She reached up and pulled at a small lever marked 'Oxygen'. Willoughby checked himself for gashes or bruises before turning to help her. As yellow oxygen masks dropped down from the ceiling, he grabbed one and fastened it over O'Grady's mouth. There was a soft hiss as oxygen pumped through the mask. Sydney grabbed the man's wrist, trying to feel a pulse. The oxygen worked its magic. The doctor's face, which had seemed tense and chalky white, began to take on color and relax. O'Grady's breathing became more regular as well, though his arms continued to tremble from the occasional spasm. He remained unconscious, slumped forward in his restraint.

"Do you think he's okay?"

Sydney frowned. "I don't know. We've got to get him warm."

Willoughby made his way to the back seat and pulled O'Grady's backpack from behind his seat. He pulled it onto the seat beside the doctor, flipped it open, and grabbed a thin, thermal blanket. Sydney helped him tuck it around the unconscious man. When they turned back, and Willoughby climbed back over, into his seat, Sydney turned and clicked the emergency button again.

"*H.S.! H.S., where are you?*" There was no answer, only the canned music, which had clicked back on soon after the craft righted itself. She slammed her fist down on the button and turned to Willoughby. "He should have answered. Something's wrong."

"I know," Willoughby said quietly. "At least the auto pilot is back on. Maybe we'll get some answers when we get to the station."

It wasn't a calming reassurance. It was an attempt to overcome the knot of fear in his stomach. What were the words his step-father Klass had repeated to him as stepped aboard the *Absconditus?* He could hear the words echo in his mind. "*I felt so big going off to sea. But then the night was dark, and the waters deep and this big sailor felt suddenly very small...*" Willoughby thought of the engraved pocket watch his family had given him. It had been in his cabin on the *Absconditus*, the same craft H.S. had ordered sunk. There had been no time to retrieve it once the hijacking began. He sighed. Home seemed a lifetime away. The craft continued its slow, circling descent, the hiss of oxygen making the dark seem suddenly alive and even more sinister.

Was it twenty minutes, an hour later, that they caught their first glimpse of the station? It felt like a long time as they anxiously searched the dark. The station appeared, at first, as a tiny prick of light in the darkness and grew. The craft arched slowly down and gradually, what had seemed like a single light became the outlines of a large complex. Willoughby glanced over at Sydney and nodded.

"Wow," was all he could manage as they leveled out and began their final approach. The size and complexity of the underwater station fascinated him. The exterior was fashioned like a multilayered bicycle wheel. Numerous spokes spiraled down from a sprocket-like central core. Directly below, within the wide radius of the spokes, the waters were agitating. He looked over. Sydney was staring out the window as well, lost in her own thoughts. He wondered who she was thinking about.

The craft glided toward a high curved band near the top of the structure. Landing docks ringed the band, allowing twenty to thirty submersibles to dock at once. Willoughby carefully studied the band, but could see no other crafts. The facility looked completely empty and fully automated. No message welcomed them over the intercom. No human face peered out from a control tower. The only sounds were the canned music and the hiss of the oxygen masks.

About forty feet away from the docking door, the craft spun and backed in, flawlessly locking into position. After a hiss of depressurization, the back hatch opened. Warm air flooded in. Sydney pulled off Dr. O'Grady's oxygen mask and held a small vial to his nose. He bolted upright.

"Relax," she said, constraining him. "We've docked safely. There's no danger."

The little man's eyes darted around for a frenzied moment before he began to relax.

Sydney loosened her grip. She grabbed her violin case and pack. "Come on, doctor. We'll get you some food and a cup of hot tea, and get you to the medical facility."

Dr. O'Grady nodded, not seeming to be in a hurry to move. Willoughby noticed that his hands were still shaking. He stayed while Sydney started toward the open hatch.

When Willoughby finally helped O'Grady out of his restraints and into the station, shouldering both of their packs as he came through the hatch, he saw Sydney just exiting the short airlock and starting up a wider hallway on the other side. O'Grady seemed disoriented as he tried to stand, his legs trembling. "Guess I made quite a spectacle of myself, aye lad?" he whispered, his eyes fastened on Willoughby.

Willoughby helped the older man hobble forward. He opened his mouth to respond, but stopped. No sooner had they taken a few steps than the hatch door behind them sucked shut. Seconds later, they heard an engine whirring into life, and a sound like a dozen soda cans being opened. "Look," Sydney pointed.

Through the oval observation windows, they could see the submersible slowly backing away from its docking platform. It spun and disappeared, angling up steeply.

"It shouldn't be leaving so soon," he said. "We better find out what's going on."

Sydney had already whirled and was marching down the lighted hallway without even consulting them. Willoughby looked to Dr. O'Grady. "Are you able to walk, or do you need to rest?" Dr. O'Grady pointed after Sydney, and Willoughby shrugged, helping the doctor toward the wider hallway. The hallway curved slightly to the left and moved into a gentle incline. After a dozen yards or so, O'Grady was panting heavily. Willoughby, still carrying both packs, decided to hang back and make sure the doctor was okay.

"Go on without me, lad," O'Grady insisted, stopping to polish his glasses. "I've been nothing but a nuisance from the beginning."

"No. We're a team." Willoughby said. "Sydney just forgets that sometimes."

O'Grady nodded, putting his glasses back on. He rested for a moment and then pushed on. The hallway continued up for maybe 200 more yards and then opened into a small lounge with chairs and couches and a kitchenette, ending with a railing that looked out over a large, circular room. Willoughby and O'Grady stepped through the lounge to the railing and looked down. The circular room was roughly 150 to 160 feet in circumference. It had a high, domed ceiling, banks of inset lights, and a narrow walkway that ringed the edges for a full 360 degrees. Below him, the floor fell away in a steep, funnel-like slope that seemed to eventually disappear into a black void about ten feet across. A high, circular window bordered the walkway and gave the room a panoramic view of the dark sea. At intervals, almost as if at the four points of the compass, the walkway widened and sunk into small lounges identical to the one they had just walked through. Willoughby could hear Sydney on the other side of the room. He motioned to O'Grady and they started moving down the walkway to the right.

They stopped for a moment at the next lounge. Willoughby noticed that O'Grady's hands were still trembling. "Let's, uh, stop for a minute and get a coffee or something," he said, motioning toward the lounge. O'Grady shook his head but stayed near the railing, staring out the huge, panoramic window. Willoughby threaded his way through the overstuffed chairs, couch, and low end tables to the cabinet area and found a steaming pot of coffee. He poured some into a Styrofoam cup, mixed in a little cream, and grabbed two little packets of sugar. When he handed the cup to O'Grady, the man stuffed the sugar into his pocket and sipped at the coffee greedily. His hands were shaking so bad that he had to hold the cup with both of them in order to not spill it. Even with a Styrofoam cup, Willoughby noticed O'Grady turn the cup a quarter turn after each long sip. He opened his mouth to ask O'Grady about it, but then heard Sydney's voice, shouting loudly.

"We just got here," she yelled. Her voice was fuming. "Oh, and in case you're wondering, it was *not* a pleasant trip."

Willoughby looked over to the next lounge area. Sydney had stopped walking and had her head angled down, like she was talking to someone seated in one of the overstuffed chairs. Willoughby couldn't see who, as the chair was turned away from him. He started toward her, Dr. O'Grady following, having almost downed his entire cup of coffee already. On their way, he couldn't help but glance again over the rail. The floor of the room looked almost like an inverted cone. The sides were made of a silver metal that glared like polished armor in the bright lights, but a black void in the center of the cone seemed to absorb everything.

"*It must be the hole,*" Willoughby mumbled to no one in particular. He thought of the electromagnetic pyramid that had boosted the power of the hole that had taken him back in time to a cave looking out over an early Jurassic sea. He noted the inverted cone shape of the huge room. *Could they actually be inside an inverted electromagnetic pyramid?* He turned back to the thick, clear glass of the circular windows. The ghostly stillness of the deep seemed somehow more terrifying through the enormous windows. He touched the smooth wall that bordered the walkway just below the window. He could sense no electricity in the walls or beams of the room—at least, not here on the walkway. There was certainly no sparking and smoking like he had witnessed at the top of the Certus Grove building, or along the outer skin of the pyramid in the heart of the prehistoric cave he had visited. Dr. O'Grady followed at a slight distance, watching him curiously.

As they reached the other lounge and slowly circled around the overstuffed chair, they saw that Sydney had been speaking with a hologram of H.S. The man looked imposing, as always, but also strangely tired and concerned. "I want to know," Sydney said. "All of it." She spun, walked over to the small couch, and sat. H.S. tensed, nervously sipping at his tea. Before Willoughby could say anything, however, the lights dimmed. A muffled cry rang out behind him.

"*Willoughby!*" Dr. O'Grady gasped, his face ghostly white. He pointed at a sudden glow outside the great window. Willoughby stared, trying to see what he was pointing at. The dark waters outside had changed. They had turned from black to more of a dim blue—*how was that possible?* The water flickered again, turning a lighter blue this time, and then back to a darker blue. It was like watching under sea lightning. Then, Willoughby saw something large and dark moving through the blue water in the distance. It appeared to be a submarine of some sort. Then the blue water was gone altogether and the deep sea returned to black stillness. A huge, florescent blob floated by. Willoughby didn't know what to make of this strange world—the flickering hues of water, the passing submarine. He wanted to turn and get answers from H.S., but he was worried that Dr. O'Grady would fly off into another panic. He started back toward Dr. O'Grady, keeping his eye focused on the glowing creature floating by.

"It's a Siphonophore, a sort of deep sea jellyfish," he told O'Grady as he approached. "I studied them this year while doing a report on marine biology. They're harmless."

"*No,*" the doctor hissed, rifling through one of his books. When he looked up, his eyes were wild. "*Did you not see it?* When the waters were vacillating?"

Willoughby frowned. The lights flickered again, but this time, came immediately back up. After standing with O'Grady for a moment, he turned and headed back toward the lounge, determined to hear as much of Sydney's conversation with H.S. as possible. Before he could reach the chair, however, the waters changed again. This time, Willoughby had an impression that they were much closer to the surface. It was as if he were peering at a body of water locked under thin sheets of ice.

"*There!*" Dr. O'Grady pointed. The distant dark shape he had seen earlier was clearer this time, passing by them around 130 to 140 yards away. A flash of running lights gave clear indication that this was, in fact, a submarine, pushing silently through the dim blue. The water flickered again, darkening and seeming to settle down. The sub disappeared. Willoughby turned away.

"I want you out of there, NOW!" the hologram of H.S. sputtered. "The facility's no longer safe. It's acting on its own without our commands. Your submersible should not have left without you. I don't want the same thing happening to the rescue craft we've sent down. It should dock at bay twelve in the next twenty minutes. I want you there waiting."

The power went off again. The dim blue waters indicated that they were floating somewhere below the same vast ice sheet. Willoughby looked for the submarine. He found it a short distance away, only this time; *it was headed straight at them.*

Dr. O'Grady screamed, pointing. "*It is*—It's the Komsomolets, SEE? K-278."

Willoughby's eyes widened. "What's the, the Kom—"

"Why is it coming at us?" Sydney shouted, approaching them at a slow trot. "How can we be flickering between different spaces? *Can that thing see us?*" Sydney had snatched up her pack and violin and had almost reached them.

"Why are you asking me?" Willoughby replied, annoyed. "You're the one who raced here so you could be first to speak to H.S." As he spoke, he moved back, away from the window glass.

"This flickering is not just space, Lassie—it's *time*. That's Russian. It's a nuclear class sub. I, I read about it in me book." He looked like he was about ready to lose it again. His voice squealed higher. "I remember the number of this one. Lost it was—lost with all hands in the Baltic Sea in October 1989." Dr. O'Grady's face went white.

"AND IT'S NOT PULLIN' UP! *It's going to ram us...*"
He threw himself back against the rail, his eyes wide with
terror.

The submarine was barely 100 yards away. It seemed
to be trying to angle up, but it was moving too fast.
Willoughby pushed Dr. O'Grady up onto the rail. "*Jump!*"
he screamed; "*over the rail and into the hole—it's our only
chance.*"

O'Grady didn't hesitate. He hopped down onto the
sloping surface of the cone with surprising agility and
started sliding rapidly toward the black tip at the center of
the inverted silver cone. Sydney started to protest, but one
look out the window sent her clamoring up onto the rail.
"We go together," she dictated. "You go now," shouted
Willoughby, giving her a good shove. She barely held on to
her pack and *Stradivarius* case as she tumbled down the
slope. Willoughby reached to grab his own pack. He
glanced behind him as he hopped the rail. The sub was
only thirty yards away and closing fast. *Did he have time to
make it?*

As he hit the slope and began to slide, he saw Sydney
whoosh the last few feet toward the hole. "Sydney," he
cried out, trying to fumble with the flap of his pack. "You
need me." He immediately punched himself. *Why had he
said that?* He had meant to say, "You'll need my direction,"
referring to his skill with the molecular computer. But that
wasn't what he said.

Sydney had glanced back at him, arching her head
just enough to mouth the words "*need* you?" She vanished
into the black.

Willoughby didn't have time to dwell on the
disastrous exchange. He had a more immediate crisis. As
he tried to gain control of his descent, an attempt to open

his pack caused him to jack-knife and then begin to tumble as well as slide down the slope. He was finally able to push onto his back. He had lost time. *His descent was taking way too long!* The sub should be slashing into them any moment now, and he would be crushed as the facility collapsed into itself. He braced himself for the worst, running the calculations in his head—estimated speed, time until impact—3, 2, 1…

But nothing happened. *Why? Had the sub disappeared? Had they flickered out of its way at the last moment?* Willoughby hadn't noticed the hue of the water change. Why wasn't the room imploding, collapsing in a huge deluge of breaking glass and buckling steel? Then, the light in the room *did* change. Instead of dim blue, everything went black. He heard a horrible burst of shattering glass, of collapsing steel, but almost at the very moment the sound reached his ear, his arms jerked from the sudden pull of the hole. It ripped him from the chaos, from the certain destruction, ripping him apart, yes—but in a way he was familiar with—a way that gave him hope that he would come back together, that he would be whole again on the other side, wherever and whenever that *other side* might be.

20

Mummies on the Mountain

In the blink of an eye, the blackness of the time hole became blinding white. Willoughby had not been able to reach the crystal computer. His attempts to grab at the flap of his pack while sliding the silver slope had almost cost him his life, and once in the hole, there was no movement, at least, not at first. There had been a few moments after he felt himself slammed back together when he just felt the falling sensation and saw narrow streaks of light zooming past. He knew from his earlier experiences with H.S. that these were number strings. One glowed more brightly than the rest, but the numbers were moving too fast. He impulsively reached out to slow them. The second his finger touched the glowing stream, the light streaks exploded outward, and he found himself falling to a world of brilliant white. He felt wind rushing by him and slammed down into a cold wet. *Where was he?*

The thought barely had time to form in his mind as he continued to roll and slide. He couldn't seem to stop and pain ricocheted down his arm from his shoulder. He'd almost forgotten about his injury while sliding down the silver slope at the underwater facility, but he sure noticed it now. The surface he had landed on was not only soft and cold, but it was also sloped. As he continued to tumble, tiny ice crystals stung his face like needles. He hit a stretch of slick ice and spun sideways and then tumbled again, onto his side and onto his back as he slid off the ice and down a steeper slope. He clawed for a handhold but only broke the crust of the wet, white snow. Finally, his thigh rammed into something hard. He clung to it with his good arm, closing his eyes tight so the world would stop spinning. Pain burned down his arm. *Where was his pack?* Where was he for that matter? He sucked in great gulps of air, trying to focus his eyes and mind.

"*Mountain,*" he wheezed. "*Fell onto mountain—air is thinner.*" For a terrifying moment, he thought he would suffocate. No matter how much air he sucked in, he couldn't seem to get enough oxygen. Slowly—achingly slowly—his lungs adjusted. Feeling dizzy and sick, he leaned over, wretched, and then squinted into the glare.

The icy cold nipped at him. He shivered, really feeling it now. *Where was he—what mountain, what country, what year?* He searched for anything that could give him a clue and could see nothing but blinding, dazzling white, punctuated now and again, he saw, with bits of black rock. He saw a semi-dark lump a few yards from him in the snow and recognized his pack. It was half buried maybe ten yards away.

He forced himself to move, half-hobbling—half-swimming, through the cold, powdery snow. He finally reached a point at which he could stretch out across the snow and grab the pack. He dragged it back the way he had come, finding what little protection there was from the wind behind the thick ice outcrop that had broken his fall. The wind howled. He leaned back heavily against the ice, gasping for breath, and yanked the pack open, pulling a thick tunic, a pair of work boots, a pair of wool socks, and a thermal windbreaker from it. He threw the layers of clothes on as quickly as his almost frozen fingers and sore shoulder allowed, and then forced his hands into a pair of thermal gloves he found in one of the windbreaker pockets. He tucked the hood of the windbreaker tight against his ears. He felt weak and light-headed still, but a little warmer. He knew the warmth wouldn't last, though—that it was partly a result of his lunging crawl to the pack. *Had he escaped death at the bottom of the sea only to freeze to death on an icy summit?* He sat motionless, panting again, scanning the horizon.

"Sidney! O'Grady!" he called with all the strength he could muster. His hoarse whispers were swallowed by the howl of the wind. He knew there was something else he should be doing, something critical to his survival, but it took great effort to focus his thoughts. Things had happened too fast. His body was numbing and his brain was in shock. *Where was he? What was he supposed to do?*

Sticking out from a small crack in the ice—a crack he had caused when he slammed into it, he noticed a bit of dark cloth. He examined it more closely. It seemed somewhat primitive, but hand woven. Dark red and black threads colored thick lines, with small weavings of gold zigzagging through them. Apparently, he wasn't alone on this mountain. "*Someone's been here,*" he whispered. He pulled at the corner, brushing away snow. Blackened sticks protruded beneath what looked like a wrapped shawl.

What was it? A stack of supplies someone abandoned?

Whatever it was, he had no time for casual exploration. Taking his bearing, he noted that the sun was already dipping toward a horizon dominated by white jagged mountains. The range extended for as far as he could see with only shallow valleys between the snowy peaks. He needed to find a way out of here fast. He doubted he could survive the night on a frozen mountain. Remembering the crystal computer, he pulled it from his pack, pushing the pack up against the outcrop. Flicking the computer on, he read the longitude and latitude. He was somewhere in South America—Chile, perhaps, or Peru. The machine sensed no time-hole nearby. *What was its range?* He realized, with a sudden sense of horror that he didn't know. He stood. A time hole had deposited him here. *Where could it be?* Was it further up the mountain? How long had he fallen before he hit the mountain? If it was located high off the ground, he would never be able to reach it. He would have to find another one. How frequent were time holes? Should he start down the mountain? He knew he would never make it down before nightfall. *How would he survive the night?*

He rummaged around in the pack and found an ice pick. Watching the read-out on the crystal, he began to ease down the icy mountainside. The snow was deep, coming up almost to his waist, making the going slow. His legs were mostly numb, but he pushed on.

Coming over a high snow ridge, he glimpsed a faint flicker from the crystal computer. It was far to his left. He turned in that direction, took two or three steps, and then felt the world fall from under him. A loud crack boomed and the snow around him gave way. He spun, fighting to find a hand-hold or foot-hold in the sliding snow and ice, the computer flung from his hand. In panic, he grabbed at his pick with both hands and swung it down hard ignoring the pain in his shoulder as he jerked to a stop.

Luckily, his ice pick had struck a thick sheet of ice. Ice and snow continued to pour over his head for a good forty seconds or so, threatening to dislodge him, but he hung fast. Finally, when the small avalanche had subsided, he looked behind him, seeing the trail of snow had shot out over a bare cliff barely twenty feet below. Holding tight to the ice pick, he dangled precariously from a steep slope of ice that bordered the cliff. Using all his strength, he pulled himself up and eased his knee onto the top of the pick. He searched in his pocket and pulled out a handful of loose change. He fanned out the two quarters, dropping the pennies and dime onto the ice, and began to dig out a shallow foothold.

"Stupid!" he hissed at himself. This was no rock-wall at an amusement center. This was a high, deadly mountain. He had to *think!* He had to be more careful! Slowly, he eased himself up the steep incline, alternating between gingerly easing the pick free and pushing up from his footholds, to swinging it down hard, snagging the ice further up, and pulling himself to the next set of footholds. His shoulder throbbed and he was pretty sure it was bleeding again, but he had no time for the pain. He cleared his mind of all thought, focusing on this sole task—pulling himself to safety.

Once again, ice gave way and he slipped, groping blindly with his hand for one of the holds. He lost the quarters. Luckily, the ice that had given way revealed a jutting bit of rock. He was able to grab hold of the rock, work his pick free, and with a mighty heave, plant a final step that allowed him to push himself over the lip of the slope and back onto level ground.

Once clear, he rolled over onto his back, panting heavily. He dropped a hand carefully over the ledge and worked his pick free, then crawled from the place, moving slow and cautious. He did not push to his feet again until he was several yards away from the ledge. He then began to cautiously retrace his steps back down to the ice outcrop where he had left his pack.

When he reached it, he crumpled to his knees, leaning against where he had brushed the snow away from the woven cloth. Tears stung his eyes. He was sweating, his damp clothes letting the cold in, but all he could think about was his computer. *How would he get home now?*

He sobbed until his body gave a violent shiver from the cold. "*Stupid,*" he mumbled again as he took stock of his situation. He wanted to be home. He wanted to be watching a stupid old movie with his Mom, or chasing the girls, or talking math with his Step-Dad. He wanted to be anywhere but here. He breathed in, shaking his head, forcing the thoughts from his mind. Now was not the time. Now, he had to come up with a plan to survive. He thought of the watch his family had given him when he boarded the *Absconditus*. Where was it now? Had it sunk with the ship? He wiped at his tears. His muscles hurt. He was exhausted and cold to the bone, but his mind was fixed on the watch. What had the inscription said? "*Chasing the moment, someday you'll find—you yearn for a place where memories bind.*"

Forcing himself to concentrate on his current predicament, he brushed snow away from the mound. The sun had already begun to sink behind the distant ridge, and he could feel the temperature dropping. Uncovering the secrets of this ice mound was no longer a curiosity. He needed to make camp and build a fire. There may be fuel and supplies under the woven cloth. There may be clues to exactly where and when he was, so he could better assess his situation. He rummaged in his pack, found a Swiss utility knife and pulled out a blade. He chipped frantically at the mound, working the woven cloth free. Even though his fingers throbbed, he continued to stab at the ice until he managed to chip away enough to peel back a few feet of the cloth. It was larger than he had anticipated—large enough to cover three or four stacked boxes of supplies. As he continued to peel back the frozen cloth, he pulled at a second layer of cloth. This layer had a faint sour smell. Willoughby wrinkled his nose.

Leaning away slightly, he used the end of the knife to scrape away some dead grass behind the dry cloth. The sun had set completely now, leaving a dim twilight that made it hard to see what he had uncovered. He pulled a flashlight from his pack. He pointed it into the dark crevice beneath the grass and clicked it on. Something white glowed back. He used the edge of his knife to pull more grass away, and then gasped, lunging backward, dropping the flashlight. Staring back at him had been the frozen glint of a human eyeball. A mummified face had twisted down into the covering of dead grass. Willoughby jerked his knife up and quickly pushed the dead grass back into place. This was not just an ice outcrop. *This mound was an ice grave!*

Recovering from the initial fright, he leaned and began to push the cloth back into place. He must be somewhere in South America. He remembered seeing pictures of the pinched, leathery faces of mummies left frozen on the mountain. The face he had glimpsed was small, possibly a child of ten or eleven. He stared at the mound for a good minute, fascinated as much as he was horrified. If he cleared away more sticks and grass, he would probably uncover a squatting, naked body unbelievably preserved. The young, dark-skinned mummy would have been propped in a fetal position, with knees brought up to just below the chin and arms crossed over the front legs. The cloth would be interwoven with beads and small charms. Insulated by the grass and sticks inside the cloth, outside, the cloth would collect snow that would melt and fuse until it became a solid shell of ice.

Willoughby could only hope the mummy had died first. He noted that they were on a bit of a ridge and that the squatting figure sat with its back to the point where the sun had set. That meant that the frozen face pointed to where the sun's rays would first break over the mountains. He imagined the frozen body waiting, like a silent sentinel.

Perhaps the boy had been some sort of warrior and had been set here to guard some sort of sacred religious site. He studied the landscape all around. Whatever its grand purpose, to Willoughby, this was a grave and he had no desire to further desecrate it. He pushed snow back over the cloth and patted it down with a chunk of ice. Then, he grabbed his pack and pick and moved warily away, trudging cautiously up the mountain, checking each step before committing his weight. His body ached and his thoughts were a foggy jumble. He was so tired. He just wanted to sit down, to take a rest.

"*No! H-h-hypo-th-thermia!*" he shouted aloud, slapping himself. "*K-k-keep moving!*"

He tried, but minutes seemed to drag on for hours. Then, he managed to see in his flashlight beam a section of low, jutting rock. Half-frozen, he stumbled over to it, falling at least a half dozen times, but forcing himself back onto his frozen feet each time he fell. When he reached the shallow overhang, he began scooping snow out. If he could only create a space under the jutting rock—a space large enough to crawl into—he could lay out the thermal tent from his pack and crawl in it.

The night was completely dark. He felt fat flakes of snow, swirling onto his face and the wind had picked up. He packed the snow tightly against the sides of the space he was digging out with heavy, numb hands. When he deemed it large enough, he pulled out the thermal tent and wriggled inside the packed snow, pulling his backpack in after him. The space he had dug out was cramped— perhaps three feet wide and six feet deep, with no more than two and a half feet clearance between the snow floor and the sloping ceiling of rock. He struggled to get the tent laid out and to roll onto it. He didn't even feel the pain in his shoulder now. It was numb from the cold. He took several long moments to get the front zipper opened, and he had to push back out of the hole in order to wriggle in. Finally, he pulled his backpack in after him and lay, panting, the tent entombing him.

He felt too frozen and cramped to turn around, but he knew that he must. He had to zip the tent closed to seal in what little heat his body generated. The effort was so painful, so exhausting that he sobbed the whole while. Finally, it was done. He reached down and struggled with his pack, fighting with dogged determination to grip the zipper and pull it open with his frozen hands.

"*Too cold, too tir-red,*" he sobbed, his throat thick and his words slurred. He had been talking to himself for some time, trying to stay coherent. He had to change his sweat-laden clothes since they were no longer an effective insulation for his body heat. He shivered uncontrollably as he pulled the pack further up toward his chest, trying to remember what he was supposed to do. "*Dry clothes-s,*" he chattered as he suddenly remembered. He managed to pull out a shirt, a thin, thermal blanket and a sweater. With great effort, he peeled off his jacket and tunic. It took forever to pull off his boots and strip out of his coveralls. He pulled on a dry shirt, shaking uncontrollably, feeling more and more claustrophobic in the cramped space in the dark. He was so tired. He just wanted to lie still for a moment, to sleep. He forced himself into a dry pair of dark breeches.

"*No!*" he yelled at himself. "*It-t-t's h-hypo-th-thermia!*" He struggled to pull a dry tunic over his shirt, and then fought for what seemed hours to get the jacket back on and zip it up. He had to take off his wet gloves to clasp the zipper. He covered his numb hands with dry socks.

Once he had his hands covered, he blew on them for awhile until they started to tingle as if from tiny pin pricks. He tried to bend the fingers, but they felt fat and swollen. He used the back of his hand to push the wet clothes to a far corner of the tent and fold them under an unused section of tent. He then tried to roll the tent around him as best he could, curling up into a ball. Emotions that had continued to well up inside him boiled over. "*So stupid,*" he mumbled over and over.

Why had he let his curiosity, his thirst for adventure, push him into all this? So, here was the real face of adventure: hijackings, time-traveling demons, zombies, near death at the bottom of the sea, arctic survival on an icy summit. He might die here and his family would never even know. He bit his lip, finally allowing himself to think again of home. What he wouldn't give to be talking with Klass on the train, or teasing Densi, or turning away from his mom when she tried to plant a kiss on his cheek. He had never felt so alone, so miserable, in all his life. *I'm not tough enough,* he thought. *I'm not tough enough for this kind of life. What was I thinking? I'm no hero. I only want to go home.* He didn't like being lonely. He didn't like feeling responsible for other people's lives. Were Sydney and O'Grady faring better than he? What about Antonio and James Arthur? He was heart-sick and broken. He couldn't bear the uncertainty of facing death again and again. He just wanted to be safe again, to be left alone.

He wedged himself tighter into the shelter. His eyes drifted shut, and no amount of fighting could keep them open. "*H-home*," he murmured. "*H-h-home...*" His last thoughts were of Sydney, barefoot and smiling, dancing, dancing, dancing in brilliant, white moonlight. His mother was there. His sisters came up beside him. One took his hand. She led him away from the white, toward a dim hole. A figure in a dark hood stood against a rock wall, holding a glowing staff. The figure waved the staff and a dozen frozen mummies broke from their ice graves to stand. Willoughby could not see a face, but he felt that he knew the stranger. It was the man responsible for everything that had gone wrong in his life.

The hooded man turned. "*Hello, Willoughby,*" a soft voice said. "*My name is Michael de Nostradamus...*"

21

Thief of the Desert

James Arthur drooped along the bottom edge of the cot. No matter how hard he tried, he could not seem to keep his eyes open, even though he desperately wanted to take in the grandeur of *Petra* as it came into view. Worn out from the heat and exhausted from his focus on healing his body, he curled into a ball, one foot hanging off the edge of his cot as the camel, oblivious to its passenger, shuffled lazily on.

A hand on James Arthur's neck made him jump. *The Sig* had widened into a sandy expanse. His eyes darted wildly before he finally recognized that it was only the man with the big head—the one who had given him water earlier. The man held up a fresh water skin to him, and Dr. J grabbed it, throwing it to his lips and swallowing down cool water in great gulps, sucking in air as he drank. More quickly than he could have imagined, the last drops of water were gone. He handed the empty skin back, feeling at first light-headed and suddenly nauseous. He bent down over the side of the cot to vomit, causing his benefactor to give a whooping laugh. The man slapped him on the shoulder and said something in his strange language. The camel snorted, as if in agreement. James

Arthur tried to clear the cobwebs from his head. On one hand, he thought he should thank the man for the water. On the other, it had made him vomit. He wondered if he had just been poisoned. His confusion must have been detectable.

"He say, '*You drink so fast when weak from heat, you give it back to the desert.*'"

The voice had a high-pitched, nasal quality. James Arthur looked up, shading his eyes. The wiry, gap-toothed face of the man with the shovel grinned down at him.

"So, you speak English," Dr. J managed. "You always carry that shovel? I hope you're not stupid enough to try to hit me with it again."

"Yes, yes," the man said; "Very much. You come to side now."

James Arthur realized that the man didn't have quite the command of English he had hoped.

"Come to side?" the man repeated.

He looked where the man pointed. The camel had stopped in a wide opening in the rock. Craning to see around the camel, he glimpsed a stunning rock wall that had been carved into a building front with enormous Roman columns and intricate roof details. "The Khazneh, the treasury..." he mumbled.

The Khazneh was the best preserved of all the carved facades of Petra, due in part to the surrounding rock walls that kept it safe from wind and sand storms. Popularized by a series of dramatic photos in *The National Geographic*, the façade went on to become one of the most recognizable images in all of Jordan. Dr. J stared with awe at the porch above the first floor roof with its central rotunda and carved reliefs. The entire two-story facade, carved delicately into a wall of solid sandstone, stretched up for at least 100 feet. Named *The Treasury* because of legends that claimed it was home to secret treasure, the building survived both the ancient Nabataeans and later, the conquering Romans. The state of preservation was incredible. The ruins looked much newer than the photos he had seen from early explorers. He surmised that he may be seeing the ruins before the camera was in wide use, somewhere in the early to mid-1800s.

"Yes, Yes," the wiry man beside him shouted, gesturing wildly, "come to side!"

Dr. J cocked his head, trying to divine what the man meant, when a booming voice startled him from behind. He glanced back to see the giantess stride up, grinning broadly. She didn't even slow down, but barked something at the wiry man as she bent with surprising agility, and snatched James Arthur up under one arm. She rolled him onto her hip, pinning his arms to his sides.

He struggled, screaming and kicking wildly, trying to work his arms free. She seemed completely unconcerned, striding on toward the steps that led to the rectangular entrance to the facade. Dr. J strained to look up.

"I—don't like," he panted, "to do this—to a girl—but... "

He sank his teeth into the woman's arm, biting down as hard as he could. The sweaty taste was revolting, but he gnashed the teeth, determined to have an impact. The huge woman laughed, hiking him up a little tighter into her armpit. He felt her squeeze as she began to mount the stairs leading to the dark, square opening. Dr. J saw that he hadn't even broken the skin. He spat, gasping for breath. As she entered the dark doorway, her grip slackened slightly. He saw his opportunity and took it, pushing out in a sudden and violent heave. Before she could react, he had wriggled free.

She stopped and looked over as he scrambled to his feet. He backed against the stone of the door frame. Her face broke into a broad grin, and Dr. J heard peals of laughter as she barked something in her language, then strode off. He followed the sound of the laughter, peering into the dim light of the interior.

A completely square room was lit by a single torch. In a nearby corner of the room, huge dogs paced restlessly. James Arthur remembered having seen them run by, but they were much larger than he had realized. In the opposite corner, the rich man sat on a portable chair made from sticks and animal hide. He picked daintily at a cooked chicken, throwing tidbits of skin and meat to the dogs. Two of his guards stood slightly behind him, one to either side.

"She likes you," the rich man said, looking at him, amused. "She says you have—how do you say—you have high spirit." He chuckled, looking down to take another bite of chicken. He tossed the bone so that it landed only a few feet from Dr. J. The closest dog pounced on it while the other jumped forward too, snarling and showing its teeth. "I advise you to leave that area," the man said between bites. "You're standing right where I generally feed my dogs. They might think you are part of the meal."

James Arthur backed cautiously away from the dogs, making his way in a wide arch toward the fat man and his guards. "Who are you?" he asked, his voice still gravelly. "How is it that you speak English?"

"I will ask the questions here, *son-of-the-future*. Now—how is it that *you* speak English? You are black. Are you a runaway slave? You do not speak with the accent of Africa or of Britain."

"I'm American," James Arthur said.

"Ah! From the colonies!" the man exclaimed. He thought for a moment. "Perhaps you can tell me what you are doing hundreds of miles from your country, in our tombs? Mahadin swears you appeared from nowhere."

"I don't have to tell you anything," James Arthur said.

The man smiled.

"Are you hungry, *son-of-the-future?* Would you like something to eat?"

Dr. J realized that he had been eyeing the chicken with longing. He gave a short nod. In truth, he was famished. It felt like he hadn't eaten for days. The rich man turned and barked an order at one of the guards. The man quickly produced another wrapped chicken and a skin of liquid. James Arthur pressed the skin to his lips. It was a sweet wine. With shaky hands, he unwrapped the chicken, seating himself on some bare, sand-covered stones a few feet away from the rich man. The man threw the rest of his own chicken carcass to the dogs, who attacked it, fighting viscously. He wiped his hands and mouth on a napkin and then turned to regard Dr. J, who was eating almost as voraciously as the dogs.

"I know English because I am a trader," the man said. "The English pay well for my, shall we say, *trinkets*. To them, I am known as *Al-Jerusha, thief of the desert.* "

James Arthur wiped a hand across his face. "Are you a thief?"

Al-Jerusha raised an eyebrow and cocked his head. "It depends on who you believe. If you listen to the desert witch, then yes, I am a thief. To my associates, I am more a businessman and an excavator."

"Ah, the woman we saw—the one who melted into the stone. Is she really a witch?"

Again, the man cocked his head; "Are you really a *son of the future*? She is, indeed, the woman we saw at the mouth of the entry. We have seen her three times now in as many days. Before that, she slept. We saw her rarely, usually only around the winter solstice when she summoned dark faces, and they converged upon the tombs for some sort of secret ceremony. We make sure to be well away from here around the winter solstice." He gave a long sigh. "But, now, something has awakened her. Do you know what that something might be son-of-the-future? She has commanded that we bring you to her. You must be worth a great deal if you are enough to wake her."

"Okay, let me get this straight," James Arthur began, things becoming clearer. "You guys are tomb robbers and you're stealing from tombs that are haunted by a witch?"

"We prefer the title of *tomb excavators*," the man smiled. "As the woman we call the *Desert Witch*, we cannot say what she is. We know she can appear and disappear, almost at will. We know she can appear old or young and is in league with the snakes and can be deadly if you cross her. Some of the weakest of my group call her *Al-Uzza*. Are you familiar with the name?"

Dr. J shook his head. The squat man played with his jewels for a moment before looking up. "Al-Uzza is an Arabian fertility goddess, one of the three goddesses of Mecca. She stands beside Dushara as one of the primary gods worshipped by my ancient people—the Nabataeans. Whether this woman is really her, I cannot say. She claims to be servant to Dushara, and she has an underground temple where she worships him. She has her tricks, and as I've said, she can be deadly. This I know. But I have never seen any evidence of her master, and if she was truly all-powerful, I doubt we would ever get anything out of the tombs."

James Arthur was already putting the finishing touches on the chicken, picking the bones clean before tossing them to the dogs. "Why would she want to see me?"

Al-Jerusha looked at him, somewhat bemused. "That is the question."

Dr. J took another swig of the sweet wine. He was already beginning to feel his strength return. "Well, sorry to disappoint you if you think I can help you. I haven't a clue who or what she is. If she can look old, as you say, she might be the one who saw me escape after your thugs stripped me and walled me up for dead in an empty underground shaft. Once she saw me, she pushed me off a sand cliff." He looked up. "Which reminds me—your men tried to kill me. Why should I trust you?"

The fat man sighed. "Yes. Mahadin has been scolded for his, shall we say, lack of kindness. You must forgive him. He thought you a competitor, trying to muscle in on our trade."

"Uh huh. That's why you, personally, had me tied up and dragged, without any food or water, behind a flatulent camel."

Al-Jerusha laughed a belly laugh. "A regrettable oversight. Tell me, son-of-the fut—"

"My name is James Arthur," Dr. J said pointedly.

"All right—James Arthur, are you friends with this woman who calls herself Al-Uzza? Are you her spy?"

"No," James Arthur said. "As I told you, I haven't the faintest clue who she is,"

The man leaned back, satisfied. "Good. Then I have a proposition for you. A business alliance could benefit us both."

"A business alliance?"

"Yes. The witch has cost me good men and much profit, due to the heavy toll she demands for what we are allowed to take. I want you to find the key to her tricks. Find the source of her powers, and you will be, not only a free man, but a rich one."

"Why would I risk my neck for you?"

Al-Jerusha smiled. "A good question. Perhaps you want a ticket out of the tombs. She has commanded we bring you to her diocese of snakes—the place where we first found you, oddly enough. It is a good distance underground. She will enter it from her ground level entry. It is in the only standing structure in the city built of brick stones and not carved into the rock. I have studied the witch and her ways for a long time. I know exactly how to snatch you, and smuggle you away, should your discussions with her turn, shall we say, *ugly*."

"Which brings us right back to the same question. *Why should I trust you?*"

Al-Jerusha gave another hearty laugh, slapping James Arthur on the back. "Because, my friend, you have no choice. I'm—how do you say—the only game in town."

James Arthur thought for a moment. The man may be a self-serving thief, but he was right. The thought of being trapped underground with the cobra woman was not exactly exciting. "And if I refuse?"

Al-Jerusha shrugged. "You try to run, I let my sister have you. She loves a play-thing." The twinkle in his eye told Dr. J exactly who his sister was. He only wondered if the man shared a father or a mother with the behemoth.

The thief of the desert had already turned away, as if the discussion were closed. He motioned to his guard and followed him to a far corner of the square room. The guard knelt carefully, brushing away a layer of sand. James Arthur felt a poke in his back and stood, commanded by grunts and gestures from the other guard. He was directed to the same corner. By the light of the single torch, he made out a raised, flat disc. As the guard continued to clear away sand, James Arthur saw that a symbol was etched onto the face of the disc—*the same symbol H.S. had shown them earlier, at their mission briefing!* The symbol was tattooed on the necks of those who had been responsible for the St. Petersburg break in, and belonged to some ancient, dark brotherhood, according to H.S. His mind raced; *what was the symbol doing here?* The guard brushed the sand completely clear, grabbed the disc, and began to twist.

The stone under the disc slipped down into the floor. About six inches down, it cleared the edges of some sort of opening and continued sinking, sliding down the smooth face of a massive stone pillar into cold darkness. When the guard had sunk a few feet below floor level, he stood, took the torch from the other guard, and twisted himself through a small opening to one side of the stone pillar. Al-Jerusha motioned for James Arthur to go next. Squeezing through the gap, Dr. J found himself in a low, narrow shaft. Al-Jerusha came right behind him. He struggled to get his belly through the opening, but once in the shaft, he was the only one able to stand more or less erect. Everyone else had to hunch low in order to keep their heads from scraping the rough rock of the ceiling. The second guard lit another torch and followed a few steps behind.

"You see, we do have our secrets," Al-Jerusha said, his voice echoing in the empty shaft. They began to scuttle forward, the front guard kicking away beetles and scorpions. "Soon, we'll come to know yours," the squat man added, seeming to enjoy James Arthur's discomfort in the cramped space.

"What if I decide to make an alliance with the witch?" Dr. J grunted as he was prodded to go faster.

"I wouldn't recommend it," Al-Jerusha said. "The witch is one woman. I have a camp of over 300 men."

"Why don't you deal with the witch on your own, then?"

"Another good question," the fat man said thoughtfully. "The witch watches me closely, James Arthur. But, perhaps not close enough. I think at last," he said with some relish, "we have a way to catch her by surprise... "

22

Gustav

Willoughby's eyes seemed welded shut. He struggled to force one after the other open. He thought he saw fire. The image of flames was not a dream. The blaze seemed close. *Shouldn't the flames burn him?* For some reason, they did not. They seemed to have an odd quality—they flicked in and out of a misty haze and flared when viewed from the corner of his eye. He pushed to his elbows. The tent he had zipped around him for warmth was crumpled with his backpack a few feet away. The small crevice he had wedged himself into to keep from freezing had widened and deepened somehow. It was now a small rock cave. He looked again toward the fire. The opening of the cave was large—much larger than the narrow crevice he had dug out of the snow. Ash flickered in and out of the mist and he thought he saw lava glow red in the distance. Then the warmth faded and the harsh ice mountain he had barely escaped from appeared in the mist. Then the two scenes mingled as if two movies were being projected on top of each other. A clump of scrub brush was burning right at the mouth of the cave. As he stared into the flickering haze, he caught glimpses of other landscapes. The glint of small glaciers and the swirl of snow falling upon mountain green. The realization hit him. *He must be in a junction.* He stretched out a hand to touch the flames, but a voice stopped him.

"*Aucun*—no. You must not touch. The flames, they would take you to a time of fire. You do not want to be in that place." The voice continued. It sounded rough and haggard, with a heavy French accent and a hint of amusement. "Of course, I would not have, eh, *choisi, chosen* your ice mountain either. Not at night."

Willoughby tried to turn his head. It was stiff and sore. He pivoted, slowly. "I," he rasped, barely audible. "I didn't choose it. I didn't plan to be on this mountain."

"Where did you plan to be?"

Willoughby thought for a moment. "I don't know." He peered in the direction of the voice. "Who are you? I can barely see you." Willoughby finally located a dark shape in the shadows of what appeared to be a rock cleft near the back of the cave. The shape pushed forward, grunting as it moved. It was obviously a man, tall and angular, though heavy-set with age. The face was partly obscured by the hood of his thick, monk-like robe.

"Please," the old man said. "*Le fini.* It is not good to leave a thought...alone."

Willoughby was taken back. His father—his birth father, Gustav—had told him that once. He still remembered. The man gave him a slow smile, motioning for him to continue. "I," Willoughby gulped; "I was...under the sea, near a natural time-hole. The observation tower was collapsing. I—we barely escaped."

"*We?*"

"There were two others. I don't know what happened to them."

"So, you are here. You can, eh, freeze to death on an ice mountain, or make a better plan. Perhaps, you should think where you want to go. If you do not know—"

"—where I want to go, any road can take you there. Yes, I've read *Alice in Wonderland*. So, who are you? Why did you create this junction?"

"The *passage du temps*—the *intersecter?* I suppose it was made because the temperature here drops to thirty degrees below Celsius. You were wet. I had to get you warm."

"Why?" Willoughby looked around. His mind was spinning. He understood what the man was saying. The junction, by mixing time points between his frozen ice mountain and a time of volcanic activity, had raised the mean temperature, making it warm enough to let him thaw and dry out. But why did the man care about him? *Who was this man?* Another thought struggled into his consciousness. "Did I form this junction?" he asked aloud.

The man seemed to consider this. "You, you create the *intersecter?*"

Willoughby made a hopeless effort to rise up on his arms. Every muscle in his body was screaming and sore. His clothes were dry, though, and he no longer shook with the biting cold. A small stain of blood near his shoulder wound throbbed. "How long was I—" he struggled to ask—"how long was I out?"

"There is no time here," the man said, "but a while, I think." He approached closer, holding out a shaky stone cup to Willoughby. "Drink," he said. "You are not all, eh—healed. You were...you were *shaking*. We only got to you just."

"*We?*"

271

"Ah," the man smiled. "Yes. I did not—*you* did not make the *intersecter*."

Willoughby studied the man. "Why are you helping me?"

The man pushed the hood of his coarse robe back. His hair was matted and gray. It fell in wild tangles beside an unkempt beard, but his eyes were intense. They sparkled with a deep, marbled blue. "Should I not try to, eh, *rescue* my son?" The man smiled weakly.

Willoughby succeeded this time in pushing to a sitting position. He studied the old face, probing for something familiar. He found it in the intense eyes. "*Gustav?* But you're, you speak French."

The man nodded at the stone cup he was offering. "Drink."

Willoughby took the crude cup. It was filled with a dark liquid. He held it for a moment in trembling hands, and then gulped the liquid down. It burned and tasted bitter. Wincing, he looked up. The man had already begun to speak.

"I look French, I speak French, because I have lived in France for over forty years."

Willoughby shook his head. "You've only been gone thirteen years. You were in your thirties. How could you be so, so—"

"Old?"

Willoughby nodded. He pointed to the cup, wanting to change the subject. "What is it?"

The man's eyes twinkled. "I cannot say—afraid to ask." He eased himself down onto the stone floor beside Willoughby. "My friend, he prepares it from roots, herbs—he is a good *healer*."

"Nostradamus?"

The man frowned. "You *know?*"

"I know you fell in a time-hole. You were working for H.S. Then, he found a staff and a letter from Nostradamus. They also found a chain, but only the chain."

"Yes," the man said. He was not surprised that H.S. found only the chain. The man exhaled deeply. "It is true. Michael told me you were a time-traveler. I did not want to believe…"

"H.S. wanted us to find you. I was—assigned to study Nostradamus. He thought you might have masqueraded as him and wrote his prophecies." Willoughby realized he was speaking fast, trying to keep from looking at, from thinking of the wheezing old man in front of him. He blinked, feeling a sudden stab of emotion. *This wasn't the father he wanted to find.* This was not the vibrant, decisive man he had dreamed that he would find, that he would somehow save. "I," he started, but his voice faltered momentarily. "I need to… Why did you leave? Why did you stay away so long? Why come find me now?"

His father looked at him with a steady gaze. "I am not what you hoped to find." The man said quietly. He looked away for a long moment. Finally, he turned back. He gave Willoughby a tight smile. "I had to, Willoughby. I had to stay away. If I loved you, if I loved your mother, I had to stay away from you."

"Why?"

"It was necessary."

"Is that all you can say? You walk out of my life, never come back, and tell me *it was necessary?* Why come now? Why as an old man? Is it guilt, an attempt to make up for what you've done?"

The man shook his head. "No. I come now because the reason I stayed away is no more. I come now because I could help to save your life one last time. I have lived seventy-six years of life, though not as much time as has passed for you. My body has not aged so much as that—something to do with being from a, eh, a different time. I have used *produits chimiques*, eh, chemicals to gray my hair, but my body has become sick. I am dying. I am sorry, Willoughby."

"Seventy-six years old? Dying? I, I don't understand? I just found you." Willoughby said, feeling a sting in his eyes. He was blinking fast, wiping an arm across them.

"No, you do not understand," the man said, looking away. "I am sorry that you have had to come face to face with the reason I stayed away."

Willoughby stared at him, sniffing. "You're not making sense. How did you find me?" he finally choked out. "You spoke of Nostradamus. Is he still alive? Why isn't he here?" Gustav reached up and caught a tear from Willoughby's cheek. He brushed it away with a trembling finger.

"*Celui qui est mon coeur...*" Gustav said softly. "It means *one that is my heart*." It was his turn to sniff and blink his eyes tightly. "I asked to have this moment with you. You have had to face far too much, far too young." He looked out at the flames licking the cave. He continued staring away as he spoke, as if seeing something on the far horizon. "There is much you need to know. Nostradamus is part. He is a friend. He will fight with you."

"*Fight* with me?"

Again, there was a long pause. Then Gustav turned back, shaking an already trembling head. "*Struggle* with you, maybe...We struggle, Willoughby, so that there may be order, so there may be life. Many struggle—you, me. Some do not even know they fight. Some do not know what side they are on. We do. We fight, we struggle because we *must*, because we know what hides in the dark."

Willoughby could not help but think of the spyglass, of when he raised it to look at Beelzebub's chest, of the black strings he saw, pulling in toward a black hole that should have been his heart. The intense eyes of the old man were on him now.

"This...*le conte*—story is long. I will not tell all, but some. Will you listen?"

Willoughby looked at this wild, old man whose eyes burned with such intensity, such vibrant energy. *Of course he would listen*. He gave his head a quick nod. He no longer wanted to scold or cry. He only wanted to know. He pushed to his feet. The initial pain caused him to cry out, but pulling on his father's shoulders, he steadied himself on his feet. The pain lessened. "Could you help me to a place where I can sit and lean back?" Gustav smiled, and the two began to hobble toward the opposite side of the cave.

When they had reached a rise of warm rock, Willoughby turned and helped Gustav sit before sliding down beside him. Behind and to the sides of him, Willoughby noted for the first time that the dark walls of the cave were alive with tiny, dancing strings of light. Peering closely, he found them to be whirling, spinning bits of equation. They winked to life, and then, just as quickly, twisted and vanished. Shadows moved at the far edges of the cave before disappearing. On one wall, not far from where they sat, Willoughby could faintly make out a hazy view into some sort of room. There were small windows with moonlight streaming in and candles lit on the wooden tables. Partially filled bottles and jars punctuated stacks of crinkled parchment across the table. There was an old brass scale, and a small kerosene burner at one corner of the table, a low flame heating a battered tin plate.

As his eyes swept the entire space of the cave, only the old man, only his father, remained constant. The man's face was lined and leathered, but kind. As Gustav leaned back, the movement seemed to cause him pain. He took a moment to recover his breath. Then, he reached out to touch the bloody stain on Willoughby's shoulder. Willoughby winced. Gustav fished in a pocket of his robe and pulled out a packet of something damp, wrapped in a bit of white cloth. The packet smelled of spice, and leaves, and forest. "Hold this to the wound. It will, *accélérer*— mm, how you say—*speed* the healing." Willoughby slowly did as he was instructed. He leaned back as well as Gustav began to speak.

"Tell me about Willoughby, about your mother."

Willoughby stared forward. "I don't know where to start. You left and never came home. We searched for years, but we never found any trace of you. Finally, Mom remarried. He's a good man, Gustav. He takes good care of us. I have two half-sisters. As for me, I'm, I'm a bit of a math whiz. After I solved the Riemann Hypothesis, I was approached by a secret organization called Observations, Inc."

Gustav looked over, his eyes narrowing. "You—the, the *Riemann Hypothesis?*"

Willoughby shrugged, looking up with a sheepish grin. "It was a few years ago. Just before I was twelve."

Gustav shook his head in slow wonder, mumbling. "Before you were twelve…" A smile spread across his face and his eyes danced. "It is true—everything Michael, everything *The Friend* has told… "

"*The Friend?*"

Gustav shook his head. "He is another one who fights."

Willoughby sucked in a breath and looked away again. "Well, solving the Riemann brought me to H.S.'s attention."

"I would think it would," Gustav said, still smiling.

"—that, and the fact that I was your son. They knew somehow. They watched me for a while, and then took me through a time hole to see a real plesiosaurus in the wild. They said they would take me to observe all kinds of cool moments in history. My first assignment was supposed to be to go back to early France and find Nostradamus. This was before I knew anything about the staff, or your involvement with H.S. This was before I knew that the real reason we were searching for you was to find a crystal computer H.S. claims you took from him. Then, our ship was hijacked by these thugs that have a dark tattoo—the same mark that Nostradamus talks about in that letter that was hidden in the staff. Most everyone was killed, except they kept me and the Observations, Inc. team alive for some reason, and we all ended up escaping through a mobile doorway built into the ship. Two of the team are lost somewhere in time. We postponed the trip to France and were going to put all our efforts into finding them. Then, our facility at the bottom of the ocean went weird and started to implode, and the only way to keep from being drowned was to jump into the time-hole, only this time with no control. So I ended up on this mountain, and found a frozen mummy, and—well, you know the rest."

Gustav's eyes twinkled. "Then you find this old man and wonder, could he be your father? How old are you?"

"I'm sixteen."

"Is this everything?"

"Yeah… Well, no. There's one more part. When the organization was checking me out by having a guy named Antonio pretend to be a barber and cut my hair, well, one time I saw numbers floating. They were just floating in the air. I had sort of seen them before, but this time, I could see whole equations, and then a brilliant light ripped open in the air, and this creepy guy stuck his head through, and everything was frozen around me. I mean, the fly hung suspended in air in front of me—that sort of frozen. I saw this guy again when I was walking to meet Mom, and then he visited me after I got off the ship. That time, he formed a junction around me—one like this, but he claimed I formed the first junction, and he said I called him. He calls himself Beelzebub and he says he's your father and my grandfather."

"He is not. He *twists* the truth."

"You know him then?"

"Yes. He is at the heart of much I have to tell. Did he hurt you?"

"No," Willoughby shook his head. "He seems to want me to join him or something. I'm not sure why. I'm not sure what he wants to do. He visited me again on the ship before we transferred to the facility on the sea floor. He threatened that if I didn't join him, bad things would happen. He said something was waiting for me. He had this strange girl with blackened eyes with him. He said the people of her time called her the *desert witch*. He seems to be able to travel time at will and he has all these strange people stashed in different places, zombies and witches and stuff."

"He would spread, eh, *chaos*, Willoughby. That is who he is. You say H.S. *believes* I am Nostradamus?"

"I think so. He located the chain he claims you took from him with a staff he claims belonged to Nostradamus. I already told you this. There was a letter hidden in the staff and numbers carved on the outside. The letter was signed by Nostradamus. It mentions Beelzebub and something called *the cult of the dark edge*. It had the same symbol that is tattooed on the hijackers. All this was found in a cave in Scotland, along with your," he turned to look at his father, his voice lowering, "your bones... I, I don't know if I should be telling you this. Maybe I could change the timeline somehow. H.S. says that's not easy to do, but—"

Gustav leaned forward to touch his arm with a grim smile. "I am aware of the cave. I know why I must be there. There is no need for your—your concern." He leaned back with a heavy sigh. "I know much about you, Willoughby." He looked over with a grin. "Michael has told me. The Friend has given details. *But to see you!* To hear your voice..." The old man made no attempt to stop the tears from sliding down his face and falling to his robe. He smiled again, blinking hard and patting Willoughby's knee. There was a long silence, and then Gustav spoke, his voice trembling a little.

"Are you ready to hear the sad tale of Gustav Helmand Von Brahmer?"

Willoughby felt a pang in his chest. *Was he?* He nodded.

Gustav stretched out his legs. He suddenly seemed old and frail. "Here is the reason you seek, Willoughby— the reason I stayed away from you and your mother. The reason that no longer exists…" He leaned back, resigned, haltingly, and began his tale.

23

Things Broken

There are words that come from somewhere near the surface, that come quick, and easy, and are painless to speak. There are also words that are stuck deep inside of us, that have to be searched for, and prodded, and only come out in halting, pain filled pauses. Gustav's tale was the latter. It seemed to take him forever to finally find all the words he wished to say and speak them. "Each person, how you say, *shapes*," he began, "a world around them. We may think that what we see, the space we choose to, to be in, is the same for everyone, but it is not. The world begins to change as soon as we step into it. We make it like us— we make it...*unique.* Before I met your mother, my world was broken—a thing my hands and mind could not fix. I did not know comfort. I did not know home. The walls of my room were cold and bare. The eyes who watched me were filled with, how do you say, *le cruex*...emptiness. I knew want and I knew fear. I was fed. I was dressed. I was *never* loved. If I did not prove myself brilliant in every way, I was beaten and scolded and starved."

Gustav went on to describe a cold, barren apartment in East Germany. He explained his school years, that he excelled at math and logic. By the age of nine, he was already known in his small village as an *inhabituel*—an unusual boy. Bauman University in Moscow recruited him as a novice of only fourteen. It was the year he left his house for good and began to make his own way in the world. His state-assigned guardians, an austere couple in their late fifties, noted his great achievement in a one paragraph note, pinned to his things on the porch. They had taken it upon themselves to pack for him and place his things just outside the locked front door. He did not ring the doorbell to tell them goodbye. There was no point.

When he asked his guardians about his true parents, he was told that he had no mother or father because they had tried to escape East Berlin and had been gunned down, which is more than they deserved. He learned not to ask more. "I was my own man," he said. "I gained a reputation—the boy who could fix things. Anything..." He sighed. "Anything, that is, but his own heart."

The year before he graduated from the *Bauman*, he was hunted down by the man who raised him. The man admitted to lying to him. He said there were reasons for the lie, but he wouldn't say what they were. He said that Gustav's mother had died giving birth to him, but that his father was alive. The man was powerful and secretive. He had given instructions, which were obeyed. Now, the man wanted to meet his son. On an unknown day in the future, a car would arrive to take him to the rendezvous.

"Five months later, a car arrived well into the night. The driver knocked on my door. He was a strange man. He did not seem to breathe and he did not speak. He wore dark glasses, even at night. He gave me a card that said, 'I am to take you to your father.' I followed him to a long limousine. That is where I met the being who professed to be my father. The tall man had pointy teeth, and introduced himself as *Aribert Heim*. Does that name hold any significance to you, Willoughby?"

Willoughby shook his head, content to just listen for now.

"Aribert Heim was a—ah, what is the word? He was a *célèbre*, a famous Nazi accused of experimenting on the Jews before they were killed. He is said to have been trying to, how you say, *la collure*, eh, *splice* human genes to add German features to Jewish bloodlines."

Gustav went on to explain that the man had escaped after World War II and was never caught. He had learned this by researching the name after his first meeting with the man. There were other meetings, but he soon came to the opinion that something was wrong. If Aribert really were the Aribert Heim of the Third Reich, he would have to be close to 110 years old. Surely, the man who visited him wasn't older than sixty or sixty-five. The Nazi, Aribert Heim, had to be dead by now. Or did he?

"Aribert Heim said he had not finished his *la recherché*—his research. He claimed to be more than one man. He said he was Vlad, the Impaler, Tomas de Torquemada, and a hundred other names. He said it was part of his *la recherché*. He wanted me to be a part of this."

"'You expect me to believe you are, eh, *immortelle,* unable to die?'

"He looked at me and said, 'I don't care what you believe.'

"'*What are you?*' I asked." He looked at me for a long moment. "Your father," was all he said.

"I told him I was an Engineer. I had a talent for design. I could see how to fix things, how best to build things, but I had no interest in genetics. He asked strange questions—could I see holes in space? Could I move in time? I thought he was, eh, *farfelu*." Gustav touched a finger to his head, indicating that he had thought the man to be crazy. "Before we finish the third visit, he told me he will not see me for a while. But, he said he would be watching me. He wanted to know when I found someone, when I had a son. He gave me a number to call."

Gustav told of finishing school, of getting a job offer in the United States, and secretly moving there. Then, he told of how he met a beautiful girl named Lillian, one who had a heart that could fix anything… *Willoughby's mom*.

"Your mother, Willoughby, was a new world to me. She was everything I had never known. She was more brilliant than I. *How I loved her.* She fixed even this broken boy. In time, we were married. I remembered Aribert Heim and his number. I did not like the man. I did not trust the man. I decided to cut all ties with the man who claimed to be my father. Then, you were born. You were so beautiful. You were everything perfect—there was nothing for me to fix in you, Willoughby.

"Then, it began. At first, I was not so worried. I received a letter forwarded to a PO box from my Munich apartment. The man who raised me was still alive. The crazy man who claimed to be my father was looking for me, he said. He told me this man was not pleased. Somehow, he knew of you. He wanted me to bring you so he could play the role of Grandfather. I remembered my conversation with this crazy man. How did he know I had a wife and son? *What did he want with you?* I remembered he said he would watch me. How else could he have known I was no longer alone? Already, I could see that you had unusual abilities. I left to go back to Germany. I did not want your mother to know where I was—to try to follow. I was going to confront this madman once and for all."

Gustav's face was ashen as he described his last meeting with the man who claimed to be his father. They did not meet in Germany, but in Bermuda, on an abandoned dock behind a dark warehouse. Another of the strange men with dark glasses was there, one who was very large, with massive arms and neck muscles. The air was cold. The man told him again that he was no ordinary man. He claimed to be Lord of Demons—*Beelzebub*, a creature beyond time. "He said that my coming," Gustav continued; "was not enough. He wanted me to bring you to him. I asked why. He said he had to know if you had the gift."

"I asked him what gift? He did not answer. I told him I had no intention to bring you to him. I did not think he knew where I lived, where you were, or he would have already visited instead of trying to find me through the old guardian. I refused to tell him. He became angry. He said he would find you—that he would find his grandson. He said I could not stop him. He said my usefulness may be at its end."

Gustav looked down at his hands. "The man was threatening me. I did not know what to do. My thought was only to protect Lillian, to protect you. I had purchased a gun and hidden it in the pocket of my coat. I pulled it out and pointed it at the man. I told the man to stop. The man laughed and told me to shoot. He kept coming. I had no choice but to fire at him to protect myself. But the bullet did not stop him. I fired at him again. It did not even slow him down. He grabbed the gun from me and flung it away. He then picked me up and held me high in the air. 'With one word from me,' this Beelzebub said, 'I could have him crush you. You have lost my trust, Gustav. I was wrong to give you space and time. You will not be free of me again.' He nodded to the big man and I was thrown at least forty feet into a pile of garbage bins. As I struggled to get back to my feet, there was a blinding light. Peering over the edge of the bin, I saw the man rip open the air and then he and the brute who could not die were gone."

Gustav became silent. "So, what happened then?" Willoughby asked. "How did you connect up with H.S.?"

The old man looked over with a sad grin. "I wondered if I was mad. I wondered if I had, eh, *imagined* the whole thing. A man who does not die? A man who steps into a rip in the air to disappear? It was *fantastique*. But I could not risk letting them find you and your mother. I decided I would not go back to my home until I knew for certain the threat was no more. That is when I stumbled upon a strange man in a back alley shop. I had heard music played with such *passionne* that I was compelled to follow. The strange man told me I was a '*good customer*.' He pushed me into his shop, led me to his register, and handed me a business card. It said on the card, Hathaway Simon, Observations, Inc."

"*Empty Spaces to Distant Places*," Willoughby interjected, remembering the business card H.S. had given him at their first meeting.

"Yes," Gustav gave a brief grin. "I see you must have his card too."

Willoughby stared at his father intently. "Was the name of the strange shop the *Lucky Seven Emporium*? What was the music you were hearing?"

Gustav looked up, thinking. "The man told me the music was not for sale. It was a violin, playing Vivaldi if I am not mistaken. I... I do not remember the name. The shop was hidden in, eh, how you say, *la niche*. The keeper was Asian. He had a funny name."

"How Loa," Willoughby said in a matter-of-fact tone.

The old man's eyes narrowed. "Do you know him?"

"I saw numbers in the air, like I sometimes see when there is a time hole. I found the shop just like you did, in a hidden alcove off a narrow alley. The Asian man, How Loa, said I was a *'good customer'* too. He gave me things— an odd, brass spyglass that lets me see things."

"*See* things?"

"I, I don't really understand it, but it seems to let me see things outside of my time. Like, I saw you walking toward the shop when he first gave it to me. You were, you were younger..."

Willoughby's words trailed off. Gustav looked away, and then back, putting a hand lightly on his shoulder. "Yes. I was much younger."

After a long moment, Willoughby looked up. "Did you give him something—something to pass on to me? Did you give him a jade box with no key?"

Gustav frowned and shook his head. "I was interested in the music. He said it was not for sale. Then, he gave me the business card. He said this man was the one I need to see. I left the shop and called the man on the card."

Willoughby was quiet for a moment. How had indicated that the man who left the box for Willoughby had been glimpsed through the spyglass. Willoughby had only seen two figures in the glass, Gustav, and...

"Wait," Gustav said, absently rubbing at his chin. "The shop keeper did give me something." He fished out a small, polished rock from a purse at his belt. He handed it to Willoughby. The rock had a carved symbol on it that he had never seen before. It showed a curved line with arrows spreading out from the top of it like rays of the sun. Below the line were three dots, arranged in pyramid fashion. Willoughby looked up. "What does it do?"

"Do?" Gustav responded.

"Doesn't it do something? What is the symbol for?"

Gustav shrugged. "It is only a rock, Willoughby. "The symbol did help me when I found Michael." He grew quiet for a moment. "Michael knew the symbol. He said it stood for a place—the Library of Souls. He knew of the place."

Willoughby handed the rock back. He looked down, blinking hard suddenly. He sighed. "I don't know what any of this means. It's like somebody is giving us clues, but for what? I can't see the patterns. What am I supposed to do?" He looked up at his father, this man who was old enough to be his grandfather.

Gustav met his eyes. Willoughby wanted to turn away. It was as if the man's gaze could bore right through him. "*Réagissez, stoppez, ou changez le monde ...*" the man whispered calmly. His lips paused. He wetted them. "In English; '*React, quit, or change the world.*' You are not the first to find the path difficult. Does difficult make the path pointless, or does it give the path *more* meaning? You are the one to decide. You hit back, angry at life. You can quit. You didn't ask for your situation. Or, you can stand and face what will come. You may not always be the tallest, or wisest, or *solide*—strongest, as some say of the hero. You may just be a boy. But sometimes, this is what the hero needs to be."

"I'm not a hero. I'm just...Willoughby."

"Yes, but you are Willoughby," Gustav said softly.

The hot rush of tears stung Willoughby's eyes. "Does it really matter what I want? I wanted to have a father at home. I wanted some adventure—to know something of the wonders of time—but I didn't' know it would put my friends, my family in danger. I want to go back. I want to undo what I've done."

Gustav was quiet for a long time. His hands were working in his lap, bending, curling, weaving, as if he were tinkering, trying to fix something. His eyes were focused far away. He seemed completely unaware of what his hands were doing. He looked down. "Time, it gives us the moment. To wish that moment away is to waste a gift. There is no way to change what is meant to be. It will find a way to happen. Maybe there are things you learn from decisions you make, but you cannot create a future while living in the past. The future does not wait. If you do not act upon it, it will act upon you."

Willoughby shifted, wiping his eyes. "So, Mr. Loa helped you meet Michael."

Gustav watched Willoughby. "Yes. I think this was meant to be. H.S. looked in to my background. He hired me, but would not give me the full, eh, *la vue* of the project. I figured it was a device to affect time. I wanted to disappear so you and your mother could be safe. I found the time hole. H.S. caught me and we fought. I started to fall into the hole. I grabbed for H.S. but only caught the necklace and pendant. When I woke in a muddy field, I stumbled to my feet and tried to find where I was. At a nearby village, I find it is France and it is the fifteenth century. When I tried to trade the coin I carried for food, it was the rock with the symbol that seemed to catch the eye. I was taken to Michael, who had a small practice in the village. I told him my story. He believed me.

"As we ate, he told me why. He was one who could see the future—like looking out of some other man's eye. One day, he saw that his wife and child would die from the fever. He struggled to become a healer to save them, but he was not able to save his family. It broke him. He left France, wanting to escape his visions. But, they still came. He found a monk in a high mountain who told him of a people who could help him. He climbed to a hidden monastery, high in the mountains and found the order of this monk. They told him of the Library of Souls, the symbol on my rock. They told him this library knows of him. They taught him to, how you say, to *compartimenter*—to separate the visions of future from the rest of his brain.

"Michael stayed with them for many months. Then, he came and set up his shop in this village. A visiting monk who calls himself the *Friend* told him to watch for the symbol of the Library. He told Michael there will also be an extraordinary boy. Michael is convinced, Willoughby, that the *Friend* was speaking of you."

Willoughby had been listening quietly. "Why?" he asked, looking up.

Gustav shook his head. "Michael does not tell me all. I have been his assistant for many years, since he was a man in his twenties. I go by the name *Chavigny*. A monk from the monastery visited and asked what I would want of him. I told him I would want to see my son one last time."

Willoughby looked down. "What do you mean *one last time?* You're coming back with me, right? We can get you to a hospital. You can get better—"

"No," Gustav said, flashing a tight smile. He shook his head gravely. "There is no healing my sickness. I have a part to play still. I, eh, told you I know of the cave."

"I can find you further back in time—before you get sick."

"You have some skill with time? You learn from H.S.? If you come to me sooner, our enemy may know of me. I will not be ready. It could destroy everything."

"Ready for what?"

Gustav paused. "Ready to face what each must face."

"What does that mean?"

Gustav let out a slow, heavy sigh. "I do not have that answer for you, Willoughby. The monks tell Michael that you have a destiny known to them. I am not here to affect that destiny."

Willoughby stared at the hands in his lap. He was surprised to see them moving, slowing mimicking the empty movements Gustav had been making, as if to repair something only he could see. "Why are you here?" he said softly.

Gustav looked at him for a long moment. "Because," he said slowly, "A father has a right to let his son know that he loves him. That he always has and he always will."

Willoughby felt hot tears coming again. "That's a long way to, to…"

"Yes," Gustav said, his hands working again, probing the blank air as if reaching for something, tinkering, fixing… "I, eh, wish I could have been there with you, Willoughby. *Solving the Riemann!* I have today, though— this moment, this cave outside of time. This cave will always be here for you." His hands stopped moving just long enough to point a finger at Willoughby's chest. Then, they were active again. "When you visit in your mind, perhaps I can be younger." He smiled. "I was handsome once, you know. Love is a thing outside of time. It fills the gaps between every lonely moment." His hands slowly stopped moving again, this time for good. He lowered them to his lap, wiping a teardrop from his nose. "Don't forget, you have a mother who loves you, a step-father and sisters you say? You also have friends, Willoughby—powerful friends. When it is time, you must seek out the *Order of Padmasambhava.*" Gustav bent forward and spelled the word in the dust of the cave floor.

"Padmasambhava?" Willoughby repeated, staring at it. "What do you mean, *when it is time?*"

Gustav smiled his tight smile again. "You will know."

"I wish you could meet my friends," Willoughby said. He was thinking of Dr. J, and Antonio, and H.S., and T.K. But, most of all, he was thinking of Sydney. He couldn't but wonder if the music that had led Gustav to the Lucky Seven Emporium was Sydney's violin. It had led him to her through the time grid. What was it about Sydney's music? It seemed to have a quality that transcended time.

"Yes. I would have liked that." Gustav's smile was genuine this time. He wiped a shaking arm across his eyes. His fingers were moving again, trying to mend the air. *What is he doing?* Willoughby thought. It was if he held some, something small and intricate, probing it, adjusting it, turning it. Gustav looked over, still oblivious to the movements of his hands. "It is almost time. For me, it is the night of July 1, 1566. I have much to do."

Willoughby recognized the date. It was the night Nostradamus was recorded to have died.

Gustav looked up apologetically. "I must keep my part of the bargain. I must hide Michael's bones. Then, I must travel to the cave as Michael has foreseen. There, I will die."

"*Wait*," Willoughby pushed to his feet. "Can't you stay just a little longer? I haven't—there's so much more to, to talk about. Things I want to tell you. Things I want to know. There was a number sequence—"

"Yes," Gustav managed with a weak grin. "It is a message—a puzzle for you. You remember the puzzles I would give you? Think of me when you solve it." Gustav pushed to his feet and turned. Willoughby reached to grab him, "Can I, can I touch you?"

Gustav's hands shook where he held them, just above his waist. They were close together, the fingers working—pulling, turning, tapping—relentlessly, as if frantic to fix a hidden thing that had become suddenly exposed. But his voice remained steady. He held his arms out and nodded. Willoughby rushed into them, feeling the man's thin frame in his embrace.

"There are moments," Gustav whispered, "that burn inside us like fire that will not be still. This embrace will burn inside me, Willoughby. Find that fire in you and know I am there. Then, we will never be lost to each other again." The man let his gaze fall for a moment and then he gave a pained grunt. He reached up, using the wall to steady himself. As he raised his shaking hand toward a numeric equation that had begun to grow brightly, he gave Willoughby one last glance "You see, *un de mon cœur*," he said, "we have changed the world, you and I. Already, it is less empty."

Willoughby felt his chest tighten and his throat go dry. He opened his mouth to speak but no words came.

Gustav let his shaking fingers touch the bright equation at one and then two distinct points. The candlelit table became brighter and clearly more visible. He spoke almost in a whisper over his shoulder. "All that is worth knowing wants to be known. If we choose not to see, if we leave ourselves distracted, what is important can easily be lost. Like the *arpenteuse,* the inchworm, we must pull ourselves in to gain the power to stretch out. You must listen as you pull your thoughts in, Willoughby. Life's great victories are won or lost inside, on the battlefields of the soul."

He touched the cave wall one last time and then turned, his eyes glistening. "I go now. Let few know of our meeting—you came upon an old man. You thought he might be Nostradamus. He gave something to you. When you wake in the ice, it will be with you, wrapped carefully at your feet. Study Michael's verses. Arton is a clue... " The man's voice faded. His hands were in front of him again, working, building, fine tuning... Willoughby could not take his eyes off the hands. As tears streamed from his face and this old man, his father, began to pass through the rock into the small room, and then fade, he noted his own hands, fingers moving again, mimicking the man, caressing a shape the size of a heart.

"Already," he whispered, the words shaky and barely audible, "*we change the world...*"

When the room had completely vanished, and Gustav was gone, and the cave was dim again, the silence hung thick around Willoughby. It felt suffocating. The flickering firelight just outside the cave held no more warmth. Wiping at his eyes, he turned searching the cave floor. When he found the pile of tent that he had zipped himself into, he went to it and dropped to his knees. Sobbing, he crawled inside, pulling himself down, wanting to leave this silence, wanting to smother himself in a colder

corner of time. *Like an inchworm*, he thought to himself—
like an inchworm I pull myself inside. Tears fell hot down
his cheeks, and in his heart, he did not know if he could
ever, *ever* stretch out fully again.

24

H.S.'s Secret

It took Antonio several long moments of gasping and sputtering to re-oxygenate. As his chest slowed from its heaving and his breath returned, he felt a sharp jab on his arm. He turned to find T.K.'s eyes furiously boring into him. "*What was that all about?*" She shoved him again. "You almost got us killed!"

He stared at her, still breathing rapidly, trying to comprehend the question. "I," he started, "I—was trying to distract it. To give you a chance—buy you a little time."

"Yeah, little is right," T.K. shot back. "You might have bought me thirteen seconds while the thing chewed you twice and swallowed. That was an insanely stupid thing to do! What was your plan? Ram it with your incredible bulk? Give it an underwater slug with your mighty hammer fist? Antonio, I can't keep saving you every fifteen minutes!"

Antonio stared, thunderstruck.

At last, T.K. sighed. "But," she added. "It was very brave. I've never had anyone jump in front of a speeding bullet to save me before—especially not one that weighed a few thousand pounds!" She gave him a weak smile. He returned the smile, but already, his mind had moved beyond the conversation. The beast howled again, but this time, its cry was muffled by several feet of thick rock. It was on the *other side* of the stone wall. He groped at the rough walls, which followed a fairly cylindrical curve. The enclave seemed to be about eight feet across and was partially flooded with water.

"What is this place?" he mumbled.

T.K. was mirroring his gaze. "It almost seems manmade—like someone expanded a natural fissure in the rock wall."

Antonio's hand brushed against something cold, hammered into the rock. A faint, greenish light powered up from the shallow water below. He stared in amazement. T.K. was right. *This small enclave was not a natural phenomenon!* As his eyes adjusted to the light, he recognized that his hand had found a metal ladder, bolted to the rock at the far back corner of the enclave. It extended up into darkness.

"We should have explored our cave more carefully," he whispered.

T.K., at the flare of the strange greenish light, had squeezed in tighter beside him. "I," she said, matching his soft tone, "just thought it was a normal crack in the rock at first. Then, I saw it was a tunnel of some kind, and that it headed up. I thought there was a good chance it might rise above water level. I looked around and you weren't behind me. I went back for you. What do you think this place is?"

"It is cleverly hidden, no?" Antonio said. "Let us see where the ladder leads." He motioned her toward the steel rungs. She began to climb and he followed. About sixty feet from the bottom of the enclave, they came to a metal platform. As soon as they stepped onto the platform, another greenish light glowed from a small rock overhang.

Antonio's eyebrows rose. "I seem to recall," he mumbled. "H.S. and I once spoke of hiding outside accesses to some observation windows. He had mentioned hiding steps in a fissure—a doorway in a crevice." His eyes had landed on an ancient-looking door. It was completely oval, like the doors in a submarine. A wave of anger flooded him. *Why hadn't he thought of this before?* They had been surviving on bland weed and fighting monsters for days. He had almost died. They both had. *For what?* Had it been there all the while? Had they been only yards away from the safety and relative comfort of an observation window? He bit his lip. "I am suddenly wondering… H.S. built an observation window near a Jurassic sea. It was the first project his company built. It is one of the few windows I have never visited."

T.K. considered his words, leaning against the edge of the platform. "You mean, this could lead to one of your outposts?"

"Possibly"

"Then, why wouldn't your friends have seen us? Or where they just observing us, waiting to see if we lived or died?"

Antonio did not miss the bite in her tone. He realized that T.K. was not a full member of Observations, Inc. "Most of our observation windows are fully automated, *Senora*. They are completely unmanned. We use them for specific purposes. With the attention of the group on medieval France, our arrival here could have gone completely unnoticed. I do not remember seeing this back-door in any of the schematics. It is possible that this is merely a maintenance access to the hole—one that is seldom in use. If I recall, the window itself looks out into the wider sea. There would be no reason to monitor the cave except to note how frequently the hole is active."

Antonio pushed to his feet and walked to the huge steel door. Flakes brushed away as he put his hand on the large, metal wheel at its center. It smelled of crusted salt and rust. He pulled on the wheel, but it didn't move.

T.K. suddenly held up a hand for silence. "Did you hear that?" she asked.

Antonio listened. There was another roar from the beast, and then a sound that almost seemed like yelling or screaming, drowned out by roars this time from both beasts. Antonio looked at T.K. "You think the two beasts are fighting?" he whispered.

T.K. shrugged. "This alcove may be safe, but I still want to get on the other side of that door."

Antonio nodded. He sucked in a gulp of air and strained against the wheel. "Please, my friend," he panted, when the wheel didn't budge. "I am needing your assistance."

T.K. came up beside him and grabbed the wheel as well. Together they pulled and pushed, but still, the wheel wouldn't budge. "You're right—this door hasn't been used in a long time," she said, blowing out a huge breath. Antonio picked up a rock and gave a couple of sharp bangs on the wheel. Finally, with an enormous thrust, the two succeeded in getting the rusty mechanism to budge. They rested, panting.

"I'm wondering why this door was not in the plans for the facility," Antonio mused.

T.K. shrugged. "You might find there's lot of things H.S. failed to tell you. I told you, he's a snake, Antonio."

Antonio considered the comment. He nodded at T.K., and the two attacked the wheel with renewed vigor.

Together, they managed to force it to turn. Finally, the bolts unlocked and the heavy door creaked open.

T.K. pushed through first. Antonio followed. At the end of a pitch black passage, they came to a set of smooth stone stairs. With no light, they groped slowly along, feeling the walls.

"The wall light must be broken here," Antonio said quietly. They soon came to another metal door. It opened easily, throwing a wash of blinding light into their eyes. As they slowly adjusted, they found themselves in a cramped storage room. Machinery parts and cleaning supplies lined the walls. In one corner, crisp wetsuits hung on pegs above shiny scuba tanks and spear guns. There was also a stack of white workmen jumpsuits.

T.K. took one of the jumpsuits and handed one to Antonio. "I wouldn't want anyone to see us like this," she mumbled, pointing at the ragged remains of her clothes. Antonio looked down at the tatters of rag that still hung around his own shoulders and middle. "What?" he said; "You do not like my tailor?"

T.K. did not answer. She had zipped up her jumpsuit and was rolling up the pant legs. She carefully scanned the walls. "Hey," she said, "how do we get out of here?"

Antonio hurriedly threw on his own coveralls and began probing the storage closet. He found a narrow door hidden in a section of seemingly smooth wall next to a brass plate with 313 over spiraling triangles. It opened when he placed his hand over the triangles. He ducked through. T.K. followed, but insisted on leaving a metal air cylinder to keep the door wedged open. "If we have to make a fast getaway," she explained, "I don't want to be searching smooth wall for a plaque and a door."

They followed a narrow hallway into a wide corridor. Lights instantly sensed them and flicked on. The sides of the hallway were metallic and the floor was polished and smooth. T.K. walked a few steps behind Antonio. Near a sharp bend, he stopped at a set of double doors. A sign over them read, *Clean Room Traffic Only.* He clicked the intercom located just to the right of the doors. A wall video screen flicked to life.

"H.S.? Anyone? Hello, *Amigos?*" he shouted into the intercom. "We are needing attention! Please respond!" There was a moment of static, and then a somewhat startled face appeared on the video screen.

"Antonio? Good heavens, how did you get to the Jurassic facility? We checked it thoroughly only days ago— I'd, I'd given up hope." Antonio stared at the man blankly.

"Did you check the back door?"

H.S.'s face crinkled with confusion. He stared dumbly for a moment, and then his eyes lit up. "Good Lord, I'd forgotten about that door... You were in the cave, then?"

"Yes," Antonio said dryly. "Your pets have not forgotten about the cave."

H.S.'s eyes widened. "The plesiosaurs? You're lucky, then, to be alive." He shook his head, visibly angry with himself. "I can't believe I didn't think to check. That door hasn't been used since—well, since the facility officially came online twenty years ago. The cave has never been used as a destination preset—the doorway on the *Absconditus* must have malfunctioned. I don't think the search team even knows about the cave."

Antonio tried to control the anger welling up in him. "Why should they? I looked over the plans for this facility—there is no 'back-door' identified."

"Of course not," H.S. replied. "The concept was to create hidden escape doors should a facility become compromised. All our windows actually have them. We have a separate architect design them onto a piece of the facility, but they never get to see the full facility plans. The primary architect never sees the plans for the secret door. Once again, it is a safeguard." H.S. pursed his lips, thinking. "I wonder if…" He left the question hanging.

There was a stunned pause. Finally, H.S. looked up, pulling himself back to the present. "I'm sorry, Antonio," he said, shaking his head. "*The cave…* You're lucky you're alive. I attempted to use that cave while they were building the internals of the post. I thought it might allow me to study the plesiosaurus up close, but I found them far too aggressive. I had to actually kill one before locking that door for good." He caught a glimpse of T.K. as she bolted from behind Antonio and started up a set of spiral stairs to the next level. "Who's that with you? Is James Arthur with you?"

Antonio stared at H.S. The man was sitting in the boardroom of his yacht, the *Pesci Piccoli*. "No. James Arthur used the time door before we did. We found no trace of him in the cave. I have T.K. with me. She's the cabin girl from the ship, the captain's adopted daughter. She rescued James Arthur and I and helped us escape. What is the situation there? You are no doubt aware of the killings on the ship. What has happened while we have been here? Did Willoughby and the rest of them get off the ship alive?"

"Willoughby, Sydney, and Dr. O'Grady got off the ship okay, but there have been—other complications. We had hoped James Arthur would be with you. If he is not, then he, also, is missing."

Antonio felt suddenly exhausted by his ordeal. "What do you mean, *also missing?* What are these other complications, my friend?"

H.S. didn't seem to hear the question. He frowned. "You say James Arthur came through first, and then you and T.K. came through together?" He had concern written on his face.

"Yes. Dr. J must have stepped through alone. The cabin girl and I, we stepped through together."

"But we tracked three separate pulses, each about fifteen minutes apart."

Antonio did not know what to say.

H.S. shrugged. "We…shall have to look at that later. The important thing is that we've found you and T.K. With your help, perhaps we can track down the others. We have much to discuss. Come up to the observation level. I believe we can scare you up something hot to drink and some biscuits. You probably need a good night of rest as well. How did you get that scar on your forehead?"

"A gift from the brutes on the *Absconditus*," Antonio said quietly as he unconsciously reached his hand up to touch the healed skin of the scar. "You have not told me who else is missing."

"I'm heading straight over," H.S. said, this time purposely avoiding the question. "Out."

Antonio stood for a moment, staring at the blank screen. Then, he turned and headed up the staircase after T.K.

He had barely stepped onto the floor of the observation window when T.K. accosted him. "Did you really expect to get a straight answer out of him, Antonio? Almost everything he says is either a direct lie or only a partial truth. I hope you can see that. He doesn't care about you or James Arthur."

Antonio barely heard her. He was too taken aback by the incredible view. "Unbelievable," he mumbled. "I saw the schematics—the plans, but the view…" They stood quietly for a good ten minutes, neither speaking, just staring out the dramatic, curved window. Patchwork greens swayed in the pristine water for as far as he could see. Streams of sunlight glinted on the seafloor, highlighting all manner of strange plants and incredible creatures. They slowly paced the interior of the huge, hollowed out room, their eyes flitting briefly across the furniture or computer equipment before being drawn back to the window. Finally, they were standing side by side again. Antonio spoke.

"*It is as fantastic as Willoughby described it,*" he whispered, watching the hypnotic sway of the seascape.

"Atlantis had windows like this," T.K. mumbled. "But not with—"

"*Atlantis?*" The quiet of the room was shattered by an energetic voice from high above. Their eyes turned to the upper landing of a long, zigzagging stairway. H.S. stood at the top, hands gripping a metal railing. He peered down, brandishing a brass tube in his right hand, his brow furrowed.

"That's a primordial sea, young lady—Jurassic period to be precise. Why would you bring up a myth like Atlantis?"

T.K. turned and looked him full in the face, the fierce blue of her eyes sparkling. "Because I lived there, as you might remember, *Haubus Socees*. I lived there the same as you, and I have no intentions of calling you H.S. You are a murderer and a thief. You know as well as I do that

Atlantis isn't a myth. It's the mispronounced name of an ancient city, *Aert Olaneas Tis.* A city, I might add, which spawned the technology you have so brazenly stolen."

H.S. stared, wide-mouthed and unbelieving. Antonio couldn't help but be curious about the brass tube he was holding. It appeared to be an antique spyglass—the kind British Admirals once used. He had never seen H.S. with it before. T.K., however, focused only on the man's face. "Will you admit to the murder, Haubus?" she said calmly. "Was Kunna-Bactu right? Were you plotting to murder my father, Abbacar Kielhar, the whole time you pretended to be his loyal scribe?"

H.S. cocked his head. "*What did you call me?* Where, where did you hear those names? How do you, you..." He let his gaze drop for a moment and breathed in deeply, his expression somber. "You were the daughter of Captain Voight—"

"*No!* Not birth daughter—only adopted daughter. My name is Tainken. My father was Abbacar Kielhar, leader of the blue-eyes! Don't pretend that you don't recognize me, that you've never seen these blue eyes before. You were my father's scribe. I want the truth. Did you kill him yourself, or did you push the dirty work off onto Belzarac?"

H.S. seemed stunned, barely able to breathe. His eyes darted from Antonio back to T.K. "Ab-Abbacar Keilhar? Kunna-Bactu? Haubus? *Belzarac Treec?*" He leaned heavily against the rail. "Tainken—Tainken, *is it you?*"

The question hung on the air, caught in the chill of T.K.'s stare.

25

Hark! What Light

Willoughby wasn't sure how long he had slept before he opened his eyes again. Light filtered through the loosely shoveled snow at the opening to the crevice he had wedged himself into. He felt cold and stiff, but his clothes were dry and he found, with some effort, that he could move. *He had survived the night!* His visit with Gustav came back with stinging clarity. *Had it really happened? Had he dreamed or hallucinated the whole thing?* He had been in bad shape when he dug into this crevice. Slowly, he pulled the thermal gloves on his hands down tighter around his wrists, unzipped the tent, and began to push the snow back, forcing it out of the opening of the crevice. Before long, he broke through the thin layer of white and felt the cold, white light of the sun shine onto his face. He noted that his cheeks were stinging, reached up and plucked small icicles from under his eyes. *From tears* he wondered, staring down at the thin strand. Then he remembered his father's words about the gift.

He reached down toward the bottom of the tent, rummaged around, finding his boots and putting them on. There were two other small bundles there. *The visit with Gustav had not been a hallucination—it had happened.*

As he pulled the bundles up, he found one to be something bundled in tied bits of thick fabric. The other bundle was wrapped with heavy brown paper and tied with string. He opened the paper bundle first. It was a block of some sort of heavy fruit cake. He wasn't usually a big fan of fruit cake, but as he stared down at the cake, his stomach rumbled and he realized that he was hungry enough to eat shoe leather at the moment, so he took a bite. It was hard and dry, but he didn't think he had ever tasted anything so good in his life. There were also a few apples in the bundle, a little flask of some sort of juice, and a small bag of nuts. He downed the juice and pocketed the nuts and half of the cake, devouring the rest. He then began to untie the cloth bundle.

The last layer of cloth was deep crimson velvet. Lying in the center of the velvet was a large, flat crystal that had a hole drilled in the top of it where the chain had been. Willoughby held the crystal up into the sunlight to more closely inspect it. The pendant was long, thin, and rectangular, made of a lightweight substance that seemed neither metal nor plastic, but somehow organic. He ran a hand down its strange, smooth sides. It was the brightest, oddest looking object he had ever seen.

"*The crystal computer…*" he whispered.

It was the final gift from his father. Spider threads of light snaked across it in flickering, pulsing flows. The roughly rectangular object seemed to be alive with frantic little nerves of light. A number flashed bright above it in the air, blinking in unison with a bright pulse from inside the strange crystal. He heard a high pitched scream seeming to emanate from the very air, followed by a girl's voice. He didn't understand the language, but knew the voice. The equation started to fade. Without a second thought, he jerked his hand up and touched it. A blinding light seemed to rend the air. Quickly grabbing his stuff, rolling it into the tent and throwing it into his pack, he threw the strap of the pack over one shoulder and held the crystal out in front of him. The tear in the air was beginning to close. He pushed to his feet with a grunt and dove into the blinding light.

For a moment, there was the sensation of being ripped apart. Then, he tumbled down onto a lip of ice. Luckily, the night had left a skiff of softer snow to help break his fall, but still, it was painful. A bright haze enveloped him. When it faded, he began scanning the terrain around him.

He was lower on the mountain, but not much. Down to his right, he could see an ice bridge that spanned a deep chasm. To the left, he saw what looked to be a packed trail in the snow. Four moving shapes, dark against the sparkling snow, trudged along the path heading up toward a high ridge.

Three of them were large, covered with thick skin coats and hats. Their faces were dark-skinned, but adorned with paint, and their ear lobes were weighted down with large, gold rings. Two of them carried gold-tipped spears. The third held, what looked like, a crude whip of some kind, which he used to prod forward the fourth and smallest figure—a girl with dark hair in mismatched clothes.

Sydney!

The brute with the whip lashed out again, yelling in his strange language. Sydney responded by swatting the whip away and spitting in the man's face. The man wiped off the spittle and then slapped her hard. She screamed. The man grunted at the other two. One grabbed Sydney, slamming her down, and began to force her knees up against her chest. She fought him like a lioness. The other spear-holder began to pull at her clothes. Willoughby realized with horror that they were trying to force her into the same naked, squatting position as the mummy he had unwittingly discovered when he first landed on the mountain. Perhaps frozen mummies adorned many of the crests of this mountain—some sort of pagan welcome to the rising sun.

He had to do something, *and fast*. The man with the whip laughed as Sydney landed a good kick on the man trying to tie her hands. The second spear-holder, the one trying to pull her windbreaker off, suddenly yelped, pulling back his hand. Sydney spit at him too, after apparently biting him. The man used his good hand to pull a stone club from his belt.

Willoughby reacted instinctively. He raised his arms, holding them high, and screamed, "*Stop!*"

The men paused, looking over. They were on higher ground than Willoughby. One of them seemed confused, and then quickly, afraid. He pointed frantically at the snow around where Willoughby stood. Willoughby threw a quick glance around, trying to figure out what the man was pointing at. Then, it dawned on him that there were no tracks at all in the snow around him. To the men, it must seem as if he just appeared out of nowhere, or pulled up from the ground. This gave Willoughby an idea.

The closest man, who seemed to be some sort of Shaman or priest, puffed out his chest and stepped forward, trying to look menacing and doing a pretty fair job of it. *What should he say?* These natives wouldn't understand a word he spoke. But then, maybe they didn't need to. He stabbed a finger into the air.

"*THOU ART MOST FOUL!*" he screamed, with all the volume he could muster. He scowled, holding the crystal computer out before him. The man with the whip cocked his head. The other men mumbled to each other, trying to make sense of his words. He waived his arms again.

"BEHOLD…" He pointed toward the sun, breaking over the peaks of the distant mountains. "*Soft; what light in yonder window breaks! Tis the east, and Juliet, the sun…*" He held both arms out, as if beckoning to the sun itself. He could easily imagine Sydney's arched eyebrows. She made an attempt to turn toward him, but the man with the whip barked at her, raking her so hard with the back of his hand that he knocked her to the snow. He grunted at the other men, cracking his whip. They promptly grabbed their lances. Willoughby gestured wildly; "*ARISE FAIR SUN!*"

He tried not to panic. *If this went south and they attacked him together, how would he defend himself?* The only things he had at hand were snow, ice, and the crystal computer. He swept the computer through the crisp air before him, taking note of any ripples that could be floating number strings. In a half dozen places, he identified number equations crowding the air. In some places, the equations were barely visible. In others, they were larger and more plentiful. Larger holes, he thought to himself. He selected one and reached the computer toward it, studying the strings at the spot and willing the number string to somehow connect with him. With a crack that seemed almost like lightning, the space between he and the equation strings bent, allowing him to stretch out and touch the numbers, and he was suddenly there—yards away from where he had been standing.

He heard the two men with spears shout in alarm. They pointed frantically at his old place in the snow, now empty, and to the new spot where he was standing, which was closer to them. The man with the whip however yelled loudly, cracking the whip angrily over his head. He motioned to the two spear bearers to move forward. They did.

Willoughby was actually as surprised by his success as the natives were, though he tried not to show it. It must be the skimming technology H.S. had told him about—the technology that had allowed he, Sydney, and Dr. O'Grady to transfer to a different point in space instead of a different point in time. Yet, the machinery behind the technology he had seen at the Jurassic Observation Post was massive. He had seen a huge electromagnetic pyramid, helping to focus gravitational strings of an existing time hole. What energy had he channeled to make *this* leap in space? Surely, the energy couldn't be coming from the small crystal computer.

His thoughts were cut short as he noted the natives creeping close. The man with the whip had pulled Sydney back to her feet and was holding her out in front of him. Frantically, he searched the holes nearby. Could he do the trick a second time? H.S. had seemed fascinated with his ability to instinctively find equation variation on the fly. Finding a target string, or the mathematical representation of a time hole, wasn't easy. Yet, the variations stood out to the point of almost glowing to Willoughby. He found a hole that seemed brighter than the others to him and reached for it.

Again, the space before him seemed to bend. He touched the string and was jerked, as if by a bungee cord, to that point. "Just keep still, Sydney," he muttered, trying to maintain his balance so he didn't fall over into the snow face first.

The men with the gold-tipped spears had seen enough. They fell to their knees, prostrating themselves on the snow. The man with the whip, however, wrapped it savagely around Sydney's neck.

What happened next was instinctive for Willoughby. H.S. had taught him the mechanics of the skimming technology. The normal flow of time through matter creates a force known in physics as the *strong force*. When this force is disrupted within a controlled time-wave, a bubble is formed. All things within the bubble become detached—no longer tethered in space. The bubble can then be directed toward a target point with minimal effort. Even the slight pull created by a time hole, or a person out of time, can set the bubble in motion, skimming forward like a puck in a game of air-hockey. Willoughby saw the number string he recognized as Sydney. He heard Sydney choke as the savage man yanked tight on the whip. He grabbed at the number string.

Almost immediately, there was a blinding flash as the air ripped open, and then a bone-rattling jerk as he leaned into the rip. He felt his body slam against something solid. His vision cleared to find the terrified savage before him on the icy trail. The whip still hung limp around Sydney's neck. Willoughby waited a moment, giving his limbs time to recover, and then looked down, scowling. He put his thumb to his front teeth and flicked it forward.

"Sir," he said menacingly, "I do prick my thumb at thee!"

The man had scrambled to his feet and backed away, bent low, trying to hide his face. His two friends were already a good thirty yards down the side of the frozen mountain. The bent man quickly turned and sprinted off after them. Willoughby stretched out his arms and cried with triumph.

"*ARISE YE FOOLS AND KILL THE ENVIOUS MOON! FOR SHE IS ALREADY SICK AND PALE WITH GRIEF—*"

Sydney had managed to pull the whip from around her neck and flung it after the fleeing savage. "*Coward!*" she screamed. Then, she turned, eased herself down onto the snow, and collapsed into sobs. She wiped at her bloody lip.

"Hey, they're gone," Willoughby said, bending down to her. He wiped at the tears and blood on her cheek.

"I know," she said, pulling herself back under some semblance of control. "Thanks."

"But I'm not done yet," Willoughby intoned dramatically. Standing again, he held out an arm.

"Willoughby, believe me," Sydney said, wiping again at her cheeks, "you're done."

He pretended not to hear. "*Her eye discourses. I will answer it!*"

"Willoughby!"

"*She speaks, yet she says nothing, what of that?*"

"That line is supposed to come two lines earlier than your last line."

"*I am too bold, tis not to me she speaks: see how she leans her hand upon her cheek—*"

"I'm wiping mud and spit from my cheek!"

"*Oh, that I were a glove upon that hand!*"

"*Willoughby!*"

Willoughby dropped the arm and shrugged. "Well, I don't suppose this is the best time to hear about your *vestal livery* looking *sick and green*, is it?"

He glanced down with a slight grin, but saw that Sydney had looked away, her head hung low. She was sobbing again, spitting blood out onto the white snow. He lowered to his knees. "Hey," he said, softly pulling her chin up. She fell into him, burying her head into the crook of his neck.

"They, they tried to strip me," she said. "They were going to tie me and, and, I don't know…"

"I think they were going to just let you freeze. I've seen other frozen kids bound like that up here. I think it has something to do with sacrificial rites or something."

"It was horrible, Willoughby."

"I know," Willoughby said softly, and then just held her.

After she had cried out, she pushed him away. "Go ahead," she mumbled, grabbing some snow to wipe across her cheeks and eyes. "Say it."

"Say what?"

"That I *did* need you," she said, sniffing.

Willoughby smiled. "Well, every Juliet needs a Romeo now and again," he said.

It was her turn to grin. "Yeah, I guess you're okay every now and again—Shakespeare and all. You know the play pretty well. When did you memorize all those lines?"

"Eighth grade," Willoughby sighed. "It was while I was standing around being a tree. I was sure I could be a better Romeo than the joker they cast, and Juliet was seriously hot. I had to stand perfectly still while tall, suave Buck Larsen stood beside me twanging through his impassioned pleas like a banjo picker at a bluegrass festival." Willoughby put on his best hillbilly accent. "'*I take thee at thy word. Call me but love and I'll be new baptized...*' The guy seriously hammered it up. It was hard to keep a straight face."

This got a choked chuckle. Sydney sniffed. "Lucky for me, one tree has an exceptional memory."

"Lucky for me, I saved up my best performance for when the real Juliet came along." Sydney did not react to the compliment. He continued. "Besides, those lines were better than *"I love you, you love me, we're best friends like friends should be."*

This got a genuine laugh—albeit small. Sydney looked up, scanned the snow, and sighed, seeming to let go some of the tension she had bottled up. "I don't think they would have found those words particularly frightening."

Willoughby relaxed a little. It was good to hear her laugh. "Well, they're definitely more frightening when sung by a purple dinosaur...Anyway, what did you do to tick those guys off so much?" He stood, narrowing his eyes to look out over the ridge. The native men had disappeared.

Sydney was quiet for a while, before she finally spoke. "They said I woke the devil," Sydney answered, her words a little slurred.

Willoughby frowned. "You could understand them?"

Sydney pulled back at her matted hair. "Some. I should have listened to you, Willoughby. I should have waited so we went into the hole together. I was stupid." She tried to sound unaffected, though her voice trembled. "Did it take you long to find me?"

"I had help," Willoughby said, suddenly serious. "How long did they have you? Are you hurt anywhere?"

"Yes," Sydney mumbled, tears forming again in her eyes. She gulped a great lungful of air. "They only had me a few hours, but my ankle is badly twisted. That big one with the whip kept shoving me, and one time, my foot got caught in a crevice. I don't even think he noticed. I think all of them were drunk. The ankle burns like fire if I try to put my weight on it. When they found me, I surmised from what snatches of their language that I could understand, that I was trespassing on sacred grounds. The guy who was responsible for my ankle was sort of their leader. He told the others that the Fire God had to be appeased." Her lip still trembled. "Being left alone up here to freeze on this mountain—what a horrible, pointless death…" She sniffed again and then looked up at him, trying to compose herself. It was no good. Tears came afresh. "And on top of everything else, *they called me ugly!*"

Willoughby raised his eyebrows. "Wow. They were drunk."

Sydney forced a smile.

"They're sun worshipers, I think," Willoughby said. "That spot where they were trying to put you was on a small ridge, right in line with where the sun first strikes when it comes up between those two peaks, this time of year, see?" She looked and nodded. He pocketed the crystal computer and reached over to clear a strand of hair from her face. "You have a bad ankle, a fat lip, some scratches, and I wouldn't be surprised if you end up with a black eye. Nothing serious, but I don't think you'll be hitting *Vogue* for a week or two. Maybe *Rolling Stone*…" He stood and helped her up onto her one good foot. "Can you put *any* weight on the twisted ankle?"

Sydney tried, but fell back in a spasm of pain. Willoughby was barely able to catch her. He eased her back down into a sitting position. "Well, I guess we're not walking home. Of course, it's a pretty long walk from Peru anyway, and I'm not sure they've invented the automobile yet. "

Sydney sucked in a breath, fighting the pain. "They were speaking a pre-Aztec dialect. I guessed these were the Andes. By the way, that was a neat little trick back there. How did you do it?"

"Do what?"

"You transported almost twenty yards without a gateway."

"Ah," Willoughby shrugged. "I improvised."

Sydney shook her head, impressed. "Can you get us out of here?"

"I don't know. I'll try. Any sign of O'Grady? We'll have to find him before we leave."

Sydney dropped her head. "When I first got here, I glimpsed him just disappearing over a ridge. I followed the fresh tracks. It took ages, but I finally reached the spot where he had been standing. He was gone. The tracks led up to a sharp cliff. I carefully made my way down and scoured the ice and rock below, but there was no body or blood. Weird, huh? I thought maybe a giant condor had snatched him or something. I decided to go back and try to wait for you, but the sun was going down. I knew the mountain would get cold fast. I'd glimpsed an ice cave while searching for O'Grady, so I went back there. It was a lonely, terrifying night."

Sydney wiped her eyes again, fighting back more tears. Willoughby breathed a heavy sigh. "Yeah, I hear you. It was a rather long night for me too. I don't think I would have made it through, except for my, my father. He pulled me into a heated junction."

"A *what?*"

Willoughby shook his head. "A junction of time streams…" His voice faded away, as if to other thoughts. He gave his head a sudden shake. "Anyway, he gave me the real crystal computer that H.S. wanted us to find." He reached into his pocket and pulled out the crystal, running a finger over it. Sydney's eyes widened.

"That's the crystal computer and it was given to you by your *father?* I thought he was in France with *Nostradamus.*"

Willoughby exhaled sharply. "He is. Well, was… It's a long story. Right now, I think we need to find a way out of here."

Sydney didn't want to let the topic go. "You haven't seen your real father for years. What was he like?"

Willoughby hesitated. "He wasn't what I expected. He was, uh, he was cool—the kind of father you hope for, only…older. Are you able to walk?"

"I want to hear more about your father. Promise me you'll tell me when we're safe?"

Willoughby nodded.

She sighed; "Okay. First, I need to drop by the ice cave. I left my violin there. I don't know if I can put weight on this ankle or not."

"Is it far?"

Sydney considered. "I don't think so. I think it's only a few hundred yards in that direction." She pointed to a path of trodden snow angling down steeply toward the ice bridge he had seen earlier. Willoughby sucked in a deep breath, pocketed his computer, bent, and scooped her into his arms.

"Your chariot, *Madame,*" he said, staggering to maintain balance on the snow. Sydney wrapped her arms tight around his neck, wincing slightly from the swift movement. He started forward, cutting a rather hap-hazard trail into the snow. His breath came sharp and ragged. Carrying Sydney intensified the challenge of navigating through knee-high powder in thin, high altitude air.

"I'm not *that* heavy," Sydney complained.

"It's the combination," Willoughby huffed; "this snow comes pretty high up." He gritted his teeth and pushed on, pausing every few steps to catch his breath." Maybe I should just go get the violin myself and be right back."

"Right... What if you slip and fall and knock yourself out, leaving me to crawl after you until I'm a frozen hood ornament? If I'm going to freeze, I'd rather it be with someone and not alone."

"*Someone* or just *anyone?*"

Sydney smirked. "You'll do. Please, let me down. While I appreciate the sentiment, I think I'll do better hobbling. Do you mind if I lean on you?"

"You can lean on me anytime—but let's take a short rest first." He let her down easily onto the snow and sat beside her. They were quiet for a few moments and then he looked over at her. "Here's a question—have you ever heard of a place called *Arton?*"

"Arton?"

"Yeah." Willoughby flexed and stretched his arms. "Nostradamus refers to it in one of his quatrains. The book I was reading said the word was sometimes used by alchemists to refer to the city of Atlantis."

"*Atlantis?* That seems a bit out of the blue. What does the quatrain say?"

"I don't remember all of it. Something like a phalange would go by sea from Arton. *Phalanges* are bones in the finger or toe."

"I know what phalanges are, thank you," Sydney said. "Go by sea to do what?"

Willoughby leaned back onto the snow, racking his brain. "No good," he finally sighed. "I can't remember. But I did earmark the page. I thought it might mean something."

Sydney narrowed her eyes. "The *Absconditus* was designed for arctic exploration. One of the popular theories about Atlantis is that it's buried under tons of ice on the continent we call Antarctica. Some scientists have suggested that the crust of the earth shifted a couple of thousand years ago. When it did, it caused the ice cap to slip down to a more temperate climate. They speculate that this could have been the cause of the great flood. At the same time, a more temperate land mass, Antarctica, shifted to the polar region where it became nothing more than a barren land of ice. H.S. had the *Absconditus* built because he believed he would find a prime hole there."

"Wait, I remember reading something about this— the Einstein-Hapgood papers!"

"What?" Sydney rolled to her side, careful to couch her bad ankle on a fresh cushion of snow.

Willoughby sat back up. "It's kind of crazy, but there's a lot of supporting evidence. Even Einstein got involved, claiming that such a shift was possible. Legends from Japan and India tell of a lost island that was hidden by the sea and became a frozen waste. There's also a map, drawn by a monk named Kircher. He claimed that it was a map he copied from the Library of Alexandria, a map of the continent of Atlantis. The land mass the map outlines almost perfectly, matches the shape of the island below the ice that we call Antarctica."

"You know a lot about this," Sydney commented, pushing up onto one elbow.

"I like puzzles." Willoughby grinned. "The most recognized theory about *Atlantis* is that it was a volcanic island near Crete—one that exploded, bringing an end to Minoan culture. The Minoans always seemed a bit lackluster to me, though, when compared with Greek descriptions of Atlantis."

Sydney cocked an eyebrow. "Okay, but what does any of this have to do with getting us off of this frozen mountain?"

Willoughby straightened. "I don't know—maybe nothing." He fidgeted a moment, unsure of what else to say, and then leaned over to have a closer look at Sydney's ankle. "It's pretty swollen," he said, pushing to his feet. "We need to get you someplace safe so we can cut that boot away."

Sydney winced as she pushed to a sitting position. "Yeah," she said. "Help me up. We're almost to the packed path."

Willoughby locked an arm around her waist. "I'll still have to lift you every other step," he said. "There's no way you'll be able to kick through this snow with one foot."

"Watch me," she countered, her face determined. She pulled on his shoulder, and with a hopping motion, kicked into the snow. To Willoughby's relief, they hit the well-packed path quickly and Sydney was able to hobble with more grace, though she still winced with almost every step. He tried to think of silly things to distract her, but ended up speaking to himself a good share of the time. When Sydney did answer, her responses were short—spat out between quick breaths and clenched teeth.

The path continued level for a while and then dipped below a high snow crest. He helped Sydney navigate the slippery slope into a steep gully. Half-guiding, half-carrying Sydney, he finally got her to the glistening ice bridge at the bottom of the gully. She pointed to a dark crevice. "The violin is in there," she said, panting. Willoughby eased her into a sitting position, taking care to elevate her foot. He then made his way to the crevice. Sydney's backpack had been dumped onto the ice to create a sort of cozy nest.

He decided to leave everything except the violin—it was all replaceable. If he could use the computer to find a big enough time hole, he was convinced he could get them off of this frozen waste to one of the observation decks. He had memorized the signature of every operational deck during his training, and H.S. had also told him that there would still be a trace connection linking him with the Jurassic-era deck he had actually visited. He just had to find a time hole big enough.

Crawling out of the crevice, he made his way back to Sydney and placed the violin beside her. He dropped to her side.

"The stuff in the packs is replaceable. I'll just take my crystal computer."

Sydney flushed. "You mean, and the violin, of course. Willoughby, I'm not leaving the violin behind. This instrument and I have been through a lot together. It's an original Stradivarius, very old and—and very much *a friend*. It would be like leaving behind a part of me."

Willoughby sighed. "I thought you would say that." He looked out over the blinding white terrain. Judging from the sun, he guessed it was fast approaching mid-day.

"Didn't you say you stayed somewhere near where O'Grady disappeared?"

Sydney nodded and pointed to a drop-off just beyond the other end of the ice bridge. "The cliff is just over that ridge. Be careful. It comes up quickly, and the edge is slippery. His tracks went right over the side."

Willoughby took the crystal computer from its pouch and held it at eye level. Numbers appeared in a wild array. Out of the corner of his eye, he glimpsed Sydney's astonishment. *She could see them!* The numbers were in short strings that winked and swam, then disappeared as new strings became visible, some very bright.

"Do you see the floating number strings?"

"Yeah," she said, "four or five of them. They're very dim." He considered this for a long moment before putting the computer down. She wasn't seeing near what he saw, but she *was* seeing something.

"There's some kind of disturbance in that direction, but no sign of O'Grady—at least, none that I can see. I'll need to get closer." He jumped to his feet. "I'll be back." Before she had a chance to protest, he stepped over her and carefully navigated the length of the bridge. He climbed the far snow ridge and began scanning the area. It didn't take him long to find what he was looking for. Grinning from ear to ear, he headed back over the ridge toward Sydney.

"It's a huge hole! That's why O'Grady disappeared. He found the hole! It's hovering in the air about half way down the cliff. That's why you found no trace of him. He jumped off the cliff into the time hole. Mapping time-holes was his specialty, wasn't it? He was supposed to help us find an alternate hole if we somehow got into trouble. Maybe he thought you and I didn't make it out of the underwater facility. I wonder how he expects to find an Observation Deck, though, without a computer."

Sydney's eyes narrowed. "He must be pretty good. I know he's been to several of the decks, some of them more than once. Maybe he's memorized some of the signatures. Look how fast he found this hole. When we were talking once, he told me he had charted more than 100 natural holes worldwide, some no bigger than a pin-prick, some large enough to swallow an army. Maybe he recognized this mountain and knew right where the hole was."

"That's the strange part," Willoughby said. "He told me he used star charts to locate holes, but it clouded over last night and snowed. This hole wouldn't have been easy to find at night. Like I said, it's located about half-way down the wall of the cliff. We'll have to jump."

"*Jump?* You expect me to jump from a five-hundred foot cliff?"

"We'll only fall about eighty feet or so before we hit the hole. The trick is to clear the edge of the cliff safely so we're angled right."

"*You're crazy!*"

"Well, we could wait around until we freeze to death—or until your buddies return with reinforcements."

"Willoughby, I—I *can't* jump! Look at my ankle. I'm no good with heights."

Willoughby noted her ashen face. She was terrified.

"Okay," he said. "I'll carry you on my back—we'll jump together. Let me grab some of the clothes from your pack. I'll grab an extra belt so you can strap the violin to your back. Then, we'll make a path with the clothes to make sure we don't slip and to guide us to the edge."

Sydney gulped a huge breath of air and nodded her head. "I must be insane."

He grabbed the things from Sydney's pack and then helped her to her feet. As they worked their way over the ice bridge and toward the cliff, Sydney turned to him. "Why do I get the feeling I should compose a requiem before we jump?"

"I'd prefer a knee slapping victory dance."

She forced a grin. "Tell me with a straight face that you *don't* have concerns about this? You'll have an extra hundred pounds on your back and only one chance to leap from an ice cliff and hit a hole that's what—ten feet wide? What if you slip? And what's to say this hole will even work? It's not like people are just disappearing all the time because they walked into some invisible time hole. At the observation decks, there's a ton of high-tech gear behind our jump into the time-stream. This is just some invisible hole that you think might be strong enough to suck us in if we hit it right."

Willoughby ignored the comment and helped Sydney up the other side of the narrow gorge, up to the top of a winding snow ridge, and over a slight embankment. They were facing the cliff straight on now. He took the clothes he had pulled from Sydney's pack and the crystal computer and busied himself stretching the clothes into a kind of runway that led right up to the edge of the cliff. He packed down the snow beneath them and make sure they lay perfectly flat so that there would be no chance of tripping. The truth was that he was terrified. If he looked too long over the cliff, he knew he would never jump. But it had to be done, so he kept himself busy and only looked down enough to judge, using the computer, where the center of the hole was. When everything was ready, he trotted back over to Sydney.

"Okay, maybe a requiem is a good idea, but keep it short, okay? We need dry eyes to find the jump point. By the way, the hole is only about six feet wide." He paused and then gave her a wry smile. "I don't plan to slip, but just for the record, if I do, I can't think of anyone I'd rather plunge to my death with."

"Willoughby!" Sydney said. "We don't have to do this."

"Actually," Willoughby said, "I think we do. We aren't prepared for this kind of terrain. We can't walk far enough or fast enough with your ankle to get off this frozen mountain before we either fall into a crevice or freeze to death, and I would be surprised if it takes long for the natives to regroup and be back with a bigger welcome party. On the flip side, Dr. O'Grady jumped and he's one of the most skittish, nervous guys I've ever met. He seemed to make it okay. Also, people seldom get jerked into time holes from their natural time because we have a certain attraction or cohesion with our natural time. It takes a lot to jerk us out of that. Here, however, we are not in our natural time. Thus, a much smaller pull can displace us. Lastly, I'm learning to trust my senses. You see a fraction of what I see when I pull out the crystal computer— sometimes, I don't even need the computer. There are equations everywhere, but somehow, I know, I recognize the ones that I need. I feel that way about the hole over the cliff. I don't know if this makes you feel better but this is how I see it."

Sydney was quiet, considering the words. Finally, she said. "Let's skip the requiem."

Willoughby smiled. "Okay," he said, helping her up. "Climb on. We'll practice running over the path and make sure this is going to work."

Sydney slung her violin onto her back and let Willoughby heft her piggy-back style. They made a trial pass along the far end of the runway, taking time to make sure every inch of the path was well packed and stable. Finally, Willoughby stopped. "We'll need more speed, but I'm not going to worry about that now," he said. "I don't want to run to the very edge of the cliff. It could crumble from the weight of both of us. I think we should leap about eighteen inches from the edge. I used that spindly red-heel thing to mark the point."

Sydney thumped him on the shoulder. "I'll have you know that your *spindly red-heel thing* is a $200 pair of Guccis!" She broke into a whimper. "They looked stunning with my $2600 Donna Karan gown!"

"Oh, you mean the black and maroon thing?" Willoughby pointed. "I put it there—it covers a surprising amount of ice. By the way, what were you going to do with that in medieval France?" Willoughby turned as began walking slowly back toward the beginning of the runway.

Sydney sighed. "I know, it was stupid, but you didn't see what H.S. had me wearing on this assignment! He had me dressed like a street urchin! I couldn't dare go without bringing at least one real outfit—even if I only wore it at night, to sleep in. And you never know how things will turn out. Street urchin clothes don't make very good ice-cliff runways... "

Willoughby took a deep breath and began down the runway again, going faster this time. On the third stride, he tripped, careening face-first into a bank of snow. He came up sputtering, rolling Sydney gently off him. After an initial bark of pain, she broke into giggles and then hysterical laughter. Willoughby was still trying to get himself untangled from her, wiping the snow from his face.

"What's so funny?"

"I'm going to die," she said. "I'm going to die playing horsey with my boyfriend on an ice cliff!"

Willoughby fought a grin. He liked the sound of that—*boyfriend*. "You are not going to die. *We* are going to get up and try again, and we're going to keep trying until we get it right."

Sydney stopped laughing. "Killjoy," she said and gave a loud sigh. Willoughby started to rise, but she pulled him back down. "Wait a minute," she said. She pulled him toward her. "I think you need some, some motivation." She pulled him closer and kissed him.

The kiss was long, and slow, and very different from the one on the submersible. Blood rushed in his veins. He pulled away feeling stronger, more confident, and more determined. He pushed to his feet, helped her up and onto his back again, gripped the crystal computer, and went back to the start of the runway. He set off at a trot and rapidly picked up speed. He felt adrenaline surging through him. *This was it*—he knew it! This would be the jump!

"We're not stopping!" he yelled over his shoulder. Sydney squeezed his neck so tight that he could barely breathe. He leaped off the cliff.

For a moment, there was only the sickening, sinking feeling that comes with falling into a sudden, unchecked plunge. Willoughby gritted his teeth, forcing himself to concentrate on the readout from the crystal computer. Number strings swirled about, twisting around them like an odd funnel. Suddenly, there was a chest-crushing jerk. The white world around them winked out.

26

The Witch's Throne

James Arthur tasted blood and recognized, with surprise, that he had been biting his own lip. The underbelly of Petra wasn't really to his liking. Narrow, cramped passages twisted chaotically, intersecting dozens of other similarly cramped spaces. Even climbing through the air ducts on the *Absconditus*, he hadn't felt as hemmed-in. With Al-Jerusha's breathing on his back and the rank sweat of the guard ahead, he had to breathe through his mouth to keep from recoiling from the tunnel's pungent odors. Solid rock pressed in on him from all sides, sometimes less than a few inches away, and the passages seemed to get progressively smaller with each turn. His shoulders ached, his calves burned from stooping, and the blended smells of sweat, stale dust, and torch smoke, made his eyes water and his stomach churn. He struggled to find a way to get his mind off the pain and nausea.

He thought back on his days before joining Observations, Inc. In hindsight, his life had been pretty carefree. He had grown up only blocks from California's famed Malibu beach, where he spent many sunny mornings with his surf board, the dolphins, and the waves. He closed his eyes to savor the memory. So why had he accepted H.S.'s offer to come work for this crazy, clandestine organization? Maybe it was the dream that life could be a grand adventure day after day, or the thought that facing unknown challenges could give him tools to make the world a better place. Of course, there was also New Orleans. The girl with the blackened eyes had somehow inspired in him a desire to heal, to press beyond the bounds of what is known and come face to face with the unknown. *Or did it go deeper than that?* There was no getting around the fact that he had sensed in Observations, Inc. a chance to come to terms, once and for all, with who he was and why *he* had been singled out by the girl with the scarred face. He had sometimes imagined she was a witch.

Caught up in his thoughts, he stumbled, falling heavily into the guard a few feet ahead of him. The guard spun, ready to pounce, but Al-Jerusha skillfully calmed him, redirecting his attentions to a coming bend in the tunnel. The *Thief of the Desert* had an uncanny ability for navigating in the underground maze. He relayed instructions with calm confidence, often cautioning James Arthur about coming obstructions or guiding him around hair-pin turns when the torchlight was momentarily lost.

"You seem to know these tunnels well," James Arthur mumbled when the passages widened. "Did you and your men dig them?"

Al-Jerusha barked a short laugh. "You are funny, James Arthur—clumsy, but funny! We are in the catacomb passages. They wind in and out of hundreds of tombs that have been carved into the hills. The Nabeateans were fond of caring for their dead. A worker would always stay inside the tomb after it was walled up to help the deceased ancestor find its way home. After all rites had been completed, the worker needed a way to escape from the world of the dead, hence the secret passages."

"Huh." Dr. J considered. "Secret passages come in pretty handy for thieves, too," he muttered.

Al-Jerusha laughed again. "Precisely."

Around another slight turn, the ceiling lifted, leading into a widened area where six passages came together. James Arthur sighed with relief at being able to straighten to his full height. He put as much space as possible between himself and his companions. He breathed in deeply.

"Why do we have to cram so close in those passages? I thought I was going to suffocate."

Al-Jerusha had taken one of the torches and was inspecting the side walls of each of the passage entrances. He turned.

"We've tried leaving more space between us before, but we always seem to lose one or two men. There will be a scream, a torch will go out, and the man has vanished. Only once did we hear the scream and have a man return to us. He claimed the passage wall opened and the bone-arm of a dead man grabbed at his throat." The thief turned, matter-of-factly, back to his inspection of the passage walls. James Arthur stared after him, forcing a grin.

"Ah, mummies... You don't really believe that, do you? Dead men are dead. They don't walk through secret passages in the walls."

Al-Jerusha looked at him and gave a small dip of the head. "You are the best chance I have found for dealing with this witch, James Arthur, and I don't intend to let you feed the dead in some dark passage." He swung the torch around and pointed to a symbol chiseled on the inside wall of the smallest of the passages. He said something to one of his guards in his own tongue. The guard took back his torch and bent low, starting into the passage. Al-Jerusha looked back.

"Son-of-the-future?" he motioned, pointing toward Dr. J.

James Arthur faked a short laugh. "It figures that you'd pick the smallest tunnel." As he crouched and waddled into the passage, he saw the symbol Al-Jerusha had been looking at up close. It was the symbol of the Beelzebub...

After what seemed an agonizing hour, the passage opened into a wide, high arena. As Dr. J stretched, trying to untangle his tensed muscles, he recognized the arena. He had looked down on when he exited the tomb-like cavern the time-door had deposited him in. A semi-circle of tiered levels rose almost to the cavern's ceiling along its back and sides, and the huge, carved head of a striking cobra overshadowed the smooth face of the front wall. What had looked from high above like a circular stage was actually an odd, circular floor, made of a glass-like substance. What had appeared to be twelve carved cobras surrounding the glass circle were really chess pieces, with carved giant snakes wound tightly around them. Across the glassy floor, James Arthur could make out the squares of a chess board.

A hiss started from the top tier of the arena, issuing out of the dark alcoves that dotted each tier. It was followed by a rattling that sounded like bones. The sound spread quickly down until it reached the arena itself. A rush of wind brushed James Arthur's cheek, even though he saw nothing that could have caused it. A shoulder-high chess piece near him sputtered. Blue flame poured from the mouth of the stone cobra that wound itself up the length of what appeared to be a queen, her crown prominent upon her stately head. The rest of the odd carvings flared to life, one after the other. James Arthur could now see that each represented a different style of queen, bound by a giant carved cobra whose hooded head towered over the queen's stone crown. The rattle and hiss reached a deafening climax.

"Stay close, James Arthur," Al-Jerusha whispered. One of his guards shouted and pointed.

In the dark alcove, beneath the head of the cave wall cobra, hundreds of weaving eyes reflected the glow of the blue fire pillars. A great hissing issued out from the eyes as all other sounds faded. Golden fire burst up from two flat bowls to either side of the fanged cobra, freezing the weaving eyes in place. The fires settled into low, bright glows, and James Arthur saw that the eyes were actually part of an elaborate throne. The throne was enormous, and seemed to be made of the twisted bodies of hundreds of snakes. The snakes appeared to be carved of stone, but their eyes glistened, as if precious jewels. The Desert Witch sat placidly on the throne. She absently caressed the head of one of the stone snakes.

"Stay where you are, *desert thief*—and keep your thug with you. I will deal with you later. Now, *son-of-the-future*—approach."

James Arthur looked to Al-Jerusha, who motioned him forward. He looked back at the witch and took a step toward the strange throne. "I'll give her this," he mumbled to no-one in particular, "she knows how to make an entrance."

27

Haubus and Hannuktu

Walls of solid number wove around Willoughby as he desperately tried to find something he recognized. "*They're whirling by too fast!*" he wanted to shout, but there was no speaking in the time hole. He felt a surge of panic—he couldn't recognize any of the number strings. Then one sequence of numbers flared, pulling at him as if by some invisible connection. He threw a hand up as the sequence whipped by. The second his hand came in contact with it, the numbers winked brighter as he felt a sudden jerk sideways. Sydney gave a slight gasp as she let go of his neck and the two crashed against hard stone.

Sydney hit on her shoulder, landing half on top of Willoughby. Luckily, he had been turned enough to cushion her bad ankle, but her good leg was tangled in his. He had also been trying to protect the still glowing crystal, which had taken the brunt of the impact with his hip and arm, sparing his bad shoulder somewhat. The collision with the stone surface still hurt, though, and it had knocked the wind out of him. He struggled to push Sydney away gently, gasping for breath. She sat, reaching down to nurse her ankle. They were both dizzy and disoriented.

"Well," Sydney said, finally catching her breath. "That was—*painful. B*ut, hey, we're alive. I think we—"

Her voice stopped in mid-sentence. Willoughby tried to turn toward her, but something cold and round pushed up against his skull.

"Well, well—full of surprises, are we?" a raspy voice whispered; "Very impressive, lad."

There was a sound of struggle in the dimness and Sydney jerked free. "*Let me breathe!*" she hissed. The pistol at Willoughby's head drilled into him and there was a sound of a click. "Keep the voice down, Missy," the harsh whisper threatened. "One more sound from you, and I'm afraid your friend here will be quite dead. Lucky for you, there's a heated debate in the works, or you might have given us away already."

Willoughby had finally recovered enough breath to speak, though his voice was barely audible. "O'Grady?"

The dark shape didn't answer. It ripped Sydney's violin from her as she attempted to slip it from her shoulder. The violin was pushed behind them, safely out of reach. Willoughby tried to casually put the crystal computer back into his pocket. The man with the gun snatched it from him and held it up, trying to study it in the dim light. "Well, now—looks like the two of you have been busy. You found the crystal. *Where did you find it, lad?* Tell me softly," the voice rasped.

"I met an old man," Willoughby replied. The words stuck in his throat. "I think it was Nostradamus."

Other voices faded up from below. Willoughby craned his head toward them as his eyes adjusted. He had already caught a glimpse of the fuzzy barrier behind them. The strange phosphorescent gases looked just as he remembered them from his first visit here—from the day he had been recruited. The last time he had been in this dim corridor, he had been frightened, confused as to how he got here, and concerned at what he had gotten himself into. While some things were very different, others were not. He felt again the lump of fear in his stomach and the sense of confusion at the turn of events. The rock corridor extended about fifty feet before turning in a sharp bend. A dim light filtered around the bend.

"Well, I underestimated you," the dark shape said dryly. "You've proved quite resourceful. I might find...Ah—*what am I thinking?* I've no time for extra baggage. You are right, lad. Say hello to good old bumbling Dr. O'Grady, who's not quite the skittish fool he's pretended to be."

Willoughby tried to get his mind around the idea that O'Grady was not who he seemed. *Was he some sort of traitor—was he the inside spy?* "It was you. You were behind the hijacking. That's why they didn't put you with James Arthur and Antonio."

The gun pressed against his skull. "You stop right there," he snarled in a whisper. After a moment of quiet, he continued. "I had no part of the killing and the hijacking. I was looking for the crystal. I planned to find it first, and then lose ya, but events pushed my hand. I faked my panic in the submersible, thinking you might leave me somewhere to recuperate so I could slip away. Ya didn't, but a little premature panic at the sight of an approaching sub obliged me nicely. I gambled that neither of you knew the nature of a real time junction. Without a tethered fix in a timeline, the facility was like a floating cork. Events could push it about a bit, but there was nothing for real matter to connect with. We were all perfectly safe all along."

"No."

"What are you saying, lad?" The pistol was pushed so tight against his skull that it hurt.

"The facility imploded—I only just made it to the time hole," Willoughby managed, keeping his whisper barely audible. "One second more and I'd have gone with it."

The man panted softly. "Huh... That shouldn't have happened. It's going wrong. It's all going wrong..." He blew out a breath. "I'm not sayin' I believe ya, lad, but there are peculiarities. Something has been stalking us for some time. Things aren't as they should be." He sucked in another breath. "Perhaps I won't kill ya, then. Perhaps you'll be useful... "

A voice flared from below. There was a gasp and then another voice. "No—you must listen to me, *senorita!* This is not the way. If you wish for me to believe your story, you must loosen the knife from his throat. You must let me hear his side too, my friend."

Willoughby jerked his head. *It was Antonio's voice.* A louder voice sputtered and coughed. "Whether you believe it or not, I am who I say I am, Tainken Keilhar. My name is Hannuktu Shantdka!" The voice lowered considerably. Willoughby could only catch snatches, but he was sure the voice belonged to H.S. "...Third Seat, Minister of Science, on the council. I can prove it. The night after mid-solstice feast—and then, I came to see you and your brother. You were nine and he was barely eleven. I brought a present for each of you—intricate. Yours was a mechanical sea creature."

"A silver and gold dolphin," replied a girl. *It was the voice of T.K.!*

A longer pause and then the voices became too muted to make out. Willoughby glanced over at Sydney, his eyes wide. The man behind them shifted position. Sydney's soft whisper broke the silence.

"I came looking for you. I followed your tracks to the cliff. I thought you were dead."

"As ye can see, I'm not," The man hissed back, curtly. "Just the blundering doctor is dead. The wretched O'Grady was created for me academic life, for me cloak and me cover. I'm finally free of him! I can speak my real name again—and I can speak it with pride, knowin' that the great Elder, Hannuktu Shantdka, has been mistaken for me, Haubus Socees!" He chuckled softly to himself.

Willoughby was trying to listen, but he wasn't following much of this. It was like tumbling out of the rabbit hole into Wonderland. "Who is Haubus So—"

"Socees." The man with the gun completed, keeping his raspy hiss low and close. "It's a long story, lad—one I have no intentions of tellin' ya. Suffice it to say, I don't belong to your century, and neither do H.S. or the girl T.K. You hear them both down there, squabbling, right now? Well, she would be the Princess Tainken Kielhar, Princess of the blue eyes! I recognized her the moment I stepped aboard the *Absconditus*. I must admit, I thought *she* was behind the hijacking. The other is the mighty Elder of the blue eyes, Hannuktu. The man you call *H.S.* is, in fact, a distant relative of mine. He would have recognized her too had he been more observant, had he been less interested in savin' the world. Aye, that'd be why he failed to recognize me as well."

"*Princess? Elder?*" Sydney whispered.

The conversation from downstairs became audible again. "Then tell me—*why?* Why is Belzarac here?"

Haubus pushed to his feet lightning fast. He clipped Willoughby with a sharp blow from the butt of his gun, watching him drop like a rag doll onto the cold, stone floor. H.S.'s voice also seemed to pounce on this news.

"*Belzarac is here?*"

***

Things were happening too fast. Sydney stared at Willoughby, crumpled on the cave floor, in horror. The man calling himself *Haubus* now swung his gun quickly, pointing the barrel at her face. Seeing her tense, he smiled. He gave Willoughby a sharp kick. "Not dead," he mouthed. "At least, not yet…" He bent down to whisper in her ear. "Now, lass—you stay here, and you stay quiet, and I might let him live. Do I make myself clear?" Haubus pulled a rag from his pocket, poking the pistol into his waist. He forced the rag into Sydney's mouth, tying it tight. Pulling her arms behind her back, despite her struggles, he bound her wrists with a thin cord. The voices below became audible again.

The clear, accented voice of H.S. bellowed loudly, "I don't know him! At least, I did not know him well. I never met him. I only knew of him. I knew he was a ring-leader of the unfortunates who were not pure bloods. The last communication I received suspected him in the murder of your father. Part of our city had sunk into the sea. The holes were becoming sporadic and difficult to travel. Then, the natural holes to *Aert Olaneas Tis* stopped functioning altogether. In the blink of an eye, the city was gone. As history subtly changed, a myth was born—the story of Atlantis. At that moment, I knew they had gone too far. I have spent my life trying to heal time, to undo the damage."

"Why were you exiled, then? You were away. You visited rarely. I heard Father say you were old, as old as my grandfather."

The voice of H.S. remained steady and surprisingly audible.

"I knew the original travelers, Tainken. I was born shortly after they arrived on this planet. My parents were two of its highest ranking members—my mother, a geneticist, and my father, a respected physicist with interest in the emergence of ancient culture and its affect on the interstellar time continuum. I saw people come and go between Earth and our home world—I saw the original door working.

"My father and I were not banished from *Aert Olaneas Tis*. We chose to distance ourselves from your city. My father believed that a time of chaos from our home world poisoned our time-stream and that the safeguards built into the time door shut down the connection to protect this world and its timeline. He worried that if the council were ever successful in re-establishing the time door link, it would only spread the destruction that engulfed our home world.

"I chose to stay with my Father even though my mother and sister did not. My mother felt the family could be a voice of reason on the council. My father and I visited the city when she was still alive. When she died suddenly of an Earth disease, only I continued to go back to visit my sister and inform the council of our work and concerns. When my father also died, I chose to continue his work. My sister held our family view that continuing the work to re-establish the time door would only bring disaster to our people, a view that was proven correct when the city was destroyed. She argued that *Aert Olaneas Tis* had become part of a time period and should adopt *its* technologies and ways. She married a Greek merchant and minor philosopher. They had a son, Haubus Soceess... "

At this, Sydney saw the silhouette of Haubus stiffen in the dim light. He edged a few steps farther down the rock corridor.

The voice of T.K. was still skeptical. "Antonio told me you are still trying to find this prime-hole. *Why?*"

H.S. gave a heavy sigh, as if the words he now spoke caused him pain.

"I want to find it, T.K., to make sure the time door your city rebuilt is destroyed. I have reason to believe there are others who somehow know of its existence—who, even now, search to find it. I believe that is why we have been targeted and infiltrated, why the *Absconditus* was hijacked. You can't image what could happen if that technology were found and perfected by the wrong hands."

Sydney heard only a shuffling, as if players were repositioning themselves on a court. Then, H.S. spoke again.

"You accused me of being Haubus a few minutes ago, and you asked if I murdered your father. Why did you say that? What has Haubus to do with the death of your father?"

There was a long pause and then T.K. spoke, though only parts of what she said were audible.

"...brother believed they were working together... I saw him, coming out of the room shortly before, before my father was found."

"Where is your brother?"

Haubus seemed to have had enough of the conversation. He turned moved further down the corridor, quiet as a cat.

Sydney waited until he was out of sight and then scooted along the rock floor toward Willoughby. Shouts and commotion broke out suddenly below. At first, she thought someone may have heard her moving. She froze. Next, she thought the man they had known as O'Grady must have stepped into the open, but she heard a new, gruffer voice. H.S. cried out in stunned surprise. "*Who are you? How did you get in here?*" As she strained to hear, she saw the dark form of Haubus ease back into sight, hovering a few feet from the bend in the tunnel.

"Well, well," the gravelly voice boomed from the room below, "Bats in the belfry, have we? I hate to break up this touching reunion, but seems I have finally caught my ghost...Don't try anything Haubus."

"*Haubus?*" H.S. yelled indignantly

T.K. cried out. "Put that thing down, Belzarac. He's telling the truth. He's not Haubus. He's HannuktuShantdka, Haubus' uncle."

Belzarac chuckled. "Yes, and I'm the penguin from Mary Poppins ...didn't pin you as one so gullible, Princess, but then you were a might young when you left our fair city."

"Ah, so you are the troublesome Belzarac," H.S. began. "I—"

"Stop, Haubus! I'm not listening to your babble this time. Your fancy words cost me a good bit of my life. Stay put and shut up until I decide what to do with you. That goes for you too, Antonio. You were pretty quiet through that whole load of rubbish about infections. Perhaps it's because you realize, as do I, that the one infection in this world's timeline is right in front of us—Mr. Haubus Socees... Now, let's all get nice and cozy. We've got a bit of business to conclude Socees. You be real good and Reiss, here, might not have to bloody his hands. Not yet, anyway. Why, only hours ago, he was an upstanding member of your fine ship's crew."

A deep, rumbling chuckle underscored the man's measured words. The chuckle eased into silence. A new voice sounded over the silence, *"Miss me T.K.?"*

"Charmed, I'm sure," the gravelly voice of Belzarac went on. "Reiss hasn't been able to keep his mind off of you, Princess. He spent all those nights in the brig thinking about what he would do to the captain's little pet when he had the chance. I'd advise you to run back to your cave as soon as you have the chance. The beasties out there may be quite a bit tamer than my Reiss... " There was another low chuckle. "Oh, and in case you don't know, these spear guns are lethal for a two ton shark. Imagine the hole they would leave in a pretty, young thing like you, or for that matter, to a scrawny pretzel like you, Antonio. Why, this here pin-shooter would even pierce the hide of a fat pig like you, Haubus." There was a pause and then the voice added, "Hoped you were rid of me didn't you? Oh, no—the good Princess led us right to your door. We heard her voice as soon as we surfaced in the cave. Mind you, it seemed to come from behind solid rock. But the cave wasn't quite hospitable, as you well know, so we investigated. You would build a technological castle in your cave, eh, Haubus? Why of course. It makes perfect sense. You sit here in this fine room, all toasty and safe, while you let others die in your companion cave, in your own secret torture chamber. That sounds like you. Only, I didn't die, Haubus. T.K. didn't die. Now, we're all back together again. What do you make of that?"

There was a pause. The other new voice spoke. "Good of you to leave the light on and the back door open for us, T.K. And what a nice gift—spear guns hanging right on the wall for us when we climbed through…"

"Why do you believe I am Haubus?" H.S. spat. "There was never any great resemblance."

The man laughed. "Sure, you've masked yourself well. I must admit, you had me going for a while. You have more weight and less hair—but then it has been what, fifty years? And all that time, while I've been aging far too slowly in this time, I've had time to think of what I know of Haubus Socees. He has a very peculiar trait, one that's very distinctive. He always, *always,* turns his teacup exactly one-quarter turn when he's setting down his tea. I asked him about it once. He said it was a tradition, handed down from his rightful family. I've watched you drink your tea more than once, H.S… "

"Of course he knows tea etiquette!" H.S. shouted. "For heaven's sake, Haubus is my sister's son. Did you ever visit him at his home? You would have learned that most blue-eye pure bloods have strict tea etiquette. It's a tradition handed down among our people. You were never taught that as a boy? You are half Atlantian, are you not?"

"I am my own person," Belzarac spat. "I never claimed allegiance to your lot."

H.S. boomed a reply. "No, you just stormed my ship and slaughtered my innocent crew."

The gravelly voice of Belzarac chuckled. "Well, I would say we have different opinions as to what constitutes *innocent*, old friend. Now, why would an uncle of Haubus be here in some far future time—the same time I followed the real Haubus to, mind you—building up his time-travel empire, the same empire he used to fill my head with dreams of untold wealth and treasure. I risked my life to help you steal that technology, and here you are, living the life of luxury in your secret organization while I scrape through barely able to pay the rent. Sort of pulls at the heart strings, doesn't it?" The question hung in the air and then the low voice grumbled, "Tie 'em up Reiss."

The silhouette of O'Grady, or Haubus held his gun high in the dim corridor. Sydney watched him make his way back around the bend, out of sight. As soon as he had been gone for a full minute, she scooted the rest of the way over to Willoughby and nudged him. His eyes opened slowly. He pushed a finger to his lips. He sat, wincing somewhat as he moved his head. He leaned toward her. "Good thing it's dark in here," he whispered, rubbing the bump already rising where O'Grady clipped him. "He sort of just grazed me, but it was still painful, especially the kick. I thought I was going to vomit." He scooted closer. "I haven't caught everything, but it's crazy! O'Grady's real name is Haubus? H.S. has a nephew by that same name? T.K. is a princess?"

Sydney grunted, straining at her gag. Willoughby suddenly noticed it and started to move to untie her. Then, thinking better of it, he held up a hand for silence and crawled stealthily forward to the bend in the tunnel. Sydney gave an irritated moan. One peek around the bend, and Willoughby hurried back. He whispered as he pulled off her gag and untied her.

"*Atlantis?* Time travelers from another world? It's all too much. Did they say *Riess?* Riess was the tattooed guy who was spying on Antonio's shop. I told Antonio I thought I saw him on the *Absconditus.* Come to think of it, he may have referred to this Bellzar or Belzarac guy once too."

Sydney had been spitting silently to the side. She sucked in a deep breath. "Thanks for just leaving me with that foul thing in my mouth!" She tried to keep her voice low despite her irritation.

He ignored her, working to undo the knots that bound her hands.

She calmed herself. "I find the T.K. thing outlandish—a Princess in coveralls, as a cabin girl?"

Willoughby had to bite at the knot, but was finally able to loosen it with his teeth. As he sat back up, he spoke directly into her ear. "O'Grady, or Haubus, or whoever, has stopped about twenty yards away, right at the edge of the stairway. This is the observation deck H.S. originally brought me to, which is probably why I was able to get us here. This entry tunnel widens onto a metal platform a little way around the bend. The platform is about three stories above a large room with an observation window looking out on a Jurassic era sea."

Sydney nodded.

H.S.'s voice boomed again from downstairs. "So what do you want?"

"I want to go home, Haubus," the gravelly voice snapped back. "I want to go back to *my* home, the one *I* never wanted to leave. If you hadn't taken what was rightfully mine—if you hadn't tricked me—I would have never followed you. For the record, I did not kill your crew. Funny thing, but I found a rival organization to yours. They wanted to find you as much as I did. They branded this little tattoo on my neck. It was their leader who insisted on eliminating your crew. I just pretended to look the other way. If I'm not mistaken, you've sent them to the bottom somewhere near the base of the Mid-Atlantic Ridge."

Sydney threw a sudden glance at Willoughby whose eyes had narrowed and lips tightened into a definite frown. "*Their leader?*" Willoughby whispered. "Is he referring to the black brute Gates, who seemed to be in charge on the *Absconditus,* or was he referring to the leader of the cult itself—the man who claimed to be his grandfather?

A sound of slow clapping rang out from the tunnel mouth above the observation floor. Apparently, Haubus—a.k.a. O'Grady—had finally stepped out onto the metal platform. A shout greeted his appearance, followed closely by a loud pop. A spear came whistling into the tunnel as the platform creaked with sudden movement. Two shots were fired from O'Grady's gun. A heavy thud sounded as something fell to the floor. Antonio seemed to be the first to recover.

"Dr., Dr. O'Grady?"

Willoughby finished loosening the bindings on Sydney's legs. She rubbed her sore ankle and wrists while he turned back toward the bend in the tunnel. She saw that Willoughby had already begun to creep forward on hands and knees. He motioned for her to follow.

"I hate to disappoint ya," the man who called himself Haubus said. "You see, O'Grady never really existed." Willoughby peered around the bend just in time to see the man peel off a long sideburn and drop it to the steel floor of the platform. He took off his spectacles and dropped them too. Peeling off the other sideburn, he smiled down. "Now, if I take out the contacts that turn me eyes dark brown instead of deep blue—don't move Belzarac. You've always been quite the coward and a fool. I've been practicin' and, I must say, I'm a good shot..." He blinked the contacts out, one at a time. "If I still had me full head of hair and hadn't lost the young man's physique, well, don't you see now? Still, I find it humorous that I've a *loving* uncle who worked right beside for me for years and never guessed who I might be. Imagine what the council would say, Hannuktu, if they knew you'd been teaching sacred technology to a half-breed. You know the code—section fifteen-twenty-three, or was it twenty-four? That's death, starin' ya right in the face, man!"

"*Haubus!*" A horrified H.S. hissed.

The man started down the staircase, disappearing from Willoughby's view. His voice continued to ring out clearly. "A wee-bit slow on the up-take, but the great Hannuktu will usually get there. Got ourselves quite a reunion going, have we? Tainken Keilhar, Belzarac—seems almost like old times. Ah, but you filled out nicely lass. Barely out of diapers when I saw you last—when was that? I think our friend, Belzarac, said over fifty years, is that right? Yet H.S., you've hardly changed at all—still the same old walrus as ever. We'll have to meet your nutritionist."

Sydney's eyes widened at the implication, suddenly comprehending the comment. She stopped, a few feet from the edge of the metal landing. "*Fifty years?*" she mouthed. As Haubus paused to let the words sink in, she lifted her hand to touch the bleeding gash at the side of Willoughby's head. He flinched. "How bad?" she mouthed. Willoughby waved her off. He still seemed a little nauseous from the kick to the stomach and his head looked like a cold-cut that has been over-tenderized, but he was coherent. He pointed to her ankle, a question in his eyes.

Sydney bit her lip and shrugged. She tried to smile, but it came out as more of a grimace. Willoughby edged forward to the point where the end of the tunnel connected to the metal platform. Sydney pushed silently up beside him. She gave an inaudible shudder as she took in the grandeur of the huge room and the panoramic view. The metal was perforated, giving a limited view of the vast room below. As Sydney quickly scanned the scene, she saw Antonio and T.K. They were standing toward the back of the room, near the lounge area. H.S. was toward the top left corner, near the window. An ugly brute—probably Reiss—was on the floor in a pool of blood, and another man was kneeling on the floor grumbling, a still-loaded spear gun dropped about ten feet away. The man held his hand, which dripped blood. Haubus slowly descended the last flight of the zigzagging stairs.

"Stop your grumblin', Belzarac," Haubus barked, pausing at the foot of the stairs. "You'd have never had to leave had you done the job you were paid for."

T.K. piped up. "Murder my father? Is that the job he was *paid* for?"

Haubus paused, swinging the gun over at T.K. He mimed pulling the trigger and then smiled.

"No. Actually, I rather liked your father, Tainken. Belzarac here was hired to get a key—that's all. Just get a key for me, right Belzarac? I wanted to unlock the chamber where they kept the plans for the time-travel technology. I planned to copy 'em. Then I'd disappear… You see, lass, it occurred to me that someone with this travel ability might be able to amass a small fortune, stealin' antiquities from time itself. Oh, I could be sensitive. I did believe as Hannuktu has said, as me dear mother believed. I felt the council was headin' for ruin. My plan was to leave the fair city, learn to use the technology, then take from time only what would be lost anyway. That was the plan. Then, this bumbler accidentally killed your father."

"*Accidentally?*" T.K. echoed.

"Aye. I've not the stomach for answerin' that one... Answer her, you blubberin' fool!" He shouted at Belzarac, pointing the gun back at him.

Belzerac looked over at T.K. grudgingly. "He did not have the key on him as Haubus said he would. What he did have was a knife, and he went for me. In the scuffle, he, uh, fell. There was no murder involved. But who would have believed me? Who would have believed either of us?"

Haubus gave a nod. "Well, I must agree with that—a known thief and half-breed workin' for another half-breed, it wasn't a pretty picture. I decided the best road was to disappear into the past. Turns out I was quite adept at usin' the technology. I had been slowly learning how to use the hole, buyin' the information bit by bit. My plan was to disappear with Belezarac, then leave him and find me way back. The crime would be laid to his feet, and if he wasn't found, they'd know nothing of me. I had him knock out the guards. The plan might have worked had the cave of horrors not been the first stop in our adventure through time."

The man on his knees began to swear. "You *planned* to leave me? I thought you just got scared of the beasties. I thought you saw one take a nip at my leg, and turned sickly yellow like the coward-dog you are. I, I ought to... "

"You ought to what, Belzar? Seems I'm the one holding the gun. Before I put a bullet in your brain, though, I would like to know how you got away. You must have been more ornery than the beastie."

"Leave him be," a small voice said, stopping Haubus cold. He was standing near the middle of the room, about half way between where T.K. and Antonio watched and where H.S. stood. He was only a few feet away from the kneeling man, with Reiss's unmoving body far to his right. Sydney scanned the room for the new voice and gave a slight gasp. Her eyes caught hold of an explosion of dark, wavy hair directly below them. Skinny, brown arms held a spear gun only a few yards from Haubus' back. She knew that dark, wavy hair. *It was the girl who helped them escape from the Absconditus.*

"My father didn't murder anyone. If he says it was an accident, it was. He wouldn't have been a thief if you and your kind hadn't ridiculed him and left him to starve because he wasn't pure enough for you. He wouldn't have recruited the tattooed men if *you* hadn't stranded us here in the future, apart from our family, from our rightly home."

Haubus threw a quick glance behind him. It was a girl holding the spear gun, her arms trembling. His smile widened. "I was wondering when I'd see you. I do owe you for helpin' us escape from the hijackers. But a *rightly home?*" He chuckled softly. "Why, Belzarac, I don't recall you havin' a family in our fair city—just a no-account father who didn't seem to want to claim you. Nor did you have a little girl with you when you chased me into the time door. How did you convince this little *urchin* that you're her father?"

"I am her father," Belzarac said.

"Who was her mother? She had to be from here. Where is she?"

"She, uh—she died," Belzarac mumbled and then grew silent.

The girl shook her head, poking Haubus. "No. No, she's alive. She's, she's in Atlantis, waiting for us. You promised that, Belzarac. Tell him. Tell him the story you've told me every night of my life—about the beautiful woman you were forced to leave, that you love more than life itself. *Tell him!*"

The spear gun quivered in the girl's hand. She wiped her cheek on her shoulder. Sydney racked her brain trying to think of the girl's name. It sounded something like hottie, only it was spelled different, with an a-u-t-i. She was a girl Willoughby had first met at his High School. She had then shown up on the *Absconditus* and saved their lives.

Belzarac stared down at his bleeding hand. He said nothing.

"*Tell him!*" The girl continued, her voice angry and trembling. "You weren't a murderer! You always wanted to be an explorer, right? You met mom, and you were in love, and you wanted to leave the city, to get away from them, but they wouldn't let you. You knew too much. They wouldn't let you learn their technology and they wouldn't let you leave. You said I must've gotten my brains from Mom. She was bright and beautiful, and she will be waiting for us when we get back there, right? No-one would have gotten hurt on the ship if the Men of the Mark... "

"I'm sorry, but you been lied to, miss. If you truly are his daughter, it wouldn't surprise me to learn that he had a hand in how she died." Haubus had not lowered the barrel of his gun. He pointed it directly at the trembling figure of Belzarac. "Now, my old friend, I want you to tell the girl the truth. I'll know if you're lying. I knew you for almost twenty years."

"I didn't kill her, you dog. She died giving birth."

"Possibly," Haubus mused, "but you know as well as I do that the lass has no fair city to return to. Atlantis, after all, is just a myth."

"We, we can go back!" Belzarac stammered. "We can go back to before the city disappeared. We can escape the island this time and live somewhere in Greece or Macedonia."

Haubus sighed. "I have no time for this, Belzarac."

Belzarac looked up, a cunning gleam in his eye. "That's not what the Men of the Mark say. Things from the city still exist—powerful things. They hired me to find one."

Who are these *Men of the Mark*?" T.K. asked.

"They're stronger than you," Belzarac spat. "They're stronger than any of us! They wanted me to deliver something to them—something called a, a *crystal computer*. They promised me more wealth and power than I could ever use. I wasn't interested in their money, but I was only interested in finding you and getting what you promised me."

"Yes, but I wonder what would that get me?" Haubus mused. "A knife in me back? A lunatic wreaking havoc in the time grid? You're a fool, Belzar. Folks like you are bad to do business with. I learned my lesson on that. You're daft enough to be dangerous, old friend. That's why I'll have to kill you."

Haubus spun quickly, lunging for the spear gun and then slamming it and the girl against the wall. He grabbed the girl roughly.

"Leave her alone!" Willoughby shouted down through the platform grate. He shoved Sydney out of the way just as Haubus swung his pistol up and sent a bullet whizzing up through the platform floor. A whooshing sound ended with a meaty *thump*. Haubus gasped. His gun fired again and then a tense silence ensued. Sydney, at last, peeked down into the room, despite Willoughby's attempts to stop her.

The girl was crumpled, frightened, on the floor. Haubus, a spear protruding from his back and out through his gut, stumbled to turn around. "That was—stupid," Haubus choked.

Antonio tried to edge forward, but froze as Haubus swung his pistol erratically. H.S. stepped in front of T.K. to shield her. The gun barrel jerked to the right and fired. The kneeling form of Belzarac, still holding the now empty spear gun, crumpled to the floor, blood trickling from his forehead. Hauti, the girl with the wild, dark hair, screamed and tried to stand, but Haubus gave her a viscous kick that sent her crashing back down to the floor. He swung the gun barrel down to point at her but didn't fire. He kept it trained on her, however, as he stumbled away, toward the window.

"Haubus," Antonio finally spoke. "She is not your enemy. None of us are."

Haubus turned. "No," he said weekly, blood oozing from his nose. "To kill her would make me no better than Belzarac." He swung the barrel to point at Antonio, and then over to point at H.S. and T.K. "I had—thought to force you—to teach me, Hannuktu. I thought we could—find a way to make up for the mess our people—created. I was always brighter than you gave me credit for. You didn't want to see it—because I'm not a pure-breed of your *great* race." He moved slowly to the opposite corner of the observation window, away from the bodies, and from the stoic form of H.S. He fumbled in his pocket and tried to pull out the crystal computer he had snatched from Willoughby.

"We have—it, you know. Willoughby found the—"

The small, sleek computer tumbled to the ground. Haubus' hands were beginning to shake badly. He made a half-hearted attempt to lean to pick the crystal computer back up, but grimaced with fresh pain. He pushed back up straight.

"I loved your mother, even your father," H.S. said. "I tried to help you. I suggested you for that posting as scribe to the council. You should have come to me."

"I—I tried," Haubus said. "Wouldn't let me leave—" Haubus shrugged, forcing a hideous grin. "Now, it ends— it all ends—here. That's fittin', don't ya think? It's fittin' it should end..."

Haubus held the gun almost steady, despite his heavy breathing. The only sound in the room beyond his rasping breath was Hauti, who sobbed quietly over her father a few yards away. She had crawled to Belzarac's side, lifted his limp hand, and held it tightly. Haubus fell to one knee, pushing out from the great, panoramic window. "It could have—been different..." He rocked wildly, the gun barrel shaking. "Too late, now... Someone must clean—this— mess..." Swaying, he swung the gun around. He fired twice, point blank, at the same point in the heavy glass. The thick pane didn't shatter, but almost immediately, spidery threads formed around the deep gash the bullets had made.

Haubus fell over, dropping the gun to the floor. Lightning fast, T.K. leapt in toward the window to grab it. "*No!*" H.S. shouted, just as a loud pop sounded and sprays of water spurted in from the weakening pane.

Before anyone could move, before anyone could even think, a siren blasted, red lights flashed, and a huge, metal shield slammed down—an air-tight barrier closing off the full length of the panoramic view. Just as it was falling, Sydney glimpsed a swirl of dark in one corner of the glass. "The beasts," Willoughby shouted. "The beasts—they heard it, *they heard the window crack!* T.K. and H.S. are cut off!" Everyone stared at the metal barrier, at the heavy shield protecting them while dooming their friends. The thought of the window giving way on the other side of that barrier, of the monsters lurking in the shadows, but rushing forward as soon as the massive panes of glass gave way, was too horrible to contemplate. How could they help? *What could they do?*

28

Into the Flame

"*Tainken!*" Antonio screamed. "*H.S.!*" Lights flashed. A metallic voice warned. "Window breech is imminent. Automated safety protocols have been engaged." Antonio raced to a wall control, punched a series of buttons, and sat back, watching as a small keyboard slid out from the wall. He began typing furiously. A flat-screen monitor became visible. The rock pattern that had disguised it faded to reveal a cross-section of camera feeds.

Willoughby took the metal stairs two at a time. "What's happening?" he shouted.

"Automated safety protocols—they won't let me raise the shield!" Antonio shot back, frustrated. "*I can't get them out!*"

"What can we do? We've got to do something," Sydney screamed. She had pulled herself to her feet and was hobbling frantically down the metal stairway, holding tight to the rail.

Willoughby reached Antonio. "Is there a back door— something?"

"It would take too long to get to them, my friend, and the beasts..." Split-screen images flashed up on the monitor. One view showed the cracked observation window. Willoughby could make out a swarm of plesiosaurus in the distance, agitated and circling closer. "The shots, the cracking glass," Antonio mumbled. "Willoughby, the cloaking mechanism has been disabled— the beasts can also *see* them…"

Willoughby studied the monitor. T.K. and H.S. were huddled together, bunched against the steel barrier that cut them off from the observation lounge. Could he—*could he form a junction? Could he stop time through the steel barrier, stopping the rush of water, the movement of the beasts?* Before he could try, though, H.S. looked directly at the camera and called his name, slow and deliberate. Antonio quickly keyed in another bank of commands. A low, metallic voice clicked to life, coming from the speaker in the monitor.

"…lip reading software will allow you to hear me. Don't try a rescue. There is not enough time. There is hope for Tainken, but you must listen carefully. Willoughby, her chance lies with the crystal computer. Tainken has the necklace I told you about—the one I thought was lost. Joining them will activate the prime-hole door if it is still functional. It will attempt to retrieve the one holding the device if that person's DNA matches any from the council. I was never officially on the council, so it won't work for me, but the moment the computer and necklace are connected, T.K. should be pulled to the prime-door. This makes it all the more imperative to find that door. It was built to withstand any kind of natural disaster and to house the full council for weeks, so T.K. will have food, water, and air for a time, but not forever. You are the one who must find her. Find her, and find James Arthur. You need your team. Something is coming, Willoughby—something that you are already a part of. The prime-hole door must be destroyed, but that may not be all. Everything happening is connected. Somehow, you are the focal point. I wish I could be here with you, fight with you, but my time is gone."

"I can try to create a junction—" Willoughby started, but H.S. cut him off.

"*Listen to me, Willoughby! That will not be possible!* This is bigger than me. I have lived longer than I should. It is my time. Do not mourn me—this is how I would want to go, saving one I love, fighting for what I believe in. You must be strong. Can you do that?"

Willoughby paused a moment, breathing hard. "How do I destroy the door?" he finally said. He saw the skin of one of the beasts sweeping close by the leaking window.

H.S. let some of the tension drain from his voice. "Tainken is the key. Only one with pure DNA who holds the other keys can deactivate the door and trip the auto-destruct mechanism. She will need your help though—"

H.S. was interrupted by the deafening thud of one of the beasts slamming the glass. The leak from the window grew. Any ordinary glass would have surely burst already. Willoughby did not let himself consider what material the window was made from. H.S. recovered his balance and started waving his hand excitedly. "I have sensed forces trying to help us, Willoughby. You will need to reach out, to ally with them. The spyglass you were given may be from such a source. I brought it—you should keep it with you. It is on the coffee table."

Another collision shook the cave. Willoughby gulped. A huge plesiosaurus with an infested, milky eye swirled past the camera. The water was over H.S. and Tainken's knees. The beast hovered for a moment, watching H.S. with its one good eye. It spun unbelievably quickly and then slammed forward, fangs barred. Its body slapped against the glass. The whole observation room shook again.

"TAKE CARE OF SYDNEY, SHE, SHE IS QUITE UNIQUE—ANTONIO, KEEP THE TEAM TOGETHER. I'M SORRY I—THERE, THERE IS MUCH MORE I—"

The window groaned. H.S. spun, grabbing hold of T.K., who had been just out of camera view. He pulled her toward him. As the water sloshed around them, he took the crystal computer she had been holding. T.K. fumbled to pull a small, crystal necklace from her neck. H.S. grabbed it and held it up against the side of the computer. Willoughby couldn't see clearly, but he knew the man was trying to slide the small necklace into a narrow groove near the top. He said something to T.K. She tried to argue, but he stepped back, yelling. She looked up at the camera, her fingers pushing down on the necklace. "Antonio," she called, her eyes wet with tears. At that exact moment, the window burst—water, metal, glass, and debris pounded in, slamming against the thick barrier shield. Two camera feeds winked out immediately. One lingered a few moments, showing swirls of dark water and debris. A dark shape swept into the camera's view, cutting off all else. Willoughby wanted to glance away, but he couldn't. His eyes were riveted. The last thing he saw as that camera, too, went dark, was a brief, intense flash of light. The flash caught the beast open-mouthed and poised to attack. Something smashed into the camera only seconds after the light faded, taking it off-line. Willoughby stared, unmoving, at the blank feeds from the various cameras.

A second thud rang out as something massive slammed against the barrier. A few moments later, one of the beasts slammed into it again, this time hitting the metal shield so hard that it knocked everyone off balance. Antonio was the first to recover. He started typing frantically on the keyboard. There was a screech of metal, as if something were ripping at the webbing of the destroyed window. Antonio finally got one of the cameras to come back up, pointed after a flood light that had flared above it. Willoughby gasped. A swarm of at least four plesiosaurs were digging at something through the torn and shattered remnants of the window webbing. Swirls of dark tainted the water, diffusing into muddy shades of red. There was silence in the room.

Willoughby stared in shock at the screen. Antonio pushed away from the small keyboard and slid down the wall. "*Gone!*" he wailed, "*both of them—gone!*" He dropped his head to his hands. Willoughby reached forward and turned the monitor off. A deafening screech sounded as one of the beasts tore again at the metal webbing. There had been no sign of anyone alive—only the beasts and their prey.

"Willoughby?" Sydney called out. She limped painfully across the floor toward the monitor, wiping her eyes. No one said anything. "Willoughby, why did you turn it off?"

Willoughby looked up, tears brimming in his eyes. Sydney screamed.

"No! *NO!*" She crumpled to the floor, banging her fist against the polished stone, tears streaming down her face.

Willoughby felt that he should go to her, but he didn't. He couldn't seem to move, he couldn't seem to think. A few feet away, the dark-skinned girl sat, quietly sobbing as well over the lifeless body of the man she had called *father*. Another beast slammed against the safety plate, sliding across it.

"How long will the plate hold?" Willoughby heard his voice ask. It sounded detached, emotionless.

"I am not worried about the plate," Antonio finally replied. "It is a special metal—it will hold. Willoughby—did you see the flash? Do you think Tainken…"

Antonio seemed unable to complete the question.

"You mean, do I think Tainken escaped?" Willoughby said as he looked back up at the blank screen. "I don't know. If this prime-door exists, maybe. But it could be buried under ice, under a mountain, at the bottom of the sea."

Antonio nodded weakly. "I feel so helpless, my friend." He was sobbing now. "We had no way to help them." He dropped his head again.

Willoughby looked across the room again. He didn't know what to say to Antonio. He didn't know what to say to Sydney. He finally got his legs to work and walked over to her. He bent down. She grabbed at him and held him. He let her, wrapping arms around her tight. Everything seemed so *unworldly*. It was almost as if he wasn't sure what had really happened. It was as if he were a character in some macabre play. Sydney didn't say anything. She just continued to hold on. After a while, he became aware of the brown-skinned girl. She had looked up from her lifeless father. Her eyes stared at him and through him, blank-faced and empty. He tried to meet them.

"Hauti, I'm sorry," he said. She focused in a little and gave a slight nod. Sydney pushed back, turning to look at the girl behind her, trying to echo Willoughby's sentiments. It came across as just a nod and a tight smile. She turned again, wiping at her eyes.

"How long before you have to go after her?" Sydney said.

"Go after her?"

"T.K... He said—H.S. said that you have to find her. Maybe she can help us to, to make sense of all this." She spun quickly, wiping at her eyes again. "I have to get Hauti out of here—away from, from the body and the blood," she said softly so that only Willoughby could hear. "I imagine there's a kitchen or a lounge somewhere." Willoughby gave a curt nod and pointed. Sydney hobbled away from him, gently approaching the other girl.

For a long moment, Willoughby stood, frozen. *Did Sydney mean for him to leave now?* The more he mulled it over, the more it felt like the right thing to do. Sobbing wouldn't bring H.S. back, but if he had something to do, some task or goal, maybe that would help him make sense of things. His eye fell on the spyglass on the corner of an end table. Slowly, he stood. He walked over and picked the instrument up. He held it for a moment, then turned with purpose and strode to Antonio.

"How can I tap into the raw time-stream from this facility—so that I have options beyond transporting directly back to the door above the Certus Grove building?"

Antonio looked up, dazed. "What are you talking about?"

"T.K.," Willoughby said emphatically. "What if there was a way to reach her, to save her? H.S. seemed to believe I could do it."

"Maybe," Antonio said tiredly, "if you had the crystal computer. But you do not, my friend. H.S. did not have the time to teach you. Yes, I most certainly heard what the man said, but I believe he meant that we study the problem and come up with a most excellent plan."

"Antonio, things happened while you were away. H.S. knew that I don't really need it. What others use the crystal to interpret, for some reason, I see it in my head. I can locate her trail in the time grid. *He* knew I could."

"I cannot let you do this, my friend. As senior member on this team now, I am forbidding it. I listened to H.S. once before, and it got us separated and could have gotten you killed."

"You don't understand!" Willoughby was spitting the words out with vehemence. "I don't have time to tell you everything. The hijacking, Nostradamus, probably even the whole Atlantis connection—it all revolves around *me*. I didn't start any of this, but somehow, I have to be the one to stop it. If I don't, they'll just keep coming. They'll come after everything I know, everything I am, unless I can stop this!" Tears were flowing freely from his eyes now.

"Stop what?"

"I don't know! That's the thing—I don't even know what this war is all about. I only know that, somehow, I'm supposed to stop it."

"We are explorers, Willoughby. You make it sound like it is a war."

Willoughby lost control. "I don't know what it is, Antonio. I only know that I have to stop it. I can't sit here and do nothing." He started off toward the smooth curve of wall that he knew hid a sliding door. As he approached, it slid open.

"Willoughby!" Sydney cried, still prying Hautie away from her father.

Antonio was on his feet. "No, think Willoughby! You must think. You could be lost in the time stream, or pulled into a trap. Who will help us find James Arthur and T.K. if you are no longer with the team?"

Willoughby kept walking, moving quickly toward the planetarium he knew lay ahead and the slowly revolving pyramid that lay beyond it. He heard the door swish open behind him.

"Willoughby!" Antonio ran to catch up with him. "We are not talking about silly house rules. The time-stream is dangerous. *What if you are wrong?* What if you can't read the stream as well as you think? What if H.S. was wrong? He was certainly wrong about Dr. O'Grady."

Willoughby had broken into a run. He wasn't listening. He clasped the brass spyglass tight. Without a word, he raced toward the familiar buzzing sound near the end of the corridor, and the darkness of the planetarium. He would use the fiery arc above the great electromagnetic pyramid to enter the time grid. He would peer at it with the spyglass first, and if he saw T.K., which he felt sure he would for some reason, he would jump into the flame— the *slender flame.* He remembered the words suddenly. It had been the words Nostradamus had used in the letter to his son. He thought back to reading about the seer on the *Absconditus.* It seemed a lifetime ago. *"Unless aided by a voice coming from limbo,"* the letter had said; *"by means of the slender flame..."* Willoughby slowed to a brisk trot.

Antonio entered the corridor behind him. "Listen to me, Willoughby. Just stop for a moment and let's talk this out."

Willoughby found the planetarium door. He remembered how H.S. had explained the interstellar relationship between time and gravity to him here, his eyes brimming. He wiped an arm across them, his vision blurring momentarily, and bolted through the dark room, straight to the thin catwalk that reached out across the automated machinery of the post. He knew he couldn't stop to think, to discuss things with Antonio. If he did, he would lose his nerve, he would miss his chance to find T.K. The electromagnetic pyramid turned, arcs of electricity buzzing across its surface near the end of the walk. A flickering flame seemed to warp the air a few feet above its tip. It would be about a ten foot leap. Antonio, with his long legs had already reached the planetarium. It would be close. Willoughby paused, his body tense, his hand holding to the railing of the catwalk. He raised the brass spyglass to his eye.

At first, he couldn't see anything. After a moment of adjusting, something came into view. In the eyepiece, he saw a dim glow. He couldn't make out what or where it was, but there was movement. There was a sound as well— breathing, a cough. That was all. But that was enough. *T.K. was alive!* He was sure of it. He lowered the spyglass.

Antonio thundered onto the catwalk. "*Willoughby! Wait!*"

Willoughby sprang forward. Could he beat his barber friend to the arc that buzzed across the open air, leaving in its wake a haze of acrid smoke? *This is the only way,* he told himself. *I have to act.* If he was the focus of all this, if he was the one who could end it, he had to trust his instincts. Every fiber of his being told him this was the right thing to do—*he had to jump…*

Gaining speed, he hurdled toward the end of the metal catwalk, Antonio right on his heels. *He couldn't let Antonio catch him.* If he was stopped now, somehow he knew that the opportunity would be lost. Who knew how long T.K. could survive in that—well, in the place where she was at? He had to at least *try* to find her.

Antonio bounded closer, reaching out toward him. He dove and caught him by the wrist just as Willoughby dove off of the end of the platform. The two sailed through the air, sucking in the sharp tang of acrid smoke. Antonio held tight. Willoughby felt as if everything were moving in slow motion. He thought of Klass, his step-dad, and of his mom, and his half-sisters, Densi, and Cali. For the third time in less than twenty-four hours, he was risking his life. He thought of the watch his family had given him. "*Make you the moment, only to find, a yearning for home and memories that bind.* He knew for certain, now, what he had begun to understand on the frozen mountain—adventure can be cold, and hard, and unfriendly when you are living it. It has a justice, a path of its own, one that made his own yearning for home, for the simplicity he once thought of as boring and mundane, all but pointless. He was in the thick of it now. This was the life he had had been given. *Perhaps destiny isn't a thing to be found,* he thought, *but a thing that finds you—that comes out of nowhere to hit you like some runaway freight train.* For better or worse, destiny had closed around him, holding him tightly, like a lifeline, or perhaps, a noose.

The hum of the metallic pyramid was deafening. It revolved somewhere below. Black gases bubbled around them, and then they connected with the raw, flickering power of the arc. He closed his eyes. He heard in his mind the broken rasp of Gustav and tried to picture his face. "*Already,*" the shaky rasp rang out, "*we change the world.*"

The flame crackled. There was a flash and a familiar tug. He felt the pressure of Antonio's grip on his wrist. Then the world around him seethed with glowing numbers.

29

A Friend in Need

Willoughby sucked in a sharp breath. He felt panic—*once again, the number strings were too plentiful and moving too fast.* Exhaling slowly, he tried to steady his eyes and focus. This time, however, no string snapped onto him, pulling him forward. He had no crystal computer to help him identify a known thread. All he had was his mind. *Calm,* he though; *calm...* At first, there was no change. The numbers curled around him, flying past in undecipherable waves. He closed his eyes and forced his mind to picture T.K. clearly. When he opened them again, a number string did slow. It curved, flowing toward his head. He had time to read it. It was not a string he recognized, but the experience helped him focus. More strings slowed, both close to his face and further away. Some glimmered or sparked. He had no idea what T.K.'s string would look like, or if he would actually hear her as he had heard Sydney's music, or see some representation of her floating among the numbers like a jellyfish in a warm current.

A string snaked through the others, heading straight for them. It glowed slightly. Willoughby *did* recognize this number sequence—*it was the signature of James Arthur!* H.S. had introduced him to all the number signatures of the team. Memorizing them had been part of his homework while learning how to use the crystal computer. He hesitated. *This number sequence belonged to James Arthur—not T.K.!*

The string curled around him. He had only a moment to decide whether to go after his friend Dr. J or hope that he could identify something in the time-stream that would lead him to T.K. On impulse, he raised his hand, parting the collision of spinning, flowing number strings. He felt as though James Arthur's sequence were calling out to him amid the sea of abstract equations. He hesitated only a moment, and then grabbed at James Arthur's number sequence. It flared, jerking him forward the moment he touched it. As the bright flare faded, he felt a sudden sense of falling. The other number strings vanished as the string in his hand seemed to shatter into spinning patterns of light and shadow.

Antonio hit solid ground first, slapping onto a spongy, dim surface. Willoughby tumbled down on top of him, and the two struggled to get untangled from each other and sit up.

"Willoughby, I am hoping you are...okay," Antonio hissed. "Because then, I am thinking I will *kill you myself!* What fool thing have you done? Where might we be?"

"I don't know," Willoughby groaned as he rubbed at his shoulder and leg, "I didn't ask you to come, Antonio. You grabbed my wrist, or don't you remember?" He sat up and looked around. "All I can say with some certainty is that we're not in the age of dinosaurs anymore."

Antonio rolled to his knees and started to wipe a thin layer of chalky dust from his arms. He looked around. "You are right... It looks like a tomb."

Dim light reflected through a rounded doorway highlighting piled artifacts, clay pots, and dust-covered statues. In one corner, closer to the doorway, white bones gleamed. Antonio pushed away from the woven baskets and bits of crumbled pottery and made his way to the opening. He peered out for a long moment. Willoughby crept up behind him. "Did we take a wrong turn?" he whispered. "This does not look like what I would envision for a prime-door. That is where H.S. said the homing device would take T.K., did he not?"

Willoughby dropped his head. "I, uh, I stayed in the time-stream as long as I dared, Antonio. I couldn't find any trail from T.K. or her homing beacon. You were right. It's going to take more than just my skill to find her. I thought, from what H.S. said that, somehow, I would know where she was once I got into the time stream. But I didn't." He looked up. Antonio was looking away, biting his lip. "You really like her don't you?"

Antonio nodded. He forced a sigh. "So, why are we here?"

Willoughby glanced around. "I *did* find James Arthur's signature. I grabbed hold and it brought us here." He continued to let his eyes roam over the inside of the tomb-like chamber. A row of small clay bowls housed low burning wicks, providing a flickering glow to the crude walls.

Antonio began to stand. "We do have to find her, Willoughby. But we are here now. If we can find our friend, James Arthur, and can get back to the Observation Deck before the girls get worried, I will not kill you just yet."

"Gee, thanks," was all Willoughby could manage. They stood, brushing themselves and each other off.

"We have much to catch up on," Antonio said, conversationally. "How did you escape the *Absconditus?* When did H.S. teach you how to navigate the time-stream? How did you find the crystal pendant? O'Grady, or Haubus, or whoever he was, said you found it. Did you get it from Nostradamus?"

"Yes, and no—listen; there isn't time to go through everything. I mean, I want to know stuff too. Like, how did H.S. find you, and why did T.K. call out your name just before the window exploded?"

"Ah, yes, well, we…became better acquainted. As you say, now is not the time, my friend." He peeked out from the chamber. "Let us find our most illustrious friend, the good Doctor, and return ourselves safely to the Observation Deck. Then, we can share our different tales. Maybe a plan for finding T.K. will become clearer as we share and contemplate. Things have been moving a…a little fast for me today."

A part of Willoughby, the part that was still a fifteen year-old boy, wanted to grab his good friend and one-time barber in a big bear hug, letting him know that he was glad to see him. But another part of him had aged twenty years in the past three weeks. He just nodded at Antonio's words, picked up the brass spyglass, tucking it in the small of his back, and followed his friend out of the chamber.

The chamber connected to a much larger cavern. Willoughby stared in shock. The place was enormous, shaped into six distinct, half-circle tiers that descended to a lit arena. All in all, it looked like some kind of underground amphitheater. Each tier consisted of a wide shelf, with dozens of rounded doorways dug back into dusty, sandstone walls. A single stairway led down from the top tier to a strange, glassy floor at the center of the arena.

The floor was checkered with light and dark squares. It was ringed by a circle of enormous stone figures. "Chess pieces," Willoughby whispered, awed at the sight. "It looks like they're all Kings—no, Queens. What is that woven so tightly around them?"

Antonio squinted, looking at the thick bands entwined around the figures. At length, he straightened, raising an eyebrow; "I think they're giant cobras," he whispered. "At the ends—those are the flared hoods." An oddly consistent blue flame flicked from a fanged mouth, punctuating each curved hood. The flames lit the cavern with a cold, bluish glow. Behind the arena floor, a much larger Cobra head shot out from the back wall. The cobra's mouth was open wide, its fangs barred, as if it were in the act of striking. Beneath its amber eyes was a throne. The throne seemed to be woven from twisting vines or cords, with twinkling stones embedded like eyes, sparkling in the glow. A mark had been burned into the slab of stone forming the back of the throne. Willoughby studied it a moment, and gasped. *It was the mark of the Beelzebub!*

Waiting a moment for his heartbeat to slow, Willoughby took a step forward. Antonio grabbed his shoulder and pointed wordlessly toward a far corner of the glassy floor. A cloaked woman had stepped out of the shadows, towering menacingly over the crawling figure of a dark-skinned man—*James Arthur!* Dr. J appeared injured. He struggled to push to his feet. Slightly behind him, four other figures stepped into the dim light. Two looked like Bedouin guards of some kind. The shortest of them looked like some sort of desert Sheik. The fourth figure was tall and broad. As Willoughby squinted to see, he noted that this was not a giant of a man, but rather, a *giant woman!*

She towered over the group, easily nine or ten feet tall with thick, muscled limbs and a huge head. The giantess spoke.

"Why you do this? This man already weak. There is no need."

The cloaked woman barked a short laugh. "She speaks! Wonder of wonders—and in English no less." Her words carried a heavy European accent. "I guess you do have a brain in that big head. Well, don't worry about son-of-the-future." She reached down and raked a bony hand through James Arthur's hair. "I have heard he has the power to heal himself. Interesting, isn't it? Should we test than power? How much healing can you do, James Arthur?" She bent down until she was at eye level with him, raising his chin. She smiled at him. "You see, you and I have met once before. Pain is mostly what I recall from that meeting—horrible pain. You did not help me. I did not feel any of your *luck*. Do you recall that day, son-of-the-future?"

James Arthur did not answer.

She let his chin drop and stood. For a long moment, the only sound was Dr. J's heavy breathing. The woman stepped back, looking down at the kneeling man. "Of course you recall. Pain is the most timeless of emotions. When it is exquisite, it cries out, penetrating eons, transcending the barriers of time itself. Why did I think you would help me, James? I foolishly thought that one who could heal would heal. Instead, you stood there, staring at me like a lost puppy, a skinny, quivering boy. Now, you kneel before me, a quivering man. I will know the extent of this healing gift. I will acquaint you with exquisite pain, the kind I live with…unless you want to tell me where your friends are. Where is the boy, James

Arthur?" She bent down again. "If I take you to that exquisite pain, it will call him from across time, *oui?*"

"I don't know where he is. I wouldn't tell you if I did," Dr. J rasped. "I was too young when we first met. I didn't understand...healing." His words were slurred, as if he had marbles in his mouth.

The cloaked woman turned away. "Yes, you did tell me that. Such a pity..." She motioned at the others, speaking in some sort of desert language. The short man seemed to be trying to debate her, but as the woman started to raise a hand, he thought better, bowed, and turned. The others followed him, back into the shadows, out of sight—all except for the huge woman. She stood, staring at the cloaked one for a long moment, even though the smaller man called to her. She clearly did not want to go. Finally, with a grumble, she turned to go. The cloaked woman walked back to James Arthur, who had pushed himself to a sitting position.

Dr. J looked up at her. "You're older. Why do you want Willoughby?"

"Older?" The woman laughed, stepping forward to once again rake her hand through his curly hair. "Because, he is valued by the one I hate. So, I must crush him. I must destroy him. I am good at destroying things."

"He's only a boy," James Arthur grunted.

"What is this '*only a boy,*' James!" The woman threw back the hood of her cloak. "Boy or man makes no difference. I was only a girl when I first met you, but that did not keep me from burning, from destroying all I loved. Now, I suppose, I must destroy you." She lifted up her chin, pulling the hood back. All the skin around her eyes was charred black. She waved a hand over the floor, and immediately, her eyes began to glow. The glow increased until bright light shot from them. It cracked, like a bolt, striking James Arthur. He cried out. Willoughby screamed.

"*No!*" His voice echoed through the cave. The woman waved her hand. The bolt of lightning stopped. She turned and looked up to where Willoughby and Antonio stood. Willoughby could see her clearly now. It was the woman with the scarred eyes—the one Beelzebub had called Carolyn, the one that James Arthur was supposed to know. He tried to remember the thin man's words; "*So, Willoughby, a test—a chance to prove the superiority of your own right and wrong. Should James Arthur try to save this poor, lost soul? Let us say that you control this reunion. I warn you thou—she plans to kill your friend. He failed her. He must pay the price…*"

Okay, so maybe Beelzebub wasn't bluffing. Maybe James Arthur's life really was on the line. What should he do? The being claimed that thousands of lives may be at stake, not only Dr. J's. Should he form a junction? The woman's powers didn't work properly in a junction. How did he form one? He had done it once before, but it had been an accident—he didn't know how he had formed it. Stalling for time, he began, numbly, to move toward the stairs. James Arthur had fallen back to the glass floor. He was shaking and gasping for breath, but at least, *he was alive!*

"Ah," the woman smiled. "I knew he would come, but why so quickly?" She turned to Dr. J. "James Arthur and I were just getting reacquainted…Pity, son-of-the-future, already, your friend has come to save the day. What is his name?" She cocked her head, looked up, and gave a tight smile. "Yes, Willoughby, is it not?"

"Yes."

"Well, Willoughby, how would you like to die?"

Willoughby stepped down another stair.

Antonio caught him by the arm. "Stop—this is, this is out of our league."

Willoughby jerked his arm away. "It's okay. I've met her before. Trust me."

The cloaked woman laughed again. "You are either very brave or very stupid, Willoughby." She moved languidly toward her throne. Willoughby could see, now that he was closer, that the throne was not carved vines, but hundreds of carved snakes, each with glittering jewel eyes inset into the stone. The woman sat as she reached the throne. "Do you recognize my floor?"

Willoughby glanced at the squares again. "It's, uh, it's like a big chess board."

The woman smiled. "Bravo, though this is no ordinary board. It is pieced together from different points in time." She sat. "In fact, there are eight different time-lines from my life living safely on this board. Each active time-line does not endanger the others."

Willoughby cocked his head. "The Eight Queens puzzle."

The woman raised an eyebrow. "Right again. You are a marvel. See, James Arthur, what a *boy* can do?" She shifted, draping one leg up on the throne's arm. "Since you impress me, Willoughby, I'll tell you what. I'll give you a sporting chance. Not to live, really, but a chance to not die so horribly. Pick one of the eight squares correctly, and instead of instant death, I will let you face the destruction that square controls." She smiled brightly. "I'll even throw in a hint—the eight placements are from a fundamental solution where no three queens are in a straight line. If you know all the fundamental solutions to your puzzle, you know which solution I speak of and where the eight squares are. Sounds fun, doesn't it?"

"Why would you want to kill me?" Willoughby said, only one tier above the glass floor. "The being who calls himself Beelzebub is not my friend."

"Yet, you came, just as he told you to," the woman said. "He controls you and you don't even know it."

"I came to rescue my friend. I could have called Beelzebub, but I haven't," he fudged. In truth, he wasn't sure if he could call Beelzebub. He had never tried.

"He does not frighten me, but he does control me. I am unable to use my power in his junctions. If I do not do as he says, I am locked in that place. You have no idea the pain when the power builds inside me, and I am unable to let it go. It is a pain that reaches to infinity."

"What if we could help you?"

The witch laughed. "Yes, I thought that once, too. I thought, maybe I could find someone to help me. I trusted the winds of time in which I was born. They brought James Arthur to me. You see how that worked. The dark edge does not want me healed."

"The *dark edge?*"

"It is what the cursed man who controls us is."

"What is he after?

The woman cocked her scarred face to one side. "He wants to use you, to add you to his collection, I think. Believe me; I am doing you a favor. You are better off dead than in his clutches."

"Maybe we could face him together. Maybe we could stop him."

The woman shrieked with laughter. "Oh, my boy, you do not understand what it is you speak of. With ten times our power, we could not face that one. He is older than time itself. He toys with you. Perhaps he wants to take your form, which is his way. You have no chance against him. Nor do I. So, I do what I am told, what I do best. I kill. I destroy. I don't like it, but...Sometimes, I make things uncomfortable for him, I make him angry. I am punished, but, what is more pain to me? That is the best I can do. I am resigned to my fate. Enough talk. Let the game begin. Or do you need a little demonstration with your other friend?"

"I am not afraid of you," Antonio said, stepping boldly forward. Both he and Willoughby had reached the glass floor now. Again, Willoughby held him back. "Trust me," he whispered, speaking directly to his friend. Antonio, at length, gave a curt nod.

"The cave," Antonio whispered, "it uses a four dimensional architecture. The power is being focused onto this board. The general design indicates that this is some type of elaborate time-door."

Willoughby raised an eyebrow. "Go to James Arthur," he said hurriedly. "Try to make your way to the center." He turned back to the woman with the blackened eyes. His mind churned wildly. He did have the beginnings of a plan formulating in his mind, but he needed time to think it through. He needed to stall. He decided to play along with her game. He thought of the Eight Queens puzzle. There are ninety-two *distinct* solutions to the Eight Queens Puzzle and twelve *fundamental* ones. She had said that the squares were aligned as the "only fundamental solution" where no three queens were in a straight line, so the eight squares connected to her timelines were arranged according to one of the fundamental solutions. But which one had no three queens in a straight line? He envisioned the twelve solutions in his mind. Finally, he spoke. "What if I'm wrong?" he said.

"Then, you and your friends die immediately," the woman said.

Willoughby took a deep breath. "D-4," he said, his voice a little shaky.

"*Excellent!*" the woman cried. "What a great selection! You get to meet my warriors!" The woman stood and walked to D-4. She stopped on the square for only a moment, waving a hand over the clear square. Her fingers bent and she flicked her wrist, then turned and strode back to the throne. *Had Willoughby seen a bright flash the moment she flicked her wrist?* The woman seated herself again, sucked in a great breath, and cried out, her words ringing through the cavern.

"*EXCITO VOS SILENTI!*"

There was a tension, a crackle of electricity in the air. Willoughby remembered enough from his Latin class to get the gist of her words—"*Wake you, the dead!*" A sudden swirl of chill air rippled across the glass floor. It seemed to scale the tiers of the cave one by one and penetrate each of the tomb-like chambers. There was a sound of clattering.

Willoughby glanced over just in time to see Antonio reach James Arthur and help him to his feet. Dr. J was the first to see one of the *warriors*. He pointed a shaky finger. Antonio turned to look.

"Ah, we have trouble, *amigo*," he mumbled in a low breath. Swirls of dust rocketed in and out of the doorways of each tomb, tier by tier. There was a sound of stirring from the tombs and dust winds soared back down toward the glassy floor.

30

Eight Queens Down

Willoughby looked frantically around the amphitheater. An army of animated skeletons had begun to emerge from the arched entrances of each chamber. Clad in rags and holding weapons from different time periods, the forces of the dead appeared at once ruthless and ferocious. A faint hint of their former bodies and selves clung to weathered bones like ghosts who could control their own bones. Willoughby glanced back, seeing Antonio lead the injured and shaken Dr. J toward a square near the center of the board. Just as the first of the rag and bone troops reached the checkered floor, the giant woman stepped in from the shadows brandishing a huge curved sword. She smote the first wave of the creatures, scattering bones across the board. Willoughby slowly backed up to stand with Antonio and James Arthur, his eyes wide. The giantess put a foot on a dropped, rusted javelin and a rusted sword and scooted them toward the three.

"*Fight!*" she commanded. She gave a crooked smile. "James Arthur, he make me laugh."

Willoughby gave a curt nod, bent, and grabbed the rusted sword. He handed it to Antonio, realizing for the first time that he had absently grabbed the brass spyglass with his other hand and was brandishing it like a club. The attackers saw the giantess holding off a knot of slicing, jabbing bone warriors at the foot of the stairs and began to drop down the cave tiers directly, bypassing the stairs. The first wave reached the edge of the checkered floor and spread out in a line. They seemed intent on isolating Willoughby and his small group in a corner to the left of the throne. James Arthur was standing on his own now. He picked up the javelin, using it as a crutch as well as weapon, and pushed Antonio away. "Help Willoughby," he said, his voice thick.

Antonio ducked forward and swinging the sword the giantess had shoved across the glass floor. As he brandished it, he motioned for Willoughby and James Arthur to retreat a few steps. "Is this part of the fine rescue, my friend?" he hissed.

"*Fine rescue?*" James Arthur forced a weak grin. "Is that what this is?"

Willoughby ignored both of them. He had looked back toward the woman on the throne. She raised her eyebrows, the smile evident on her face. She was enjoying herself.

"Care to guess again?

Willoughby narrowed his eyes in concentration. Sweat trickled down his face as he fought a sense of panic. *What was he doing?* He didn't know how to deal with this kind of stuff. He was going to get them all killed. A bone warrior lunged at him. He could see a man's bearded face faintly, as if a slightly visible covering to the yellowed skeleton. He kicked away the warrior's spear and thumped him on the head before James Arthur used his javelin to scatter the warrior's bone legs. A thought occurred to Willoughby. He looked up at the witch.

"It's a junction. You've created a junction, combining a time when the warriors were alive with two or three time points where there are only bones! The bones align themselves with the movements of the living being."

The witch frowned. "I told you to make your second choice or the game will soon be over."

"But if it's a junction, you can't use your killing powers."

The witch laughed again. "Care to test that assumption, young Willoughby? First, there are many ways to die. Second, it is not the same if *I* create the junction. Now, your second guess."

Breathing in deeply, Willoughby forced himself to pull back under control. He had a puzzle to solve. He thought over the fundamental solutions to the puzzle he had selected once again. "E-2" he said softly. The cloaked woman actually clapped. "Oh, you are good!" she said, the smile returning to her blackened eyes. "You have chosen my favorites!" She slowly stood from the throne and walked dramatically to square E-2. Willoughby glanced behind him. The bone warriors were closing in, despite the giantess pulling back from the stairs and Antonio brandishing his rusted sword with a fierceness that was almost shocking. Clashes of metal against metal and metal against bone rang through the cavern. The witch turned when she reached the square. She waved her hand and flicked her wrist again. Willoughby noted that she stood over a clear square and that there was a brief flash this time. "Now," the cloaked woman said, turning toward him, "you meet *my* pets..."

A warmer swirl spun in from the edges of the board. It tugged a moment at the woman's cloak and then whooshed through the throne of carved snakes.

Willoughby stared in astonishment as the seemingly stone snakes changed color and began to writhe. The throne, in a matter of seconds, had turned various hues of brown and black. It moved, melting to the glass floor in a tangled mass of writhing serpents. Willoughby stepped back. "To your right," was all he could think of to say. Antonio and James Arthur glanced over as dozens of the snakes slithered toward them. James Arthur, who had begun to swing the javelin from side to side, groaned.

"*Snakes!* This rescue just keeps getting better."

"Well," Antonio said, "we could have left you to your ladies." He indicated the giantess and the witch. The giantess had pulled a second curved sword from the strap on her back. Her skill with the two long, curved blades was evident by the number of bones skittering to the floor in front of her. Soon, snake blood was also dripping off them. She had formed a barrier to the right of Willoughby and James Arthur while Antonio was a slightly less impressive barrier to the left.

"*Willoughby!*" a tired voice shouted. "Thanks for rescue and everything, but—you guys need to *go back!*" Willoughby looked over at James Arthur, swatting at a lunging snake. He slapped it away with the spyglass and dazed it just enough that Dr. J could spear its head with the tip of his javelin.

"There's a plan—" he started, but his words were interrupted by a grunt of pain as a detached skull hit him square in the back. He shook it loose. "That thing bit me!" He said, slamming it away with his foot. Antonio had glanced up a moment to wipe sweat from his brow. He was standing in front of a headless skeleton that had twisted around and was now attacking its fellow bone warriors.

"Sorry!" Antonio called with a sheepish grin. He turned back just in time to duck an ax swing from a particularly short and wide bone man in rusted Norse armor. He shaved off the bone arm wielding the ax and sent the weapon flying, implanting itself into the back of a large bone man trying to raise himself from the floor. The large bone man collapsed. The grinning, one-armed skeleton that had just lost his ax, pulled a long-bladed knife out of his belt with his remaining arm. He swung it at Antonio, who hopped behind one of the stone queens and swung his own rusted sword down with a mighty blow. It cracked the bone warrior's skull in half, and the warrior fell into a heap of bones. He continued to swing from his hidden vantage point—snakes' snapping at his sword's every swing.

James Arthur dove, shoving Willoughby aside as a stone hammer barely avoided smashing into them. The giantess leveled the bone warrior that had thrown the weapon. Willoughby caught the huge woman's eye and nodded his thanks. For just a moment, he thought he saw her mouth twitch up into a crooked smile. A huge skeleton, with bits of tattered robe hanging from its ribs, had stepped up to the stone queen Antonio was hiding behind and waved another enormous hammer. Antonio jumped back and let the hammer strike the pillar. The weapon snapped in two. The skeleton seemed shocked as it looked up at Antonio, who had already sent his own sword sailing through the bone man's rib cage to shatter the spine. The thing, still staring at him, fell to the floor, little more than a writhing heap of splinters.

James Arthur glanced over at Antonio. "Was he like this cutting hair," he asked Willoughby.

Willoughby smacked another snake. "Uh, well, he was very good with scissors." He looked over at the smiling witch. It was time to pull his trump card. He could see Antonio was tiring and Dr. J was already weaving slightly, leaning on the javelin whenever he wasn't using it to stab at bone warriors or sweep away snakes. Even the giantess was becoming slower, sweat pouring from her huge body, and yet the snakes and the warriors kept coming.

"Seven-G," he called out toward the cloaked woman, who had faded back into the dark shadows at the side of the glass floor. She stepped out, pushing aside a small pile of bones. For just a moment, her face seemed to register a hint of concern. Then, her lips relaxed into a tight smile.

"Ah, pity. That is not one of the eight squares—but then, you know that, don't you?"

Willoughby did not answer. He was busy making his way, slowly, to a point between squares 1-C and 2-E. He stopped there, slapping away a snake. As he positioned himself, he looked up and matched her smile.

"I do know it is not one of the eight queen placements for the fundamental solution you chose. But it *is* the only square that appears in six of the twelve fundamental solutions, which is why you chose it to hide the location of your time door, the center of the golden spiral you used to construct this cave."

The smile on the woman's face vanished. "It is time to end this," she said irritably. "I tire of the game." She stepped closer, her eyes beginning to seethe and glow. At that moment, the giantess felled the final bone-warrior facing her and spun. She threw one of her curved swords directly at the cloaked woman. The reaction was immediate. The cloaked woman flicked her wrist and there was a flash. Her form was now a few yards away, far enough to watch the sword clank harmlessly against the cave wall. *It was the same trick Willoughby had used to frighten the drunken priest who was trying to sacrifice Sydney on the frozen mountain. But the cloaked woman did not have a crystal computer—or did she? Could it be somehow built into the glassy floor?*

The giantess grunted. She sheathed her other sword and reached down to take a rusty javelin from one of the fallen bone-men. She began to swirl it around like a massive propeller blade and moved toward another crawling thicket of bone men. The cloaked woman turned to Willoughby.

"Was that your big plan?" She smirked. "Goodbye, Willoughby. It is your time to die." Leaning her head back, she let the glow in her eyes grow bright. As soon as she had looked away, however, Willoughby put into action a plan of his own. He stretched out both arms until a hand rested in the space over both 1-C and 2-E. Just as bright light cracked from the charred eyes of the cloaked woman, Willoughby gave his wrists a quick flick at exactly the same time. There was a single flash. Everything froze. The light died in the cloaked woman's molten eyes. Her head snapped up as her gaze darted around the cave.

"You have called him!"

"No. I did not call him. I formed my own junction, linking two of the timelines you're linking in this cave. I guessed that you have carefully designed this cave so that junctions are created but contained to specific areas of the cave. I noticed that you stepped away from the throne before letting it appear to melt into snakes. I was right, wasn't I? This whole glass floor is connected to the time-door, isn't it? It acts as a sort of computer. I watched how you activated the squares. I activated two timelines at the same moment, bridging between them to form a link."

"This, this should not be possible—for a boy."

"When you visited the yacht with Beelzebub, I remembered how your eyes seethed, but you could do nothing. He said you were born in a junction, so the raw energy that can course through you in temporal time does not in a junction. Your carefully planned horrors are set up so they leave you protected spots in the cave outside of the junctions, am I right? You tried to bluff me, to say it is different if you form the junction, but that isn't true, is it?"

The cloaked woman narrowed her eyes. "*You are dark edge!*"

"Dark *what?* I followed science here—I followed logic! There is no *dark* anything. I'm not trying to kill people. I'm trying to save them—even you."

The woman stared at him for a long moment. "*Science!* Science is only a playground for your kind." She bent a picked up a rusted sword. "No, Willoughby, you cannot save me—even if you wanted. You are clever. At least I understand now his interest now. I promise your death will be swift." She hefted the sword. "Prepare to die, young master."

Willoughby stumbled backwards. He glanced quickly behind him. The glass floor was surreal, littered with bones, sliced and speared snake bodies, snake gore, and weapons. The giantess, frozen in mid-swing, sweat glistening in beads on her face like diamonds, had a large bone-warrior on her back, a dagger poised to come down at her throat. Antonio was frozen stumbling back toward a corner where an angry nest of cobras were frozen with hoods flared and fangs extended. Dr. J had been pulled to one knee by a decapitated bone-warrior. His face was frozen in a look of utter agony. Willoughby turned back just in time to duck the first swing by the cloaked woman. The sword whistled only inches over his head.

"You don't want to kill me," Willoughby said. "I know you don't. Let us help you. I only want to get my friends safe."

"*Safe?*" the woman gasped, struggling to swing the heavy sword again. "No one is safe with your kind. The dark edge only manipulates, only destroys. I will not be tricked again."

"Why do you keep saying, *my kind?*" Willoughby continued to back up, dodging the woman's erratic swings. He moved past James Arthur, toward the opposite corner of the board. "What do you mean by that? My father has fought that, that being—Beelzebub—his entire life. My mother lives outside of DC with my step-father and two half-sisters. I'm a boy, *that's all.*"

The woman swung again. This time, Willoughby had to use the spyglass to fend off the blow. The blade still grazed his arm. He felt warm blood trickle down to mingle with the spattered snake remains, dust, and sweat he was covered in.

"Today maybe you are a boy, but what about tomorrow? Your kind slips in and out of time like a child slips in and out of a winter coat. You bring beasts into being like *me.*"

"I don't do any of that. I'm not that sort of person."

"You're one of them." The woman swung the sword again. "Or, you soon will be." Willoughby tried to fend it off again with the spyglass, but the force of the thrust sent him flying backward. He tried to jerk his head out of the blade's path, but its tip caught his cheek. This time, he did not even feel the blood. The woman stood over him, panting. He tried to back-pedal, pushing away from her through the gore and mess covering the glass floor. The woman followed him, raising the sword for a final strike. "I will stop you here, before you can start." She brought the sword down. Willoughby did the only thing he could do. He held up the spyglass to fend off the blow.

The sword hit the spyglass near its center. The brass tube finally snapped, releasing a shower of glass, cogs, wheels, wires, beads, what looked like jewels, and other specific trinkets. The blade continued through but was deflected just enough to allow Willoughby to twist out of its path. Then, Willoughby looked up and saw the woman's scarred eyes, wide, but not from anger or fear. They seemed wide with—*wonder*.

31

You like, You like!

At first, Willoughby wasn't sure what he was seeing. A bright glow illuminated the cloaked woman's face, but it didn't come from her eyes. The dust, jewels, trinkets, and bent pieces of the brass spyglass had not fallen to the ground, but hovered in the air. Then, Willoughby noticed that certain trinkets were floating through the air. They seemed to position themselves, one over each of the specific squares that represented the eight solutions to the *Eight Queens* puzzle. The face over him was also changing. Its features were getting younger. Within moments, the witch holding the sword had become only a girl, her eyes frozen on one of the floating trinkets—what looked like a rabbit's foot. Her hands let the sword fall away and clank to the floor.

Willoughby rolled away from the girl and rose to his knees. The light which illuminated the girl's face was coming from the square he had been lying on. Out of the corners of his eye, he noted that the other seven squares were also glowing, light shining up from the glass floor, breaking through the bones, snakes and gore.

Beside each square, a semi-transparent image of the witch at various ages stood. A ninth square lit up, and another child appeared, kneeling on it. She was the youngest version of the witch. A locket charm of a cross hovered over this square. As Willoughby noted the position of the square, he realized it was 7-G.

"My rabbit's foot," a raspy voice said.

Willoughby looked in the direction of the voice. It was James Arthur. He had pulled himself away from the headless bone-warrior and was using the javelin to push to his feet. Willoughby stared at him. Why wasn't he frozen? Then he realized—the rabbit's foot belonged to James Arthur. It had somehow called him, connected him to this junction.

"There must have been something inside the spyglass from each of the timelines she connected to here. The trinkets activated the timelines," Willoughby mumbled.

"Where," Dr. J coughed; "Where did the spyglass come from?"

Willoughby shook his head, trying to clear it. "It's a long story. We've got lots of long stories to discuss."

"Yeah," James Arthur agreed, hopping over to his side. "You're bleeding. Are you okay?"

"I'll be fine," Willoughby said.

"By the way," James Arthur added with a grin, "Good to see you. Thanks for the rescue."

"Well," Willoughby said. "You're not rescued yet. I'm still trying to figure out why you aren't frozen. This is a junction."

"A what?"

Willoughby ignored the question. "You say something among the trinkets belonged to you?"

"Yeah," Dr. J answered. "That rabbit's foot was mine. I gave it to her when we first met. I was just a boy. She was a girl. She wanted me to heal her. I didn't know how. I gave her the rabbit's foot instead."

Willoughby cocked his head. "You're part of one of the timelines—that's why you aren't frozen. But then, the girl in that timeline shouldn't be frozen either." They looked again at the girl in the white dress with gloves on her hands and a horribly scarred face. She had turned and was staring at them.

"You *are* the one then? You can help me?"

Willoughby started to answer, but James Arthur held up a hand. He moved to the girl. Placing the javelin down, he raised his hands to her face. "Healing is a matter of aligning your being to the time and place where you belong. I can try." She watched his every move. He placed the hands over her eyes and bowed his own head, eyes shut in concentration. The girl stayed still.

At first, it seemed that nothing was happening. Then, Willoughby noted great drops of sweat breaking out on James Arthur's forehead. His body shook as he groaned. The lights from the other squares flickered. The other figures seemed to fade a little. James Arthur breathed heavily. He cried out, agonizing pain in his voice.

"*Stop!*" Willoughby yelled, hitting James Arthur hard to knock him away from the girl. Dr. J crumpled to the floor, still breathing, but only semi-conscious. Meanwhile, the girl was changing. She glowed brighter. The other squares of light winked out and the other figures disappeared, all except for the youngest girl. The figure that James Arthur had placed hands on moved toward the one lit square, her features melting to match those of the youngest witch. The bone-warriors clattered to the glass floor. The remaining snakes turned to stone. The trinkets from the other squares floated to this one and formed a circle, hovering around it. Willoughby watched as the two young girls—now their features all but identical—melded into one form, one being. The little girl's feet left the ground. She floated higher and higher into the air, growing brighter and brighter until she seemed only a glow of pure energy. Her skin was translucent, like glass, but the blinding light was warm. Willoughby had to shield his eyes from the brightness.

"You *were* the one," a soft, sing-song voice spoke. "I thank you, James Arthur. You have set me free—aligned me with the place where I belong. I am my own singularity now. The raw energy that burst from me, at last, is controlled in me. I can to do no harm. I am free. I can no longer be held by your time, by your world."

"What are you?" Willoughby asked, trying to see her even though the glare was physically painful. "Where will you go? Is Carolyn your true name?"

"No. I told the demon, Beelzebub, that. I did not want him to know my secret name. I am *Pi*. I would like to think I am as you will be when you are come," the voice paused, looking down at Willoughby. "I was wrong. I see that now. You are one of them, but not one with them. That is the difference."

"I don't understand," Willoughby said.

Pi seemed to consider and then gave an answer. "A dark edge is rising, Willoughby. Choices must be made. *Go!* He is coming. He holds no danger for me now, but he did not mean for you to leave this chamber untouched. He is strong here. Take your friends, now, and go." She floated down and touched Antonio. He fell back, landing atop the hooded stone cobras. He groaned, blinking, and trying to take in the spectacle of the being, the fallen bones and the stone snakes.

"Antonio, we need to leave," Willoughby said, trying to pull a barely conscious Dr. J to his feet.

"What—" Antonio began, but Willoughby cut him off.

"No time. We need to get out of here."

Antonio pushed to his feet with a sigh. "I thought you were going to say that, my friend." He helped heft James Arthur to his feet. The three of them stepped over to the G-7 square.

Just as Willoughby gave a flick of his hand, the soft voice said in his mind, "She will always wait for you, Willoughby. That is your comfort."

There was a sense of tumbling backward, then streaks of light whizzing by. Willoughby noted the numbers, but they were coming too fast. He felt Antonio, holding tight to his arm, and James Arthur with an arm around his waist. He closed his eyes a moment. He was suddenly exhausted, hungry, weak, and sore. He opened them again. The number strings swirled around him, *but they were still too fast!* He was too tired to focus, to concentrate. Nothing looked familiar. He tried to think of H.S., of Sydney, of Hauti, blank-eyed over her dead father, of the damaged observation platform. *He had to get back there!* Still, nothing was familiar. His heart pounded. Sweat ran down his back and dripped from his forehead.

Suddenly, a string curled around his face. It was 7-7-7, repeated over and over. He breathed in easier, reaching forward to touch it. A hand grabbed his before he could.

"No refunds! I tell you, read fine print!" How Loa's voice rang out in his mind. His eyes followed the bony fingers to the image of How Loa, moustache and gray hair crawling with tiny lines of 7-7-7 equation.

"How?" Willoughby said, the streaks of number string swirling and spinning past him.

"Wrong question," How's voice said. "You not very good with questions!"

"You never told me to read the fine print," Willoughby smiled.

"Oh, I tell you much. You listen little. No fault to me—you choose not to listen to what I choose not to say. Very good, yes?"

Willoughby tried to think the words through, but decided he was just too tired. "How," he asked, his voice full of the pain and exhaustion he felt, "how do I get back?"

"Yes, you get back." How raised an eyebrow. "Then, you come to shop, make you very good deal, yes?"

Willoughby smiled again. "Not this time," he said. "I can't. People are waiting on me. They're depending on me."

"Hmmm," How said. "Okay. Very good, chop, chop. You no smell very good anyway! And you friends, they falling all over you. If I take you to shop, it be '*Clean up, aisle seven.*'" How smiled. "But, as I say to you, no refund, but got great news. You like, you like. Only for good customer, got best ever exchange. It in left pocket right now. I take back glass, I fix. Chop, chop!"

Willoughby grinned, "You don't need to How—just help me get back to the, the observation post."

How stared up at Willoughby, his yellow teeth smiling as the 7-7-7 number strings continued to swirl around him. "But, you still got box with no key! Deal is deal. You good customer! I do good trade. You check right now—it left pocket."

Willoughby managed somehow to reach his left hand down and push it into his pocket. He felt something round and hard. He pulled it out. It was the watch his Mom had given him the day he left on the *Absconditus*. Through moist eyes, he read the inscription on the back—"*Chasing the moment, someday you'll find—you yearn for a place where memories bind.*"

How was gone. He put the watch back in his pocket. A warm feeling spread through him. That is when he heard it. A tune he recognized. He looked up. He didn't have to pull an obscure number string out of the hat to get back to Sydney, to his family, to home. There were places, cryptic spaces, indelibly engraved on his heart. He suddenly knew beyond a shadow of a doubt that he would always be able to find them. He looked at the flying, curling number strings with renewed energy. One flashed with the rhythm he heard and knew. He smiled, reached out, and grabbed it.

32

Cryptic Spaces

Light and sound immediately burst around them as Willoughby and his friends tumbled out of the same arc he and Antonio had jumped into earlier. In some ways, that seemed a lifetime ago. The first thing he saw as they slammed against the lattice-work mesh of the catwalk was Sydney, lost in her music. She stopped playing abruptly as the three fought to recover their breath and began to untangle themselves from the heap. James Arthur groaned, holding his head and mumbling. "I'm done for. Tell my family, my brothers… What should I tell my brothers?"

Antonio pushed out from under him. "Tell them you have gained weight," he panted. "Most of it in that puffed up head."

Willoughby pulled to a sitting position. "Thanks, Sydney. I heard you—I, I saw your music." He wasn't sure he could be heard above the automated machinery of the huge chamber and the crackling arc behind him, but Sydney smiled. She lowered her violin and wiped at her cheek.

"You're lucky I don't smash this violin over your head for leaving me like that. If it weren't a Stradivarius…" She wiped again at her cheek, and then continued, softer. "I didn't mean for you to go *now*. I pushed the music out. I had to find you. I wove the music tight. I had to pull you back."

Their eyes locked. A groan from James Arthur broke the spell. He had pulled back his robe to reveal a jagged and bloody cut. He winced, looking over at Willoughby. "Not pretty, but I'll live. Okay, I'll say it. *You are the man, Willoughby!* You got us back—" Dr. J looked around. "By the way, where are we? And who was the Chinese guy we picked up along the way?"

Antonio pulled to his feet and bent to help Dr. J. "Yes! I was wondering that too, *amigo*. But I think that can wait until after a shower, a long sleep, and a hot meal. Someone at headquarters should have picked up our automated signal by now."

"Automated signal?" James Arthur grimaced, pushing to his feet. His voice was still harsh and weak. "Mutiny, tombs, witches, snakes, spears, dead warriors, we had a simply wonderful time, didn't we? I think I'll find H.S. and thank him." He looked over at Sydney. "Where is the old man?" He looked at Antonio. "And where is T.K.?"

Antonio took him gingerly around the waist and helped him down the catwalk. "H.S. is dead, James Arthur. T.K. is missing."

James Arthur bent, shocked, grabbing at the rail. "*What?*"

Willoughby pulled himself up, listening to Antonio explain as he once again pushed James Arthur forward toward the dark entry to the observatory. "Much has happened in little time," Antonio said. "We are all tired and some are injured. I am feared we will be untangling this tale for some time. But for now, James Arthur, you need medical attention." He looked over his shoulder.

"And you, Sydney, you were limping." He looked down. "Your ankle is swollen. Is it broken?"

Sydney shook her head. "I don't think so."

Antonio sighed. "Perhaps we should get back to our own time and get some food and rest before we begin to untangle the events that have happened to us."

Hauti, her wild black hair waving, ducked her head out of the shadows of the darkened observatory. Dr. J looked her way. "Who is that?" he asked. When Antonio didn't say anything, James Arthur looked back to Willoughby.

"Uh, she was in one of my classes at school," Willoughby began.

James Arthur held up a hand to stop him. With a shake of his head, he rasped. "Just...get me home."

"Her name is Hauti," Sydney said. "She helped us escape the *Absconditus*, and her father—at least, we think he was her father. He, he... She—"

James Arthur gave Sydney a weak smile. "Tylenol? Food? A bed? Don't answer anymore questions, okay Sydney?" He croaked

The dark-skinned girl stepped back into the shadows.

Sydney dropped her eyes. "It's just that she—she has nowhere to go."

Antonio motioned for them to follow and continued down the catwalk. "We will take her with us, then," he said, trying not to sound as tired as he felt. "Come, let's get some rest. Then, we must discuss how we plan to find T.K."

"She's a little young for you, isn't she Antonio?" James Arthur said, trying to lighten the mood.

"She is over fifty, my friend."

Dr. J roared. "I think you might have gotten a few too many bumps on the head," he grinned. "What would a spunky gal like that see in a broken, slightly dotty old barber?"

"I wouldn't have too much to say about being broken at the moment," Antonio replied. "And was I mistaken, or did I not hear that very big woman say something about how you '*make her laugh?*'"

"Well," James Arthur dropped his head in a grin. "I make everyone laugh, my good man. It comes with being such an irresistible guy—especially to the opposite sex. I can't be responsible for the effect I have on women, can I?"

"Yes—and *what* a woman!"

Dr. J sighed. "Well, if you want some pointers, all you got to do is ask."

Antonio's genuine laugh did lighten the moment. Willoughby noticed for the first time that Sydney had pushed closer to him. They continued to listen as James Arthur and Antonio continued their good-natured ribbing.

"I think I am too skinny for your kind of woman, James Arthur," Antonio said.

"She was built," Dr. J agreed. "Talk about a brick house… "

"I think, my friend, she was a brick coliseum! And what a fighter!"

"She was that," James Arthur agreed again.

As Antonio led James Arthur off the catwalk, Willoughby moved to embrace Sydney. She gave him a tight hug, and then pushed him away.

"Yuck! You're sticky. Good thing my nose is stuffed up or I might be gagging."

"Yeah, you're not the first to mention that," Willoughby said, remembering about the snake blood, dust, sweat, and his own blood.

Sydney reached up and touched the slash on his cheek, and the cut on his arm. "You were only gone maybe fifteen minutes and you managed to get yourself further beat up," she said, tearing up again. "It was a long fifteen minutes."

"Yeah," Willoughby agreed. "That is was." The two were silent for a moment before Sydney spoke, almost in a whisper. "Is it finally over?" she asked.

Willoughby looked away, over the rail of the catwalk, watching the automated machines below. "No," he said blankly. "I don't know that it will ever be over, Sydney. There's a lot more to my involvement in this than you know—than even I know. There are forces causing these events that are still out there. They'll come for me again."

"For us again," Sydney corrected. "Who are these forces?"

"I'll tell you everything I know, but not now. I don't want to think about it right now. I want to focus more on not being alone."

Sydney scooted closer.

"How's the ankle?" Willoughby asked.

"Throbbing." She looked up. "Listen Willoughby, I, I wanted to come after you, but I thought my music—"

"You did the right thing," Willoughby interjected.

"I wasn't the only one who wanted to help. I had to physically hold back that girl, Hauti, or whatever. How well did you say you knew her at your school? She would have jumped straight into the flame—"

"Some girls are like that," Willoughby cut in, smiling. "Thanks for holding her back. She would have probably gotten lost in the time-flow. Even if she had somehow managed to reach us, the friendly reception we got in there was less than overwhelming." He smelled the smoke and could taste the acrid tang of the arc flame as he breathed in—such a different taste from the first time he met Sydney, breathing in the fresh tang of the open sea. He raised Sydney's arm, gently put it around his shoulder, and took firm hold of her waist. "Come on. Let's get you home."

There was silence. Willoughby concentrated on taking most of Sydney's weight so she could hobble with her good foot as painlessly as possible. A few yards from the observatory door, she stopped him, tears again stinging her eyes. "Willoughby," she whispered.

"What?"

"I need to know," she started, "that I'll be a part of, of—I don't know what I'm trying to say… I need to know if I'll be with you—if I'm part of why you won't face things alone."

Willoughby stared at her.

"I mean, I was hoping you'd still *want*—" She took a moment to compose herself. "I guess it's not the kind of life you expect for a mathematician, and—you know, mathematicians and musicians… I, I just have to know you won't go back to, to your world and leave me in mine, all *alone* with the screaming fans, and…" She looked into his eyes, blinking away the emotion.

Willoughby could not escape those eyes. He never had been able to. Even if he tried, they pulled him, they enveloped him, and they consumed him. They had been there in the music he heard in the time grid, he realized. They were as much a part of him now as his own breath. They were the stuff of his dreams, of his hopes, of those most cryptic of all spaces where hearts beat softly, pulling in before venturing to stretch out. Despite all that had happened, those eyes still set him ablaze. When he looked into them, he was always falling, and time did not matter. With deafening machinery around and smoke highlighting the brilliant arc behind him, he felt a tug inside stronger than any time-hole. He leaned down, ignoring her protests, and kissed her. Flame crackled. Smoke billowed in velvety puffs. When he finally pulled her away, she looked up at him, trembling.

"You really do need a shower," she finally said.

Willoughby felt the corners of his own mouth twitch. He bent down and swept her dainty frame into his arms, lifting her from the catwalk. "Now, we'll both need one," he said.

She leaned her cheek flush against his shoulder, locking her arms around his neck. "I guess there are worse things," she said, this time with an airy finality. "I won't be in front of the press any time soon with this ankle and my bruised cheek."

Willoughby made his way toward the exit door.

"We've got to call my dad," she sniffled, wiping at her nose. "He'll get us out of here, let us clean up, and come up with a cover explanation. By the way, I've decided I'm okay with Von Brahmer."

Willoughby pursed his lips. "Johansen," he said. "I'm going to take my step-father's name."

Gustav would want it that way. His thoughts trailed for a moment to the watch in his pocket and to his family. He smiled. He *did* have a girl to introduce to Klass. Mom would love that she was a classical violinist. Densi and Cali would be enchanted by the ping and tinkle of her layers of bangles and bracelets.

"*Ah!*" he said suddenly, thinking of Densi and Cali. They had passed through into the observatory. "I have to get my stuff from the *Pesci Picolli* before I go back. I picked up some souvenirs for my sisters. They'll be heartbroken if I don't bring them back something."

"Oh, that's no problem," Sydney said, almost cheerfully. "Do they like bracelets?" She rattled the trembling hands she held around his neck. "Anklets? Bangles?" she whispered. "I can fully accessorize them ..."

Willoughby walked on beneath the star-filled ceiling. He remembered the first time he had viewed this enormous room—the guts behind the time travel technology. H.S. had been by his side. He felt a pang at the thought of H.S. So much had happened, so fast. He bit his lip. Behind them, the mechanized room continued to whir and sing as it always had. The huge steel pyramid spun, the brilliant arc zapped. The noise around the catwalk was as deafening as it had always been. But Willoughby blocked it all out. He wanted to hear only one thing right now. He wanted to hear Sydney's heart, beating softly beside his chest. All he did hear, though, was her voice, her words droning on…

"…and I can throw in the boots too—oh, they're to *die* for! I first wore them at Carnegie Hall when I was six, you know. And maybe we can do some cooking together…"

Willoughby stopped, balancing Sydney's weight on the railing.

"Don't tell me I'm too heavy already," she said, still holding tight to his neck.

"Well, it was sort of a long, rough day," Willoughby began.

"Oh, I've seen worse, Sydney jumped in. "I had two concerts in one day once. The day started in Central Park, and ended with an outdoor concert in Paris. They had to give us police escort from the airport and I had to dress and tune up in the limo. You should have seen—"

Willoughby bent forward again and kissed her, long and hard. When they finally came up for air, she wiped a timid smile from her lips.

"Uh, what was that for?"

He just smiled, lifted her back off the railing, and continued down the catwalk. He thought of the answer in his mind, but he didn't want to speak it aloud, not yet.

Besides—how else could he get her to shut up?

Cryptic Spaces
Dark Edge Rising

The blink of an eye…an average person blinks every five seconds. That is roughly 17,000 blinks in a day or 6.25 million blinks in a year. Little usually happens in the blink of an eye, but Willoughby discovers that an entire world can change in one blink. In this, the third installment of the award-winning series *Cryptic Spaces*, the *Dark Edge* is finally ready to show its hand. In a single blink, Willoughby is told, one he holds dear will be gone. Who is the target? What is the reason? As Willoughby, Sydney, Antonio, and Dr. J race to find and save their friend T.K., dark things are racing too, tracking them, watching them. Ghosts and banshees, alchemists and priests, the *Edge* has many cards to play. So, the game continues; from mountain monasteries in Bhutan, to lost temples in India; from Kubla Khan's lost fleet, to haunted halls in Tasmania, the action moves toward fever pitch, and then, *blink!* Everything Willoughby thought he knew, everything he had thought he had, *everything* changes.

Coming in 2016, the stakes move ever higher in *Dark Edge Rising* as Willoughby fights to save his friends, his family, and the girl he has come to love. One blink and someone does not walk away.

Who?

CPSIA information can be obtained
at www.ICGtesting.com
Printed in the USA
FFOW04n2234241114
8969FF

9 781600 474774